KT-570-060

DANGEROUS DECISIONS

Helena Standish knows that a good marriage would enhance her father's social status. The wealthy and enigmatic Oliver Faraday is considered an ideal match, so why does Helena have faint misgivings? Nicholas Carstairs has little patience with frivolous pleasure-seekers or an upper class that closes ranks against outsiders. Why then is he entranced by the lovely 'girl in the window' – a debutante who would appear to be both of those things? A champagne celebration at Broadway Manor marks the start of a happy future for Helena, but no one can predict the perilous consequences of her decision or the appalling danger it will bring.

DANGEROUS DECISIONS

DANGEROUS DECISIONS

by

Margaret Kaine

Magna Large Print Books
Long Preston, North Yorkshire,
BD23 4ND, England.

British Library Cataloguing in Publication Data.

Kaine, Margaret
    Dangerous decisions.

    A catalogue record of this book is
    available from the British Library

    ISBN   978-0-7505-3915-9

First published in Great Britain in 2013 by Choc Lit Limited

Published in Large Print 2014 by arrangement with
Choc Lit Ltd.

LP

Magna Large Print is an imprint of Library Magna Books Ltd.

Printed and bound in Great Britain by
T.J. (International) Ltd., Cornwall, PL28 8RW

For
The Romantic Novelists' Association
in appreciation of their support and friendship.

Acknowledgements

As always my gratitude to the talented members of JustWrite for their perceptive critiques and friendship, and to Biddy Nelson for her 'fresh eye' when reading my draft chapters. The Staffordshire Regiment Museum was once again helpful with research and I owe much to Helenka Fuglewicz and Julia Forrest for their valuable insight.

It has been a pleasure to work with the welcoming Choc Lit team and I can only add that this novel has been a joy to write.

'Evil can hide behind a mask of perfection.'

Anon

Chapter One

'This is a most unsuitable area, Helena!' The
tone was one of outrage as a flamboyant woman,
her face a mask of paint and powder, swept by in
a cloud of cheap scent.

Helena was gazing at the creased face of a
costermonger and admiring his jaunty cap, fas-
cinated by everything, from the raucous shouts of
the stallholders to the scent of flowers and the
smell of both fresh and rotting vegetables. The
people too – some looked pinched and tired and
many lined with age, but others were jolly with
florid cheeks and firm, muscled arms. Surrounded by Cockney voices, Helena breathed in
the pungent atmosphere, loving every minute of
it. 'Just fancy standing out here in all weathers!'

'Well I fancy sitting down if you don't mind.'

Immediately contrite, Helena said, 'I'm sorry
Aunt Beatrice, I forgot about your feet.' Reluct-
antly she turned to lead the way through the
crowd and out of the vibrant market so that they
could search for a hansom cab. As her aunt lifted
her skirt to climb into the fusty, tobacco-smelling
interior, Helena gave the driver their address in
Cadogan Square and once inside sank back
against the creased leather upholstery. As she
half-listened to the clip-clop of the shaggy horse's
hooves, she remembered how when younger her
visits to the capital had been limited to historical

15

landmarks, museums and art galleries, her life constrained; even her pleas to be sent to boarding school curtly dismissed by her father.

Jacob Standish was implacable. When twenty-five years ago he had bought Broadway Manor, a country estate near Lichfield, he had been under no illusions. Money alone would not achieve the social standing he craved; the establishment had their daughters educated at home and so must his be.

Now in London for her coming-out season, Helena was determined to take advantage of her new freedom, to explore not only leafy squares but side streets and alleyways, to discover the real city, the one where ordinary people lived and worked. The glamour of being presented at Court may have been exhilarating, but the following whirl of receptions, parties and balls was beginning to pall. She glanced across to her aunt with resignation. 'So what are our plans for this evening?'

Beatrice told her. 'And do make more of an effort this time – at least you could try to look animated.'

'It all seems so false somehow.' Although there had been some point to Queen Charlotte's Ball, which raised funds for unfortunate mothers and babies. 'Anyway,' Helena went on, 'it's becoming tedious dancing with what you call eligible young men. Some, I might add, with very few brains. Even papa wouldn't want grandchildren from any of those fools.'

'Helena, do you deliberately try to infuriate me? Just remember that a bored expression is hardly an inspiring one. And I find your radical views bewildering.'

'No you don't,' Helena said, 'not really. After all, I am my father's daughter.'

Beatrice drew her eyebrows into a frown above her long nose. 'Men are a different species. They are allowed, even applauded for having strong opinions, but as you know very well it's considered to be most unbecoming in a young woman.'

'Maybe I don't wish to be "becoming", as you call it. It's 1905 for heaven's sake...' Helena's voice tailed off as the driver drew to a halt outside the tall house that her father had rented for the summer months. A young girl came up the steps from the basement, her thin face pale and drawn. Clutching a small carpet bag the shabbily dressed figure hurried away.

As soon as the cab left, Helena stood before the black iron railings and swung round to Beatrice. 'What on earth...?'

'It's just a scullery maid; a domestic matter.'

'She looked as if she'd been dismissed.'

'Indeed she has.'

'Why, what has she done?' Helena waited with impatience until a footman had taken their gloves and hats. When seated in the morning room Beatrice answered her question. 'She was stupid enough to get herself into trouble.'

'You mean she's pregnant?'

'Really, do you have to be so forthright in your language?'

At the age of fourteen, desperate for company of her own age, Helena had become friendly with a new young maid who loved to read 'Penny Dreadfuls', so she had become quite familiar with such predicaments. 'She hasn't been turned out without a reference? Have you any idea what hardship that brings?'

'She should have thought of that before she indulged in immorality, and as this house is only on lease, she's neither my concern nor yours. If we were at Broadway Manor it would be a different story.' Beatrice turned as two parlour maids came in with a silver tea service and buttered toasted teacakes beneath a domed dish, and then once they had left she sighed. 'Thinking of this evening, I think I'm getting a bit old for all this gallivanting.'

'Now, you know you love it, all that gossip with the other chaperones.'

Beatrice's tone was dry. 'Helena, I'm a spinster. Tolerated maybe, but never truly included.'

Helena gazed at her as she bit into a teacake. Did her aunt ever regret the sacrifice she had made? In coming to Broadway Manor to support her brother and take care of his motherless baby, there was no doubt she had missed any chance of a marriage and family of her own, but she knew that Beatrice would never answer such a question.

It was later that evening when Helena, feeling pleased with the way her hair had been arranged in soft wings and gathered in a loose coil at the nape of her neck, wandered to the window of the drawing room and glanced down into the square. Unusually she found it deserted except for a tall man carrying a doctor's bag, walking below along

18

the tree-lined pavement. Probably about ten years older than she was, he was dark-haired and clean-shaven with an unmistakeable air of authority. She thought what a sensitive and handsome face he had, yet how tired he looked. But then practising medicine must be a most demanding profession.

Maybe it was the sun glinting on the glass or his need of a distraction from his concern about a suffering patient, Nicholas Carstairs never knew what made him glance up to that particular casement window. In the evening warmth and gentle air, he could see a young woman framed, stunningly beautiful in an ivory satin gown, her slender throat encircled with pearls. She was gazing down at him with an expression that seemed full of compassion. Surprised, his step slowed, but weary after a difficult and harrowing day, Nicholas merely gave a slight nod of acknowledgement before continuing home. Yet strangely, her image remained vividly with him, lingering even during his cold supper left by his housekeeper.

As he went over to the heavy carved sideboard and lifted the decanter, he thought of her again. She had been almost unutterably lovely ... but then he told himself as he poured a drink and cradled the brandy glass in his hand, she was almost certainly a debutante and as such belonged to the narrow social circle he despised. Nicholas had scant patience with such frivolous, pleasure seeking lives.

That same evening Oliver Faraday's decision to

attend the ball at Grosvenor House was a desultory one but once he saw the slender girl with honey-blonde hair, his interest never waned. It had not only been her appearance that had attracted him, although he approved of her simple ivory gown with its modest décolletage, it had been the tilt of her head, a challenge in her stare, the slight air of boredom. Innocence combined with spirit and perhaps a taste for adventure. It was an intriguing prospect that he had not expected to find in this hothouse of social graces and his pulse quickened. Unobtrusively he began to move closer, to a point where he could observe undetected. The girl's complexion not only bore the bloom of youth, it was satisfyingly unblemished, and with deliberation his gaze went down to her bare shoulders and upper arms. There too the skin was clear and smooth with no unsightly moles or imperfections. It was frustrating that elbow-length gloves concealed her wrists and hands, but he was full of purpose as he threaded his way back behind the clusters of partygoers to stand in a prominent position by glass-paned double doors.

When a few minutes later his closest friend came in, Oliver caught at his arm. 'Johnnie, tell me – that young lady over there, by the woman in fussy purple, do you happen to know who she is?'

Johnnie Horton glanced across the room. 'Gosh, it *is* a frightful frock. You mean the vision of loveliness. That's Helena Standish – the cream of Staffordshire.'

'What do you know of her background?'

'Well one wouldn't call them old money. I believe the father's in trade.'

'And tell me...' Oliver lowered his voice, 'have you heard any rumours, any whispers?'

Johnnie snorted. 'Not a chance old boy, you're out of luck there. As far as I know, she's as pure as the driven snow.'

Helena, aware of the tall stranger's searching gaze, was beginning to find it intrusive. Once again partnered on the dance floor, she glanced up at her round-faced perspiring partner. 'Hugh, do you know who that is – standing just inside the doors?'

He turned his head. 'The man with a fair moustache? I know who he is, though we are not acquainted. That's Oliver Faraday, the well-known "man about town".'

'Stupid expression,' Helena said tartly. 'I've never really known what it means.'

'Me neither. But I don't think it implies gainful employment – not like me, unfortunately.'

'Come on, it has only been for a few months.'

'Long enough,' he said, guiding her somewhat clumsily around a corner.

'Well, I'm sure it won't do you any harm.' She smiled at him. 'You always were lazy.'

'You know me too well. It is a distinct disadvantage growing up in the same county as a smashing girl. I don't suppose if I made an offer...' Her look of horror was enough to make him splutter. 'I'm only joking, you daft thing.'

Helena glanced over to the double doors to the ballroom. Oliver Faraday was still watching her and she felt a prickle of unease. A few seconds later the space he had been occupying was empty.

Chapter Two

If Oliver Faraday had one passion in life, it was his ancestral home, Graylings. And his interest in Helena Standish sprang from the shock of an unexpected funeral earlier that year. The deceased was a close friend, a man of a similar age who had appeared in perfect health yet suddenly succumbed to the wretched London fog that plagued them all. As Oliver stood in a cold and musty church in Highgate half-listening to the droning voice of the parson, he came not only to the sober realisation of his own mortality but conscious of the appalling consequences that could follow. Were he to die today or even within the year, then Graylings would become the legal property of his first cousin Selwyn Faraday. A man he loathed, whose dissolute gambling was notorious; it was even whispered that he was in debt to money lenders and the banks had refused him credit. Therefore, while the rest of the congregation sang the 23rd Psalm, Oliver's mind wrestled with the fact that he must delay no longer. As soon as the burial was over, he strode out of the cemetery full of purpose – he needed a son. And the London season would provide the ideal and fruitful market in which to find a suitable wife.

His search had been a frustrating one until he saw Helena Standish. She would seem to be ideal; she not only had beauty, but youth and robust health – he had bred enough horses to know that promised fertility, and there had been spirit in her demeanour – he had no desire to be married to a mouse. He had waited until his lawyer reported on his investigation into the Standish family. There was apparently no scandal attached to the name, and although it was a pity that Jacob Standish had made his money in brewing, unlike many of his contemporaries Oliver was perceptive enough to recognise that times were changing and the future would depend on industry rather than on inherited wealth.

Now free to make his approach, he became impatient for the next event on the social calendar. As he entered the glittering room, he saw her immediately, looking cool and elegant in white satin trimmed in blue, while her nearby aunt was wearing a brown frock almost as ugly as the last time. Swiftly he searched for Johnnie Horton, and seconds later the two men began to thread their way through the partygoers.

Helena had been aware of his presence as soon as he had arrived, had instinctively known that this second time he would approach her, and in answer to his request, held out her silk-tasselled dance card. When it came, their dance was almost a parody of silent meanings. It was there in the way that Oliver held her, the expression in his eyes as he gazed down at her, the slight movement of his thumb against her palm as he held her gloved hand. He held her so closely that she could feel the warmth of his body as he said softly that he understood that her mother had died when she was born, a misfortune they both shared. 'But I see you have an excellent aunt,' he said, 'who certainly takes her role as chaperone seriously.'

Helena glanced across the room to see Beatrice watching them, her expression one of stern disapproval, and laughed. 'It's because you're holding me too close. I'm afraid she's terribly old fashioned.'

However, later, Beatrice's reaction was an unexpectedly warm one when Oliver invited them to walk with him the following day in the Botanical Gardens. 'That would be delightful,' she said and with an approving nod, gave him their address. As his tall figure then left the ballroom, Beatrice said in a low voice, 'I've been making enquiries about that young man. Not only is he extremely eligible but do you realise that he didn't dance with anyone else?'

It was a month later when Jacob Standish received the letter from his sister. He wandered on to the large stone terrace overlooking the park-like grounds of Broadway Manor and adjusting his spectacles, read through it once again. A powerfully built man in late middle-age, he murmured aloud the name – Oliver Faraday. This news from Beatrice was a matter for his lawyer to look into because if this man was showing a serious interest in Helena, then certain discreet enquiries would need to be made.

Jacob glanced again at the letter.

'I believe his family are landed gentry and his seat is Graylings in Hertfordshire. He is certainly taken with Helena. I must confess that I too find him charming.'

That may be so, Jacob thought, but though his sister had many admirable attributes to her character, experience of the male sex, particularly with regard to women, was not one of them. He went back into the drawing room and going over to the ornate Adam fireplace, gave a tug on the silken bell cord.

When the silver-haired butler entered the room, Jacob said, 'Ah, Bostock. I shall be leaving for London on Friday. Would you tell Fraser to pack for at least a week?'

'Very good, Sir. Might I enquire whether Miss Beatrice and Miss Helena are enjoying their time there?'

'I'm delighted to say that they are. And you may tell the rest of the staff that Miss Helena is a great success.' Jacob saw a slight smile pass on Bostock's normally impassive face. Helena was enormously popular with the servants; Beatrice often protested that she was far too familiar with them. As the heavy mahogany door closed behind his butler, Jacob went to sit in his favourite winged chair, the one that Helena laughingly called his 'thinking chair'. And he had much to consider. If all went well and a marriage did take place then a member of the 'landed gentry' in the family would not only assure its social standing, but could even be beneficial for the business. Jacob made a steeple of his hands and drew his brows together. His interest nowadays was spreading tentacles into a wider field, one that needed influence and contacts; surely such an alliance could only bode well for a man with political ambitions.

The day before her father was due to arrive, with Beatrice having retired to bed with a headache, Helena was feeling both bored and restless. Much as she enjoyed being in London, especially lately as Oliver had taken her riding in Rotten Row, she missed her chestnut mare Blaze and the graceful manor house where she was born. And the capital could be so unbearably hot. She wandered over to sit on the velvet-covered seat by the open window, in no doubt of the reason for her father's visit.

Not that Oliver had given any formal indication that he was about to propose, but Aunt Beatrice seemed to be convinced of it. The other debutantes with whom she had become friendly were blatantly envious. He was certainly attentive; each day brought more flowers or chocolates and there was no denying that he was devastatingly attractive. Yet Helena sometimes felt what she could only describe as a slight uneasiness.

She leaned nearer to the open window hoping to feel even a hint of a breeze. And it was then that she saw a dejected-looking horse struggling to pull a delivery van. Thin flanked, his coat matted, he looked half-starved. Infuriated to see a whip raised, within seconds Helena was dashing into the hall, through the front door and out into the road. Startled by her sudden emergence and waving arms, the horse immediately baulked and the driver was thrown forward and let out a stream of curses.

'How dare you so ill-use an animal,' Helena yelled. 'You should be ashamed of yourself!'

'Yer stupid bitch!' The burly man gave a vicious jerk on the reins. His fleshy face was beaded with sweat and he lifted his red neckerchief to mop at his brow, then with a dismissive shrug he flicked his whip again over the horse's swayed back. 'Get out of me way.'

'Leave that horse where it is.' A resolute male voice came from behind Helena and as she hurried to the shafts, a man went forward to seize the reins. 'And I'll thank you to watch your language before a young lady. Are you the owner of this van?'

'That's none of yer business.'

'Whether you are or not, I've made a note of the name on it so that I can report you to the authorities.'

Helena was gazing in distress at the horse, its eyelashes yellow-encrusted while froth at the corners of its mouth was flecked with blood caused by the sharp, cruel bit. It was with grim satisfaction that she heard the sudden fear in the driver's voice.

'Oi, there's no need to go doing that. It ain't my fault. I've only just bought the beast.'

Helena turned to glare at him. 'Well, I for one don't believe you.'

'Are you calling me a liar?'

'Yes I am. Nobody would try to sell a horse in this state. I'm sure this gentleman will agree.' It was only then that Helena turned to look up at her companion and her breath caught in her throat. Surely ... yes, he was the same young man she had seen from her window last month. She hadn't realised he was quite so devastatingly handsome.

With his black bag on the pavement beside him, he was looking up at the driver. 'Where do you stable him? Come along, man, answer me, I can easily find out.'

With some reluctance, the driver muttered the address.

'Now that is most convenient, I often pass that way. I won't warn you again. If I see any further sign of this or any other horse on those premises being ill-treated then the police will be paying a visit.' He released the reins and stepped back to stand beside Helena.

As the horse plodded away, she turned towards him. 'Thank you so much for coming to my assistance.'

He smiled down at her. 'I think you were very brave.'

She smiled back. 'And you were very effective.' She remembered him so well from that earlier evening when she had seen him walking along the pavement. He seemed less tired now, his clean-shaven face alight with warmth, his brown eyes holding her gaze. Helena felt a rush of attraction so strong that heat rose in her cheeks. 'I think I saw you...' she had intended to ask if he had a patient nearby, but her sentence remained unfinished because an outraged Beatrice was already hurrying towards them.

'What on earth do you think you are doing?'

28

Ignoring the man beside he,r she seized Helena's arm to hustle her away, and within seconds they were both back in the house and in the morning room. 'I've never heard of such a thing, out on the street talking to a stranger, whatever were you thinking of?'

Helena flashed, 'Did you have to drag me away like that? He was a doctor who had, if I may say so, dealt with an unpleasant situation in an exemplary way. You didn't see that poor neglected horse.'

'Maybe not, but have you never heard of white slave traffic?'

Helena stared at her in astonishment. 'And you accuse me of having a vivid imagination. I hardly think they come looking for victims in this part of London.'

'There are rogues everywhere, Helena. You are far too trusting.'

'Maybe I am, but Aunt Beatrice I'm not a child any longer. I'm capable of making my own judgments and decisions.' Helena was livid. If only her aunt had not interfered, then at least she could have discovered the man's name.

Nicholas, who had continued on his way to visit a regular patient, had immediately recognised the furious girl confronting the driver of the van, and knew that he too would have intervened. He hated cruelty and neglect wherever he found it, but it was unforgiveable in the case of a defenceless animal. And once again that evening he found his thoughts returning to the girl who kept lingering in his mind. She may be a debutante, but she was neither shallow nor frivolous, not with spirit and courage like that. He smiled as he recalled her slight figure confronting the burly driver, but then he gave a regretful shrug and returned to his newspaper. Belonging as she did to a social class that closed ranks against outsiders it was unlikely that their paths would ever cross again, and yet... Raising his head Nicholas stared unseeing across the room.

Chapter Three

That same evening, not too many miles away, Cora Bates was getting ready for the coming night's work. She felt no shame at her profession. Her view was that if men were daft enough to offer money to relieve their urges, a woman who was short of cash would be mad not to take it. Besides, sex was better than scrubbing floors for toffs any day. Cora knew a lot about toffs; when they came to her they were more than likely half-drunk and free with their talk. And she had her regulars. In their minds, she was just an un-educated whore and Cora was careful not to let any of them know that she could read and write. Several of the girls could, but not even they knew about her daily scribbling; the record she kept. Cora was looking out for her future because she had no intention of going on the streets, es-pecially when her face was raddled and her body grown thick. Her shabby journal was hidden behind a loose brick in the wall of her bedroom, concealed by the only picture she had, a cheap print of a flower garden. Cora had never been in a garden but as a young girl, she had worked on a flower stall in Petticoat Lane. Not serving but helping to unpack the stock and to fetch and carry hot drinks and food from the market cafe. It had been Sid the burly red-faced stallholder, who had encouraged her to work at her letters. Cora had learned her alphabet during her rare attendance at the board school, but it had been Sid who had helped her to write more than her name. Surrounded by the fragrance of flowers, she had sat behind the stall on an iron bucket and during slack times, he had used his pencil stub to correct her mistakes. She would always be grateful to him, and despite the difference in their ages, he was the only man she had ever felt any affection for. If he hadn't gone and died of apoplexy before she reached an age when ... but then everyone knew that life was built on *'ifs'*.

It was stiflingly hot, had been for days, so Cora decided to wear her latest muslin, a frock she had recently bought second-hand, and it had been an easy task to change its virginal look. She had always been good at sewing; it was about the only useful skill they'd taught her in the workhouse. Of course, there she'd worked with rough calico, not fine and flimsy material. Just a rip to lower the bodice, a few flounces, a shortening of the skirt, and if she wore it without a petticoat, its transparency would drive the punters wild. Not that she wanted any rough trade. That was why she lived in Camden Town at Belle's brothel. Belle, still an attractive woman despite her now blousy figure and hennaed hair, kept her charges high. Her discriminating clients were well able to afford an extra coin or two for a girl who satisfied them.

'Cora...' Belle, whose shrill voice could shatter glass, shrieked up the stairs. 'Ain't yer ready yet?'

'I'm comin' now!' Cora straightened the flower print and then closing her door went along the landing among a cloud of scent left by the other girls.

The house never opened until midnight. As the upper classes dined late, and would only seek diversion once they had fulfilled their social commitments, there seemed little point in beginning a night's work too early. As always, Belle was waiting in the salon; it was her custom to check the girls as they came down. She would brook no stained clothes, insisting that she employed a laundress and expected them to use her. Nor lack of personal hygiene. Her rules were strict and the girls knew better than to flout them.

'That looks good, ducks!' Belle glanced with approval at Cora's muslin dress then added in a sharp tone, 'but yer late and one of yer regulars is waiting.'

'Sorry.' Cora turned to give a warm smile of welcome. Young Johnnie – the clients never revealed their surnames – didn't seem to have a perversion or nasty habit in his nature. He was no trouble at all. But although after his last visit she'd found his white lawn handkerchief beneath her iron bedstead, she had no intention of returning it. Instead, with its fine monogram of the initials J.F.H. it was folded and safely tucked away behind the loose brick – just in case.

Oliver Faraday did not share Johnnie's fondness for what he called 'ladies of the night'. To Oliver they were simply whores, a crude word for an ugly but necessary profession. His own fastidious needs he dealt with in a different way. He rented under an assumed name, an apartment in St John's Wood, and a red-haired and pleasure-loving young woman called Sybil was the current occupant. Oliver demanded in return only that he retained exclusive rights to her white-skinned and unblemished body and the arrangement had suited them both perfectly. The apartment in St John's Wood and its occupant had served him well in the past, but he had no plans to renew the lease. Now that he wished to marry he could ill afford even the whisper of scandal and with her services no longer needed, a generous final payment was as much as Sybil could expect. The girl was no longer his concern.

On the afternoon following Jacob's arrival in London, Helena, her outward composure calm, felt slightly nervous as she joined her father and aunt in the drawing room to await Oliver's arrival. With every confidence in her father's judgment of character, she was watchful when Oliver was shown in and went with outstretched hand to take Jacob's proffered one.

'Please – do take a seat.' Jacob indicated an armchair opposite his own.

Oliver, his appearance impeccable, smiled at Helena while Beatrice said, 'We're delighted you

33

could join us for tea, Mr Faraday.'

'An invitation much appreciated, I assure you.'

The two men embarked on pleasantries at first, then Helena, who knew her father so well, gave an inward smile as she heard him asking what she knew he would consider to be vital questions. 'I was sorry to hear that you had lost your father two years ago,' he continued after a parlour maid had brought in tea. 'You must find it a heavy responsibility to run the estate on your own. You have several farms, I understand.'

'I am fortunate in having an excellent estate manager.'

'And do you spend much time in the country? Or do you prefer London?'

Oliver smiled. 'I am content in both places, as I think Miss Helena is too.' Helena, lifting the silver teapot to pour tea for them all smiled at him. 'Yes, I am. But to have the choice is the best of both worlds.'

Sitting with Oliver in the sunny room, seeing him so comfortable with her family Helena began to feel ashamed of her misgivings. After all, how much experience did she have of men of Oliver's age, or of any age really? As she listened to the intelligent way he conversed with her father, her gaze played over his hands, watching the swift way he moved them to illustrate a point, remembering the frisson she felt when his fingers occasionally touched her own. Then suddenly an image came to her of the handsome features of the tall doctor she had met in the square, his air of confidence and determination. Even the remembrance of his deep almost musical voice made her long to hear it again. Helena felt utterly bewildered. Why was she thinking of a complete stranger when Oliver was not only a few feet away, but being so utterly charming?

That same evening before the others came down for pre-dinner drinks, Helena found herself once again standing before the casement window and thinking of the young doctor. What useful purpose did she serve? How did she help humanity? Beatrice deplored such serious thoughts, declaring that these matters lay in the male domain, but this notion irritated Helena. She was convinced that she had more to offer than simply being decorative and having an ability to speak French and to play the piano. She glanced down into the square still hopeful that she might once more see him, that this handsome, professional man might look up and see her. He might even smile...

Nicholas, a strong believer in the value of exercise, had instructed his cab driver to stop a short distance before his destination. He often did this when a call was not urgent, especially if it meant he could enjoy a stroll along a leafy road or through a pleasant square. And within minutes, he saw Helena's outline by the window. Even from some distance, the sun caught the brilliance of her blonde hair, which as before he thought almost the colour of honey.

This lovely girl – why was it that she haunted him so much?

Not a man inclined to what he regarded as 'flights of fancy', Nicholas was finding his inability to dismiss her from his mind increasingly frustrating. He felt his steps begin to slow as he came ever nearer, fighting against the temptation to glance up, perhaps even to exchange glances, to make some connection. But that'd be the action of a fool; after all what would be the point? Nicholas walked on only to immediately regret his decision and it took all his self-discipline to prevent him from turning.

Helena remained at the window long after the young man had walked past and once he was no longer in sight, turned away in bitter disappointment. Why should she have expected anything else? He was probably married anyway.

It was a few days later on a perfect summer evening that Helena followed Jacob and Beatrice out of the house and down the short flight of steps to where Oliver's carriage awaited them. Helena had received his invitation to the opera with pleasure, Beatrice with fortitude who found sitting in one position for long periods difficult, and by Jacob with resignation. His own taste leaned more towards music halls, a fact he kept to himself.

Nicholas Carstairs often reflected on the cruel turn of fate that made him turn into the square at that particular time only to see the elegant carriage waiting in front of the house at the exact spot where he had come to the assistance of his 'girl in the window'. There was a small group of people clustered on the pavement, the two men in evening dress – one carrying an opera hat – but his gaze was drawn only to a remembered lovely face above a vivid green cloak. She was smiling at her companions, her expression one of youthful anticipation as she followed an older woman.

Nicholas, finding his way blocked, came slowly to a halt only feet away. Then suddenly she turned. His gaze directly met her own and in that one intense moment there came a flash of mutual startled recognition. Her eyes – those wonderful hazel and gold-flecked eyes – widened and in that one fleeting instant there passed between them a connection so intense that he instinctively took a step forward. But already the pavement was clearing and the younger and taller of the two men was holding out a gloved hand. 'Helena?'

At the sound of her name Nicholas drew back. He saw her cast a bewildered glance at him over her shoulder, but then she was inside the carriage, the coachman was flicking his whip over the backs of two splendid grey horses, and they began to trot away.

Helena could only sink back against the plush seats of the coach and avert her burning cheeks. As her father began to recount his earlier visit to the National Gallery, she scarcely heard a word. Any confusion she had ever previously felt was as nothing compared to the chaos of her emotions now. What had happened back there? That sense of connection, even of intimacy with a man who was almost a complete stranger. *He* had felt it too – of that she was certain. Helena lowered her eyelids, not wanting anything to disturb her thoughts. Such vivid, evocative images; even now she could see his eyes, so brown, warm and expressive, the set of his mouth, those broad shoulders...

Oliver's voice came as if from a distance. 'Are you quite well, Helena?'

As she looked at across at him, her first thought was: he is so fair, so different from... 'Just a slight headache,' she said. 'It's disappearing already.'

'But you are looking forward to the performance?'

'Yes of course.' Helena doubted whether she would be able to concentrate on a single moment.

Chapter Four

A few evenings later, Oliver felt his first flash of jealousy. Whether it was sheer protectiveness of his future plans, or simply seeing Helena with a young Lifeguard's officer, he didn't bother to examine. He only knew that having come to search for her in the plant-filled Conservatory the scene before him filled him with an unreasoning fury. He had been aware that as an heiress Helena would have other suitors, but it was the delight in her expression, the flirtatiousness in her manner that so startled him. Oliver took a deep breath, forcing himself to remember that she was only eighteen and her reaction to flattery was simply a natural one.

Helena was enjoying being with the good-looking young Lieutenant, despite the fact that she considered he had the intelligence of a flea. However, he was funny and charming. Already he had proposed to her twice – not that she had revealed this to Beatrice – but she had no intention of accepting him. 'I think, Tristram,' she was saying with suppressed laughter, 'that you think more of that horse of yours than of anyone else. And whatever made you call him Gladiator?'

'Because he's got such powerful shoulders – am I talking of him too much?' He gave a rueful smile. 'You know I'm not very successful with young ladies.'

'Oh, I don't know,' she smiled up at him. 'You're terribly good-looking, you know.'

He brightened up. 'Really? Then…'

Helena shook her head. 'No, Tristram. Please don't ask me again. Besides…'

'Yes, I know. I don't stand a chance against … oh, glory, here he is.'

She turned to see Oliver walking stiffly towards her. 'There you are, hiding away in here. Your father and aunt have already gone in to supper.'

Helena heard the edge in his tone, and said swiftly, 'Sorry, I hadn't realised the time. You know Tristram Wade of course?'

'No, I don't think I've had the pleasure.'

'My fault – I'm afraid I kidnapped her,' Tristram said good-naturedly.

'Did you?' Oliver's voice was chilly. 'Well, I can't allow that, can I?'

Helena felt a surge of resentment. She was not engaged to him and even if she was, she had no wish to be 'owned' by anyone, something she had once declared to Beatrice. Her aunt's reaction had been one of ridicule. 'A woman stands before God on her wedding day and vows to love and honour and obey her husband. That's the natural order of things and has been for hundreds of years.'

If so, then Helena sometimes wondered whether

she wanted to get married at all. However, as society and the church dictated that if a woman wanted to have children and a home of her own – and she did – then she had no other choice. Although why it should mean a woman relinquishing her right to an independent mind... She gave Tristram a brilliant smile. 'You know I was a willing captive.'

His answering grin faded as Oliver, with a granite expression, offered his arm to Helena. 'Don't you think we should join the rest of our party?'

Even though she acquiesced, Oliver could sense a chill in her manner. He frowned to himself. It had been unwise to forget that independent streak; he must be more careful – at least for the next few months.

Three weeks later, on her last evening in London Helena sat before the triple oval mirror on her dressing table. Tomorrow morning they would be leaving for Lichfield, while Oliver, who had accepted Jacob Standish's invitation to visit Broadway Manor, would soon follow. Her father had no further plans to rent the London house, insisting that if in the future they wished to visit the capital, then a hotel would suffice. With a sigh, Helena rose from her velvet-covered stool knowing that she finally had to accept that she was unlikely ever to see the intriguing dark-haired doctor again. Since that night at the opera, not an evening had she let pass without standing at the window to gaze hopefully down into the square. She may never discover his name, but she knew that she would always remember him.

Slipping off her peignoir, Helena lifted the already turned down silken coverlet on the bed.

There was no explanation for it, none at all.

In a less than salubrious area of London, Nicholas Carstairs was examining a child with a severe case of scabies. He glanced around at the filthy room knowing that the bedding should be boiled in order to kill off the mites that caused the condition; but from their appearance, the thin and grubby sheets were only fit for the dustbin, while the ticked flock pillows bore no sign of any covering. He looked down again at the weeping sores on the small girl's legs, with the rash spreading over her buttocks and back. Cleanliness, soapy water and fresh air were a desperate need throughout all these tenement blocks, but Nicholas had seen too much abject poverty not to know that it bred first despair and then apathy.

'I'll give you some lotion to relieve the itching,' he said to the child's mother. 'But if you could manage to provide a sheet or a pillowcase...'

She looked at him with empty eyes in a grey tired face, a frail baby suckling at her breast. Nicholas, knowing that the situation was hopeless, struggled with an urge to leave a few coins behind. Experience had taught him that it would be a foolish and idealistic gesture. Word would swiftly spread that he was a 'soft touch', resulting in an increasing and often needless demand for his services. Instead, with a feeling of reluctance mixed with shame, he took the meagre coin offered in payment and made his way down the steep dark stairs and out into the welcome daylight.

He attended both the wealthy and the poor, and it never ceased to amaze him that each class had so little knowledge of or even interest in the other. We live in a truly divided and unfair society, he thought wearily as he trudged back to his rooms. He was longing for a bath; it was always his fear that he would pick up some infection, but how was he to treat the sick without exposure to the bacteria that caused their condition?

Later, unable to concentrate on his book, Nicholas read again a letter he had received a few days before. He was not an impulsive man, preferring to give careful consideration to anything that might affect his professional life. With his practice becoming established did he really wish to accept an extra responsibility, however influential in advancing his career? This offer from a Harley Street physician had been unexpected, apparently arising from the gratitude of a barrister who six months ago had collapsed in Kensington High Street. In the area on a rare shopping expedition, fortunately Nicholas had been swiftly on the scene and diagnosed a heart attack, his decisive action saving the man's life. He knew that he could learn much from a respected man such as Dr. Andrew Haverstock, but he was wary, suspecting that his own interest in the care of what he thought of as the 'more unfortunates', might not be viewed with equal sympathy. Determined to keep his independence, his freedom to practise medicine as he wished, he read the letter again, finding it rather ambiguous. If it was merely an offer for him to work with Dr Haverstock on an ad hoc basis, assisting him in certain cases, then it could prove to be an attractive proposition indeed. And that, he thought as he got up and propped the letter on the mantelpiece of the mahogany fireplace, is the crux of the matter.

But now, he would go upstairs to slide beneath pure cotton sheets, and thank the good Lord that he had the good fortune not to have been born in one of those wretched areas only a few miles away. That young woman in those cramped rooms, already with two children, could not have been much older than Helena. Yet the gulf between them was such that they might have been born a different species.

Nicholas closed his mind against even her name. He could not risk another sleepless night, lying awake to stare into the darkness, wondering whether he should try to see her again, knowing that it'd simply be futile. The carriage with its connotations of wealth, the assured man who had ushered her inside, the fact that the London season was coming to its end – the scene told its own story. Even if she was not yet engaged it was crazy to be thinking along those lines. Had those hazel eyes robbed him of his intelligence? What could he offer? He had neither social standing nor an established income, but Nicholas knew that he wasn't going to find it easy to remain true to the decision that he'd reached; to relegate his 'girl in the window' to nothing more than a poignant memory.

On the morning when Helena's suitor was due to arrive at Broadway Manor, the servants' hall was buzzing with curiosity.

43

'I bet he's really handsome,' Annie said.

'And what makes you think that he'll notice the likes of a scullery maid?' Cook snapped.

But Annie was used to such caustic comments. Mrs Kemp's bark was always worse than her bite. Not that Cook had ever been a married woman – her title was an honorary one. 'Just think – what if he proposes while he's here?'

Molly, the under-housemaid, a quiet dark-haired girl, leaned forward. 'What I'm wondering is, who will she take with her if she gets married and goes to live in Hertfordshire? As a lady's maid, I mean.'

'Miss Helena is of an age when she will need her own maid, whether she marries or not.' Enid Hewson was a thin, harassed looking woman of forty with pretensions of gentility, and crooked her little finger as she sipped at her tea. 'It was hard work in London, I can tell you, with two of them to take care of. Looking after Miss Beatrice is what I'm paid for.'

'Do you think you could train *me* up?' Molly said, with more hope than conviction. 'I'm a quick learner.'

Enid drew her thin eyebrows together. 'It's not as simple as all that, you know. There is the question of age. Most lady's maids are older than me, never mind you.'

'Aren't you all forgetting something?' They all turned to look at Ida, whose round face beneath her white filled cap was flushed with indignation. 'As head parlour maid, if anyone should be trained up it should be me.'

'But you're sparking with that corporal at Whittington Barracks,' Molly protested, 'you're not going to want to leave him behind. After all,' she gave a sly glance at the others, 'he might be your last chance.'

Ida glared at her. 'I'm fully aware of that, thank you very much. But that's my decision to make.'

The butler, sitting at the head of the long kitchen table as the staff took their mid-morning break, glanced up from his written notes for the forthcoming visit. 'Don't forget that it's possible a new member of staff might be brought in, someone already experienced.'

'Still, if Ida does decide against it, and you think there's a chance, would you speak up for me?' When Molly had joined the household six years ago at the age of fourteen, she had never expected the daughter of the house to become her secret friend. It still astonished her that no-one at Broadway Manor had guessed that she and Miss Helena, especially in the first two years, had spent so much time together, even meeting in the vast grounds sometimes. There, when Molly had a half day, they would sit beneath one of the large oak trees and read aloud to each other from a current romantic novel and exchange others.

Molly gazed at Miss Hewson. She had always envied her, the way everyone treated her with respect. To accompany Miss Helena when she got married, to go and live in another part of England – now that really would be exciting. She had no doubts of her abilities; learning to dress hair and care for beautiful clothes couldn't be that difficult? It would be a damn sight better than everlasting dusting, polishing and making beds.

'Well there's one thing for sure,' Annie said, and they all turned at the bitterness in her voice. 'It's a job I'll never be able to do.' When she was a child Annie had been jostled near a bonfire on Guy Fawkes' night, and lost her footing. Despite being hauled swiftly from the hot coals, she had suffered severe facial burns and an ugly puckered scar disfigured her right cheek. She knew, as they all did, that despite her hard work and quick mind, her appearance would preclude her from ever being promoted to work 'upstairs'.

'Never mind all that.' Cook folded her hands across the stiff white apron that covered her ample body. 'While this Mr Faraday is here I shall expect all hands to the pump, because if I'm not mistaken we'll be doing a fair bit of entertaining.'

'I think we can all rely on that.' The quiet valet who looked after their master was already rising to leave. He rarely joined in servants' gossip, preferring to read in his room.

Molly looked around at them all. 'I bet Miss Helena's that thrilled. I mean it's really romantic isn't it?'

Chapter Five

Oliver travelled to Broadway Manor in his first motor car. As his chauffeur with the valet beside him concentrated on the route, Oliver, seated in the back, was pleased to find the journey far more comfortable than travelling by coach. He was also looking forward to visiting Lichfield during his stay. The cathedral was reported to be a fine one. Oliver was fond of cathedrals; not to attend services, which he regarded as empty words spoken by tedious clerics, but the buildings appealed to him aesthetically with their noble architecture and glorious stained glass windows. When at last they turned into a long tree-lined avenue of lime trees he leaned forward to see that the graceful manor house built of red brick appeared to be less than 200 years old and certainly lacked the grandeur of Graylings. However, it did offer a warm welcoming appearance, with the grounds immaculately tended, and the portico entrance fronting a magnificent mahogany door.

The noise of the engine brought two black Labradors racing around the corner from the back of the house, barking fiercely. 'Caesar, Nero, quiet!' The dogs retreated as Jacob, followed by a silver-haired butler, came out to welcome his guest personally – a measure of the importance he placed on this visit.

Oliver swung his long legs out of the car and grinned ruefully. 'Sorry about the racket.'

Jacob was walking around the 4-seater Daimler with intense interest. 'Have you had it long? What horse power?'

'Just a few weeks, and it's six. She's a beauty, isn't she?'

Jacob placed one hand on the bonnet of the car to feel the engine's warmth. 'She certainly is.'

'Shall we take your bags directly to your room, Sir?' Bostock beckoned a young footman to assist the valet, and then directed the chauffeur to drive the car to the back of the house, murmuring, 'You'll find your accommodation above the stables.'

Jacob began to usher Oliver into the house. 'Anything you need, refreshment or such, just ask Bostock. If you would care to join us for drinks in the drawing room about seven-thirty? I know Helena is looking forward to seeing you. She and Beatrice have been making all sorts of plans.'

'She's not around?'

Jacob shook his head. 'Changing for the evening, I believe. You were expected rather earlier.'

'Yes, I apologise for that. The journey took longer than I thought.' Oliver followed the butler up a broad staircase carpeted in sage green and panelled in a honey shade of oak to where it divided into two separate landings. They went along a corridor to the right and entered a spacious bedroom with its windows overlooking green parkland. He began to think that his stay at Broadway Manor was going to be a more enjoyable one than he had anticipated. There was a tranquil feel to the house and unlike some he had visited, there were none of the gruesome stags' heads on the walls, no gloomy family portraits where the oils had darkened with age. Maybe there was something to be said for marrying into the *nouveau riche,* although in Oliver's opinion, nowhere could compare with his beloved Graylings.

Helena was in a tizzy of apprehension. 'I don't know Hewson, I really don't.'

'Miss Helena, I have your aunt to dress after you, so if you could please make a decision...'

'Gosh, I'm sorry, I didn't think.' Helena pointed to a silk gown in soft rose.

'Might I suggest pearls?'

Once the maid had dressed her hair and left, Helena moved restlessly around the room. Why did she feel so nervous about meeting him again? She was terribly worried that away from the glamour of London, she might not feel the same physical attraction. Even more crucial, would Oliver staying at the Manor where they would be able to spend more time together, dispel those strange doubts she seemed to have? It was the fact that she had no basis for them that she found so disconcerting.

Helena was aware of her father's expectations; he had made no secret of the fact that he favoured the match. Aunt Beatrice, who was constantly singing Oliver's praises, would never understand Helena's misgivings and she had no wish to be dismissed as foolish and fanciful. Nevertheless, she thought as she descended the wide staircase, I shall be the one spending the rest of my life with him, and the final decision is mine and mine only.

Trying to calm her nerves, she went into the drawing room to find Oliver already there. He was standing with her father before the ornate marble fireplace and studying the striking portrait of Mary Standish hanging above. He turned as she entered and, putting down his glass, came immediately to greet her. 'Helena, you look enchanting. The country air certainly agrees with you.'

'Thank you.' She smiled at him. 'It's nice to see

you again.' He was even more handsome than she remembered, and it was then Helena decided that she was going to stop this nonsense of fretting all the time. The grounds at Broadway Manor were so extensive that surely when she and Oliver had spent hours alone strolling and talking, her mind would be put at rest.

They walked together to stand beneath the gold-framed portrait and Oliver said, 'You are very like her.'

'I just wish I could have known her.'

'I know exactly how you feel.'

Helena turned to gaze at him with sympathy, remembering that he too had lost his mother at birth. Oliver rarely mentioned his late father and she wondered whether he had been a lonely little boy. She had been so lucky to have someone like Beatrice in her life and as she came in to join them, Helena noticed that her aunt was wearing a new rust-coloured dress. Unfortunately, like most of her clothes, it hung awkwardly on her angular body but her garnet necklace – a recent present from Jacob – glowed softly against her rather sallow neck and Helena smiled at her with affection, thinking how typical it was of her father to be so thoughtful.

And so they enjoyed their cocktails seated comfortably around the fireplace, the conversation light and often witty. Helena soon realised that Oliver was socially adept at being a houseguest, striking the perfect tone of respect and interest as he asked about the history of Broadway Manor. She saw his lips twitch slightly when Jacob told him that he had bought the house and its estates only twenty-five years ago. 'Before then it had been in the same family since it was built. The last inhabitant – a young man of only thirty – was obsessed with travelling the world, exploring Africa and big-game hunting, that sort of thing. The hall was hideous, full of animal trophies. Mary hated them and so we had them all removed and replaced the dark panelling with a lighter shade.'

'What makes people think they have the right to take an animal's life just to boast how brave they are?' Helena said. 'Killing elephants for their tusks, leopards for their skins, even in this country people shoot deer to hang their antlers on the wall.' She saw Beatrice give her look of warning that Oliver may have different views. But Helena did not intend to marry anyone if it meant submerging her personality. 'And I'm afraid that was how he met his death. A distant cousin in America inherited and promptly put Broadway Manor on the market.'

Oliver's deep rooted fears and hatred of his own cousin rose to the surface. If he were by some misfortune to inherit Graylings, Selwyn with his gambling debts and weak nature would have no compunction about exposing it to land-hungry vultures. Oliver glanced again at Helena, noticing how the rose silk gown clung to hips that although slim were satisfactorily rounded. He had a sudden desperate image of white unblemished skin on the entire surface of her body. It was his constant fear that his future wife might prove to have even a slight physical defect. Yet Oliver knew that even his valet's diplomacy might find it difficult to ascertain something of such a personal and intimate nature. So much would depend on the age and discretion of Helena's personal maid.

Later, in the high-ceilinged dining room again panelled in light honeyed oak, with long casement windows flooding it with evening sunlight, Oliver found dinner to be equal in refinement and flavour to any meal he was served at Graylings. He turned to Beatrice. 'You have an excellent cook, if I may say so. The quail was especially good.'

'Yes, Bostock,' Jacob said, 'please convey my compliments to Mrs Kemp.'

Oliver was bending his head to listen to Helena. 'And we could ride,' she was saying, 'I'd like to show you the farms. I think the head groom has already picked out a horse for you, unless you would prefer to choose your own.'

He smiled into her eyes only to look away as a footman hovered at his shoulder waiting to serve the lemon syllabub.

'Helena and I have been making plans for your entertainment,' Beatrice said. 'We thought a weekend house party, and perhaps a visit to Lichfield?'

'That would be delightful, Miss Standish.'

Helena's initial nerves had vanished and she was enjoying herself immensely. It was fascinating to see Oliver so relaxed in the familiar surroundings of her home.

Jacob gazed at them both expansively. The couple looked well together; the fact that Oliver was somewhat older troubling him not at all because there had been a similar age gap between himself and his beloved Mary.

Later, once Beatrice and Helena had withdrawn, Jacob was feeling mellow as he sipped his brandy. He looked across at his guest. 'Do you hunt? I'm sure I could arrange...'

Oliver shook his head. 'Thank you, but it's not a pastime I enjoy I'm afraid.'

'The foxes do have to be culled though.'

'Indeed. But I have no desire to witness the ugly sight of hounds tearing one to pieces. I'm afraid I don't shoot,' Oliver said. 'Certainly I don't include the Glorious Twelfth on my social calendar.'

Jacob paused to clip the end of his cigar. He respected a man who had his own principles and upheld them. 'How do you feel about the present government? I wasn't altogether surprised when Winston Churchill decided to cross the floor.'

Oliver nodded. 'He's been in disagreement with Chamberlain for some time. I am pleased to say that the Liberal Party is certainly growing in strength which augurs well for the next election.'

Jacob blew out a cloud of cigar smoke, and nodded in agreement, relieved to hear that their political views were similar. As their conversation drifted to discussing the recent signing of the Entente Cordiale between England and France, he decided that this would be the ideal time to mention that if a suitable constituency arose, he would welcome the chance to serve his country. Oliver Faraday, like so many of his class, moved in influential circles.

'You should see the way he looks at her, if that isn't true love...' Molly said. She hadn't had a chance to see Miss Helena alone since she'd returned from London; once they had managed to exchange glances in the hall, but that was all.

'And is he really that handsome?' was Annie's question, whose reddened hands were already scrubbing away at saucepans.

'I should say so. Some girls have all the luck.' Molly glanced with exasperation at Oliver's valet who was enjoying a slice of Mrs Kemp's pork pie and had so far failed to respond to even one of her flirtatious looks.

'Go on,' Ida said to him. 'What's he like then, this master of yours?'

Jack Hines glanced across at Annie who had her back to him. Then he gave a thin smile. 'I'm afraid I can't say.'

The servants glanced at each other.

'And that's how it should be.' The butler came in to join them. 'Loyalty to one's employer is an attribute to be admired. Now if everything is finished in the dining room and laid up for tomorrow morning, I think we should all be off to our beds.'

Later, in the bedroom they shared, Molly whispered to Ida, 'If we're not going to find out any good gossip from the valet, I'll just have to transfer my charms to the chauffeur.' She slipped her nightdress over her head before removing her underwear then whispered as they got into bed. 'Don't you think it's a bit unusual that they're both so terribly good-looking?'

'They are, aren't they?' Ida said. 'But I think that Mr Hines is aiming higher than the likes of us. He was asking me which of us was Miss

Helena's personal maid.' She giggled. 'He'll have a shock when he meets Miss Hewson.'

Helena was finding her mind was far too active to be able to sleep. She kept dwelling on the way that Oliver, once the two men had re-joined them in the drawing room, had managed to convey a silent yet intimate conversation between them. Against a background of polite social chit-chat, sometimes his glances towards her had been full of amusement, at others quizzical, and once the expression in his eyes had been so meaningful that she had to avoid his gaze. And once when his fingers had brushed against her own... If this was how he was going to make her feel after only one evening, then Helena was rather hoping they might have some secluded times alone.

Full of a delicious anticipation she turned over and snuggling into the soft feather pillow let her mind drift ahead. How wise she had been to dismiss those silly doubts about him.

Yet strangely, that night she dreamt not of Oliver, but of the tall and dark-haired doctor, a man she would probably never see again.

Chapter Six

Two weeks later, Helena and Oliver rode through the familiar meadow in the grounds of Broadway Manor, beneath trees dappled with sunlight, and slowing down their horses after the exhilaration of their gallop, gradually came to a halt. Oliver nodded towards an ancient oak, its branches spreading wide, the clearing beneath it quiet and secluded. 'Shall we stretch our legs?' With his hands firmly spanning her waist, he helped Helena to dismount from her chestnut mare and then waited as she dusted down her riding skirt.

'Isn't it a beautiful day,' she said.

'It's a wonderful day.'

She glanced up to see an intense expression in his eyes that made her pulse begin to race. This could be the moment. Would he at last kiss her? She was longing to know how it would feel to be held in his arms. Surely he wasn't going to wait until he had proposed before he kissed her? Tomorrow people would be arriving for a weekend house party and there would be little time for any privacy at all.

She remained silent as Oliver led her over to the welcome shade of the stately tree, and Helena, leaning to rest against the rough bark of the gnarled trunk, looked up at him in anticipation. Slowly, deliberately his lips came down to meet her own and as he drew away, he lifted a hand to trace the outline of her cheek. Smiling down at her, he murmured, 'I think we'll do that again.'

This time he teased her slightly with his lips, tracing the outline of hers before their kiss became deeper than before, longer. She was finding to her delight that the experience was rather a pleasurable one. Leaving their horses to graze, they linked hands and began to stroll along the soft grass to the sound of birdsong and rustlings in the leaves above. 'These past weeks have been perfect,' he said, smiling down at her, 'but I suppose it couldn't last forever.'

'I know. But Aunt Beatrice would think she was failing in her duty not to arrange some company and distractions.'

He squeezed her hand. 'I'd prefer to spend the time alone with you.'

Being in Oliver's arms, feeling the warmth of his mouth against her own, had reassured Helena far more than all her hours of mental agonising. Then he was turning to her again, holding her close, kissing her forehead, the tip of her nose, and once more finding her lips.

And so she was in a contented frame of mind when they went back to the horses and returned to the main avenue that led to the Manor. As they trotted along, Helena waved at Annie who was trudging towards the entrance gates, and slowing down said, 'Hello, are you off home?'

'Yes, Miss Helena, just for a few hours.'

Oliver was reigning in his horse with some irritation. Really, Helena was far too familiar with the staff. It had been the same when they had visited the farms. In his opinion a nod and polite good morning was quite sufficient, but to his astonishment, Helena had seemed to know the names of not only the tenants, but also their families. In addition, each needed to be greeted and the children enquired after. She really should be more aware of her position and–

Just then as the girl Helena was bending to speak to turned to look up at him, the sunlight revealed a hideous scarring down one side of her face. His recoil was instinctive, even violent and

Helena, seeing Annie whiten with humiliation, her eyes full of distress, swung round to see Oliver's expression of sheer revulsion. The anger that swept through her was hot and full of shame. She said in a tight voice, 'Please remember me to your mother, Annie.'

'Yes, Miss.'

Once the slight, square-shouldered figure clutching a small wicker basket was some distance away, Helena turned in fury to an impatient Oliver. 'What on earth was all that about?'

'Who is she?'

'Our scullery maid – she was burned in a bonfire accident as a child.'

'And your father employs such a creature?'

Helena, horrified by the contempt in his voice, snapped, 'Why on earth shouldn't he? Her father is one of our gardeners. As for Annie, she is not a "creature" as you so insultingly call her. Really, Oliver, you might show a bit more humanity.'

She saw his expression darken, his mouth become grim, and without even the civility of a reply, he urged his horse to canter swiftly away, leaving Helena, riding side saddle, to clatter a few minutes later into the stable yard, only to find a groom leading the horse to its stable. Of Oliver, there was no sign.

Suddenly she was glad that her close friend, Dorothy Powner was coming for the weekend and that she would be meeting Oliver. The daughter of a judge who had moved into the county when he bought an estate near Stafford, she had been delighted to find a companion approved of by her irascible and strict father, while Helena, then fifteen, had always longed for a friend near her own age. Helena had great respect for Dorothy's sound common sense; she might be outspoken but her opinion was one to be valued. Would she too find Oliver difficult to understand?

'They've had a row, I'd put money on it,' Ida reported when that evening she returned from the dining room. 'Miss Helena and Mr Faraday, I mean.'

'Well I don't like him!' Annie called, coming in from the scullery. 'He's not good enough for our Miss Helena. He'll bring her nothing but trouble, you mark my words.'

In a corner, Jack Hines put his *Sporting Life* down. His voice was quiet. 'Why do you say that, Annie?'

'They were both riding down the avenue when I was goin' home, and…'

'He *saw* you?' The valet's voice was so abrupt that even Cook looked up from her task.

'He saw me all right.' Annie's voice was grim. 'Nearly came off his horse, he did. You'd think I was a freak or summat.'

Molly put down the cotton stocking she was mending and went over to her. 'Don't take on, love. Some people can be very insensitive.' She watched Annie go back to her duties and frowned. 'Is he like that, Mr Hines?'

But the valet had returned to reading his newspaper, and Molly sighed with exasperation. It was always the same every time anyone mentioned his master; the man just seemed to close down. Talk about being as 'silent as the grave'.

Jacob Standish was well aware that something had happened between his daughter and his guest, and with Beatrice recovering from a cold and having a tray in her room, he was beginning to find the effort of keeping a civilised discourse over dinner rather a trial. He glanced at Helena. She was not a girl normally given to moods, but even he could sense that she was upset about something.

Helena was feeling utterly miserable. For Oliver to behave in such a way just because of poor Annie's scarred face, and then to respond like that to – in her opinion – a justified reprimand, after the wonderful romantic afternoon they'd spent together! And now – not once had his gaze met hers, and the coldness emanating from him...

But this had happened once before. Not so marked but it had been the time he had found her talking to Tristram – which had, for heaven's sake, only been a bit of light-hearted flirting.

Yet his appetite didn't seem to be affected; even after having eaten heartily of Mrs Kemp's pigeon pie followed by sherry trifle, he was now enjoying his cheese. Were men always so unfathomable? Her father – as long as his wishes were adhered to – had never seemed to be so. Although she knew that her friend Dorothy considered her father to have so many prickles he ought to have been born a porcupine.

Jacob was coming to a decision. Much as he enjoyed Oliver's male company over their brandy and cigars, these two young people needed time alone to mend their differences, because until there was a proposal this whole enterprise could fall down like a house of cards. And for Oliver not to offer for Helena – after he had been so closely attentive for months – would be unthinkable and certain to be considered by society as a slight on the whole family.

With a frown, he gathered up his napkin and put it on to the table. 'I'm afraid I have some urgent matters to attend to,' he said, 'so if you'll both excuse me, I shall go directly to my study.' He turned to the butler who was standing in one corner of the room. 'Bostock, perhaps you could leave the coffee in the drawing room for Miss Helena to attend to, and I don't think they will need you any further.' As he got up he added, 'My apologies, Oliver.'

And it was only then, once they had moved to the drawing room and were out of earshot of servants, that Oliver at last turned to Helena. He had taken a seat beside her on the sofa and although she felt his gaze on her she remained occupied with pouring their coffee, determined that he should be the one to speak first.

'Helena, do you think we could forget that trivial incident this afternoon?'

Her temper flared. Did he think it was trivial to show such distaste at someone's unfortunate appearance? Helena remembered how she had hurried to the gardener's cottage as soon as she'd heard of the bonfire accident, how she had held and comforted the ten-year-old Annie as she screamed with the agony of the painful burns. Beatrice too had come with salves and bandages, and her father had paid the doctor's bills. None of them had been so careless since as to show their horror at the girl's appearance, and Helena could only imagine how Annie had felt at the shock and disgust on Oliver's face.

'I hardly think it was trivial, Oliver,' she said quietly. 'I would have expected better of you.'

'Helena, she's a servant, a mere scullery maid, it's of no consequence, and you must accept that I won't have my behaviour commented upon.'

She put down the coffee pot and turned to him. 'Oliver, I may be a woman, and a very young one, but I'm entitled to my opinion.'

He looked at the flush of determination on her face and suddenly realised that if he wanted this girl to marry him and provide him with an heir then he needed to make amends, at least for the moment. Any temperamental differences between them he could deal with once she was his lawful wife, and judging by her delicious response to their kisses that afternoon, then perhaps his best option was...

Gently he took her hand. 'Shall we agree on that point? Shall this be our first lover's quarrel?'

As Oliver raised her fingers and brushed them with his lips, Helena found herself softening at the phrase 'lover's quarrel'. Had she exaggerated his reaction in her mind? She knew that an over-active imagination was a fault of hers, both Beatrice and her governesses had frequently told her so. For a few seconds she struggled with her resentment but then relief won. It had been hateful to have such an atmosphere between them.

'Damn the coffee,' Oliver murmured, 'we won't

be disturbed, your father made sure of that.'

His hands were warm on her bare shoulders as he drew her towards him and she could taste wine on his lips. And then his mouth became more demanding, arousing within her a passion that drove all other considerations out of her mind.

Chapter Seven

The house party was proving to be a great success. Although a cold autumn had been predicted, as Helena reclined on a garden chair with her feet raised, her face shaded from the sun by a wide straw hat, winter seemed far distant. There was a doubles match being played on the tennis court, with the relaxing sound of ball on racquet, the occasional shout of 'Sorry!' and the umpire's call of the score. It was, she thought, a perfect English afternoon. Most of all she was enjoying the chance to spend long hours with Dorothy.

'Come on,' she persuaded, 'You've been here over a day so you must have formed some opinion of Oliver by now.'

Dorothy, two years older, was regarded by many as something of a bluestocking, even a born spinster. She was handsome, rather than pretty, refusing to curl her dark hair which she always wore in a chignon and preferred plain clothes and quiet colours. Instead of immediately answering the question Dorothy said lazily, 'How did that brother of mine behave himself in London?'

'Hugh behaved perfectly to the best of my knowledge,' Helena told her. 'Jolly useful too, because when he danced with me I could ask him who Oliver was.'

'He may have known his name, but he seems to know little else about him.'

'They probably don't move in the same circles.' Helena stretched. 'I hope they won't be long with tea, I'm starving.' She twisted round. 'You still haven't answered my question. I've given you the time you asked for – so again, what do you think of him?'

As Dorothy gazed at her, Helena could see a frown puckering her forehead.

'You don't like him!'

'I didn't say that. I think he is incredibly handsome, but Helena, I'm just not sure. I cannot fault his attitude towards you, nor his charm in general. But...' she hesitated, 'I can't help thinking that there's another side to him. I find him a bit of an enigma. But then, maybe that's one of the things you find attractive.' She laughed. 'I mean even I can see that it would be more exciting to marry a man like Oliver rather than Hugh, fond though I am of him.'

Helena's peal of laughter rang out. 'You're just talking like a sister. Hugh's one of the nicest people I know...'

'Maybe,' Dorothy said drily. 'But he's hardly the dashing hero. Still, I'm sure there's some nice girl out there who will think he's wonderful. At least I hope so.'

'But you can understand why I'm tempted,

with Oliver I mean?'

'Who wouldn't be? All I can say, Helena, is that if you're looking for a tranquil marriage, then I suspect he's not the man to choose.'

Helena really hadn't wanted to hear this, not least because it echoed her own feelings, particularly after that ugly scene the other afternoon. And yet when Oliver held her in his arms she had longings she hadn't known she possessed. Sometimes she felt guilty, wondering whether she should be allowing him to kiss her before they were betrothed. Was her heart ruling her head, was that what being in love meant?

Dorothy was thoughtful. 'Is your Papa keen on the match?'

'He has made no secret of it.'

'And Beatrice – how does she feel?'

'She thinks he's wonderful, and that I should consider myself fortunate.'

'Don't let yourself be unduly influenced by family pressure, Helena. Mind you,' Dorothy glanced sideways at her, 'he *is* quite a catch!'

'You make him sound like a fish!'

They began to laugh and Dorothy said, 'All I can say is that if you do marry him, I shall expect an invitation to Graylings. I've never been to Hertfordshire.'

Helena was wondering whether to confide in her friend about the strong attraction she had felt to the dark-haired doctor during her time in London. Dorothy would approve of her intervention on behalf of the abused horse, but would she dismiss as romantic nonsense that after all this time, Helena still felt haunted by the memory of a man who was almost a stranger? Then while she was hesitating, Bostock and the maids came out of the house carrying trays and tiered cake stands to put on the white cloth covered table in the shade. When he rang a bell to summon guests from all corners of the garden and house, Helena felt a sense of relief, deciding it was wiser not to say anything after all. Cook's delicious lemonade accompanied by cucumber sandwiches, scones and other confections was just the distraction she needed.

Once everyone was comfortable in the drawing room that evening, at Jacob's request Helena seated herself at the grand piano. Oliver remained standing, leaning slightly against the wall in one corner. A parlour maid had been in to light the oil lamps and in their golden glow Helena's expression was absorbed as her long, slender fingers rippled over the keyboard. Oliver, finding her sensitive interpretation of Beethoven's 'Moonlight Sonata' a delight, closed his eyes. The room was silent, captured by the beauty of the melody and Oliver imagined the same scene in the setting of the large music room at Graylings where the Steinway piano was surrounded by a circle of velvet chairs – the perfect frame for a lovely hostess. Eventually the piano keys became silent, and Oliver opened his eyes to gaze directly into Helena's slightly quizzical ones. He gave a warm, appreciative smile and it was in that moment that he realised that the eighteen-year-old girl he had chosen to be his wife was going to develop into an exceptionally beautiful woman.

'Jolly accomplished, isn't she?' Johnnie Horton said later, as Oliver strolled over to take a seat next to him on the sofa.

'She *is* a bit special.'

'Topping, old chap. I must say I'm having a smashing time. I suppose I was invited because I introduced the two of you.' He glanced around the room. 'Mind you, I could have done with a bit more female distraction.'

Oliver laughed. 'You're not enamoured of Dorothy, then?'

'Too clever by half, and the other two girls are hardly beauties.' He lowered his voice. 'I shall be visiting the luscious Cora when I get back to London.'

Oliver frowned at the indiscretion – this was hardly the time or place to speak of such matters.

'Mind you,' Johnnie said, 'Hugh's a decent sort.'

'Indeed he is, so don't go leading him astray.' Oliver's comment was automatic; his interest lay in an intense conversation taking place nearby.

'If you're really interested in standing, then you need to be putting out feelers now.' The man speaking, whose weather beaten face looked like creased leather, was apparently an old friend of Jacob's. His rather stout wife was on the other side of the room chatting to Beatrice.

Jacob's tone was confidential. 'I thought it might be a bit early.'

Geoffrey Blundred shook his head. 'I don't think so. Jacob, I hope you realise what a minefield politics can be. There's a fair bit of skulduggery goes on.'

'I still think there's a place for an honest man.'

Oliver tucked the useful nugget away as Johnnie nudged him. 'Are you listening, old boy? I was saying how well old Standish feeds us. That mutton was the best I've tasted and the salmon was excellent.'

In the servants' hall, everyone was exhausted. 'I don't know why anyone needs eight courses,' Molly said. 'I've never had more than a dinner and a pudding in me life, at least not at the same time.'

Cook was resting her swollen ankles. 'I can't deny it's been hard work these past few days. I told you we would have to entertain. Mind you, at least there should be some tasty leftovers for the rest of us.'

'I suppose that valet of Mr Horton's is packing, ready for the off tomorrow, same as Miss Dorothy's maid.' Ida flopped in a chair. 'Gosh, I'm tired.'

'Yes, well, tired or not,' Mrs Kemp snapped, 'I want this kitchen spick and span and ready for tomorrow morning. There's another full range of dishes to prepare for breakfast *and* kedgeree.'

'I don't know where they put it all.' Annie was toiling at the sink. 'They ought to share it out a bit. When I think how some people have to manage on bread and scrape...'

'There's one world for us and one world for them, surely you know that by now,' Molly said.

'You know, Annie, in some kitchens the scullery maid would be seen and not heard. You're far too fond of expressing your opinions.' They all turned as the butler came into the kitchen.

'Take no notice, love,' Cook said once he had left carrying a bottle of Madeira. 'He's just tired, like the rest of us. And once all this is over, it'll be even busier, in fact a flaming nightmare, what with having some of that new-fangled electricity installed.'

'Just think, though,' Ida said, brightening up. 'It'll be a lot less work for us, without so many wicks to trim and everything.'

'Yes, well I still think the light from oil lamps was kinder. My sister says her employers got this electric and it shows up her wrinkles something rotten.'

'I wonder what it must be like,' Ida said chin in hand. 'To be one of them. You know, to go away for a weekend with everything done for you. Waited on and pampered, not even having to do your own packing.'

'Nor having to pay a penny for your keep,' Annie said. 'When we used to go and visit my granny we had to take our food with us – and a bit extra for her.'

'Yes well that's real life,' Molly said, 'something the upper classes know nothing about. I just hope the guests leave some generous tips when they leave, although I suppose the footmen will get most of them, at least that's what usually happens.'

Two days later, the excursion to Lichfield proved a great success. Jacob was absent, having had to attend a business meeting, while Beatrice, after her initial nerves, enjoyed being driven in a motor car into the small but historic town. The medieval cathedral's three graceful spires had been visible from some distance and Helena told Oliver that while locally they were known as the 'Ladies of the Vale,' in reality they were a symbol of the Trinity.

The three of them stood for a few moments in the serene Close to look up at the magnificent frontage, and then once inside, as Helena and Beatrice went down the centre aisle and slipped into a pew to pray, Oliver strolled around to admire the architecture, the ornate metal choir screen and beautiful stained glass windows. The existence of God he dismissed as a fairytale, but even he had to admit that centuries of prayer left their legacy in these ancient buildings.

He turned as Helena came to join him and slipped her hand into his. 'There's something I want to show you.' She led the way to the South Choir Aisle. 'It's called The Sleeping Children,' she whispered, 'portraying two sisters who died accidentally in 1812.'

Oliver gazed down at the long marble sculpture and gave a brisk approving nod. 'It is very well executed.' Startled, Helena glanced up at him. Her own emotion whenever she gazed down at the lithe sleeping forms, the younger girl with her arm around her sister's waist, was one of utter sadness at the loss of such young lives; Oliver seemed almost indifferent.

Beatrice came to join them with a slight shiver. 'It's always so cold in these places. I think I'll go outside and wait for you there.'

'I'll come with you,' Helena said, glad to follow her into the warm sunshine where, as they lingered, she tried to analyse why she felt so disappointed at Oliver's reaction. After all, how could he know that the sculpture had over the years, become rather special to her? Yet surely, anyone seeing and reading of children dying would have felt some pity, not merely remark about the skill of the sculptor? Again, she felt that uneasiness she had tried so hard to suppress, but when Oliver came out to join them, he was in such an infectious light-hearted mood that after a while she managed to put the incident out of her mind.

Later, as they walked some distance to gaze at the large 3-storey house where Samuel Johnson was born, Beatrice said, 'I read somewhere that he described Lichfield as a "city of philosophers".'

'That's true,' Oliver agreed, moving a little to give her more space. 'I'd also like to see the Nag's Head public house. Apparently he wrote some of his famous dictionary there.'

Helena, her large brimmed hat held in position by a gauze scarf, was enjoying the slight breeze on her skin, but she sensed from the frown between her aunt's eyes that Beatrice was either beginning a headache or finding her feet painful. Helena reached out and touched her hand. 'Are you tired?'

'A little,' Beatrice said.

Oliver immediately offered his arm. 'Then we'll leave the Nag's Head until another time. In fact, I think we would all appreciate a rest.'

As the car wound its way between the hedgerows on the way back to Broadway Manor, Helena began to look forward to the rest of the day with a delicious anticipation. She and Oliver now took every chance to be alone together, with Beatrice considering that it was unnecessary for her to be chaperoned within their own grounds. She turned to gaze at him seated before her beside the chauffeur, studying the back of his head, looking at the way his fair hair curled slightly at the base of his neck. This feeling she had for him *must* be love, otherwise surely she wouldn't be longing for them to be alone together? As for her lingering misgivings, she decided that she was merely proving her father right. Jacob had always professed that women were illogical.

Chapter Eight

A few days later, after her silk brocade bedroom curtains had been opened to herald another warm day and the maid had left the room, Helena leaned back against the soft pillows to savour her hot chocolate. Oliver had now been at Broadway Manor for three weeks and the whole household was expecting an engagement; even the maids were casting sideways glances. Yet there had been no hint of a proposal. Helena tried to think whether there had been any change in his attitude towards her. But the reverse was true – their private moments together were increasingly more affectionate. However, even Oliver must realise that his delay was beginning to cause her embarrassment. And when after breakfast her father asked her to join him in his study, Helena guessed correctly that he too was becoming concerned.

Jacob gazed at his daughter whose resemblance to her mother grew with every passing year and was a constant reminder of the poignancy of their loss. How proud Mary would have been of her. In a high-necked white blouse with leg of mutton sleeves and long blue skirt, Helena sat in the burgundy leather chair opposite his desk and smiled at him.

Jacob cleared his throat. 'My dear, I don't like to intrude on such personal matters, but I felt that perhaps it was time we discussed…'

Helena, seeing his discomfort said swiftly, 'Are you perhaps concerned about Oliver's intentions, papa?'

He nodded with some relief. 'He will be leaving us in just over a week, and while your Aunt Beatrice and I feel that the visit has been a resounding success…'

'You are wondering if and when he is going to declare himself.'

Helena's voice was quiet and he gave her a sharp glance. The man was inscrutable at times, but then so many of the upper classes were like that, giving the impression that they were a race apart, not quite mortal like the rest of the population. However, if Oliver had been merely toying with Helena's affections… Jacob's forehead creased in a frown. 'That is exactly what I am wondering. I'm sure you are aware of how much importance I place on this match. Tell me, is there anything I should know? Something you haven't told me?'

Helena shook her head, 'Not at all Papa.'

'And he has given no hint of his intentions, has never talked of your future together?'

Again she shook her head.

'You will obviously accept him?'

Helena felt the atmosphere between them change into one of pressure, benign in nature, but insistent. A refusal at this late stage when the county was expecting such a prestigious match would cause humiliation not only to Oliver but also to her father and aunt. It was only then that Helena realised that any doubts she had were no longer relevant. 'Yes, of course I will.'

Jacob drummed his fingers on the large, highly polished desk. 'Then I hope you are right, my dear. And that a decision is reached very soon.' However, as she came over to kiss his cheek before leaving, he couldn't help but wonder whether he should have probed more into her feelings for Oliver. Did she love him in the way that he had loved his Mary? But how could a father broach such a delicate subject with his daughter, and although he rarely had a critical thought about his sister, Jacob did wish that Beatrice, with her brisk, no-nonsense attitude could just sometimes forget her sense of duty and remember her womanly side.

And so it was that when in the late afternoon Helena found herself guided by Oliver towards the rose arbour, her heart began to pound with both apprehension and relief. In an effort to remain calm, as they reached the trellis arch she breathed in the delicate fragrance of damask roses and bent to a beautiful white specimen nestling among its dark green foliage. 'I love roses, don't you?'

Oliver smiled inwardly. Fond as he was of her, Helena was a romantic little goose, which was why he had so carefully chosen the scene for his proposal. Nothing must upset his plans, which was why he had deliberately delayed this moment, knowing that uncertainty would build pressure. His valet had already reported Jacob Standish had only that morning summoned Helena to his study.

As Helena straightened up, he took her hand and leaning forward, kissed her lightly on the lips. 'Yes, of course. And I know you will love the extensive rose gardens at Graylings.' He smiled and touched a tendril of her hair. 'Helena, I refuse to subscribe to the ridiculous stance of going down on one knee. It is so undignified, do you not agree? And I don't think my next words will come as a surprise to you.' Oliver gazed down at her, utterly confident of her answer. 'Please, Miss Helena Standish, would you do me the honour of becoming my wife?'

Helena, conscious of the warm pressure of his hand in hers and the subtle cedar wood scent of his cologne, hesitated and then said the words that she knew would shape the rest of her life. 'Yes, Oliver, of course I will marry you.'

'It's champagne in the drawing room!' Bostock came hurrying into the kitchen. 'I knew it! Mr Faraday was in the master's study for well over an hour.'

'Lord help us!' Cook sat in the nearest chair.

'he's proposed at last!'

'What's she said, Mr Bostock? Has Miss Helena accepted him?' The younger of the two footmen looked up from his task of polishing the silver, while another began to set out flutes on a silver tray.

'They'd hardly be drinking champagne if she hadn't. I think this occasion calls for the Krug.' He hurried away to the wine cellar.

'I wonder whether he went down on one knee,' Molly said dreamily.

'That man would never do such a thing, he's too full of his own self-importance!' Annie stood at the door to the scullery, her eyes full of consternation. 'And I for one wish he'd never set foot here.'

'Honestly, Annie, I don't understand why you're so against him.' Ida began to stack a pile of clean napkins inside a deep drawer in the dresser.

'Do you like him, Ida?'

She paused and then slowly shook her head. 'I'm not sure, Annie. I mean he's *"one of them"*, isn't he? And they're different from us with all their formal manners and such. Perhaps that's why he seems a bit on the cold side.'

Molly bit into a broken half of shortbread. She felt worried. 'I still think it's strange that neither the valet nor the chauffeur will give anything away about him.'

'And he does have a way of making you feel invisible. But he turns on the charm when Miss Helena's around, that's for sure. Mind you, he must have genuine feelings for her. After all, he hardly needs to marry her for her money. And he's her choice so we should be glad for her.'

'Yes, well I won't be sorry when he's left,' Enid Hewson said. 'It's not him I mind as much as that manservant of his. He's always nosying about Miss Helena.'

Molly stared at her. 'How do you mean?'

'Well, it's not direct questions as such, but – oh I don't know, he just gives me the creeps. "It must be nice to work for a mistress who is so perfect," he said, and then went on to tell me that his sister was born with an ugly birthmark on her hip. I don't know what he was insinuating.'

'What did you say?'

'Nothing – I always treat him with the contempt he deserves.'

Molly nudged Ida. 'Go on then, if a man as handsome as Mr Faraday proposed to you, would *you* turn him down?'

'My Charlie wasn't at the back of the class when good looks were given out, even if he does have a gammy leg. Mind you, if he hadn't got that in the Boer War he wouldn't have been left behind when his regiment left last year.' Ida's tone was defensive. 'Anyway, he likes being a clerk at the Depot. And he may not be rich but he'll do for me. And one of these days...' The others glanced at each other. As they often said, two years was quite long enough for a courtship to drag on.

'I'm seeing him on Sunday afternoon,' Ida said, her voice tense. 'I shall tell him then that I might have the opportunity of another post.'

'Don't you go counting your chickens, Ida,' Cook's voice was sharp.

'Maybe she sees it as a way of forcing him to make a declaration,' Molly said. 'That's the trouble with soldiers – they get all found so they don't need a woman to cook for them. At least that's what my mum used to say.'

'Molly, I do think men get married for other reasons than to have a full belly!' Annie spluttered with laughter.

'Well, we shall see, won't we?' Ida said, 'When I see him on Sunday, I mean.'

'Just don't go burning your bridges, remember what Mr Bostock said,' Cook told her. 'There might be no chance of either you or Molly being promoted. Mr Faraday might want some sort of fancy French maid to attend to his wife.'

'Miss Helena won't want someone speaking a different lingo. She'll want a familiar face from home. I can tell you that for nothing!' Molly was indignant at the thought. A foreigner indeed!

Jacob was in an expansive mood that evening during dinner, while Beatrice sat with two high spots of colour on her sallow cheeks, and Helena suspected that the earlier champagne had gone to her aunt's head. A headache would follow no doubt.

Oliver was enjoying his oyster patties. Marriage to Helena was now something he contemplated with keen anticipation. He not only had the tantalising prospect of having a young virgin in his bed, he was confidently expecting to have an heir within twelve months of the honeymoon. He was also impressed by the subtle yet efficient way in which Broadway Manor was managed; he had no doubt that Beatrice Standish would have ensured that her niece was well-trained in all aspects of running a large household. Graylings deserved a capable mistress, and despite her youth, Helena had intelligence and imagination. He was confident that she would rise to the challenge and it was with complacence that he put down his cutlery. 'Tomorrow I expect to receive a package that I would like to share with you – it will contain a painting of Graylings.'

Helena's eyes lit up. 'But that would be wonderful. I'm dying to see it, Oliver. You've told me so much about it.'

'I have heard,' Beatrice said, 'that it is an exceptionally fine house.'

Jacob didn't mention the fact that in a drawer in his study lay an image of Graylings; one he had sourced months ago. The reason he hadn't shown it to Helena was because he had wanted to be sure that his daughter's decision wasn't influenced by the grandeur of her future home. Beatrice he had kept in ignorance, thinking that she might then find it difficult to behave so naturally with their guest. Both he and his sister had been born into a background that some might have thought extremely comfortable, but he had always known that being in 'trade' brought with it a social stigma. Jacob's astute business brain had developed his father's modest brewery into a leading company and had learned that success and an air of assurance smoothed many tricky situations. He was inordinately proud of Beatrice, who was of a retiring nature and had not found it easy to take over the reins of Broadway

Manor after Mary died.

He gazed thoughtfully at his future son-in-law, knowing that there were important negotiations to take place. Their respective lawyers would of course handle the marriage settlement, and Jacob suspected that Oliver would not be the easiest man to deal with. Already he was insisting on an early wedding, a matter he confessed he had not yet broached with Helena. Jacob looked across the table at his excited daughter; he on occasions thought that she looked somewhat troubled, doubtful even. Now he felt somewhat reassured.

It was dawn before Helena eventually drifted into an uneasy sleep. The euphoria and even relief that Oliver had made his offer, thus easing her father's anxiety, had sustained her all through the evening. But once curled up beneath the silken eiderdown, she felt 'full of nerves', as one of her governesses used to say when confronted with a new experience. Her betrothal wasn't the golden picture she had dreamed of as a young girl, there still seemed to be faint shadows around the edges. Although she had always dreamed of a fairytale proposal, Helena could understand that a man like Oliver would consider it undignified to go down on one knee. Although where had been his declaration of undying love? Wasn't that what every woman, no matter what her age, longed to hear? For her suitor to say those wonderful words, 'I love you'?

Then Helena thought – but if he had, could I in truth say those words to him – that I loved him too? I think I do, but what if it is merely an infatuation. How does one know such a thing for certainty?

As an image of her 'mystery doctor' crept into her mind, she thought of the intensity of his gaze that time before the opera, then shook up her pillows with annoyance. For heaven's sake, surely now, after all that had happened, she could finally forget *that* nonsense. After all, how could it be anything else?

Chapter Nine

'Where did you say you'd bin, Johnnie?' Cora leaned up one elbow and looked down at him.

'Lichfield.'

'Where's that, then?'

'Staffordshire – you know up north, well the Midlands really.'

'I've never 'eard of either of them.'

'I can understand your not knowing of Lichfield, but surely you drink out of cups and eat off plates?'

'Cheeky beggar, of course I do.'

'Look underneath sometime,' he told her lazily, 'the words Stoke-on-Trent will probably be stamped there. It's usually called the Potteries. That's in Staffordshire.'

'I've 'eard of that – there used to be a bloke on Petticoat Lane Market from there, sold all sorts of crockery.' She glanced curiously at him. 'I thought you nobs kept away from manufacturing towns.'

'I didn't say I was there, Cora – I said that I was in the same county.' He grinned at her. 'There wasn't a girl in the place who could measure up to you.'

'A country estate was it?'

He nodded.

'You're a lucky devil, Johnnie.' Sometimes Cora felt nothing but contempt for her clients. Rich, lazy sods, most of them. But she did have a soft spot for Johnnie. He always lingered afterwards and she rather liked the way he'd relax on the pillows while he smoked a fag. She liked their easy conversation too. Although Belle charged by the hour, he never quibbled about paying any extra.

'And you're a smashing girl, Cora. Sometimes I wish...' but Johnnie didn't complete the sentence and she read little into it. She wasn't daft enough to think that she could ever play any part in his life. But after he'd left and she'd used a vinegar douche, Cora lifted the flower print and took out her journal from behind the brick. Turning to a clean page, she wrote the date and the words – *'Johnnie – last weekend – country estate near Lichfield.'*

Then she reddened her lips, gave another spray of scent, and with a swift glance over her shoulder to make sure everything was in order, went downstairs to acquire her next client. Some might shudder at her way of life but Cora was used to it and she didn't really mind, at least most of the time.

Two weeks later in the austere book-lined study

at Graylings, Oliver sat opposite the tall, round-shouldered man who had handled the legal affairs of the Faraday estate for the past twenty years. Finlay McPherson was peering through his rimless glasses at the sheaf of papers before him, a frown creasing his forehead.

'Is there some sort of problem?'

Finlay removed his glasses and looked directly at a client he found impossible to fathom. 'Not especially. We need to ascertain exactly what provision would be in place in the event of your death; which of course is the normal procedure in any Marriage Settlement. And we do have to consider all eventualities. You will need to make a new Will, of course. As you know, Graylings is entailed and in the unfortunate event of your future wife being left a widow without male issue, then the house and all lands belonging to it, including the farms, would be inherited by your first cousin Mr Selwyn Faraday.' He glanced up not surprised to see a look of hostility in Oliver's eyes. Finlay was well aware of the animosity between the two relatives and for once, his sympathies lay with Oliver. 'A situation that I think we both hope would never materialise.' He glanced down again at his papers. 'Your personal assets including the London house are, of course, in your own disposal, but I am sure you will wish to provide for your wife and any children you may have.'

Oliver nodded. 'But of course.'

An hour later, their discussions complete, Finlay said, 'That seems to have covered everything, I think.' He gathered up his papers. 'You say that you have plans to come to London in the near future so…'

'Yes, I shall be at the London house from the 5th until the 12th.'

'Excellent. I shall have the draft documents taken there by hand, and if you make any comments you have in the margin…' The lawyer replaced his folder into a briefcase and snapped it shut.

Oliver nodded with satisfaction and began to rise from his chair. 'You say you need to leave directly after breakfast tomorrow?'

'I'm afraid so.'

'Then after luncheon perhaps we could attend to estate matters. My manager tells me that some tenant or other is disputing a boundary issue.' Oliver began to move towards the door. 'The fellow's a damn nuisance apparently – one of these types who's always bleating about justice and people's rights!'

Finlay followed him into the wide hall with its black and white tiled floor. He always found visiting Graylings a most intriguing experience. The house had a grandeur normally only found in the country houses of the aristocracy. Then he reminded himself that Faradays had been a titled family for generations until three generations previously when Sir Richard Faraday died childless. Their extensive wealth originated from centuries before when a courtier in William the Conqueror's army had married a highborn Anglo-Saxon widow.

They walked into the elegant dining room overlooking a long terrace with steps leading down to immaculate clipped lawns surrounded by topiary. As Finlay took his place, he wondered what the altercation with this tenant involved. His professional advice would be based strictly on the law, which in his view should apply fairly to everyone in the country, whatever their social standing.

Ten days later, Oliver's carriage drew up in High Holborn outside the discreet offices of McPherson and McPherson and, carrying a small attaché case in his hand, went lightly up the steps of the tall building. With some distaste, he noticed dandruff on the shoulders of the grey-faced clerk who came to greet him, and then seconds later he was ushered into the inner sanctum of his lawyer.

Once their social niceties were complete, Oliver opened his briefcase and after handing over the ribbon-tied document glanced idly around the large yet fusty room lined with glass-fronted bookcases. It had been McPherson senior who had attended to Faraday affairs when Oliver's father was alive and it was apparent that nothing had been altered since, not even the inkwells.

'I can foresee no problems here,' Finlay said eventually. 'So it is in order to proceed with the finalities?'

'But of course.' Oliver leaned forward to take a cigarette from the silver box offered by his lawyer, used his own lighter and leaned back to inhale with satisfaction. 'You will of course be attending the wedding?'

A smile crossed Finlay's face. 'Most certainly, my wife is looking forward to it.'

At Broadway Manor, there was already a veritable marathon of preparation going on. An extra seamstress had been employed and the leading dressmaker in Lichfield was an almost constant visitor.

'I don't know why I need so many things,' Helena grumbled, as orders for chemises, night-dresses, peignoirs, petticoats and underwear were agreed between Beatrice and Miss Hewson. There was also to be a new riding habit, and countless day dresses and evening gowns.

Beatrice gave a sigh of exasperation. 'Helena, a young woman in your position – or should I say the position in which you will find yourself – must have an extensive trousseau. You will need to impress the staff and to portray yourself as someone of consequence otherwise they will try to take advantage of you.'

Enid Hewson glanced up from checking her list. 'I'm afraid that's true Miss Helena.'

Helena gazed at them both and said in a low voice, 'Do you know how many servants Oliver has? About twenty in the house itself, and glory knows how many more outside.'

'Well, the outside staff will not be your responsibility,' Beatrice said briskly. 'They come under the jurisdiction of the estate manager.'

'Is there a housekeeper, Miss Helena?'

'I believe so. I bet she's an old dragon.'

'Nonsense,' Beatrice said, 'I'm sure she will be as anxious as you that the management of the household runs smoothly. What you must not do, ever, is to undermine her authority. Is that not

86

right, Enid?'

'It would certainly be unwise, Miss Helena.'

Helena waited until the maid had left the room and then said, 'I've never thought of it before, but why haven't we got a housekeeper?'

'There was one here when I arrived, and an enormous help she was to me, particularly in the early days,' Beatrice said, 'but when she left to go and live with her sister in Wales, I decided to dispense with the need. After all, this is a much smaller house than Graylings and we already had an efficient staff.' She hesitated then added, 'In a way it gave me a sense of purpose to use my own capabilities, to know that the efficiency of the household lay on my shoulders. Everyone needs a role in life, Helena.'

'I can understand that.' Helena wandered around the spacious bedroom and then peered out of the window. 'I wish this rain would stop. I'm beginning to feel cooped up.'

'You will have Oliver arriving tomorrow,' Beatrice said. 'Aren't you looking forward to seeing the ring he's chosen?'

Helena bit her lip. Everything was happening so fast. 'Of course I am! Papa has hinted at an early wedding ... has he said anything to you?'

'Just an intimation, which is why we have no time to waste,' Beatrice said. She looked at her niece and her tone softened. 'You will find it hard to leave Broadway Manor; I know how much you love it. We will all miss you, even the staff.'

'I shall miss them too,' Helena said. 'I've been thinking – I shall need my own lady's maid, and I'd love to have someone familiar with me.' She looked hopefully at her aunt. 'Do you think Miss Hewson could train up Molly?'

'I've long suspected that you've been too friendly with that girl. I turned a blind eye when you were younger, Helena, but it really must cease. In any case, someone so inexperienced would not be at all suitable. And there you would have made your first mistake – one to learn from,' Beatrice said. 'There is a strict hierarchy downstairs. As senior parlourmaid, Ida would be offered such a position first. One needs to be very careful in such things.'

'Ida has a soldier sweetheart – she's hardly likely to leave him!'

Beatrice frowned. 'This inclination you have to involve yourself in the servants' personal affairs will have to cease, Helena. Otherwise, you will find it impossible to maintain respect and discipline. Remember, most of the staff at Graylings will be older than you, so things will not be easy at first.'

'I know – that's what worries me.' And, Helena thought, that's one reason why I want to have Molly with me; at least it would be someone I could confide in, someone I knew I could trust.

'You can always write to me for advice.'

'I'll probably send sheaves of letters every day.' Helena held out her left hand with its bare third finger trying to imagine a sparkling ring on it. 'Can you believe that tomorrow I shall be officially engaged?'

Chapter Ten

The looming wedding overshadowed every aspect of the household at Broadway Manor. Seated before a crackling coal fire, Enid Hewson glanced up from the fine lawn chemise she was holding. 'As I've said before, it's no easy job being a lady's maid. I mean – look what tiny stitches this needs. Talk about giving a body a headache. Mind you, mine are nothing like the ones poor Miss Beatrice suffers with; I feel really sorry for her sometimes.'

'Can't you ask that extra seamstress they've brought in to do it?' Ida fished inside her high-necked blouse to bring out the fine chain on which her engagement ring was threaded. Gently she removed it and, putting it on her third left finger, held out her hand to admire the tiny diamond.

'I attend to Miss Beatrice's things,' Enid snapped. 'The seamstress is concentrating on Miss Helena's trousseau.'

'Go on, Miss Hewson, you must have caught a glimpse of the wedding dress, what's it like?' Annie asked. She cradled her cup of cocoa in her hands. 'And the veil – is it still goin' to be the one that belonged to her mother?'

'I haven't seen a thing – not yet! It's all top secret, only Miss Beatrice and the dressmaker are allowed in for the fittings. As for the veil, yes, I believe so.'

'I wish she'd been getting married in Lichfield

Cathedral,' Molly grumbled. 'Why does it have to be in London? Do you know, Mr Bostock?'

He removed his spectacles and, taking a white handkerchief from his pocket, began to polish them. 'Not exactly, but I believe it was Mr Faraday's wish.'

A fortnight earlier Jacob was initially dismayed by Oliver's formal request for the wedding to be held in London, reasoning that surely the man was aware of the accepted order of such things. It was the prerogative of the bride's parents – in this case himself – to make these decisions.

'Let me explain,' Oliver said.

'Yes, but...' Jacob frowned. 'You have spoken to Helena about this?'

Oliver shook his head. 'No, I thought to mention it to you first.'

'Quite so, although I am sure that Helena has always expected to be married from Broadway Manor.'

'London would certainly be more convenient for many of our guests,' Oliver said in a casual tone, 'among whom I expect there to be members of the government and other politicians; although if the wedding were to be held in Lichfield Cathedral, they might consider the journey to be too time-consuming. But of course the final decision on the venue must rest with you.'

It was now Jacob's tone that became casual, 'I wasn't aware that you had so many friends in high places.'

'I certainly have several acquaintances who I think would welcome an invitation. And I would of

90

course put my London house completely at your disposal.' Oliver watched the conflicting expressions on Jacob's face. They were sitting comfortably in the older man's study, a glass of Madeira to hand to celebrate the satisfactory completion of the Marriage Settlement. Oliver had decided to wait until then before proceeding with his plans. His request to hold the wedding at St Margaret's Church in Westminster was not an idle one. They would spend the first month of their marriage in London; he did not intend to allow Helena to become fatigued by travelling. She would need all of her energies to conceive and as soon as possible. A formal honeymoon could come later after a prolonged stay at Graylings.

Jacob took a sip of his wine. He had given no hint of his own political ambitions, concluding that it would be wiser to wait until Oliver was his son-in-law before broaching the subject. Therefore, he could hardly accuse the man of using that knowledge to manipulate him. And what he stated certainly rang true: there would be far more chance of parliamentarians gracing them with their presence if the ceremony were to be held at a church adjacent to the House of Commons. On such an informal occasion, one with plentiful champagne, who knew what valuable contacts could be made? Also from a social point of view, there was enormous cachet in a St Margaret's wedding with its resultant publicity and coverage in the London national press.

He said slowly, 'The convenience of guests should certainly be a consideration.'

'So you are inclined to agree?' Oliver's voice was

smooth. 'I hope you don't mind but I took the liberty of making enquiries and the date of Wednesday, the 10th January, is available. A weekday is always more convenient I find, rather than interrupting weekend plans, and Helena and I will have been engaged for three months by then. Ideal, I thought.'

Jacob frowned. Oliver had always intimated that he wanted an early wedding. The young couple did seem very much in love and Jacob was not so old that he had forgotten what that felt like. Nor could he think of a single practical reason why he should insist on a later date, although there was one matter that troubled him. 'Oliver, before we discuss this further, might I mention that I would have liked Helena to see her future home before then. It may have escaped your notice, but neither she nor I have yet had the chance to visit Graylings.'

Oliver leaned back in his chair and smiled. 'I'm sorry but I'm afraid I have to ask you to indulge me in this. You see, I have always had this dream that when I did marry, I would bring my bride home to Graylings with the staff lining up to meet their new mistress for the very first time. Believe me, Helena will love the house and her every need will be met. You need have no anxieties on that score. And of course we will then both be delighted for you and Miss Beatrice to visit.'

He is an eloquent fellow, Jacob thought, clever too. If this was purely a business matter he would have argued his case, but such ephemeral matters as dreams were difficult to refuse.

'I would have liked to have gone from here, with the servants to see me,' Helena said. She was astounded at her father's decision. 'Surely that is the more traditional way. I do think you might have consulted me, Papa, before agreeing to this.'

'Helena, there are several advantages. Your wedding will be one of the major social events of the year. It would hardly have the same impact up here in Staffordshire.' Jacob had anticipated that Helena might demur but he had never expected such a spirited reaction.

'Such things don't greatly concern me,' Helena said with bitterness. What really irked was that such a decision had been taken between the two men, as if she was merely a – what was the old-fashioned word – chattel, that was it. After all, it was *her* wedding. Wasn't the bride supposed to be the most important person on the actual day? 'I suppose the formal announcement is already drawn up?'

'Indeed, in fact Oliver is going to arrange for it to be personally delivered to *The Times*.' Jacob was beginning to feel distinctly uncomfortable. He glanced at the portrait of Mary. Would she have thought he was being too high-handed? But women had little knowledge of politics and the importance of influential connections. 'If you are concerned about the staff, then I have no objection to the staff having their own wedding celebration downstairs.'

Helena held his gaze. 'And before we leave for London, would you agree for me to wear my wedding dress and veil and for them to gather in the hall to see me?'

'That is a little unusual, my dear.' On seeing Helena's mutinous expression, Jacob gave a resigned nod. 'If that is your wish then you have my permission. But I agree with Beatrice, you have allowed yourself to become far too involved with the servants.'

Still fuming, Helena went back upstairs where the dressmaker greeted her with an anxious smile. 'I was wondering how many tea gowns you require.'

Helena frowned. 'And may I ask exactly what a tea gown is?'

Beatrice, who was looking through material patterns, turned her head away and said in a low voice, 'I believe it's a gown where a lady does not always wear a corset.'

'In that case I'll have several!' Helena flounced into a pink velvet chair in the corner of her bedroom. She had never understood why she had to wear one of the detested garments. There might be some purpose in the flesh of a plump matron being encased in whalebone, but for someone with a waist that was already the fashionable twenty inches, it was ludicrous. Then Helena noticed that Beatrice was looking embarrassed.

'You don't approve,' Helena said. 'Why?'

'They are a garment worn by married ladies during three and six in the afternoon when they entertain socially, often alone. All supposedly respectable, but it's well known that the looseness of the dress can often lead to,' Beatrice hesitated, 'other things.'

Helena stared at her then began laughing. 'So wearing one of these tea gowns can lead to a scandalous life? Then I shall definitely have several.'

'Helena!'

'I'm sorry, I couldn't help it. From what I know of my future husband, he would brook no nonsense like that.'

The dressmaker, a spinster who always wore black relieved by a single row of pearls, coughed and said, 'Shall I bring swatches of suitable fabric, Miss?'

'Yes, please do.'

Later, Helena told Beatrice of the arrangements her father had made.

'But where will the wedding breakfast be held?'

Helena shrugged. 'Papa didn't say. I expect Oliver will already have somewhere in mind. He seems to be the one holding the reins, despite what Papa says.' She looked at her aunt in some panic. 'Everything's happening too quickly; I do think I should have been able to visit Graylings before the wedding. Don't you agree?'

'Now Helena, it's just wedding nerves, every bride has them. And as for Graylings, you have seen a painting, and Oliver's wishes are not unreasonable.'

Helena gazed down at her platinum and sapphire engagement ring, trying to imagine a gold band next to it. Was her aunt right, was this how every bride felt?

'You're being nonsensical dear,' Beatrice said briskly, 'You should be counting your blessings, not looking for problems.'

But Helena, who was beginning to feel that she was no longer in control of her own life, was still fuming.

Chapter Eleven

The rooms in Wimpole Street where Dr Haverstock held his practice were spacious, elegantly furnished, and bore an air of quiet reassurance. Nicholas had found treating patients in such surroundings an experience vastly different from his usual crowded surgery. Time was allowed for a leisurely consultation, while the facilities to enable examination were exemplary. The arrangement that was agreed was that he should assist on such cases that were likely to be onerous. The distinguished physician needed to conserve his physical strength, even though his advancing years had not diminished his medical expertise. The two men had swiftly established a respect for each other, and Nicholas knew he was fortunate to have been given such an opening.

At last, in response to a hidden button, Miss Barnes came in to usher out his last patient of the day, and Nicholas rose from behind the walnut desk and went thankfully over to a cupboard in one corner of the room. Andrew Haverstock believed in the restorative powers of the grain, and Nicholas had come to adopt his habit of indulging in a small glass of whisky at the end of the working day, with scant regard to the grandfather clock that stood in one corner.

'It wouldn't do to broadcast it, so just between ourselves, laddie,' Andrew had said, his eyes creasing with merriment above his bushy but greying beard. 'Sun not down over the yardarm and all that nonsense. It's good for the circulation, Nicholas, and after attending to the sick we deserve it.'

Now with his glass in his hand, Nicholas went over to a comfortable leather armchair and settled down to relax and to read *The Times* before setting off home. It was several minutes later that he turned to the page of notices and began to scan through them, and it was then that the name leapt out at him. Slowly Nicholas lowered the newspaper. Helena was not a common name. He thought of the tall man he had seen that night. Had he been this Oliver Faraday? Could this be 'his Helena', the girl in the casement window? He read the notice again.

The engagement is announced between Miss Helena Standish, the only daughter of Mr Jacob Standish of Broadway Manor, near Lichfield, Staffordshire, and Mr Oliver Faraday of Graylings, Hertfordshire. Their forthcoming marriage will take place at St Margaret's Church, Westminster on Wednesday, 10th of January, 1906 at 11 am.

Broadway Manor in Staffordshire, Graylings in Hertfordshire, spoke of money, of landed gentry; a far cry from his own rented accommodation, comfortable though it was. Despite what he had achieved professionally, Nicholas had no family security. An only child, his father had been an officer in the Army but on leaving to pursue a career in the City, he had discovered too late that he had no talent for business. The shame of ruin through a series of disastrous investments had broken him and he had died when Nicholas was eighteen. His widowed mother had taken up residence in Bath to live with her sister, and only a small trust fund had enabled Nicholas to finish his education and to qualify as a doctor. As he had thought so many times, a privileged young woman like Helena could never share a life like his.

Of course, it might not *be* her! Nicholas knew St Margaret's Church, Westminster, was used frequently for society weddings and lay between the Abbey and the Houses of Parliament. Getting up, he went over to the desk to circle the date in the leather gilt-edged diary.

At Broadway Manor one morning, when they were in the small library, Helena looked up from her embroidery to try to attract Oliver's attention. For the past half an hour he had been so absorbed in his newspaper that she doubted whether he had remembered her presence. She gave a tiny cough, gratified to see him glance over to her.

'There is something I would like to discuss with you, Oliver.'

'You have my full attention.'

'It's just that I'm planning to bring Molly, our under housemaid, with me to Graylings. Miss Hewson could train her up to be my personal maid.'

Oliver's expression hardened. 'My dear that's not an acceptable choice, I'm afraid.'

'Surely, Oliver, the appointment of a lady's maid lies within my domain.'

'Yes of course it does, but you must understand that as my wife you will be moving in more rarefied social circles. Such a position needs experience, not the efforts of a young and untried girl.'

She knew he was right; Beatrice and Miss Hewson also held that view and Helena had fully expected her first suggestion to be refuted. She smiled at him and nodded. 'You are quite right, of course. I should have given that aspect more consideration.'

Oliver's answering smile was approving, but it didn't reach his eyes. Helena wondered why it was that when he was being tender, even passionate, she felt completely relaxed with him, and yet at other times – such as now – he managed to make her feel while not exactly afraid of him, certainly nervous.

Determined, she continued. 'I do worry that when you are not with me I shall be among strangers at Graylings. I am sure there would be a place for Molly. Perhaps she could be an under-housemaid, with part of her duties to understudy my personal maid – in case of an indisposition. A familiar face would be such a comfort to me, Oliver.'

Oliver realised that Helena's request, couched in such terms, put him in a difficult position. To refuse would seem unreasonable, even harsh, and Jacob Standish would rightly be outraged. This was infuriating, as he would have preferred that his own strictly controlled staff serve Helena. 'You would judge her to be loyal?'

'Absolutely, I've known her for years and her work is excellent.'

'And her age is...?'

'I think she is about twenty.'

Oliver frowned. 'Which one is she?'

'Molly? She's the dark-haired pretty one.' Helena was beginning to feel bewildered by all his questions. After all, what was one more maid in a house as large as Graylings?

Oliver breathed a sigh of relief. Although he normally paid little attention to servants, he had noticed this particular parlourmaid. He smiled, 'You know I can refuse you nothing, dearest. Of course she may come to Graylings.'

'Thank you, Oliver.' Helena lowered her gaze to her sewing with quiet satisfaction.

Molly, who had come to work at Broadway Manor as a kitchen maid, was proud that she had worked her way up to her present position of junior parlourmaid. The term 'junior' in her opinion was merely to reflect Ida's longer service. Molly considered her abilities equal to any member of staff, with the exception of the butler and cook. The third child of a feckless mother and workshy father, life for Molly had been one of cast-offs, blows and a sparse diet. The day she had been sent into service had been the best of her short life. Something she was reminiscing about in the kitchen. 'I never saw a tablecloth 'til I came here, never mind a full plate.'

'That's one reason I came into service,' one of the footmen said. 'At least you can be sure of three square meals a day.'

'Yes, well that's because we've got a good employer,' Molly told him. 'It isn't the same everywhere. Believe me, I have heard tales of servants worked into the ground and ruled with a rod of iron. My cousin works for Mr Standish in his brewery, and says the men have a lot of respect for him 'cos he pays decent wages, and makes sure they have good working conditions. He says we could do with people like him in Parliament.'

She swung round as the butler came in calling her name. 'Miss Beatrice wants to see you in the morning room.'

Molly glanced round at the others, drew a sharp intake of breath and went to the round mahogany framed mirror that hung over the mantelpiece to tidy a loose strand of her hair and straighten her white lace-trimmed cap. Then she hurried up the back stairs and paused at the top to compose herself before crossing the spacious hall with its polished floor and Persian rug to tap lightly on the wide cream-panelled door.

The cool voice came immediately: 'Come.'

Beatrice Standish, seated on her favourite gold velvet chair, with its high spoon back, turned from her writing table. 'Ah, Molly, do come in. There is something I wish to discuss with you.'

'Yes, Miss Beatrice?'

Beatrice gave her a warm smile. 'It's about Miss Helena's forthcoming marriage and her subsequent residence at Graylings. She has expressed a wish that you might accompany her.'

For a second Molly could hardly speak. She had dreamt of this for weeks, knowing that it could be her one chance to broaden her horizons, to meet

101

new people, even to learn new skills. 'Thank you, Miss., I'd love to go.'

'And your family – would they raise any objection?'

'No Miss Beatrice, not at all.'

'That's excellent. Now Miss Helena's initial wish was that you be trained by Miss Hewson to take up the post of lady's maid, but after due consideration it is felt that as Mr Faraday's wife, her social standing will be such that she will need the services of someone with more experience.' Beatrice paused, as Molly couldn't control a gasp of consternation, then she continued, 'However, it has been agreed that you should be offered a position at Graylings as a parlourmaid. Also to be given the chance to understudy Miss Helena's personal maid – who is still to be appointed – with a view to substituting for her if circumstances require it.'

Molly said slowly, 'So I'd be getting a sort of training…'

Beatrice nodded. 'That is correct. I shall quite understand if you need time to give the matter some thought.'

'No, Miss Beatrice, I don't. That would be quite satisfactory.'

'Then I shall write to the housekeeper at Graylings giving you a good reference. I am sure that your pay and conditions will be equal to those you enjoy at Broadway Manor. It will be a great comfort to me to know that Miss Helena will have you with her.'

'Thank you, Miss.'

As Beatrice gave a dismissive nod, Molly turned

and went out of the room, her heart singing. She may not be a lady's maid – not yet – but this was the next best thing. Full of excitement, she raced back to the kitchen to announce her news.

Henry Bostock took off his rimless spectacles and gestured with them. 'I'm pleased for you ,Molly; it will be good for Miss Helena to have you at Graylings with her.'

'Of course, she was always Miss Helena's favourite,' Ida sniffed.

'Now then, Ida,' Cook said. 'You've got your own good fortune. But bless us, that will mean two new parlourmaids once you've got wed. Change doesn't sit well with me at my time of life.'

'I've been thinking, Mrs Kemp,' the butler said, 'that perhaps you could do with an extra hand in the kitchen. If another girl took Annie's place in the scullery...'

Mrs Kemp beamed. 'Now that is a change I'd welcome, and so would Annie. She'll be glad to see the back of scouring pots and pans in that scullery, not to mention scrubbing dirt off the veg.'

'Yes, well don't go saying anything to her yet. I shall need to talk to Miss Beatrice first – it is an extra member of staff, after all.'

'Explain it's me varicose veins, they don't half give me some gip. I could do with being off me legs more.'

Molly was only half-listening. She was glad that Annie had the chance of promotion to kitchen maid, but her brain was already running ahead. Would she have to move to Graylings before the wedding, or wait until afterwards…

During Christmas at Broadway Manor, the festivities were naturally overshadowed by the arrangements for Helena's forthcoming marriage. Oliver spent his own Christmas divided between Graylings and his London house, where he intended to remain until the day of the ceremony at St Margaret's Church. The Standish family were to travel to London after the New Year.

And as Helena had wished, on the day after Boxing Day the servants gathered in the spacious hall before the huge festooned Christmas tree to see her in her wedding finery. The outdoor staff, the grooms and gardeners were ill at ease, clutching their caps and standing slightly aside, while the indoor servants stood in a cluster to watch with pride as Helena descended the wide oak panelled staircase in her ivory silk gown with its long train flowing behind. Mary Standish's fine veil edged with embroidery was held in place by a glistening pearl tiara, and as Annie, already overcome at actually being upstairs, said later – their Miss Helena 'looked like an angel'.

Helena gazed down at the sea of faces knowing that she would never forget the scene before her, and the affection and admiration in their eyes was unbearably moving. Despite her exhilaration at actually wearing the bridal outfit, the thought of leaving them all tightened her throat. Cook, her broad face wreathed in a smile, had often welcomed her as a child in the kitchen, giving her a glass of buttermilk, warm little cakes from the oven and letting her lick the pudding spoon. The loyal Bostock, whose silver hair was now becoming sparse – he had always been there; a part of her life as much as Broadway Manor itself.

'Ooh, Miss Helena, you look a picture,' Cook took up a corner of her apron to wipe a tear from her eye.

Bostock stepped forward. 'May I say, Miss Helena, how much we all appreciate this kind gesture. And on behalf of the staff may I express our good wishes for your future happiness.'

Helena's smile was warm and happy, and briefly her eyes met those of Molly. 'Thank you all so very much and also for helping to take care of me all these years. I know I shall miss you dreadfully.'

Jacob with Beatrice beside him was standing before the drawing room door and despite his pride and emotion, it was only then he finally realised that within a very short time his daughter would no longer be part of his everyday life. There would be visits of course, between both houses, but not to see Helena's lithe figure every day, not to hear her lilting laugh ... the Manor was going to seem very empty.

He turned to glance at Beatrice and saw an unguarded expression on her face. How could he be so unthinking, so unaware? She had come to this house as a thirty-year-old spinster to tend a motherless baby. Had she ever dreamed of being a bride herself? And then there came shuffling of feet as the outdoor staff turned to leave, several of the men touching their forelock to Jacob. Helena spoke for a few moments to the female indoor staff and then soon the hall was clear again.

Now it was Jacob's turn to speak. 'You look

absolutely splendid, Helena. I'm so proud of you.'

Beatrice's expression had changed to one of triumph as she moved forward to help to raise the train so that her niece could safely return to her bedroom. Helena was feeling wonderful in the dress, designed to overlay several silk petticoats to retain warmth. With her shoulders and arms covered with Nottingham lace, she had no fears of January inclement weather. Not even a top London dressmaker could have achieved more.

Chapter Twelve

On the day following New Year's Day, Nicholas walked up the steps and past the gleaming engraved brass plate into the Wimpole Street consulting rooms and gave a morning greeting to the young woman behind the desk. As he saw her colour rise, Nicholas, as always, felt slightly embarrassed. During his hospital days there had been more than one nurse who had made it plain that she found him attractive. Even with her dark hair so plainly dressed, Miss Barnes was a pretty girl, but at present he had no interest in romance; he was too much involved with his patients and medical research.

There was only one marriage he was interested in and the ominous date was rapidly approaching. It was still an irritating mystery to Nicholas that after all these months he allowed his thoughts to still linger on a girl who could never have any place in his life. Yet every time he thought of those hazel eyes flecked with gold, at the softness of her mouth as she tentatively smiled at him, he was undone.

Only seconds later the door opened and Nicholas turned to greet Andrew Haverstock. The portly physician removed his top hat in a flamboyant gesture. 'May I wish you both a health and happiness in this New Year of 1906?'

'And I extend the same wishes to you, Dr Haverstock.' Nicholas smiled at the man he now regarded as a friend.

Miss Barnes took the hat from his outstretched hand. 'Happy New Year, Dr Haverstock, I trust you had a good Christmas?'

'Capital, capital.' He rubbed his hands together and then guided Nicholas into his own domain. 'Now then, let's see what this week portends.'

Nicholas settled himself opposite Andrew, who immediately opened his new 1906 desk diary. 'Ah, I see there are already some entries.' He flicked through a few pages and then frowned. 'Lady Trentley's name is down for Wednesday week, yet I'm sure I…' He pressed a bell beneath the rim of the polished walnut desk and within seconds, the receptionist came into the room. 'Miss Barnes, I see there is an appointment made for me on the 10th. Did I not say that I won't be available on that day?'

'Oh, I'm sorry, Dr Haverstock, I remember now. I do apologise. I'm afraid I didn't make a note of it.'

'I have a wedding to attend.'

Disconcerted, Nicholas stared at him then dismissed the thought.

Andrew turned to Nicholas. 'I wonder – Dr Carstairs, do you think you could deputise for me? That is of course if Lady Trentley is agreeable. I hardly wish to cause her inconvenience.'

'May I see?' Nicholas held out his hand for the diary. The appointment was for 10.30 am. It was impossible. How could he carry out his plan to be at St Margaret's Church before eleven o'clock? He shook his head. 'I'm sorry, I'm afraid I have a commitment at the time that I can't possibly break.'

Andrew gave a heavy sigh. 'In that case, I shall just have to eat humble pie. You may go, Miss Barnes, but in future please be more careful.' After she had left he said, 'I don't understand it, she's usually so efficient.'

Nicholas looked down at his hands. 'A wedding, you say? Is it a relative?'

Andrew shook his head as he leafed through a case file. 'No, it's a society wedding. When I was a young, inexperienced doctor, my first practice was in Hertfordshire. I assisted a London gynaecologist at Oliver Faraday's birth. Sadly, after a protracted labour the mother suffered a severe haemorrhage. He's marrying some young woman from Staffordshire.'

Nicholas managed to keep his voice one of quiet control. 'Oliver Faraday?'

'Yes, of Graylings, a fine ancestral house.' Andrew glanced up and explained, 'Afterwards I used to attend Oliver when he had childhood ailments, and as I became more respected his father even invited me to luncheon.' With dry humour, he added, 'Never to dinner, of course.'

Nicholas gave a sympathetic smile. 'These social niceties, they really are nonsensical. Yet you've been sent an invitation.'

'I have indeed. Oliver consulted me a couple of years ago – merely a minor matter – and now that I have patients among the aristocracy I believe I am considered socially acceptable.' He raised his bushy eyebrows, but Nicholas merely smiled, thinking it safer not to pursue the subject.

The morning of Wednesday 10th January dawned without a hint of rain, and Helena, although nervous, was enjoying all the attention. She breakfasted in bed, the tray before her daintily laid with a soft-boiled egg, toast and honey, and a fluted china cup of hot chocolate. Then the hip-bath before the lively coal fire began to be filled by a procession of maids carrying cans of hot water. As one tipped in rose-scented bath salts, Enid Hewson busied herself laying out a camisole, a ribbon corset, knickers with lace frills at the knee, and white silk stockings. The myriad of petticoats lay fanned out over the back of a velvet chair, while complexion creams, silver-backed hairbrush, comb and mirror were in readiness on the dressing table.

Helena was leaning against the pillows trying to close her mind to the activity around her. She loved Oliver's London house, it was not only tall and elegant but exquisitely furnished. She heard faint laughter overhead from her bridesmaids, Dorothy, and three debutantes Helena had remained friendly with, and took a deep breath, trying to calm her chaotic feelings. It was normal to feel panicky, it was just wedding nerves – every bride was supposed to have them. Yet despite the day before her, into her mind came the young doctor's image again and mortification swept over her, guilt that she could think of another man on the morning she was to marry Oliver. It must be because she was back in London and with determinedly she drew a curtain over the memory and instead gazed at the ivory dress with its guipure lace and gossamer veil hanging in splendour outside the bow-fronted satinwood wardrobe. Oliver had been so sweet, so attentive in these weeks leading up to the ceremony. She hadn't felt any of that disturbing uneasiness about him for ages. Leaning forward, Helena with resolve flung aside the blue silk eiderdown, swung out her legs and put on her peignoir and swansdown trimmed slippers.

The maid turned to bob a curtsey. 'Your bath is ready, Miss.'

Helena, whose hair had been shampooed the previous day, waited until it was pinned up, then once the ornate Japanese screen was in place, undressed. She would have preferred to bathe alone, but instead lowered herself into the fragrant water to submit to the ministrations of the excited pale-faced maid.

Hewson's voice, imperious and establishing her seniority, called, 'Miss Helena, I shall go now to attend to Miss Beatrice, but I'll be back in time to arrange your hair and help you to dress.'

Later that morning when he arrived in Westminster, Nicholas was surprised to see St Margaret's Church already surrounded by a crowd of onlookers, but then focused on finding a vantage point that would give him both an unobstructed view and a measure of anonymity. Eventually, his hat by his side, he decided to stand bareheaded amongst a cluster of people who were unlikely to attract attention and contained at least two other men of a similar height.

When the carriages and motor cars began to arrive nearby he saw Andrew Haverstock almost immediately, distinguished in morning dress and accompanied by his wife who was in pale grey and wearing an ostrich plumed hat. Nicholas tensed slightly as the couple followed a stream of guests to the entrance of the ancient church, but soon realised that the crowd outside held little interest for the elite, who scarcely gave them a second's glance. The procession of expensively dressed people seemed endless and he waited with increasing impatience until the last trickle disappeared.

'Here come the bridesmaids!' someone said. There were three young women, meeting with a murmur of approval as they walked demurely past with fresh flowers in their hair to match their lace-circled posies.

'Peach velvet,' said a tiny bird-like woman in front of him. 'That must 'ave cost a pretty penny.'

'No little ones or pageboys?' her friend was derisive. 'I don't call that much of a display.'

Minutes later the carriage everyone had been waiting for arrived. Beribboned and gleaming, it was drawn by a perfectly matched set of greys. As the coachman brought the snorting horses to a halt and the ushers moved forward with the step, Nicholas felt his throat become dry, his breathing shallow. A middle-aged man descended and, turning, held out his hand first to another bridesmaid and then the bride was in view, stepping down in her long shimmering gown, waiting while her attendant adjusted and then lifted the extensive train. On her father's arm, she began the short walk to the entrance to the church while Nicholas stared with every ounce of concentration to try to penetrate the veil that obscured her face. Was it Helena? She was the same height, he could even detect that her hair was fair, but from this distance...

'Lovely dress,' the bird-like woman said. 'And look at the size of that bouquet! Just fancy – red roses at this time of year, they must 'ave cost a fortune! Are yer stoppin' 'til she comes out, Floss?'

'Nah. I usually do 'cos I like to 'ear the bells. But it's too flaming cold.'

Once inside the church, Helena felt a momentary sense of panic as through the mistiness of her veil she gazed at the beautiful and emotive scene before her. Its congregation a sea of wide brimmed hats and ostrich plumes interspersed with the stiff backs of aristocrats and prominent public figures. Ahead she could see Oliver, the winter sun glinting on his fair head and at a nod from the Rector he moved with his best man, Johnnie Horton following, to stand before the altar. Immediately there came a rustle of movement as the remainder of the congregation rose, with Beatrice in the left front pew, resplendent in peacock blue.

Then the opening bars of Handel's the *Arrival of the Queen of Sheba* began and Helena quelled her quivering nerves. Placing a hand on her father's firm arm, ever conscious of the weight of her long train and followed by her bridesmaids, she walked at a sedate pace along the flower-be-decked aisle. A few heads turned, there were gasps of subdued admiration and then Oliver was facing her and Helena with care lifted her veil to meet his cool blue eyes and slight smile. Her father withdrew to one side and the dignified Rector began to intone the immortal words, '*We are gathered here today in the sight of God...*'

Outside, as a chill breeze sprang up, Nicholas drew closer the astrakhan collar on his new over-coat and replaced his hat. Oblivious of movements within the crowd as people drifted away and then eventually other curious onlookers took their place, he waited for what seemed the longest hour of his life. His logic was cold comfort – telling him that he had only the flimsiest of reasons for being there at all.

Then at last, there came the almost deafening peal of bells, the doors of the church opened and to the sound of rousing cheers the bride and groom emerged. Now, Nicholas could see her clearly. Framed in the flowing veil, there was the same lovely face, the same honey-gold hair. Helena, beautiful and graceful, smiled for the press photographer as he came forward with his tripod, and with laughter and high spirits a few of the guests clustered around the newly married couple. Then all too soon, among a shower of rice she was leaving, giving a smiling wave to the onlookers before being handed into the carriage by the same tall man who Nicholas had seen that night in Cadogan Square. The scene brought with it such an evocative memory that even before the horses began to move Nicholas was turning, shouldering his way through the crowd and, as he told himself with bitter finality, out of their lives.

Chapter Thirteen

Faraday House occupied one of the most fashionable positions in London. Tall, elegant and situated in Carlton House Terrace overlooking St James's Park, it had been designed for Sir Vernon Faraday, one of Oliver's more astute and wealthy ancestors. Its staff, although small compared with that of Graylings, were efficient enough to provide not only the comfort, but also the measure of privacy he considered vital for these first days and weeks following the wedding.

The rooms chosen by Oliver for their personal use were on the second floor and had been completely refurbished. There were two spacious double bedrooms inner-connected by his dressing room, a graceful parlour with tall sash windows – where they had dined on their wedding night. His own room was decorated in burgundy and cream, the curtains plain damask, as was the coverlet on his bed. There were no fringes, ornaments or what he thought of as fripperies. It was a comfortable, masculine room. Helena's bedroom had been furnished in accordance with her own wishes in soft pastel shades, the pale blue velvet carpet complemented by blue and gold silk drapes and quilted coverlet. There were plans to convert two further small rooms into bathrooms.

On the evening following their wedding, he had arranged for a light supper to be served in the intimacy of their small parlour, and he listened with amusement mixed with ill-concealed impatience as Helena chattered on about the glittering social gathering at the Ritz Hotel that afternoon.

'It was wonderful, wasn't it?' she said eventually, sipping at her champagne, aware that she was talking too much. 'In fact the whole day has been just perfect.'

'Indeed, and you my darling were the perfect bride, feted and admired.' Oliver smiled across at her, 'As I think I may have mentioned before.'

Helena held out her hand to admire the slim gold band. 'I still can't believe that I'm actually Mrs Oliver Faraday, and not Helena Standish.'

'You are only my wife in name my sweet, at least yet.' Oliver's quizzical gaze met her own startled one, and Helena felt her cheeks stain with colour. 'In fact,' he said, reaching over to remove Helena's half-empty flute, 'I'm beginning to think that perhaps it is time we should retire?'

Helena felt her throat suddenly become dry.

Her knowledge of married intimacy was sketchy; the mysteries of the marriage bed were considered too delicate a topic to be discussed with or before innocent young women. Yet remembering how she had felt when held in Oliver's arms and the delicious sensations his kisses had aroused, the night to come beckoned her as one of adventure and pleasure, rather than one to fear. Helena had no intention of being the 'shrinking virgin' so often and irritatingly portrayed in romantic novels. She intended to live life to the full. So now she merely smiled her assent to her new and handsome husband, and when he came round to her rose-upholstered mahogany chair she eased herself gracefully out of it.

Oliver smiled to himself. His gentle courtship, so carefully planned, was obviously going to bear fruit. He smiled again at the unintended pun – could it be a lucky omen? But his lovemaking that first night, and indeed for many nights to come, must be of the utmost care. While he hoped – if he had been a religious man he would have prayed – that his bride's body would be free of blemish, bitter experience had taught him that he could not, must not take the risk of an adverse discovery. To have reached this point only to fail ... he could not bear even the thought ... and so he had made his decision. Only when Helena was safely delivered of a son would Oliver permit himself to see her naked.

Helena, in a white nightdress trimmed with exquisite lace, lay in the silken-covered four-poster bed listening for any sound of movement behind

116

the inter-communicating door. Miss Hewson, who on this night of all nights had been frustratingly slow, had left some moments ago and now with her hair brushed and loose around her shoulders and her body delicately scented, Helena's anticipation was almost exquisite. There was a cosy coal fire and the two fringed bedside lamps gave a soft glow that made the room look both inviting and romantic. It was, she thought, the perfect setting for a night of love, and then as she was gazing again at the gold wedding band the door opened and Oliver came in.

Looking handsome in a maroon silk dressing gown and matching pyjamas, he returned her smile and then crossed to the far side of the bed to switch off first the lamp on Helena's side and then the one on his own. She turned in the shadowy room with its flickering fire, and watched as he removed his dressing gown before sliding beneath the linen sheets to lie beside her.

Feeling suddenly rather shy, Helena felt the familiar bristle of his moustache as his lips immediately came down to hers in a kiss that was hard, even impatient. Then immediately Oliver lifted himself on one elbow and moved to lean over her, almost roughly parting her thighs. Appalled, she felt almost crushed by the weight of his body as, with a contorted face, his eyes blazing in intensity, he achieved a silent, swift and for her, agonising consummation. As he rolled off her, Helena, conscious of stickiness between her legs, closed them defensively, only to find with bewilderment that Oliver was already flinging back the sheets. She heard the words,

'Thank you my dear,' as he bent to retrieve his dressing gown and then without even a backward glance left the room. It was then that slowly, almost painfully, heavy tears began to course down her face. She felt degraded, used, her body invaded. Her disappointment was so bitter that it hurt. Was this what married love was like – a cold and impersonal coupling?

On the morning following his marriage, Oliver, after a refreshing cup of Earl Grey tea followed by his usual dressing routine, felt in good spirits as he went down the curving staircase with its black balustrade to the breakfast room. When he went over to the silver dishes on the sideboard, he heard a slight cough behind him and turned to see the butler hovering. 'Mrs Faraday has expressed a wish to breakfast in her room, Sir.'

'Thank you, Gray.' Oliver, finding that he had an excellent appetite, enjoyed the bacon, sausages, kidneys and scrambled eggs he had chosen, and then lingered with his coffee over *The Times*. He suspected that Helena had chosen to have a lazy morning because she felt embarrassed after her deflowering. Oliver had a few qualms about that, knowing that his overriding urge to procreate had clouded his judgment. The actual act had been too swift – although surely the first time for a virgin could never be enjoyable. Next time would need to be different. Not only had he little desire for an unwilling wife, if the marriage bed was to be a fertile one then it was essential that Helena should welcome their lovemaking.

Eventually, after glancing at the ornate ormolu

clock on the mantelpiece, he decided it would now be appropriate for him to go upstairs – he had no desire to see his wife in a state of disarray.

Helena, who had slept very little, was sitting before her elaborate walnut dressing table as she half-heartedly tried to choose which earrings to wear. Aware that ladies of quality never wore diamonds during the day, she pushed one pair aside and stared into the mirror at her shadowed eyes.

Then came the half-expected tap at her door. 'Come in.'

'Did you sleep well, my love?'

Helena's voice was quiet. 'Yes, thank you.'

'And what would you like to do today? The weather seems reasonable, would you enjoy a stroll?'

'I would love some fresh air, Oliver.' She was trying to keep her voice even.

'Then later we shall take lunch at the Savoy Grill. How does that appeal?'

'Perfect.' Helena rose from her velvet stool to receive Oliver's morning kiss and straightened her back. She could hardly bear him to touch her, but she had to be adult about this. She had taken her vows before God and this man was her husband. During the long hours of the previous night, her only consolation had been a desperate hope that next time Oliver would be more tender, would show more consideration. How soon that would be, Helena was unsure but until then this was a new day, the first of her married life and all she could do was to make the best of it.

Chapter Fourteen

A fortnight later, the long-awaited day arrived for Molly to leave Broadway Manor. And to her surprise, despite her nervous anticipation and even excitement at the thought of the new life before her, she found her eyes filling with tears when, dressed in her Sunday best, she went to say goodbye to the rest of the staff.

'I'm really going to miss your cooking, Mrs Kemp,' she said in a choked voice.

'Nonsense!' Cook's broad face was determinedly cheerful. 'I wouldn't be surprised if at Graylings they don't have one of those there French chefs.'

'I don't fancy foreign food. I like your steak and kidney pudding.'

'Now then, Molly, you'll be fine once you're there,' the butler said. 'And Miss Helena will be relying on you. So my girl, a stiff upper lip if you please.'

'I don't know what you're blubbing about,' Ida looked scornful. 'I mean you were the one who wanted to better yourself.'

'I know,' Molly dabbed at her eyes. 'I don't know what's up with me.'

'I do,' one of the footmen said, looking up from polishing the silver. 'You're female, that's all. My mam was always blartin'.'

'Did you never think she might have had a reason,' Ida snapped. 'I should think having eight kids and no money was enough to make anyone shed tears.'

'Well, I shall really miss you, Moll.' Annie got up and went to give Molly an awkward hug.

'Don't forget to write.' The butler stood pointedly aside. 'And a letter now and then would be most welcome, but you mustn't keep Jennings waiting...'

Seconds later Molly was climbing into the Standish carriage, which was also transporting some of Helena's belongings. Several leather trunks were strapped on to the top, while there were so many hat boxes crowding the interior that there was scarcely room for Molly and her modest carpet bag. However, she settled into a corner and leaned back against the cushioned velvet seat to enjoy her first journey, although despite the comfort there was a certain amount of swaying and sometimes jolts when the road surface was uneven.

The passing countryside and the novelty of seeing other villages she found fascinating, but after a couple of hours she was relieved to have the chance to stretch her legs when, in a sparsely populated area, the coachman drew into the yard of an old inn. Jennings helped Molly to descend and then ushered her inside to where, in a smoke-filled room, several groups of working men were 'swilling beer' as her granny used to say, and Molly wrinkled her nose at the odour of sweating bodies and unwashed clothes. The atmosphere was a distinctly male one, with loud talk and hearty guffaws, and as she paused on the threshold, drawing her skirt away from the

121

sawdust on the floor, one burly man turned and gave her a lewd wink. Jennings immediately hustled Molly away and into a small snug, empty except for an old crone nursing a glass of stout in one corner.

'Sorry, it's a bit rough, I hadn't realised.'

Molly, knowing that he would never have brought Miss Beatrice or Miss Helena into such a place said, 'It's all right, you weren't to know.'

'What would you like to drink, love?' Jennings was a kindly man who had only recently joined the staff at Broadway Manor and while Molly sipped at her lemonade, he told her that the future was in motor cars. 'Me brother-in-law's set himself up in a little garage, and I go to help him sometimes. I've learned quite a bit, I think that's why Mr Standish hired me. He's got plans to buy one, you know.'

As he wiped his moustache free of froth from his pint of mild, Molly exclaimed, 'But what about the horses?'

'Oh, they'll be all right. He'll still keep a carriage on for Miss Beatrice.'

'Well that's a relief.' Molly looked at him. 'I suppose you and Mr Faraday's chauffeur had a lot in common then. I couldn't get a word out of him. Did he say anything to you about Graylings?'

Jennings shook his head. 'Come to think of it he did seem a bit quiet like if I raised the subject.'

'Well, I'll soon be finding out for meself.'

'That's true. Now are you ready, love, or do you…?'

Molly glanced at the disreputable looking old

woman in the corner, thought of all the men in the bar, and decided not to risk it. She shook her head, 'No, I'm all right to continue, Mr Jennings.'

Her first sight of Graylings was not a fortunate one. As soon as the coach drew up outside large ornate iron gates mounted by a lion's head and a man hurried out of the gatehouse to allow them to enter, the greying sky decided to unload its heavy burden and rain came lashing down, spitting against the windows and obscuring her view. Then peering out, Molly could just see the outline of a great country house, grey in the mist. Broadway Manor seemed almost small in comparison and her stomach tied in nervous knots.

Jennings guided the horses round to the back of the house and into the stable yard, and as she leaned down to pick up her carpet bag, she could only wish with despair that Miss Helena had arrived before her.

In London, Helena found herself becoming restless. The General Election had generated some excitement, but that was now over, with to Oliver's satisfaction the Liberal Party winning a landslide victory.

Dorothy had earlier written to her, '*In confidence, I've joined the Women's Social and Political Union. My father would have a fit if he knew! There's going to be a huge march on Downing Street to urge the new Prime Minister to introduce votes for women – why don't you join them?*' But her friend, Helena thought, wasn't married to Oliver. While he might accept the concept that women could eventually vote, he would never agree to his wife taking part in a possibly violent demonstration.

And marriage itself also involved a degree of intimacy far greater and more often than she had anticipated. Without exception, each night once the maid had left, the inter-connecting door would open and Oliver, always immaculate in matching silk pyjamas and dressing gown, would come into her bedroom. His words were always the same, a murmured 'Hello, my sweet,' and he would then ensure the room was darkened before lifting the coverlet and sliding beneath the sheets to lie with her. She had never seen his naked body, only felt his maleness inside her. And she had to admit that he was considerate of her modesty too. It had taken some time for Helena to conquer her resentment after that first appalling scene, which was never mentioned. Gradually, as Oliver's lovemaking became increasingly gentler and more prolonged, she found herself able to respond; he would even whisper endearments, telling her that she was 'his beautiful wife'. But to her continuing bewilderment and dismay, Oliver always left within minutes, leaving her alone and with a longing to be held close, for him to stay with her so that they could sleep together throughout the night. What must it be like, she wondered, to awake and see his head on the soft white pillow beside her? Once Helena had actually put her desire into words, but his reaction had been one of such sharp distaste, that she had felt stung, even humiliated.

'My dear Helena, for married couples to sleep in the same bed is unheard of in our circles. It is something confined to the working classes.

Surely, you can see that it would be not only unhygienic but also most unsuitable. One would hardly wish to be awakened by one's servant in such circumstances.'

And so each night she would watch him leave with an unmistakeable air of complacency, wondering why she felt so ... Helena wasn't sure exactly how she did feel ... but in the core of her, she sensed that something was lacking. Was it her fault? Was she too young, not woman enough?

Then eventually the time came when it was necessary for her to raise an indelicate subject. They were alone in the drawing room, where Oliver was enjoying a fine French brandy after dinner and judging him to be in a relaxed mood, it was with some embarrassment that Helena said, 'Oliver, I do apologise, but it will be several days before I am able again to welcome you into my bed.'

Oliver's hand, which was half-raised to his lips, stilled. He didn't answer at first and then said in a low, tense voice, 'Do you mean that you are indisposed?'

Helena, feeling the colour rise in her cheeks said, 'Yes, I'm afraid so.'

Again, there was a silence. 'Then my sweet, I shall rely on you to let me know when...'

Helena nodded. 'But of course.'

It was with difficulty that Oliver managed to keep his expression bland, to disguise his seething frustration. Perhaps it had been a conceit to think that she would conceive so quickly. As for her female ailment, he knew that some men could disregard such a fact; he had even heard them boast of it. However, to Oliver the act at such a time would be abhorrent, and so without the necessity of indulging Helena with a view to her nightly compliance, there was little need for him to spend so much time with her, at least during the coming week. Not, he mused, as he glanced across to where Helena was leafing through a copy of Vogue, that he had any complaints about his wife. On the contrary, he had to admit to an increasing fondness for her, but he would certainly make the most of the situation and perhaps dine at his club on some evenings, or seek out Johnnie at the gaming tables.

Helena, unaware of Oliver's brooding, resigned herself to idling the rest of the evening with her magazine, her mind running ahead. There was a romantic novel in her room, and the prospect of being undisturbed and to feel again that lovely sense of drowsiness before closing the pages and snuggling down would be absolute bliss. They would also soon be back at Graylings where there would be the chance to make new friends. She was longing now to see her new home and to meet the staff. Also it had surprised Helena just how much she had missed feminine company. At least when her father eventually came to visit he would be bringing Aunt Beatrice with him.

Chapter Fifteen

Oliver had personally appointed the butler at Graylings soon after his father's death. The previous incumbent, an elderly man of loyal service but now shrivelled appearance, had been retired on an adequate pension and replaced by a tall, commanding man with the bearing of an Army officer. Edwin Crossley believed in discipline and the upholding of high standards, his features were clean cut and to Oliver he had been the perfect choice.

On the morning of the expected arrival, a groom was directed to ride to the gates and instructions given that he should then gallop back to Graylings to give the required signal. Already members of staff were hovering in readiness, alert to leave their tasks in order to gather outside the wide frontage of the house.

'I want you to line up on each side in order of seniority,' the butler told them, 'the indoor staff on the right, and the outdoor staff on the left. The men will be bareheaded and as the master and mistress pass by the women are to bob a curtsey.'

Honestly, Molly thought with resentment. He must think we haven't a brain between us. She kept a wide berth of Mr Crossley. Not that she disliked him, but she was constantly apprehensive, as she suspected were many of the maids, of doing anything that could incur his disapproval. It was bad enough satisfying the exacting demands of the housekeeper. It was a funny place, Molly thought as she dusted a blue and white Meissen vase in the vast hall, remembering the day when she had first arrived.

Nervous and filled with apprehension, she had been offered warm refreshment in the kitchen – a bowl of soup and crusty bread – and then shown immediately to the housekeeper's office; a spacious, comfortable room with rust velour curtains and a fireplace with a black-leaded gleaming surround above a cosy fire. The woman seated behind a large and slightly shabby desk had upright posture, her sandy hair swept into a chignon. Dressed in black with white starched collar and cuffs, she waved a hand to the chair before her. 'Do come in, Fox. I hope you had a good journey.'

At first the housekeeper simply asked questions concerning Molly's experience before detailing her new duties, the hours she would be expected to work and the amount of free time allowed. Then she hesitated. 'At Graylings, we are required to observe a strict rule of confidentiality. Mr Faraday insists that if any member of his staff is found to have discussed his personal affairs or those of his household outside this house, then instant dismissal will follow. I take it you are in agreement with that?'

Flustered, Molly said, 'Of course, Mrs Birley.'

The housekeeper glanced down at an open ledger before her. 'I haven't mentioned your wages, have I? You will find that Mr Faraday is a generous employer, which is one of the reasons we are all happy to fit in with his requirements.'

She had gone on to name the most satisfactory sum of twenty-seven pounds a year and that night as Molly settled into her small attic room – the first she had never had to share – although drowsy with weariness she was elated, already planning to save for a little nest egg. Perhaps she had been wrong about Miss Helena's husband; she had even felt worried, especially in view of Annie's strong dislike of him. Although she would have to accept that it would be difficult for them to resume their original friendship, which was a pity because if she felt a bit lonely at Graylings, then so would her mistress. Molly smiled to herself at the word, because of course that's what Miss Helena was now, her mistress, not the smiling girl who had teased her in the fields at Broadway Manor.

Molly carefully replaced the vase on a polished walnut side table and while waiting for the summons to go outside, reflected that although most of the staff seemed friendly enough, she still felt a stranger among them. One of the footmen had tried flirting with her, but although she liked a bit of harmless fun, she would never risk anything that threatened her chance of bettering herself.

Helena, seated beside Oliver on the leather seat of the car while his chauffeur negotiated the roads leading to Graylings, found her nervousness mounting with every passing mile. To see for the first time – for no painting could compare with the actual experience – Graylings, yet knowing that her arrival would be the subject of many curious stares was daunting to say the least. She tucked a stray strand of hair beneath her emerald green hat, trimmed extravagantly with ostrich feathers and bought for the occasion. 'Make a grand entrance,' Beatrice had recommended, 'remember your position despite your youth. If necessary, adopt an air of arrogance. Believe me it will pay dividends in the future.'

With the coach, laden with their trunks, having set off earlier, Oliver seemed to have planned everything to the last detail. As they journeyed he told her the names of the senior members of the household, ones she would need to greet personally. He himself would introduce the estate manager and butler, who in turn would present the housekeeper and cook. 'And Helena, only a smile for your maid from Broadway Manor if you please; it wouldn't do to single her out.'

'I understand, Oliver.'

The sight that met her as the chauffeur drove up a private road surrounded by parkland was one she would never forget. Despite earlier threatening clouds, when she had wondered whether Oliver would expect his staff to stand out in the rain, the weather was fine. Even from a distance, Graylings seemed larger than she'd expected; built of grey stone in the mid-18th century of Georgian Palladium style, it was four storeys high and bore an air of almost forbidding grandeur. Helena felt a rush of inadequacy, being acutely conscious of her youth, her inexperience, especially as she saw waiting outside the magnificent south frontage opposite lines of staff; the footmen in livery of maroon and gold, the maids in black, with white aprons and mob caps.

Helena saw them watch expectantly as the car came to a halt. The chauffeur opened the rear door on Oliver's side first, and then both men walked round the car, the chauffeur standing aside so that Oliver could assist Helena. A sable tippet around her shoulders, she placed her gloved hand on his arm, lifted her skirt and, after taking a deep breath, she stepped out with a smile.

Helena was unsure whether she would ever be able to think of Graylings as her home. Accustomed to Broadway Manor with its golden oak, the almost black panelling of the hall and staircase seemed gloomy. It was a much older house of course, but although well cared for, some of the furnishings seemed to her both heavy and oppressive. She was hoping that perhaps after a decent interval Oliver would allow her to arrange some of the rooms to her own taste. Their private apartments again had an interconnecting door, and were situated in the west wing, where to her delight the view from her bedroom window overlooked the rose gardens that Oliver had described. And she had to admit that in this particular room, the furnishings chosen by Oliver's late mother were pleasing and light in colour, including a beautiful Japanese silk screen similar to that in the London House. Rosalind Faraday must have chosen that too. How strange and sad that she, like Helena's own mother, had died so young and in childbirth.

Helena felt a slight shiver at the thought, and then reminded herself such tragedies were the exception rather than the rule. There was no reason to believe that the same thing would happen to her.

They had been in residence for three days when one afternoon in the drawing room, as they waited for tea to be served, she said, 'Oliver, there is the question of my maid?'

'Yes, of course. I have not been remiss in this, Helena. Mrs Birley already has a short list of applicants for you. She is well aware of my requirements.'

Helena stared at him. 'I'm sorry Oliver, I don't understand? I would have thought that it would be *my* requirements that would take preference.'

'My dear girl, don't be so prickly. Naturally, it will be your choice. I just prefer to be surrounded by pleasant countenances. Mrs Birley will have weeded out anyone unsuitable.'

'Oh, I see.' Helena watched him leave the room, remembering how he had enquired about Molly and his relief when Helena had described the maid as 'the pretty one'. Well, there was nothing wrong in preferring beauty to ugliness, but it seemed harsh on those unfortunate ones who were not blessed with good looks. As an image of Annie flashed into her mind, followed by the disturbing memory of Oliver's expression of disgust, Helena was deep in thought as she crossed over to the silken bell-pull to summon the housekeeper. There was so much she needed to learn and to understand about this husband of hers.

Chapter Sixteen

In the East End of London, Cora was fed up with the winter. Not that she ever had to face the damp mornings, or the biting cold of early freezing winds, as since the age of fifteen, she had never risen before midday. In her profession the nights were a time for working, not sleeping. But she did like to get a breath of fresh air at some time of the day, and late afternoons would often find her wandering around the markets. Today had been an especially satisfying expedition and she let herself into the house clutching with triumph a pair of boots. Black and trimmed with silver, they showed scarcely a sign of wear. And they were kid leather too, a sure sign that they'd belonged to some lady of quality. Cora hadn't tried them on yet but she knew what to do if they were a bit tight. Stuff 'em with some damp brown paper and leave 'em for a couple of days – it never failed.

When she reached the landing she discovered that Belle had hired a new girl. Not that Cora was surprised – the room next to her own had been empty for a couple of weeks now which meant it wasn't earning its way. She paused at the half-open door to see a dark-haired girl hanging her clothes in the narrow wardrobe, her lips compressed with determination, her expression one of misery.

'Cheer up ducks, it ain't so bad.'

The girl turned, and her voice was tight. 'You might not think so. I do.'

'Never expected to end up in a place like this, is that it?'

'I haven't got much choice.'

'Same as the rest of us then,' Cora said with a shrug. 'I'm next door – the name's Cora Bates.'

'Sybil Slater.'

Cora looked at her curiously. 'First time then – in a place like this I mean?'

'That's right.'

'Well, let me know if yer need anything.' Cora walked past and went into her own room thinking that at least this one seemed sober. The last occupant had been a right gin-soak; once Belle had found out that had been the end of her. Not that she frowned on the girls having a drop, she just objected to them drowning in the stuff.

Lacing up her new boots, Cora muttered, 'Might 'ave been made for me,' and pleased, decided to wear them that evening. She was half-hoping that Johnnie would appear. It was odd, but she missed him if he stayed away too long.

The new girl seemed to cling to Cora, but she didn't mind. She was glad of the company, even though Sybil couldn't half tell a tale. One rainy afternoon, when they were in Sybil's room, lying propped up in front of the pink satin headboard, Cora probed, 'This chap, the one you say gave you all these silks and satins and jewellery, who was he, then?'

'That's none of your business,' Sybil said shortly.

134

'Fair enough.' Cora didn't like people knowing her business either. 'But what I don't understand is, if you had all this stuff, how come you ended up here?'

'Where I was living, he paid the rent, didn't he? Lovely little apartment, it was, in St John's Wood. It's very select there, you know. I had me own kitchen and everything. And I never went with anyone else, not once. But then one day he just gives me 10 guineas, and bob's yer uncle. Said he had no need of our arrangement any more. So there I was, homeless, with all these clothes and things, and nowhere to put 'em.'

Cora had seen the meagre garments in Sybil's wardrobe. 'So where are they all?'

'Well, I got meself some cheap lodgings, then one day I came back to find the lot gone, money and everything! Even the bits of jewellery that I'd hid beneath me best corset. Course the old hag running the place pleaded ignorance, but I didn't dare send for the rozzers...'

'I would 'ave done, the thieving cow!'

'No you wouldn't,' Sybil said sharply. 'They'd have asked a lot of questions, maybe even accused me of lying, of stealing the things myself.'

'You could have told them the truth.'

Sybil shook her head. 'I know for sure he used a false name. I always called him Gerald, but there were different initials on his wallet. I only saw it the once, just by chance. Anyway, it was no use crying over spilt milk so I cut me losses, made a few enquiries and heard about Belle's.'

'I bet he's got married,' Cora decided. 'That's if he wasn't already. He's probably bored to death in a big draughty house with some milk-sop miss.'

Sybil's laugh was bitter. 'At least she will only have to satisfy one man, not like...'

'I've told you, you'll get used to it.'

At Graylings, Mrs Birley presented Helena with three applicants for the post of her personal maid. 'There were initially five, Mrs Faraday, but two were unsuitable.'

Helena wondered whether that had been because of their appearance or their lack of experience. From her observation of the indoor staff – she had yet to familiarise herself with all of the outdoor – she suspected that the housekeeper was well aware of Oliver's demanding standards. The footmen were unfailingly good looking, the maids were fresh-faced and pretty, even Mrs Birley could be described as a handsome woman while the butler's leonine head would have graced any theatre. The only exception was Cook, whose round face resembled a currant bun. But it was unlikely that Oliver ever came into contact with her. Even Helena was reluctant to explore beyond the green baize door that separated the 'downstairs' from the 'upstairs'. Beatrice had emphasized that strongly. 'Your presence will not be welcomed – it will be regarded as mistrust and interference, Helena. Just for once please be guided by someone with more experience. You are no longer a child to be pampered and fussed. You are their mistress, and they will expect you to know your place, in the same way that you expect them to know theirs.'

So Helena straightened her back and prepared

to portray a dignified appearance as the first of the applicants was ushered into the morning room. This was a vital appointment because she didn't merely require someone to dress her hair, care for her clothes and advise her on which jewellery to wear. She needed an ally, someone who would be intensely loyal and who she could, if necessary, confide in.

A week later, Molly could only gaze with grudging admiration at the new member of staff as she took her seat at the long table in the Servants Hall where, between the butler at the head and the cook at the other end, everyone else was placed in strict order of seniority. As Mrs Faraday's personal maid, Jane Forrester had been shown to the seat immediately on Mr Crossley's right, displacing the head parlour maid. Mrs Birley, in view of her position as housekeeper, had her meals served in her room as indeed Jane Forrester could choose to do.

Molly decided that Miss Forrester had elegance. It was in her deportment and in the touches of white at her neck and cuffs, their soft lace portraying not efficiency but a taste for fashion. From beneath her lashes Molly watched the graceful way she used her slender hands, the polite way she inclined her neck as she listened to the butler, and judged her to be in her mid-thirties. She was nice-looking too, in a quiet way, with soft brown eyes and hair. Not at all snobby and forbidding-looking. She looks friendly enough, she decided, as she passed on the bowl of boiled potatoes to another junior maid.

What Molly hadn't anticipated was that her connection with the new mistress of Graylings would be regarded with suspicion.

'You want to be careful what you say in earshot of that new maid.' One of the parlourmaids had a strident voice, and Molly had paused outside an open door to listen in growing dismay. 'I mean, why else would Mrs Faraday bring her here, if it wasn't to spy on the rest of us?'

That was Susan, the spiteful cow! Molly had taken a step forward to confront her – then thought better of it. Why stoop to her level? Instead, she had decided to keep her head down and do a good job; they would soon learn they were wrong.

But she was settling in now at Graylings, gratified to find that the cook's expertise was not only equal to that of Mrs Kemp, but her pastry was even superior. Having been half-starved as a child, food was Molly's main pleasure in life. Her second was books. She would always bless her good luck in having such a dedicated school-teacher. Molly's attendance at school might have been spasmodic, the years short, but the elderly spinster whose mission in life was to eradicate illiteracy, had recognised a quick brain and fed it accordingly. However, the arrangement that had existed at Broadway Manor between herself and Miss Helena had left a void Molly was unsure how to fill. The romantic novels she had secretly passed on had been ones given to her by the daughter of a local minister, whose eventual elopement scandalised the parish. Although scathing of religion – Molly had seen too much misery in her childhood to believe in a benevolent God – she had taken full advantage of the custom for servants to be given two hours off on Sunday mornings to attend a service. Even sitting in a chilly church and listening to a boring sermon had proved a welcome diversion from the weekly routine.

Now Molly was beginning to wonder whether Miss Helena – or Mrs Faraday as she must remember to call her, at least in public – would, in her new position, consider it beneath her to share books with a mere parlour maid. To Molly's frustration and disappointment, she had so far seen little of her apart from a swift smile of recognition that first day.

During her first few weeks at Graylings, Helena, mindful of Aunt Beatrice's advice, concentrated on establishing her authority. It took determination, but she managed to subdue her natural friendliness and instead adopted a manner that was pleasant yet slightly aloof. And she found it gratifying to see the growing respect in Mrs Birley's eyes as Helena listened to the housekeeper's views and requests and gave clear agreement and instructions.

'I do realise, Mrs Birley,' Helena had been careful to say, 'that your familiarity with Graylings far exceeds my own. And I shall rely upon your experience and wise advice in these early days.'

'Thank you, Mrs Faraday. I can assure you that the efficient running of the household is not only my duty, but also my pleasure.'

'Then we are of the same mind.'

And since then their relationship had been one

of cordial mutual respect, and a few days before Jacob and Beatrice Standish were due to arrive, just as Mrs Birley was about to leave the morning room, Helena said, 'How is Molly settling in?'

'Extremely well, I find her both willing and efficient.'

'Good. And she will receive some training in the duties of a lady's maid?'

'In due course, Madam.'

'Indeed.' She was thoughtful as the housekeeper left the room. Helena felt uncomfortable that she hadn't spoken personally to Molly, but had thought it wise to wait until the visitors from Broadway Manor arrived, giving the perfect excuse to single out their former maid. Although whether at Graylings it would be possible to resume their old friendly relationship was a question to which she hadn't yet found the answer. She missed the way they were relaxed with each other; the fact that they had been girls together had somehow blurred the class boundaries between them. Although Helena suspected that Molly never quite forgot the difference in their status. Meanwhile, slowly she was beginning to trust the quietly efficient Jane Forrester and had already decided that her first appointment had been the right one.

But she had more urgent matters on her mind. Oliver had been absent all day but after dinner, Helena needed to choose the right moment to inform him that she was again indisposed.

Chapter Seventeen

Three weeks later the staff at Broadway Manor waited impatiently in the kitchen for Miss Hewson to join them after her return from Graylings.

'Miss Beatrice will probably expect her to unpack first.' The maid who had replaced Molly was, Cook declared, one of those people whose cup was always half empty.

'Nonsense girl, she's much too considerate for that. Ah, here she is...' Mrs Kemp lifted the large brown earthenware teapot and began to pour.

'Oh, I'm ready for that.' Enid collapsed on to an armchair.

'How about a slice of my fruit cake, Miss Hewson?'

'That would be most welcome Cook, thank you.'

'We're dying to know how Miss Helena is, and all about Graylings.'

'That's right.' Annie leaned forward on the table, one hand shielding the scarred side of her face.

'Give me time to catch my breath. It's ever so grand, I nearly got lost the first day.' She went on to describe the stateliness of Graylings with its myriad of rooms and corridors, the dark oak panelling, the huge rooms with long casement windows overlooking parkland and how many of

141

the graceful chairs were embroidered in gold-threaded tapestry. 'Lovely it is,' she said, 'although it doesn't have the cosy feel of Broadway Manor. Believe it or not, there's even a lake.'

Annie said, 'And Miss Helena?'

'She seems fine. Quite the mistress, I can tell you. Proud of her, I was.'

'Yes, but is he good to her?' Annie persisted.

Enid hesitated. 'He seems to be, not that I saw much of him. He's just the same, treats the servants as if they're invisible.'

'And how did you find the Servants' Hall?' was the butler's question.

Enid gave a shrug. 'There were a lot more staff in there, good food mind you. I can tell you one thing, though – they're a nice-looking lot.'

'So,' the youngest footman said, smoothing his pomaded black hair. 'What would my chances be then?'

'How do you mean?'

'Would I pass muster?'

'You're not thinking of leaving us?' Cook's voice rose in alarm.

''Course not, he's just fishing for compliments! Never mind that, tell us about Molly,' Annie said. 'Does she like it there?'

'She says so, although she was a bit quiet. Mind you, I don't suppose there's much she can say.' Enid leaned forward. 'Apparently, none of the staff at Graylings are supposed to talk about the family.'

'And it's quite a sensible rule; I've seen many a reputation ruined by gossiping servants.' The butler looked sternly at both footmen. 'I would

142

hope that neither of you have a loose tongue when you visit alehouses in Lichfield.'

'And what about Miss Helena's personal maid?' Ida's expression was slightly wistful. 'Have they appointed one?'

Enid nodded. 'Yes, a Miss Forrester. Lucky devil, at the beginning of May she'll be going to Italy, that's where they're going for their honeymoon.'

'Well, we're going to Colwyn Bay for a few days. Oh of course you won't have heard my news,' Ida said, her eyes shining with excitement. 'You know we were waiting for permission to marry to come through from the army, well it has! And Charlie can't see any point in waiting, so the wedding's next month. I'm really glad you're back, Miss Hewson, because I haven't got my dress sorted out yet.'

Enid brightened. 'You leave it to me. There's one of Miss Beatrice's silk nightgowns that's too tight on her. I'll have you looking like a princess.'

'Oh, thanks, Miss Hewson. I knew you'd come up with something. I still can't believe I'll soon be living in married quarters at Whittington.'

'And then that'll be another new parlour maid to get used to,' Cook said to Annie later. 'Only this time, I hope they get a more cheerful one than the last. She's a right wet blanket, and the new scullery maid's a half-wit.'

'No she isn't,' Annie protested. 'She's just jumpy, that's all, in case she does anything wrong. And it's not her fault – that Dad of hers was too handy with his belt. Daisy just needs time, that's all.'

Once her father and Aunt Beatrice had left, Helena grew restless, lacking stimulation. She had small talent for drawing and painting, and no interest in embroidery. Oliver was often out on estate matters and so far there had been little opportunity to make new friends. She mentioned this to Oliver.

'When we return from Italy, you can invite Dorothy to stay.' He raised a quizzical eyebrow. 'Or do I sense that there is something else on your mind?'

She nodded. 'I thought that before then, I'd like to have some tuition on the piano.'

'But you play beautifully.'

'Maybe, but when we begin to entertain, I feel that any recital at Graylings should be of the highest possible standard.'

As she had anticipated, his immediate response was to agree.

Oliver was absent from the house on the morning when James Longford, a music tutor recommended by another county family, first came to Graylings.

When Crossley brought to the music room a clean-shaven dark-haired man sporting a green corduroy jacket and spotted bow tie, Helena turned to him in surprise. Much younger than she had anticipated, he brought with him a breath of fresh air into the rather formal atmosphere that seemed to pervade even the furnishings. She found as they talked that James Longford had an affinity to music that matched her own, and soon

Helena took her place before the Steinway grand piano, while the tutor sat on one of the surrounding chairs to listen to her repertoire. When eventually the notes died away, he said, 'Mrs Faraday, may I congratulate you, that was an excellent performance. However, I think I can – how shall I put it – add icing to the cake? Believe me,' he hesitated and then gave an attractive grin, 'it will be a pleasure to work with a well-risen sponge rather than a flat and dry one.'

Helena laughed. 'That sounded heartfelt!'

'It was!' He came over to the piano. 'First of all, I think your position could be improved. Perhaps a little more distance?'

Obediently, Helena adjusted the stool.

'You see, already you have more flexibility of movement. And perhaps if there is slightly higher stool somewhere?'

Helena thought. 'I'm not sure.'

'Well before acquiring one, do try a small cushion or something to raise you up a little. Extra height will give you more control and you will find your touch lighter and yet more powerful.'

By the time he left, setting her work on advanced scales and arpeggios, Helena felt that she had already benefited from the extra tuition. Then as she was coming out of the room, she saw Molly at the other end of the corridor.

'Molly! At last, I never seem to be able to catch you on your own. Quick, come in to the music room.'

Once they were inside, she gave the other girl a hug. 'How are you? Are you happy here?'

'It's okay. I miss Broadway Manor though.'

145

'Don't tell anyone, but so do I.'

They both burst out laughing.

'Oh Molly, it's wonderful to be able to talk to you. I'm sorry it's taken so long.'

'It's all right, Miss Helena. I quite understand. The only thing is...'

'What, tell me...'

'You haven't got any books, have you? I'm desperate for something to read.'

'We must come up with a plan.' Helena glanced around the room. 'Do you ever come in here?'

Molly nodded. 'Yes, once a week. It's one of my duties to dust it and use the carpet sweeper.'

'Then look inside the piano stool.'

'You mean...'

'We'll have a system, just like we used to have with that cupboard on the landing. I'll put a novel in there and...'

'I'll wrap it in a duster and take it right up to my room. Oh, thank you Miss Helena, you're an angel.' Molly glanced towards the door. 'I'd better go – Mrs Birley's on the warpath today.'

Those few moments, in addition to the stimulating morning, had lifted Helena's spirits and she greeted Oliver with a smile when later that afternoon he returned for tea. 'I had such an enjoyable time.'

'Good. What is he like, this paragon of music?'

'Younger than I expected. He wears very colourful clothes – a bit bohemian really. He really was excellent. I'm afraid you will have to forebear the sound of scales being practised.'

Oliver took a scone and began to spread it with strawberry jam. 'Then I shall make a point of

146

being a long way from the music room.'

After he had left, Helena felt in a reflective mood. The past hour had been a companionable one; she had felt relaxed, happy even. She was finding that marriage – which seemed to be the holy grail of most women – was far more complicated than she had expected. So much effort and planning went into the actual finding of a husband, especially from mothers of daughters of a certain age, with accolades for any girl 'marrying well'. Yet little was heard of marriage itself, and to her despair, Oliver's brutality, his lack of consideration on their wedding night, was still tainting the way she felt about him. When they were in bed she managed to offer some response, but a vital part of their intimacy had been lost. Was her husband aware of it? What I need, Helena thought with desperation as she strolled over to the tall window to gaze out at the distant lake, is for Italy to perform a romantic miracle.

Chapter Eighteen

'Dr Carstairs?' The voice was urgent, even peremptory, and Nicholas turned to see a staff nurse hurrying towards him. 'Please could you spare a minute?'

'Of course.' Nicholas swiftly followed the rustling figure, her starched cap slightly awry. 'It's this young boy,' she explained. 'He's been admitted as an emergency and is screaming blue murder. He refuses to let the duty doctor examine him. All he can say is that he wants to see Doc Carstairs. Honestly, as if these people can ask for any doctor they like... I don't like to bother you, but...'

'I don't mind, Nurse Barton,' he turned his head to smile at her. 'It's just lucky I'm here, I rarely am these days unless one of my patients is admitted.'

'I know – we miss you. To be honest his mother looks as if she's ill herself. It's scandalous that such poverty should exist – but what do the Government do about it? Nothing!' She glanced over her shoulder at him. 'I do miss those political debates we used to have when you were on the staff.' Nicholas recalled that she had been a staunch supporter of women's suffrage even to the point of active involvement in the movement. Now, even before they reached their destination, he could hear the boy howling. 'Now then, my lad,' she said, as they went in. 'Here's Dr Carstairs come to see you.'

The small boy clinging to his mother's skirts turned a grimy face streaked with tears. Nicholas nodded at the red-faced young doctor in attendance then remembered when he had last seen them. It had been a breech birth in one of the hovels down near the docks. This boy had stood terrified in a corner, thinking his Ma was about to die. But fortunately – and Nicholas knew it was solely due to his care – the baby had been born alive and the woman had recovered. Although judging by her present appearance, it had been only to suffer even more hardship.

'His name's Robbie,' Nurse Forbes said.

'Hello, Robbie.' Nicholas bent down to him. 'I remember you, do you remember me?'

The five-year-old child gave a sob and nodded.

'So are you going to let me see where it hurts?' Nicholas lifted the boy and placed him on the bed. Talking slowly and gently, telling Robbie exactly what he was going to do, Nicholas examined his thin frame, compressing his lips at the sight of bruises and welts, and eliciting a scream when he pressed first in the centre of the abdomen, and then on the right side. He turned to the mother. 'Has he been sick?'

'Yes, doctor.' Her voice was a whisper.

'Now will you let nurse take your temperature, Robbie? She'll put something underneath your tongue, but you mustn't bite it. Do you understand?' Minutes later, Nicholas said, 'Acute appendicitis. He needs immediate surgery.' He bent down to the child and took his small hand in his own warm one. 'Now look, Robbie, you know I'm a doctor and I take care of people, don't you? Well, there are other doctors here, who are just as clever as I am, and they'll be able to take the pain away. Will you be a good boy for them, to please me?'

The other doctor came forward. 'Thank you, Dr Carstairs. He fought me like a whirling Dervish.'

'Fear,' Nicholas said abruptly. 'Did you notice the bruising?'

'I'm afraid so.'

Nicholas turned round, his voice sharp. 'Is it his father who beats him?'

Robbie's mother gazed at him with scared eyes.

149

'He doesn't mean to, it's the drink. He's not a bad man...'

'What about the baby? Does he harm it?'

She shook her head. 'There's not a mark on 'er.'

Nicholas sighed and went outside the room with Dr Sangster. 'I don't know what we can do. There's only one alternative – the workhouse – but would his life be any better there?'

Dr Sangster shrugged. 'Who knows? We can't even be sure if he'll have a life, not until after the operation.'

Later, after he had satisfied himself as to the progress of his own patient, Nicholas was about to put on his warm overcoat and top hat ready to go home when Nurse Barton appeared outside the ward. 'I'm glad I caught you,' she said. 'I'm going to hear Sylvia Pankhurst and Annie Kenney speak tonight. I don't suppose you'd be willing to come, Dr Carstairs? I may be a feminist, but I'm not blind to the fact that every male presence adds weight to our cause.'

Nicholas gazed at her, admiring her courage in the way she stood up for her principles and made a sudden decision. 'Of course I will. Just tell me where it's being held and when.'

Her face lit up as she told him. 'I knew you would if it were possible.'

There were times, Nicholas thought as he put on his warm overcoat and top hat and left to go home, when he despaired of the human race. Not only were women living in a democracy deprived of their legal rights, but the excuse of drunkenness for ill-treating a defenceless young child or abusing women, was one he often heard. Yet

150

ministering to the poor and sick as he had these past two years, he often found patients protesting that their husbands or fathers were 'good men when they weren't in drink'. Nicholas would never forget when a burly docker had lurched in from the local alehouse and, finding a doctor in attendance, had savagely thrown his tin plate of dinner across the room. The sight of an eight-year old girl crouching to scoop the mess of potatoes and meat off the floor to cram into her hungry mouth had sickened him. Yet in all conscience he could not turn his back on these people; Nicholas hadn't taken the Hippocratic oath that 'he would use treatments for the benefit of the ill', only to apply them exclusively to those with wealth. Although he was no saint; he was as ambitious as the next man, and well aware that he valued, even at times coveted, the finer things of life.

The meeting hall was large and chilly, sparsely furnished with rows of wooden chairs before a stage framed by limp, faded maroon curtains. On it stood a table behind which were three chairs. Two well-dressed women were arranging carafes of water and glasses and checking watches on their lapels. The centre chair was still empty, and Nicholas guessed they were still awaiting their distinguished guest. He glanced around for Nurse Barton in vain then saw a gloved hand wave to him from the third row. The audience held a majority of women, who were busy taking out hatpins in order to remove their large, feather-bedecked hats so that those seated behind would be able to see the anticipated speaker.

'I didn't recognise you out of uniform,' he whispered as he sat beside her.

'Just look for the nose.'

He chuckled. 'You don't change.'

'I'm a born spinster, Dr Carstairs, but not, as we're accused of being, a sour one.'

He glanced around the room. 'You seem to have very wealthy supporters.'

'You tell me how a working class woman, especially if married with children, could find the time? That doesn't mean she doesn't want the vote.'

'I take your point.'

The room was now crowded to full capacity, with people standing at the back, and then with a stir, Annie Kenney arrived, a much younger woman than Nicholas had imagined. But her words were no less powerful, her delivery no less stirring. Afterwards, a few men at the back threw out derisory remarks, but the overall reaction was one of enthusiastic applause.

'Did you notice that she had lost one of her fingers?' he said, as they made their way out of the hall.

'Yes, as a child she was a weaver in a cotton mill, and I heard it was an accident with a bobbin. Inspiring, isn't she?'

He agreed, and was thoughtful as he made his way home. The evening may have been unplanned but the experience had certainly been an interesting one.

It was a week later when Nicholas was visiting his

patient in Cadogan Square, and saw the tall four-storey house where he had first seen Helena, that the memories came flooding back. He now found it difficult to believe that he had actually gone to wait outside St Margaret's Church on that cold January morning. And was infuriated to find that as he neared the house, even though he knew there was little chance of seeing Helena – whose husband would undoubtedly have his own residence in the capital, that he found it impossible not to glance up at the casement window. And there was someone there, a small face pressed against the glass, her swollen jaw bound in a blue silk scarf, and he guessed she was suffering from mumps. The child looked so disconsolate that Nicholas smiled up at her and she gave a shy wave in return.

The house must be one of those on lease during the summer Season. It was in a way a salutary lesson, illustrating that life had moved on, and that, Nicholas thought grimly, was what he needed to do.

At Graylings, illness was also the dominant factor. Oliver, to his fury, had succumbed to a severe bout of influenza and his ill humour was affecting everyone around him.

The local doctor had emerged from Oliver's bedroom with a flushed face and tight lips, but Nurse Bowers, who remained, despite her youthful appearance, had a backbone of steel. 'We don't want any bad temper, now do we,' she said, briskly undoing the buttons on his pyjama jacket.

'You are far too familiar, Nurse.'

She ignored him as she scooped out goose fat and camphor and spread it over his chest. 'I'm only doing my duty.'

'And I can easily dismiss you.'

'Now that wouldn't be very sensible, would it? Sit up now, Mr Faraday, and let me plump your pillows.'

Oliver felt her support his aching and sweating head and felt too weak to argue. At least he had issued instructions that Helena was not to enter the room. For all he knew she could already be pregnant and there must be no risk of infection or risk of a miscarriage...

Having to rely on regular updates from Nurse Bowers during the next three weeks, Helena felt a useless onlooker, her only distraction the music lessons, her only outside company that of the music tutor.

James Longford's visits to Graylings were frequent ones. 'I'm so appreciative of your tuition,' she said to him one day. 'I already feel more confident when I play.'

'Believe me, the pleasure is all mine, Mrs Faraday.'

Helena wondered if she would ever become used to such formality. Her instinct was to say, 'Please, you must call me Helena,' but she knew that Oliver would think she was being too familiar.

She smiled at him, liking the relaxed way he sat on one of the gold velvet chairs, one long leg draped over the other. 'You never tell me anything of your personal life. Are you married, for instance?'

He laughed. 'And who would marry me.'

'I'm sure there would be several young ladies.'

'It's kind of you to say so.'

'I shall of course see you again on Friday?'

'At the usual time, yes.'

Helena smiled at him and left, leaving him to tidy away his music.

On Friday morning, Nurse Bowers came to say goodbye and to say that Mr Faraday was now well enough to resume normal life. Helena was relieved. Soon they would be travelling to Italy and she was determined to shake off the ennui that seemed to be with her so much lately.

However, when James Longford arrived for their lesson and she told him that she regretted their sessions must shortly end, he became, she thought with some mystification, like a coiled spring.

'That was excellent,' he said after she finished playing a sonata. 'As I have said before, Mrs Faraday, you have an exceptional ear. And how I envy you to be able to indulge it in this beautiful music room... I've always longed for a Steinway,' he glanced at the grand piano. 'I make do with an upright one that belonged to my father. Although it does have a mellow tone, and of course I keep it regularly tuned.'

'Did you never wish to play professionally?'

'I had dreams, yes, but I am afraid that in this world one needs patronage to succeed, even to achieve one's potential. You have been kind enough to say when I have played for you that I have talent, a gift even. But I have to eat, so that is why I...'

'Have to teach idle women such as myself.' Helena turned to him only for her sympathetic smile to falter as within seconds he was crouching before her, taking her hands and cradling them in his own. 'Mrs Faraday ... my lovely Helena ... you must know that I'm madly in love with you...'

'Mr Longford!' Appalled, she began to struggle to free her hands. At that same moment, the door opened, and on hearing Helena's horrified gasp the tutor turned to see Oliver's glowering face. Crimson-faced, the tutor scrambled to his feet.

Oliver's voice was like a whip. 'Good morning, Helena. Perhaps you would do me the courtesy of an introduction to this young man.'

She felt sick and struggled to keep her voice even. 'Oliver, this is my music tutor, Mr Longford...'

'And I am Mr Faraday, you impudent fellow. Get out! If you ever set foot on my land again I'll have you horsewhipped.'

With bowed shoulders, the tutor grabbed his music case and, after a despairing glance at Helena, hurried out.

Oliver walked across to examine the chaise longue at one side of the room.

Helena was aghast. 'What you saw was not how it appeared!'

He turned. 'Then pray what was it, Helena?'

She flung out her hands. 'The man just suddenly declared that he was in love with me... I was as shocked and surprised as you.'

'Yet you allowed him to hold your hands, to crouch before you in that ridiculous manner?'

'He gave me no choice!' She backed away as

Oliver came towards her. 'For heaven's sake, you can't think that I gave him any encouragement?'

'Didn't you? You are a beautiful woman, Helena. Did you never think that your familiarity of manner, of which I've had cause to chide you, might give the wrong impression?' He seized her wrist so roughly that Helena flinched. 'You're not a young and silly girl any more, you're my wife, the mistress of Graylings, and I'll thank you to uphold that position. Do you hear me?'

'You're hurting me!'

He let her go. She rubbed at her wrist, about to protest her innocence again, but Oliver was already striding out of the room. Utterly miserable, Helena watched the door close behind him. She slumped back on to the piano stool.

That stupid, stupid man! How could he have put her in such a compromising position! To mistake what she had offered as friendship, a shared enjoyment in music. What had he said, that he was madly in love with her? Hoping for patronage was a more likely scenario and if Oliver had not appeared, Helena would have dismissed the tutor herself.

However, what hurt most was the injustice, her husband's lack of trust. How could he even think that she would betray him at Graylings, while he lay ill in bed? How could he have looked at that chaise longue and imagined…

Helena's eyes began to sting with tears of humiliation and she brushed them away as her anger rose. She deserved an apology and unless it was forthcoming and soon, Oliver would find she had her own way of expressing her displeasure.

Chapter Nineteen

Molly, on her way to dust one of the rarely used bedrooms, found herself almost physically brushed aside. Mr Faraday, his face like thunder, was storming out of the music room. She watched him stride away along the corridor and hesitated. Should she tap on the door to see if Miss Helena was all right? It didn't do to intrude, not between husband and wife; she'd be overstepping the mark. Besides, what if Mr Faraday came back? He struck the fear of God into her, that man.

So she continued on her way to the well-furnished room to begin its routine clean, and looking at its emptiness thought of the cramped cottage where she had grown up. The whole of the downstairs could have fitted into this little used bedroom. It was unfair that many families had to struggle to lead decent lives in such conditions when others were born into great houses like this. Nor did they have the chance of a decent education. Poverty bred more poverty, but then it always had done. She shook out the dustsheets before beginning to polish the dressing table, headboard and footboard, all the time thinking of her own life, her own ambitions. Very few managed to escape the class they were born into, but she still had the hope that she might be different. One day to have a home of her own with a proper water closet – never again did she want to use a smelly outside privy next to a pigsty. Anyway, thinking back to that music room – Miss Helena was more than capable of fighting her own battles.

Oliver was in a quandary. According to the small leather notebook he kept in a bedside drawer, Helena's monthly date had been due during his illness. If she *still* wasn't pregnant, which he suspected, then the chill between them needed to be thawed. As for James Longford, he had already ensured with a veiled hint of unsuitability that man would never again find employment among decent families in Hertfordshire.

And so eventually one evening, Oliver went over to sit beside Helena on an elegant silk-cushioned sofa. 'My dear – please say you will forgive me.'

She turned to him. 'And exactly what do you want me to forgive you for?'

'I can only plead that jealousy unbalanced my reason. I should never have accused you of wrongdoing. I'm sorry.'

'You didn't trust me.' Helena's voice was tight with suppressed anger.

'I promise it will never happen again.' He reached into his pocket and withdrew a tiny leather box. 'I thought – to make amends...'

'I cannot be bought Oliver.'

'Helena, that was not my intention; I was at fault and I admit it. But this atmosphere between us, surely you agree that it cannot continue.'

For a moment she was silent then said, 'I know.'

'I wish you would accept this.' He opened the

lid of the box to reveal an antique cameo ring. 'My father gave it to my mother on their first wedding anniversary. Won't you at least try it on?'

She slipped it on to the third finger of her right hand where it fitted perfectly. It was undeniably beautiful.

'So – please,' Oliver said, 'are we friends again?'

Helena, aware what the question entailed, also knew that she had no alternative. She nodded.

However, when later he went through the connecting door to try again for an heir to Graylings, even he could see that Helena's bare shoulders were rigid beneath their slender pink lace straps. As he extinguished the lamps, Oliver could only remind himself that in less than a week they would be leaving for their honeymoon in Italy – surely even she in such a romantic country would respond to him with a passion that would result in an heir.

At Broadway Manor, the kitchen was a hive of activity, with Cook in her element as she barked orders at her helpers.

'I've never cooked for an MP before,' she said, putting one floury hand up to her damp forehead.

'Yes, and this might well be a significant occasion as he's a senior member of the new Liberal Government. There's been much talk of politics in this house during the past few months.'

She stared at him. 'You're not saying that Mr Standish...'

He shook his head. 'Forget I said anything, I spoke out of turn...'

160

But when he had left, one of the young footmen said, 'Glory, that'd be a turn up for the books, wouldn't it. Which party do you think he'd represent?'

'Don't be daft!' Annie glared at him. 'He'd hardly invite a Liberal if he was a Tory!'

'I didn't know you were interested in politics. Unusual for a girl, isn't it?'

'There's a lot you don't know about me! I believe in women having the vote, for one thing!'

They both glanced round as Enid Hewson came in, carrying some sewing. 'I thought I might come down here for a bit and have a cup of tea with you all.' She settled herself into an armchair.

'I could do with a sit down too,' Mrs Kemp said. 'What news have you got? I know there was a letter from Miss Helena.' Enid sucked on the end of a piece of cotton before threading a needle. 'Apparently they're going to Rome first for their honeymoon, then travelling on to Florence and Venice, so I suppose it'll be several weeks.'

'It must be wonderful,' Annie said, arranging slices of cooking apples in an oval dish, before sprinkling them with lemon juice. 'I'd just love to travel and see other countries.'

The two older women exchanged glances.

'I think you're better off where you're known, love,' Cook said gently.

'Where people are used to me, you mean? I certainly wouldn't want to frighten the natives!'

'Now then...'

A new voice joined in. 'It took me about ten minutes to get used to your scars, Annie, and you've got lovely eyes and hair, and a nice smile. I wish I had.'

'Charlotte, you're…'

'Homely.' The new parlourmaid gave a toothy grin. 'Don't worry, I know. I don't mind, really. I think a nice nature's better than good looks.'

'Well, talking of honeymoons, Ida said they had a lovely time in Colwyn Bay.' Annie went to wash her hands at the sink. 'And it's who you're with that's important. I liked her Charlie much better than Mr Faraday.'

The new parlourmaid was pouring out everyone's tea. 'I think I've got a bit of a tummy upset.'

Mrs Kemp glared at her. 'There's always something wrong with you! If it isn't the miseries it's your health. You'd better take a drop of Indian Brandy because there's no time for you to be ill, not with eight courses to help with.'

The following morning, Jacob Standish went back into the hall of Broadway Manor feeling quietly confident. After dinner the previous evening, the conversation over port and cigars had flowed well and his views on the Irish Question and the recent formation of Sinn Féin had found favour. There had definitely been an inference, even almost a promise of advancement accompanied by a promise of an introduction to Sir Henry Campbell-Bannerman himself.

Seated on the sofa in the morning room, her fingers busy with embroidery, Beatrice looked up at him. 'Can you think how proud Papa would have been – for you to shake the hand of the Prime Minister? We've come a long way, Jacob.'

As she bent her head again to her sewing, Jacob noticed that she looked a little pale. 'Are you feeling well? You haven't got a headache?'

She shook her head. 'I think it's just that I miss Helena. You are often away on business and... I thought, Jacob, that if you have no objection, I would rather like to have a little dog of my own – for company.'

Jacob glanced to where his own two dogs were lying, one on each side of the marble fireplace. 'You don't suppose Caesar and Nero will object?'

'They're getting old; you must have noticed that they sleep most of the time now. And I would have a basket for it in my own rooms.'

'Do you have a preference for any particular breed?'

'I'm not sure, perhaps a West Highland Terrier?'

'I'll make some enquiries for you.' Jacob looked down at his black Labradors. 'Poor old boys, they've been loyal friends.'

'Did you not think it unusual that there wasn't a single dog at Graylings? A great country house like that.'

'Actually I did query it. Like you, I thought it rather odd.'

'And what did Oliver say?' Beatrice put down her embroidery.

'That he didn't care for them, he found their habit of slobbering repulsive.'

'I think Helena's husband has rather distinctive views on many things. She told me, for instance, that he will only employ good-looking servants.'

Taken aback, Jacob stared at her. 'Are you sure?'

'That's what she said.'

He frowned, trying to quell a feeling of unease, then became distracted as Beatrice wondered aloud about the sights Helena would be seeing in Rome. 'Just think, even at this moment she could be standing in the Sistine Chapel. I would so love that glorious Michaelangelo ceiling.'

Jacob felt a stab of guilt, knowing that he had allowed his own life, his business and political ambitions to dominate his thoughts. 'In that case,' he said, 'when Helena returns, you must ask her recommendations and as soon as it is feasible I will take you.'

Chapter Twenty

'Isn't it wonderful? Look, isn't that church the Trinità dei Monti?'

Oliver came out to join Helena on the terrace with its panoramic view and gazed in the same direction. 'Indeed it is. I see you've been doing your homework.'

'I did read up about Rome before we left. There's a wealth of information in the library at Graylings.' Rested after the wearying journey, Helena's face was alight with enthusiasm.

'And you like the hotel?'

'Who could fail to?' Once a noble residence, the Grand Hotel Plaza was one of the most prestigious in Rome. The ancient city was drawing Helena deep into its heart. She even, to Oliver's amusement, tossed a coin into the Trevi Fountain. 'I want to see everything, even the Colosseum. Although I shall never understand how people could have regarded such cruelty as entertainment.'

'But not the Catacombs if you don't mind, Helena. As an atheist I have little interest in a Christian burial site.'

Here in the midst of such piety where priests in their cassocks were a regular sight and the sound of church bells so frequent, she had realised the depth of her husband's antipathy towards religion. Helena sometimes wondered whether he had felt a hypocrite when making his marriage vows at the altar. 'I had thought of suggesting that we attend one of the Masses while we're here. It seems a pity not to.'

'Certainly not, I think we should leave Catholicism to the papists.'

Helena glanced away. Oliver's arrogant habit of dismissing her own wishes increasingly infuriated her. She had wanted to lunch at a small and intimate Trattoria in one of the small squares, finding its red and white checked tablecloths appealing, but he had insisted on returning to their cool hotel.

Before ordering her favourite dessert of zabaglione, Helena allowed the waiter to refill her glass. Her aunt might advise that a young lady should limit herself to one glass of white wine in the evening, but Beatrice had never indulged in lovemaking during a siesta.

Later as she dressed for dinner, she glanced at Jane Forrester's reflection in the mirror. 'You've

165

got a glow to your cheeks. I believe you're just as excited as I am about being in Rome.'

The softly spoken maid expertly pinned up Helena's hair. 'Indeed I am. To be so near to His Blessed Holiness...'

Helena twisted round. 'I didn't realise you were a Roman Catholic. I mean, if you'd been Irish...'

Jane smiled. 'Oh, there are plenty of English people who are Catholic. The whole country was before the Reformation.'

With some embarrassment Helena said, 'Of course, it was a silly remark. And Jane, you must take every opportunity you can to explore.'

'Thank you, Madam, you're very considerate.'

'But I do think that as this is a strange city, it might be wise to ask Mr Hines to accompany you.'

Helena saw her maid hesitate. 'I insist Jane. Please tell him that I suggested it then he won't be able to refuse.'

The glorious beauty of Michaelangelo's ceiling in the Sistine Chapel almost moved Helena to tears and she lingered in the incense-laden atmosphere to watch an elderly woman in the eternal black of the widow, her lips moving in reverence as she fingered her rosary beads. Oliver was studying the 13th century gold mosaics and as she joined him, murmured, 'Remembering how you admired that sculpture in Lichfield Cathedral, I'm looking forward to showing you Michaelangelo's Pieta in St Peter's Basilica, but maybe we will do that tomorrow.'

She followed him past the colourful Swiss

Guards and out into St Peter's Square where almost immediately she shielded her eyes against the glare of the sun and exclaimed, 'Oliver, look – isn't that Johnnie Horton over there?'

'Good heavens so it is, and with his mother.' A few seconds later after threading their way through a cluster of Dominican nuns, Oliver tapped his friend on the shoulder.

Johnnie swung round and his face lit up. 'Well I'll be blowed! Mama, you remember attending Oliver's wedding a few months ago?'

Camilla Horton, a tall, aristocratic woman with silvering hair and the affectation of a lorgnette inclined her head beneath her white parasol.

'I'd heard you'd come to Italy for your honeymoon,' Johnnie said, 'but I never imagined…'

'We're at the Grand Hotel Plaza,' Oliver said, 'and you?'

Johnnie told him where they were staying. 'You must both join us for dinner tonight, don't you think so, Mama?'

'Perhaps, John, these two young people would prefer to dine alone.'

'Nonsense, they've been married for six months. They're probably bored with each other by now.'

The evening they spent with the Hortons was not the most convivial one, the conversation being mainly of Rome's historical sites; Mrs Horton told them of her earlier visit to the Pantheon, advising Oliver and Helena to visit the Cimitario Acattolico. 'The graves of Shelley and Keats are in such a tranquil spot. Yet I was saddened to see the house where Keats lived – the Casina Rossa near the Spanish Steps – in such disrepair. There is a move afoot to turn it into a hotel of all things!' She appealed to Oliver, 'The American poet Robert Underwood Johnson is trying to raise money to save it.' However Oliver's expression remained bland.

Helena was enjoying her ricotta cake. 'This is one of the most delicious things I've ever eaten. Your hotel has an excellent chef.'

'Naturally, I'm always very careful where I stay.'

And her subtle coolness towards Helena continued.

'She obviously thinks you married beneath you, because Papa is in trade,' she said to Oliver later when they were back at their apartment in the Grand Plaza.

Oliver was scornful. 'She's an anachronism. I despise the woman.'

'Why didn't her husband accompany them?'

'He suffers badly from gout.' Oliver hesitated. 'I thought you might be a little tired after our long day.'

'I am a little.'

'That's why I arranged to meet Johnnie for a drink. I think he needs bolstering.'

'Having just spent an evening with Mrs Horton, I can understand why.'

The two men met in a bar in the Piazzo Venezia. 'Did you know,' Oliver said reflectively, 'that they call this area "the heart of the city".'

Johnnie said, 'To be honest I've had enough of hearing about foreign culture. At least this time next week. I shall be back in London. I mean, how would *you* like to spend three weeks with Mama?'

Oliver's reply was diplomatic. 'Well, you will have done your duty.'

'I didn't have much choice. Don't laugh, but the person I'm really missing is Cora.'

'Not that girl at Belle's you're always talking about? She's just a whore for heaven's sake.'

'She's more than that, Oliver; to me anyway.'

'Then why share her? Why not set her up?'

'I've thought of it.' Johnnie looked morose. 'But I'm scared of it getting out and the scandal reaching my parents. The Pater's already decided it's time I got married.'

'It won't get out if you handle it properly. I happen to know of a lease in St John's Wood that is vacant.' Oliver held up a hand. 'No questions! Suffice it to say, that I can put you in touch with someone who will arrange the whole thing – for a fee, of course. But he's totally trustworthy.'

Johnnie stared at him. 'My word, you're a dark horse and no mistake.'

'You're interested, then?'

'You can bet on it.'

Oliver lit a cigarette. 'But if you decide to go ahead, I suggest you wait until I return to England and then we can discuss the matter in the seclusion of the club. Johnnie, you must understand that this is strictly between the two of us. I want no mention of it at Graylings, or at Faraday House. Is that agreed?'

Johnnie put a finger to his lips, 'Absolutely, old boy.'

The following morning as they enjoyed a stroll, Helena suddenly raised her parasol, peered further along the pavement and then, moving swiftly in front of Oliver, took his arm and pulled him into the shadow of an awning.

'Whatever is the matter, Helena?'

She put a hand to her forehead. 'I'm sorry, I just feel a little dizzy.' Over his shoulder, she could still see the two figures, the man's arm around the young woman's waist as they strolled along the Via Sacra. Helena let her hand flutter, her body slump slightly. 'It must be the heat, Oliver. Would you mind terribly if we…'

'Of course not, my dear, we shall return the hotel immediately. A cool drink and a rest is what you need.'

Guessing that he would immediately assume – wrongly – the reason why she felt unwell, she felt a fleeting stab of guilt about her deception.

It was a delicate matter, but Helena knew that she had to mention it. That evening she waited until Jane had finished dressing her hair, and then met her gaze in the oval mirror. 'I saw you this morning in the Via Sacra.'

Colour flooded into her maid's face. 'I only took your advice, Madam – you thought it safer for me to be accompanied.'

'Yes and I still do think that. However, I couldn't help noticing that you and Mr Hines were – how shall I put it – rather more than friends?'

Jane said nervously, 'I'm sorry, Madam, I've always liked him, and spending so much time together and in those wonderful places, well…'

'Romance blossomed?' Helena looked at her with sympathy. 'Don't worry, I shall keep your secret. But if Mr Faraday had seen you, it would be a different matter. You will have to be more careful, Jane, especially when we return to Graylings.'

'Oh Madam, thank you, and we will.' Helena watched the straight-backed young woman leave the room. The indoor staff knew that if any of them became involved in a relationship they would lose their jobs. Opinion was widely held that among servants only the threat of dismissal prevented promiscuity. Helena might feel the rule harsh, but she would be helpless to prevent its application.

Then a few days after meeting the Hortons and shortly before they were due to leave Rome, Helena began to suspect that she might be pregnant. Once they reached Florence, she began to grow ever more hopeful. Strangely, the interconnecting door between their bedrooms remained closed and she wondered whether Oliver too suspected. To her relief, her feelings towards him *were* beginning to soften; she did so long to be able to love him as a wife should, and if she really was carrying his child...

Chapter Twenty-one

Oliver drummed the cover of his small leather notebook, intensely aware that he had made no entry for several weeks. *Was* Helena pregnant? He glanced at the inter-connecting door as he had so many times on previous nights. If she was, he must take care not to endanger his possible heir; if not... Eventually as the days in Florence stretched into weeks, impatience and frustration won. Helena, her hair loose against the snowy white pillow, was reading, but laid down her book as Oliver crossed to an ornate gilt chair and drew it up to sit facing her. 'I thought, my sweet, that perhaps we should talk.'

She smiled at him. 'You *have* guessed!'

'I think I have. But I need to hear it from you.'

'Well I can't be sure, Oliver, but yes, I think I am pregnant.' She paused, and he saw a soft glow in her eyes. 'Isn't it wonderful?'

'But when were you going to tell me?'

'I didn't want to raise your hopes in case I was wrong.'

He rose and went over to the bed to kiss her gently on the lips. 'Then I shall continue to respect your privacy.'

Their time in Florence was for Helena idyllic; her spirit gloried in the paintings, the museums and the beauty of the city itself. They would emerge into the warm sunshine from musty old churches and it wasn't until it was nearly time for them to leave that she began to tire easily.

Then once they reached Venice she began to feel queasy, and it was not confined merely to the mornings. When one day she couldn't face Molecche – Oliver had ordered the tiny soft-shell crabs especially as apparently they were at their best in Spring – and they were forced to go back to their hotel, he was adamant. 'We must return home at once. There is no point in staying any longer – even the Gondola affected you.'

'It was the movement in the water. I'm sorry, Oliver, I know I'm being a nuisance.'

'Nonsense, Helena, but we need to consult Dr Haverstock to have your pregnancy confirmed anyway.'

They both turned as a soft knock came at the door with the familiar call, *'Permesso?'*

Oliver glanced at Helena who called back, *'Avanti.'*

She waited until the maid had left after replacing their bathroom towels then said, 'Dr Haverstock?'

'Yes, if you recall, he and his wife were guests at our wedding.'

London, despite it being the beginning of August, was damp with drizzle and it was a relief to be welcomed in Carlton House Terrace by a cheerful fire in the drawing room. The journey had been tiring and when the parlourmaid brought in their refreshment, the dainty egg and cress sandwiches were welcome though Helena was dismayed to find that she had developed an aversion to tea. 'I hope it passes,' she said to Oliver. 'A proper cup of tea was one thing I was really looking forward to.'

'I'm sure Dr Haverstock will reassure you. I shall make an appointment at his consulting rooms in Wimpole Street as soon as possible. Until then, Helena, I think you should rest as much as possible.'

'It's not an illness, Oliver. Lots of women have to look after large families while carrying a child.'

'They, Helena, are not carrying the heir to Graylings.'

Helena began to feel bored with little to occupy her but to play the piano and read. Oliver was out most evenings at his club, and she found the bookshelves in the small library distinctly uninspiring.

'I need some new books,' she told him one morning after breakfast. 'I was reading the other day that Foyle's have opened a new bookshop in Charing Cross Road.'

'I shall take you myself.'

Helena knew that Oliver would be bound to suggest worthy literature and she wanted the freedom and privacy to choose romantic novels and perhaps a few detective stories, not only for her own pleasure but to take with her to Graylings and to lend to Molly. His presence would only be constraining. 'But hadn't you planned to see your lawyer? Honestly, Oliver, I'm quite sure that if I take Jane with me, I shall do perfectly well.'

'And you feel up to it?'

She nodded. 'I seem to feel the nausea only in

the mornings now.'

The following Monday Nicholas arrived at the Wimpole Street practice just as the polished mahogany door to Andrew Haverstock's room opened. 'I shall see you in one month, Lady Maudley, when I hope to see you much improved.' Despite the warm weather, the elderly dowager's shoulders were caped in mink and as she inclined her head, Nicholas wondered where and how women of her class learned to convey so perfectly graciousness and condescension.

'We have a busy week ahead as usual,' Andrew said, and Nicholas followed him into his consulting room to where the Appointments Book lay on the large polished desk.

Nicholas glanced down, leafing through until he reached the page for Wednesday, when his hand stilled. He remained silent for one long moment, then said, 'Mr and Mrs Faraday? Didn't you attend their wedding earlier this year? When you had to postpone Lady Trentley's appointment?'

'I'm impressed you remember. They are at their London House, having recently returned from Italy.'

'Is the London house close?' Nicholas managed to keep his enquiry one of light interest.

'It's in Carlton House Terrace. I had cause to visit there once, when as a child Oliver developed measles.'

Nicholas simply gave a nod and their conversation turned to medical discussion. The morning was a busy one and it was their habit to lunch together, so it was only when his first afternoon appointment was cancelled that Nicholas was able to clear his mind. He left the practice and made his way to Regent's Park, hoping that in the fresh air he would be able to think calmly, logically. On Wednesday he had a full diary, so there could be no question of cancelling his appointments. Already the thought of seeing Helena again was sending adrenalin racing through his veins, even though he knew he was being unrealistic. It was months since that fleeting scene in Cadogan Square, so much had happened in her life. Nicholas was hoping that the magic would have gone for him too, that he would see her as an attractive young woman, nothing more. At least he would then be able to dismiss the whole episode as nothing more than a foolish fantasy. He continued walking along the tree-lined paths and reaching the lake, in an effort to escape his tormented thoughts, paused to watch and then smile at the excitement of a small boy who was trying to launch a red sailing boat. Seeing that he was hovering dangerously near to the water, his uniformed nanny leaned down and crossly pulled at his shoulder. 'Come back Master Peter, you'll be splashing your sailor suit.'

Her concern was not for the child's safety, only to keep his clothes pristine, and Nicholas disliked hearing a grown woman address a child in such a subservient way, thinking that it was hardly surprising that the aristocracy and upper classes grew up with an innate sense of superiority. The brief episode lingered in his mind, an un-comfortable reminder that Helena was a member of that privileged section of society.

As he continued on his way and eventually left the park, he knew he must face the fact that he was fooling himself. Already his every sense was impatient for Wednesday to arrive. Should he try to remain out of sight, ignore her presence? Would he be able to? The layout of his consulting room was such that his desk was not in view when the door was open, and so Nicholas had no fears that he and Helena might inadvertently catch a glimpse of each other. His hearing was acute, he could always hear Andrew's door open and the muffled sound of farewells, and so it would be easy to manoeuvre a meeting.

The thoughts continued to plague him until he felt the threat of a headache; *that* he could easily remedy, but so far no-one had invented a panacea for a lack of common sense, not when the heart was involved.

Chapter Twenty-two

On Wednesday morning Oliver escorted Helena to the practice in Wimpole Street, where they arrived exactly five minutes before the appointed time. The receptionist smiled up at them. 'Good morning – Mr and Mrs Faraday?'

'That is correct.'

'Please may I take your full details?'

'Dr Haverstock knows me perfectly well.'

'Yes, Sir. But I always check a patient's details –

just to ensure accuracy.'

'All you need to write down, young lady, is that I am Mr Oliver Faraday of Graylings in Hertfordshire.'

'And is it yourself or your wife who is the patient?'

Oliver gave a sigh of exasperation. 'Mrs Helena Faraday.'

'Thank you, Sir. I shall notify Dr Haverstock of your presence.'

Helena led the way over to a horsehair sofa, wishing that Oliver wouldn't be so arrogant in his manner. The young woman had only been doing her job. She glanced over to the gleaming coffee table where beside a vase of pink carnations were copies of magazines such as Tatler, Country Life and The Lady. There were two doors, both with a nameplate. One bore Dr Haverstock's name and the other Dr N E Carstairs. 'There is another doctor here too,' she said in a low voice.

'So it would seem. Perhaps Dr Haverstock has taken on a partner.' Oliver began to leaf through Country Life. 'I see there is a new crop of debutantes.'

'Yes, perhaps Johnnie will make an offer this year and be accepted. Can you imagine anything worse than having Mrs Horton as a mother-in-law?'

Oliver frowned. 'No names in public, Helena.'

It was a rebuff she considered unnecessary in view of her voice being almost a whisper, and she was about to retort when the receptionist rose from her desk to usher them in. Oliver had reminded Helena that she had met the doctor at their wedding breakfast, but it was only when she heard his soft Scots burr that she remembered him. He came forward, hand outstretched. 'My dear Oliver and Mrs Faraday – how are you both?'

'Excellent, and I trust you and your family are in good health?'

'We are very well, and my wife and daughter still talk of your wedding and your lovely bride.' He smiled at Helena and said, 'I believe you wish to consult me.'

She smiled back. 'Yes, please.'

He turned to Oliver. 'Then if you would indulge me and leave your wife in my capable hands...' He gave a frown at Oliver's outraged expression. 'I'm sorry, but I'm afraid it's not usual to have someone else present during a consultation, except in the case of children, of course.' He walked over to the door and opened it. 'If you wouldn't mind?'

Oliver left with ill grace. After Helena had taken a seat before him, Dr Haverstock said with a smile, 'Perhaps you would let me know the problem.'

After her explanation, he took her medical history and then asked her to go behind a screen and undress. 'Just the top layer, Mrs Faraday there is no need to be concerned; I shall merely make a short preliminary examination.'

Helena found his brisk yet friendly manner inspired confidence and once she had retaken her place before his desk and they had talked a little, he summoned the receptionist to ask Oliver to rejoin them.

Dr Haverstock rose and held out his hand.

'May I congratulate you? I can confirm that your wife is not only pregnant but in the best of health.'

Oliver shook his hand. 'Thank you. And the expected date?'

'I would expect it to be towards the end of March.'

'And I assume you will attend the confinement?'

'I would be delighted. But as babies are not always punctual I would recommend that you also enlist the services of a local doctor and midwife, just in case.'

'You haven't mentioned a gynaecologist.'

'That is rare unless there are anticipated complications. But if appropriate, I assure you I will make the necessary arrangements.'

'And are there any precautions my wife should take? I presume, for instance, that she should cease riding. I am also concerned about her nausea.'

Helena felt a flash of irritation. Did he think her a child, incapable of asking these questions herself? 'Dr Haverstock has already discussed these matters with me, Oliver.'

'I'm sure your wife will take the greatest care. Now I shall need to see Mrs Faraday in another three months, just to check that all is progressing normally.'

'I had thought at least every four weeks,' Oliver protested.

'Your wife would do better at home, rather than undergoing the constant travelling. You must trust my judgment in this.' He softened his words

180

with a smile. 'But before you go, I think it would be wise for you to meet my colleague, Dr Carstairs. I'm sure the situation won't arise, but if for some reason...' He pressed a bell at the side of his desk. 'I'll just ask Miss Barnes whether he has a patient with him.'

Nicholas was endeavouring to write up medical notes. The fact that the door to Andrew's room had already opened twice was of no concern to him – he could guess the reason. He had still not decided whether to remain in his own.

'Dr Carstairs?' Miss Barnes smiled at him. 'Dr Haverstock wondered if you could please join him for a few minutes.'

Never for one moment had Nicholas imagined this would happen. He managed to say, 'I'll be there directly.' Then he sank back against the leather upholstery.

So it had come – within seconds he would see her again. Moments later, struggling to maintain a professional demeanour, he turned the gleaming brass knob into Andrew's consulting room.

Her broad-brimmed hat was cream, adorned with apricot tulle roses and he saw beneath it her lovely hazel eyes widen in shock.

Helena knew him immediately. The same sensitive face that had so haunted her, the warm brown eyes that once again met her own with that extraordinary sense of connection. Bewildered, she watched him being introduced to Oliver, while her pulse raced madly with the effort to regain her composure. Then he was turning to her, his hand outstretched. Their fingers touched; his were firm, hers were trembling, while his

181

gentle smile was for her alone.

'Dr Carstairs, I'm delighted to meet you again. If you recall we met briefly once before, in Cadogan Square.' The practiced civility sprang to her lips even while her every emotion was in chaos.

Nicholas collected his thoughts. 'Yes, of course – a matter of an ill-treated horse, as I remember.'

Then as the three men exchanged pleasantries, Helena heard Dr Haverstock use his colleague's first name and at last, she knew her mystery doctor's full identity. His voice too, low and musical, and she tried to store every cadence in her memory.

But to her panic, all too soon Oliver was saying, 'Helena, I think we may now take our leave,' and she was forced to follow him to the door, struggling not to look back at Nicholas, but it was impossible. With her head high, her body tense, she flashed one last look at him. His face was inscrutable but his eyes... She dragged her gaze away. 'Thank you again, Dr Haverstock,' she said. 'Goodbye, Dr Carstairs.'

Outside in Wimpole Street, the Faraday coach was waiting for them and once they were comfortably seated Oliver said, 'Within ten years or so, I daresay a private coach will be a rarity in the capital, or indeed in the country.'

Helena merely said in a low voice, 'Would you mind having luncheon alone, Oliver? I'm feeling rather tired.'

Chapter Twenty-three

'What a charming and attractive young lady she is,' Andrew said. He went over to his desk and, opening the top drawer, withdrew his pipe and pouch of St Bruno Flake. 'As for Oliver, the Faraday estate is entailed so he will be hoping for an heir.'

'One of the reasons he married I expect, isn't that the point of the whole debutante scene?'

'Do I detect a slight note of cynicism?' Andrew gave a chuckle. 'But of course you're right. However, this particular union would seem to be a love match, at least according to Mrs Haverstock. Have you noticed how women get fanciful at weddings?'

Nicholas managed to smile. 'My mother always gets tearful. Now if we are to lunch together, then I should go and complete the notes on my last patient. Not that I could help him very much, apart from prescribing opiates.'

'They will give him some comfort.' As Andrew began to fill his pipe at last Nicholas felt free to return to his consulting room.

He leaned back in his chair and closed his eyes. He had seen her again – and now he knew. As soon as he opened the door and met her startled eyes, he had known. She *had* felt that sense of recognition all those months ago in Cadogan Square. She had not forgotten him. Her voice

183

was as light and sweet as he remembered it, and her perfume delicate and flowery like that ridiculous hat. He smiled; he would never see cream roses again without that lovely image. When she had turned before leaving, had she understood his silent message? Nicholas opened his eyes to stare blankly ahead as frustration and anger swept through him. Frustration that he could never love her in the way he longed to and anger with himself for not accepting the futility of it all.

The following week at Broadway Manor, the maids had opened all the windows to allow the cooling air in. It was, as Beatrice was saying to Jacob, going to be yet another hot day. They both turned as the door to the morning room opened and Bostock brought in a silver salver containing the early post.

Jacob smiled as he saw a large envelope bearing Helena's handwriting, and taking an ivory paper-knife from a small sofa table, he slit it open. 'How very odd, there is a letter here for you too. I can hardly think she needs to economise on postage.'

Beatrice took it from him and held out her hand for the paper knife. Moments later, they were both smiling at each other with Beatrice clasping her hands together with delight. 'She wanted us to read her news at the same time, how clever of her.'

'So I'm to be a grandfather.' Jacob's face creased in a proud smile.

'And me a great-aunt. Isn't it wonderful? A baby in the family. I am so thrilled, Jacob, and so must she be. She says she is well but my note is quite short, is there anything further in yours?'

He frowned. 'Just that Oliver wishes us to be discreet. He can see no point in Helena's condition being general knowledge, not until she's at least six months.'

'That's not too unusual you know. After all, it is a matter for discretion in the early days.'

'I suppose you're right. So we must be careful not to discuss it before the servants. Didn't you say that letters were sometimes sent to Molly?'

'I believe so.'

'Although how Oliver expects to keep his own staff in ignorance I don't know. If Helena was living here it would be impossible.'

'Yes, Jacob, but I feel that our house, possibly because it is smaller, is much more of a family home, and our servants are part of that family. Whereas Graylings is so vast and grand...'

'Impersonal, you mean. I do wonder sometimes whether Helena will ever be truly happy there.'

Beatrice's tone was one of reassurance. 'A child will make all the difference, you'll see.'

At Graylings Helena was unable to put the meeting at Wimpole Street out of her mind. She tried to convince herself that it was pointless to dream of 'what might have been'. Yet the expression in his eyes when his gaze met hers, the feel of his touch on her skin, the secret and silent message between them, how could she not think of it? How often did she wonder whether if they had met sooner and in different circumstances, their lives would now be entwined?

She was strolling in the extensive walled kitchen

garden, where against the warm red bricks one of the gardeners was tending fan-trained fruit. He doffed his cap as she approached and, leaning up, picked a ripe peach and presented it to her. She searched for his name and with relief found it. 'Thank you, Alf.' As she continued on her way, Helena rubbed the peach gently against her sleeve then bit thoughtfully into its downy skin and soft juicy flesh.

Was Nicholas feeling as bewildered as she was? That one glimpse, one exchanged glance, and now a few moments spent in the same room, could have such a devastating effect? Was he too trying and failing to make sense of it all? Was he married? Did he have children?

And in the late evenings when Oliver often retired to the library, Helena would feel so restless that she would meander around the drawing room, gazing out at the beautiful rose gardens and silvery lake in the distance. She was able to console herself that at least having received warm and congratulatory letters from Broadway Manor, she now felt free to confide her news in confidence to Dorothy. And this was the perfect time to invite her to Graylings. Her company would be the perfect diversion.

'I had thought, Oliver,' she said, 'that during her visit we might host a few intimate suppers after which I could give a short recital. The music room is too beautiful not to share with others. I especially love those French gilt chairs. Do you know who acquired them?'

'My father did.'

'You so rarely talk about him. I don't feel as if I know him at all.' She glanced up at the ornate framed portrait of a stiff-collared fair-haired man who bore a strong resemblance to his son.

'Then your feelings are the same as my own.' Oliver's voice was tight. 'I'm afraid he had little time for me, even as a child.'

Helena stared at him in growing dismay. 'But that's awful. You were his only son and heir...'

Oliver gave a shrug of his shoulders. 'I never understood it either. I can only think that he held me responsible for my mother's death.'

'And there was no relative, no aunt? I can't imagine what my childhood would have been like without Aunt Beatrice.'

'No, no-one. I wasn't neglected in any other way.' Oliver's normally confident tone became defensive. 'There was a nanny and later a governess. Of course I was away at school much of the time. One learns to be self-sufficient.'

Helena was thinking of a lonely little boy in this great house, starved of affection. This could be the reason for what she sensed was his lack of interest in others, his underlying coldness. What had Dorothy called him, an enigma?

'Shall we decide who to invite to entertain your friend?' Oliver asked. 'For instance, I'm sure Johnnie would welcome the chance of a weekend at Graylings.'

Helena laughed. 'I hope you aren't matchmaking. I know you said he was looking for a wife, but I can hardly imagine a more ill-matched pair!'

Oliver went on to suggest other guests and as

187

soon as the list was complete, rose to return to his study.

Helena watched him leave and thought again how unlike Nicholas he was. They were both tall, but Oliver was broader in the shoulders and there was always that air of arrogance.

But even if she *had* met Nicholas first, she doubted whether her father would have approved of him as a suitor. Helena had always known of Jacob's ambition for her to marry well, of his political ambitions, and her marriage had brought with it an entrée into the influential circles he needed. Only yesterday, he had written that he had been adopted as the Liberal Candidate in a forthcoming by-election. Glancing around the drawing room at the plum silk damask wall covering, the Georgian satinwood tables and Chippendale armchairs, Helena thought how comfortable life was for those who inherited wealth. Yet how would they fare if, like Nicholas, they had to depend on their skill for their livelihood?

Then going to sit at her escritoire and taking an embossed, cream sheet of vellum, she began to write to Dorothy. She would be pleased to hear that her often-expressed views on politics were beginning to bear fruit. Helena had spent many hours curled up in an armchair in the drawing room at Broadway Manor listening to her friend, and lately much of that conversation seemed to be occupying her mind.

Chapter Twenty-four

In London during the following week, the temperature rose to an unbearable level but Belle refused to let the girls open the windows during working hours. Cora felt the heat extremely trying and with exasperation, she flung aside the thin cotton sheet.

'Hang on,' Johnnie swiftly covered himself. 'Spare a fellow's blushes.'

'It's a bit late for that.' Cora turned on her side and studied him. 'Did you really mean it, what you said a couple of weeks ago?'

'You mean about setting you up? Of course I did.'

'I'd need to know all the details, Johnnie. Financial I mean – I've got ter think of me future.'

He leaned over and ran his forefinger over her hip. 'But you like me enough? We get on well, don't we, Cora?'

She smiled at him. 'Yes, I like you more than enough, Johnnie.' She kept her tone easy and intimate but beneath her outward calm, Cora's brain was feverish. Fond as she was of him, she would match her wits against his any day, and if she couldn't turn his offer to her best advantage then her name wasn't Cora Bates. 'So how would it work – this arrangement?'

'Well, you'd live there all the time, of course, but no other men! I mean if I'm keeping you, then...'

She nudged him in the ribs. 'Don't be daft. Even a dog doesn't crap on its own doorstep.'

Johnnie hooted. 'Now that's what I call a ladylike expression.'

'Well, if you'd wanted a lady, you've come to the wrong place.'

He leaned over and kissed her plump breast. 'I want a real woman, someone to have some fun with, not some prim and proper miss.'

Until you need a wife, Cora thought. But it was without bitterness; she had long accepted her place in the social order – not exactly at the bottom, but there were a hell of a lot of rungs above her. 'So you'd pay the rent, then? And me food and everything?'

'I'd provide all that. I don't know how much you earn here?'

With some trepidation, Cora doubled the sum.

Johnnie didn't even flinch. Instead, he lay back and linked his hands behind his head, 'How about if I add another couple of guineas?'

She stared at him in growing exhilaration. Could she extract anything further? She trailed her fingers through his chest hair. 'I'd 'ave to keep the place clean and such.'

'If you mean will I employ a maid, then the answer's no, Cora. It's too risky. And you're not to tell *anyone*, either about me, or where you'll be living. I can't afford even a whiff of scandal.'

She was quick to reassure him. 'I'll be quiet as the grave, honest. But I'll 'ave to see me friends, Johnnie. I'm not the sort to be a hermit!'

He laughed. 'I'm not keeping you a prisoner, you daft thing. But meet them away from the area and don't tell them where you live. I'm sure they'll understand.' He nuzzled his head into her neck. 'So what do you think? Shall I sign the lease?'

Cora glanced around the sparse room, and didn't hesitate.

'Yes please, Johnnie. I'll just 'ave to give Belle time to get another girl in.'

'That's what I like about you, Cora. You're pure gold, through and through.'

She smiled up at him and felt a surge of affection. 'In that case you won't mind spending a bit more to stay longer?' Cora drew him down to her and her expert hand found its target. 'Every bargain deserves sealing with something special.'

Sybil's expression was one of dismay, swiftly followed by envy. 'Well I can't say I won't miss you, but you make the most of it. Cora. What's he like this, Johnnie? I know he's quite young and not bad looking either cos I caught a glimpse of 'im once when he was waiting downstairs.' She frowned. 'Mind you, I'd bet a pound to a penny that's not his real name.'

Cora glanced down at her hands, which were smothered in the cold cream she'd bought off the market. It smelt funny and what with the misspelt cheap label, she suspected it had been made in someone's scullery. Then she thought of the handkerchief behind the brick with the initials J.F.H. Would Johnnie be stupid enough to use his real name when visiting the brothel? Cora wasn't sure.

'Probably not,' she said, 'but I don't give a toss

whether it is or not. I like him, he makes me laugh. And he's a decent bloke, he'll look after me.'

'Then I wish you good luck. And where is it – the apartment I mean?'

Cora had been taken aback for a moment when Johnnie had mentioned St John's Wood. She knew that was where Sybil had lived before her chap dumped her. But there was little chance of it being in the same building or even the same street – that would be too much of a coincidence.

'I can't breathe a word, that's one of his rules.'

'But if I want to see you…?'

'We'll 'ave to meet at a cafe or something.'

'What, by the market?'

Cora nodded. 'I'm sure we'll sort something out. But how does it work, Syb? I mean, how do you know when he's coming?'

'You don't. But it's nearly always in the evening, so you just 'ave to stay in at nights. It's not so bad, a bit lonely sometimes but at least you'll be warm and well fed.'

'So I'll 'ave a bit of time on me hands,' Cora said. 'I used to fancy learning to draw, yer know – flowers and things.'

'Ask this Johnnie to get the stuff you need, you know pencils, paper and such like. It's best to make the most of the early days, Cora, while he's keen. Believe me, nothing good lasts in this life.'

And for Cora, the dark-haired girl with her miserable eyes was a constant reminder of the fact.

Molly had already begun to suspect Helena's condition. The old saying was that in the early stages of pregnancy a woman had a 'pinched look'. And without doubt Miss Helena, since she returned from her honeymoon, had definitely been looking a bit peaky. I bet Miss Forrester knows, Molly thought; no mistress could hide such a thing from her personal maid. Still she supposed that the master, with his phobia about privacy, would want it kept secret for as long as possible. All this secrecy, Molly thought. I don't know whether he realises it, but servants are human beings too. Although the butler kept a strict rule in the Servants' Hall, there was always some whispering in corners.

At least Molly had her refuge, her solitary bedroom. She had persuaded the housekeeper to let her have a discarded silk bedspread for the flock mattress; it might be a bit faded but its ruby colour gave a feeling of warmth and cosiness. She shuddered at the thought that she might have had to share with spiteful Susan, who was a born troublemaker.

Late that same evening, Helena, knowing that Oliver was unlikely to come through the inter-connecting door, was absorbed in her current novel, one that described a deep and abiding love against a background of abject poverty. The details of cruelty and deprivation were shocking and the story so gripping that it was with some reluctance that she extinguished her bedside light.

Her thoughts drifted to Dorothy who was due to arrive the following day. She was so looking forward to seeing her. Helena might be the mistress of Graylings, but it was a lonely role with only the servants for company. With Jane, a certain relaxation of authority was possible, but there was still a distance, an unspoken barrier between them. Molly was the only one with whom Helena could laugh and joke without restraint, but their time together was of necessity spasmodic, and even then limited. However, even though Dorothy was her closest friend, Helena was still unsure whether to confide in her about Nicholas. If she was mystified herself about her feelings, how could she possibly explain them to someone else?

Chapter Twenty-five

Dorothy pronounced herself delighted that their first week together was spent almost exclusively alone.

'It won't last,' Helena warned her. 'Once Oliver returns from London, you will not only be introduced to worthy neighbours, but be forced to listen to me at the piano. Of course if you wish to sing to entertain our guests...' She laughed at her friend's look of horror. 'Then of course there will be a weekend house party just before you leave.'

'You feel well enough for all that excitement?'

'Don't you start – I get more than enough fussing from Oliver. Honestly, you'd think I was carrying the heir to the throne!'

'At least you've proved yourself. Papa's always trying to stop me studying; he believes too much thinking uses up a woman's limited physical resources and makes her womb wither.'

Helena broke into a peal of laughter. 'You're not serious?'

'He won't even consider my undertaking a university education, although I know I could get a place at Girton College. But even if I did go to Cambridge, I would have to ask permission to attend lectures and wouldn't be able to take a degree.'

Helena stared at her in disbelief. 'Why on earth not?'

'Because I'm a woman – honestly, anyone would think it was a sin! In my opinion it's just another way of keeping our sex in servitude. Oh you and I may have silk dresses and live in fine houses, Helena, but we're equally at the mercy of men as the poorest drudge in the land, just more comfortable that's all.'

They were relaxing in the rose garden, and feeling the sun move across the sky, Helena adjusted the angle of her parasol. She glanced sideways at the tall young woman next to her, at her serious face, her dark hair drawn back almost severely into a chignon. Dorothy despised frills and laces, and her white blouse was plain, the high collar devoid of even a subdued brooch.

'Do you not think of marrying at all?'

'Not unless it was to someone who treated me as an equal, although Papa is beginning to pressure me rather.' She turned to Helena. 'Tell me the truth, do *you* find that your own wishes are subservient to those of your husband?'

Helena hesitated. 'I can't deny it, but then my

father's wishes were always paramount too. Aren't we all conditioned from birth to accept it?'

'And in whose interests is it? Helena, I rest my case.'

Helena laughed. 'Dorothy, I don't think you have any idea how much I've missed you.'

'Oh, I don't know.' She glanced in the direction of Helena's stomach. 'I think you've been pretty busy!'

'Dorothy!' But Helena was laughing again, a frequent sound during the past few days. 'You know it's getting a bit too hot, I think we should go indoors for a while. Besides, there's something I'd like to show you.' Even she could hear the change in her tone and she sensed rather than saw her friend glance sharply at her.

'I am intrigued.'

'I think you may well be.'

Once they were back in the house, Helena rang for some lemonade and when they were refreshed, she led the way up the broad staircase, turned left into the Long Gallery, through a door at the end, which led into another corridor, and then paused. 'I discovered this only about three weeks ago.' The dark oak door opened with a slight creak and they stepped into a dim and darkened room. 'Please – you wait there.' She went forward to the tall windows and unfastened the shutters.

As light flooded the room, Dorothy drew an intake of breath.

'Heavens, even more portraits. How many ancestors can one man have?' She began to wander along the right wall peering at the faces, then with a thoughtful expression crossed to the other wall. Helena waited.

Eventually Dorothy turned to her. 'I confess to some puzzlement. It doesn't take a genius to realise that all of these have one thing in common. But what I find mystifying, is why they are shut away here and not with the others in the Long Gallery. If I recall, there are several spaces.'

Helena's voice was quiet. 'And what exactly do they have in common, Dorothy?'

'It would seem that each has some sort of blemish,' she indicated a portrait of a young woman who bore a strawberry birthmark on one cheek, 'although one would have thought the painter might have disguised such a thing.'

'Perhaps she wished a true image,' Helena said.

'In which case, I am full of admiration for her lack of vanity.'

Dorothy went over to another painting. 'And this man has a pendulous wart at the side of his eye ... and the others – I don't wish to be unkind, but they are prodigiously ugly.'

'Tell me, have you noticed anything out of the ordinary about the staff here?'

Dorothy turned to her, her brow wrinkling. 'Do you mean that there's not an elderly face, or even a homely one? I did wonder about that.'

'That's right. And these...' Helena waved a hand at the portraits, 'are in my opinion hidden away so that Oliver doesn't have to look at them.'

Dorothy stared at her. 'That seems rather odd. Have you never questioned him?'

Helena shook her head. 'I haven't mentioned that I've seen them. I did query once about the staff and his explanation was that he preferred to be surrounded by pleasant countenances, so I suppose that's the reason.' She paused, and then related Oliver's reaction to Annie's scarring. Sometimes Helena wondered whether her husband's reticence about seeing his own wife's body was because he feared a physical flaw. But of course she could not mention something so private, even to such a close friend.

'Sounds like a fetish to me,' Dorothy said. 'Men do have some strange ones, you know. Papa has never read any of the volumes in the library at home so he has no idea what depravity is described in some of them. However, as Francis Bacon said, "Knowledge is power."' Her lips twitched. 'Besides, it certainly livens up a rainy afternoon.'

Helena spluttered. 'You're impossible!' She went to close the shutters. 'I'll show you the Chinese room on the way back. There are some lovely hand-painted silk panels, they're extraordinary.'

'From what I am learning about Oliver,' Dorothy said, 'I think he is too. What will he do when you lose your looks – banish you to a locked room and find his own Jane Eyre?'

Again, Helena laughed, but Dorothy did not. 'Seriously, Helena, this is all a little disturbing. You are happy with him?'

'I'm his wife. Isn't it my duty to be happy?'

Helena's piano recitals received lavish compliments and on the Saturday evening of the weekend house party, once again Oliver congratulated her. 'An excellent choice of programme, my sweet.

I always think that Mozart appeals to most tastes.'

He now seemed completely at ease in the music room and Helena hoped that the unpleasant incident with James Longford was firmly behind them. 'I see that neither Dorothy nor Johnnie seek each other's company.' She glanced over to where they were seated, several chairs apart. 'And I can't see him taking an interest in either of the Redfern girls either.'

Oliver had his own views on the reason, concerns too. From what Johnnie had told him the previous evening, this girl Cora was an avaricious bitch. Oliver had refrained from pointing out that Johnnie had been a fool to agree to her financial terms, which were outrageous, far more generous than his own had been with Sybil. The man was so besotted there would have been no point in antagonising him.

Helena invited their guests to return to the drawing room where four of the men began to play bridge. Aunt Beatrice sat near to Mrs Shirley, a sweet-faced widow, while Jacob stood conversing with the guest Oliver had invited especially for him to meet, Peregrine Hurst, the new Liberal MP and the youngest member of the House of Commons. He had arrived just before dinner.

Helena strolled over to where Dorothy was lingering in front of one of the watercolours. 'I must say, our late guest is rather good looking.'

Dorothy smiled. 'I suppose you could say that.'

'And you can't say this one hasn't got a brain, otherwise he wouldn't be in the Government.'

Dorothy's peal of laughter turned several heads.

'Helena, there are more dunderheads in that place than there are in Bedlam, surely you realise that!' She glanced across to where the tall, dark haired man was talking earnestly to Helena's father. 'But I must admit he seemed reasonably intelligent over dinner.'

'Then I shall make sure you two are brought together, after all one never knows ... but remember Oliver's rules?' Helena had not been surprised to discover that her husband was scornful of the idea of women having the vote. He had also stressed that Dorothy should not use Graylings as a platform for her political views.

Dorothy sighed. 'I know. But surely they don't apply to a private conversation between two people.'

Helena shook her head. 'I don't see how even Oliver could control that.'

Several minutes later, she had gently persuaded Aunt Beatrice that she needed to circulate, and with raised eyebrows hinted to Jacob to entertain Mrs Shirley. Dorothy, with a grateful smile to her friend, strolled casually over to talk to a rather amused young man, and Helena heard her say, 'I see you saw through that strategy.'

Oliver and Johnnie had eventually gone to stand by the tall windows, which despite the late hour were open. 'Jolly hot this summer,' Johnnie complained. 'It saps a fellow's strength, if you know what I mean?'

I wish I had the chance to find out, Oliver thought with irritation. He lit a cigarette.

Helena came over to join them. 'I love the night air, don't you?'

Johnnie grinned at her. 'I don't suppose there are more gems like you in Staffordshire?'

'I'm sure there must be. Shall I ask Aunt Beatrice to begin matchmaking for you?' Seeing his look of horror, Helena began to laugh. 'I'm only joking, you idiot.' She turned to Oliver. 'I came to tell you that the Spencers are about to take their leave.'

'In that case, we had better go and wish them God speed.'

Helena stared at him, feeling that it was an odd expression for an atheist to use, but then Oliver never failed to astound her.

Dorothy was the last guest to leave on Sunday, and made Helena promise to let her know if she heard any news of Peregrine Hurst. 'Honestly, Helena, whatever could have been so urgent that he had to leave before breakfast?'

'I've told you, that was always his intention.'

'Just when I actually find someone with a measure of influence who believes in our cause, he disappears. Of course I could always write to him.'

Helena frowned. 'I'm not sure. I think to follow up your meeting him at Graylings with political pressure might be...'

'Yes, I suppose you're right, it could be interpreted as taking advantage of Oliver's hospitality. What a nuisance.'

'But if we could find some way of your meeting again... I mean from where I was standing, didn't I detect a sort of frisson between you two?'

'Helena, will you ever stop being such a romantic?' She laughed as she saw her friend's colour rise. Dorothy's tone became brisk. 'Now I don't suppose there's much point in asking you to write letters for the WSPU during your enforced waiting period? We need all the helpers we can get.'

Helena gave a shrug. 'The spirit is willing, there's just one problem.'

'Don't tell me, I can guess. Oliver?'

She nodded. 'He would only say that I was tiring myself.'

Dorothy gave a sigh of exasperation. 'You should stand up to him more. Don't fall into the trap of losing your identity, Helena, as seems to happen to so many women when they marry.'

Helena smiled. 'Don't worry, I don't let him have all his own way.'

Dorothy gazed at her, 'I'm giving you what my mother calls an "old-fashioned look".'

Helena laughed. 'And I'm not saying another word!'

However, while she was sorry to see Dorothy go, she was even more reluctant to say goodbye to her father and Aunt Beatrice. 'Good luck in the by-election, Papa.'

He nodded. 'As it's considered a safe seat I have an excellent chance. I hope so, how else can I introduce some common sense into politics? One of the problems in this country is that far too many people in government come from the ruling class. They have little if any experience of industry, nor of earning a living. I am hoping to make a difference, Helena.'

'I'm sure you will, and I shall be so proud of you.'

'Make sure you take care of yourself, Helena,' Beatrice said, 'and I shall come again soon.'

Helena stood outside Graylings and after watching the chauffeur-driven motor vehicle drive along the tree-lined avenue until it disappeared, went slowly back into the large hall, whereupon a footman closed the heavy door behind her.

Chapter Twenty-six

Several weeks later, as she was in the drawing room awaiting Oliver's return from London, Helena read again a letter that had arrived that morning. Dorothy had written,

I have received an invitation from Peregrine Hurst to say that he would be pleased to show me around the House of Commons, if I would find it of interest. I am to contact him the next time I am in London. Could I presume, Helena, would you let me know when you next intend to be in town?'

Helena was smiling to herself, thinking how clever that was of Peregrine, when the door opened and Oliver came in. He crossed the room to kiss her cheek. 'I hope I find you well.'

'Perfectly, thank you. Did you see Papa?'

'I did, we spent a pleasant evening together. He is most appreciative of being able to use Faraday House while the House is sitting.'

'Yes, Aunt Beatrice is so proud of him being

elected. I do wish I could have gone with her to the official count.'

'I'm sorry, Helena, but as I explained, these occasions can become agitated and even Jacob agreed that in your condition it was best that you abstained. By the way, I telephoned Dr Haverstock to arrange an appointment for you.'

Helena slowly put down her knitting. 'May I ask when it is for?'

'Towards the end of this month. You will then be six months into your pregnancy, which is the time he stipulated.' Oliver smiled at her. 'It will be good to know that everything is progressing well.'

'The baby is becoming more active every day.' She longed to take his hand and place it so that he could feel the tiny movements, but Helena knew that a man who averted his gaze from his wife's thickening body was hardly likely to welcome such intimate contact. As into her mind rushed the thought, even the hope that she might see Nicholas again, she said, 'While you were away, I received a letter from Aunt Beatrice inviting us to spend Christmas at Broadway Manor, and I would very much like to do so, Oliver. After all, a visit will not be possible during the following months.'

At that moment Oliver's refreshment arrived, and he waited until the door closed behind the parlour maids before saying, 'But the long journey, what if the weather is inclement?'

'I will have plenty of time to rest after our appointment in London, and we could travel in two easy stages. I am sure a comfortable hotel could be found.' Helena lowered her eyes to look down at her delicate knitting. 'I have been feeling a little low in spirits lately. It would be just the tonic I need.'

After a pause he said, 'In that case, my dear, I agree. We shall go to Broadway Manor for three weeks, returning just after the New Year.'

She smiled sweetly at him. 'Thank you. I'm sure we'll have a wonderful time.'

When she was once more alone, Helena thought again of the implications of a further visit to Wimpole Street. She had no fears about her health although it would be reassuring to know that all was well. It was the thought, the hope of seeing Nicholas again... Would he still feel the same, would he find some way of ensuring that they met? Then she glanced down at her now swollen stomach, and feeling guilty for even thinking such a thing, rose to go and write back to Dorothy.

Ever since the names *Mr and Mrs Faraday* had leapt out at him from the Appointments Book, Nicholas had been impatient for this particular Wednesday to arrive. Now, following his greeting to Miss Barnes, he saw with relief that her distinctive black inked script for today's date was untouched. There had been no cancellation.

His spirits rising, he went to his consulting room and after removing his top hat and warm coat went to stand before the window to gaze out at the grey skies. Fog would undoubtedly descend by five o'clock so it was fortuitous that Helena's appointment was a morning one.

He took out his pocket watch and after glancing at it went over to a tall cabinet to retrieve the folder relating to his next patient, an elderly man who had recently suffered a fall. Previously treated at home, it had not been easy to persuade him to come to Wimpole Street, a stage Nicholas considered essential if the man was to regain confidence. The appointment should not take up too much time and fortunately neither would the following one. All I have to do, he thought, is exactly what I planned last time, and I am certain to be able to see her.

In Carlton House Terrace the heavy brocade curtains were closed when Helena awoke. She treasured the moments of restful dimness before Jane's arrival, because they gave her time to think of the morning ahead, and of Nicholas. Yet again, she told herself that such an intelligent and attractive man must surely have either a fiancée or wife and family. Even if he had been single when they had met, then in the intervening time he could easily have fallen in love. But her doubts hadn't prevented her from planning to wear one of her favourite long coats in rose pink velvet, with a toning hat, its brim softly feathered. She knew that Aunt Beatrice would have considered it vain to wear such an impractical outfit in winter, but Helena knew that the colour gave her radiance and the style was flattering.

Just then the door opened and her maid came in, balancing the bed tray on one arm while closing the door behind her with the other. 'Good morning, Madam.' After placing the tray on its customary side table, Jane went to open the curtains before bringing it to her mistress. 'I wondered whether to bring you another drink of lemon and honey? I hope it helped last night.'

Helena's throat was a little sore, something she hadn't mentioned to Oliver. She took a sip of her hot chocolate. 'Perhaps I'll have another following my bath.'

An hour and a half later, with one hand resting on the balustrade she went slowly down the crimson-carpeted stairs and into the breakfast room where both Dorothy and Oliver were already at the table.

Oliver glanced up from his toast and marmalade. 'Good morning. How are you?'

'Good morning, Dorothy. I'm absolutely fine Oliver, you have no need to be concerned. I'm sure Dr Haverstock will find nothing amiss.'

'I was referring to the fact that I encountered your maid. She was on her way up to you with a cold remedy.'

'Just some lemon and honey for a slight sore throat.'

'Nevertheless I have telephoned Dr Haverstock and requested that he see you here, rather than you having to make the journey to Wimpole Street.'

Horrified, Helena protested, 'It's nothing, Oliver – hardly a reason to cause inconvenience.'

'It is not only chilly but damp after an early fog. Really, Helena, you should have told me.'

Her disappointment was so bitter it was almost choking her.

'Please,' Oliver waved a hand in the direction of

the sideboard, 'I want you to ensure that you breakfast well – it is always advised to feed a cold...'

'And starve a fever,' her voice was tight with anger. 'Yes, I know.' Going over to the sideboard, she began to lift the silver domed lids of the various dishes, her resentment almost uncontainable. How dare he make such a decision without discussing it with her first? She took a small helping of scrambled eggs and one rasher of bacon. Then realisation came, stark and undeniable. After today, any further medical care would take place at Graylings, at least until after her lying-in-period. What if she never had a reason to visit the practice at Wimpole Street again? That would mean...

'Helena?' She turned to see Oliver staring at her. Dorothy was diplomatically concentrating on her breakfast.

'Sorry, I was just thinking about Dorothy's visit. It's this morning that she's meeting Peregrine at the House.'

Oliver crumpled his napkin and pushed back his chair. 'Of course, do give him my regards, Dorothy.'

After he had left the room, she said, 'I was expecting to be admonished to behave myself. Is he always so forceful?'

'He's just concerned for my well-being, or should I say that of his precious heir.'

'Do I detect a cynical note?'

'Sorry, I didn't mean...'

Dorothy said quietly, 'Helena, are you sure there isn't something you aren't telling me?'

Still fighting her disappointment, she carried her plate to the table. 'No, of course not, it's just that he does fuss so.'

Nicholas was reading a medical journal while waiting for his next patient to arrive, when Andrew gave a brief knock on his door and came in. 'I shall be out for a short while. Oliver Faraday has telephoned to say that his wife has a slight cold, and he thinks it advisable that she consults me at Faraday House.'

Slowly, Nicholas said, 'That seems rather extreme.' He tried to keep the bitterness out of his voice.

Andrew chuckled. 'I think he would wrap her in cotton wool if he could.'

'And I suppose in future you will be attending her at Graylings?'

'I would imagine so, certainly throughout this confinement. Shall we meet for lunch?'

Nicholas nodded and watched the older man leave. Suddenly the day which had held such promise seemed drab, even dreary. And then he remembered that he planned that evening to go and hear Christabel Pankhurst speak. It was a year since that fateful meeting in Manchester when during a Liberal Rally she and Annie Kenney had questioned Winston Churchill and Sir Edward Grey on the subject of 'Votes for Women'. Both were arrested for obstruction and Annie Kenney, charged with assaulting a police officer, had spent three days in prison. He had considered the sentence harsh at the time, and was keen to hear a first-hand report of the event.

Now, he thought grimly, perhaps concentrating on real injustice would distract his mind from the emotional one of his own making.

Chapter Twenty-seven

It was ten days before Christmas and at Broadway Manor, there was a buzz of expectation. In the kitchen Cook finished larding a beef fillet and, going to wash her hands in the deep sink, she called over her shoulder, 'Do you know exactly what time they're expected, Mr Bostock?'

He completed the winding of his pocket watch and then said, 'According to the master they should be here in time for luncheon, that's as accurately as I can tell you.'

'I can't wait to see Miss Helena,' Charlotte said. 'I've heard so much about her.' She glanced round at them all and her face reddened. 'I've been knitting some bootees for her baby.'

'Got on my nerves, she did,' the other new parlourmaid said with a sniff. 'Nothing but click click click, it was, just when I was trying to get off to sleep.'

'Everything gets on your nerves!'

She glared at Annie. 'Well if the cap fits!'

'That's enough! I've got too much to do to be bothered with all this squabbling.' Cook's voice was sharp, her face flushed.

The butler frowned and gave her a light touch on the shoulder. Seeing him make a slight movement with his head, Mrs Kemp followed him into his small office.

'You know,' he said in a low voice, 'I can't help thinking that that girl has been a mistake.'

'We've had nothing but trouble from her, Mr Bostock. If she isn't complaining or moaning, she's stirring up trouble. We never had any of this before she came. If there's one thing I can't stand it's having bad feeling in the Servants' Hall. We used to be such a happy band when Molly and Ida were here.'

'And we will be again, Mrs Kemp, I promise you.'

Later it was Annie who first saw Molly, turning when she heard light footsteps hurrying down the stairs. With a shriek, she rushed forward to give her a hug. Molly hugged her back and then called to the others, 'Surprise everyone!'

'Well I'll be blowed,' Mrs Kemp exclaimed. 'Now you *are* a sight for sore eyes.'

Molly was full of excitement. 'Gosh, it's good to be back.' She glanced round the familiar cosy kitchen, at the long table being set for the servants' lunch, and with some curiosity at the two new parlourmaids. 'I've just seen Mr Bostock. Where's Miss Hewson?'

'She'll be upstairs in Miss Beatrice's room, fussing that little dog, I expect,' Cook said. 'How did this come about then?'

'Miss Forrester slipped and sprained her ankle. I'm to be Miss Helena's personal maid while she's here.' She turned to see a thin elfin face peering round the scullery door. 'You must be Daisy.'

'Yes, Miss.'

'You don't need to call me Miss. I'm Molly, I used to work here.' She swung round as Enid Hewson came to join them.

'You look well – Miss Helena told me you were here. All we need now is Ida, but I don't suppose there's much chance of that happening.'

'How is she?'

'Annie's been to see her, haven't you Annie?'

Lifting her head from where she was pouring boiling water into the large brown teapot, Annie nodded. 'She's got her place ever so nice. Hoping for a baby too, but no sign so far.'

'She's got plenty of time,' Molly said.

Helena too was delighted to be back. Nothing had changed except that Caesar and Nero, who were from the same litter, seemed to have lapsed into old age.

Aunt Beatrice was so absorbed in her little Westie that Helena wondered why she had never before had a pet of her own. 'I've called her Skye,' she said the morning after their arrival. 'It's somewhere I've always wanted to visit, ever since I read about Flora McDonald helping Bonnie Prince Charlie to escape.'

'I'm discovering lots of things about your Aunt,' Jacob told Helena. 'I've even had to promise to take her to Rome next year.'

The three of them were relaxing in the morning room just as they used to, and Helena hadn't felt quite so happy for ages. 'Oh do go,' Helena's face lit up. 'You would love it. And our hotel was wonderful. So was the one where Mrs Horton and

212

Johnnie were staying. I told you we met them?'

'Yes, in one of your letters. You also were less than complimentary – about Mrs Horton, I mean.' Beatrice looked reprovingly at her niece. 'One needs to be careful about such comments.'

Helena laughed. 'Oh, don't you start – it's bad enough with Oliver.'

'What is?' Oliver came in to join them.

'Aunt Beatrice is reminding me to be more discreet.'

Jacob smiled at her. 'Your aunt tends to forget that you are now a married woman, and no longer her responsibility.'

But for Helena the easy familiarity and banter changed somewhat now that Oliver was with them, and as the days drew nearer to Christmas itself, with the glittering huge tree decorating the hall and the rooms festooned with holly boughs bright with red berries, she sensed that he was restless. But Helena was loving it all; the nostalgia of Cook making her favourite puddings, sleeping in the bedroom that had been her childhood refuge, Molly keeping her entertained with kitchen gossip.

'It's just like the old days,' she said on Christmas Eve. 'Do you miss being here, Molly?'

'In some ways, I do.' Molly was struggling with hairpins. 'I don't know, Miss Helena, this just won't go right. I need more practice.'

'Here, let me help.'

Between them, with some laughter, the chignon was eventually achieved, and Molly said, 'Miss Helena, I wondered if you'd mind my having tomorrow afternoon off. I'd be back in time to dress you for dinner.'

'Of course I don't mind, Molly. It's natural you will wish to see your family.'

Yes, Molly thought as she later tidied the bedroom and brushed the grey serge skirt Helena had worn during the day. I wish to go home all right, but not for the reasons most would think. It was because of her three younger sisters. Annie had told her that one of them had been seen with a bruised face. If her dad had been laying in to them, he'd have her to answer to. Her mum was bound to be on the cadge, and Molly was prepared to give her ten bob, although it would be too much to hope that she'd spend it wisely. Perhaps, she thought as she closed the door and went down the back stairs, Cook would give her treats to take. There were bound to plenty of leftovers.

'It's been a wonderful Christmas, Papa, thank you.' Helena went to Jacob and kissed his cheek. 'Oliver and I have so enjoyed it.'

'Splendid. And your spending it with us has been the icing on the cake, hasn't it, Beatrice?' Jacob, standing before the fire in the drawing room was finding the cold weather rather a trial and lifting his coat tails to feel extra warmth.

'It certainly has.' She looked searchingly at her niece. 'I do hope Oliver has felt comfortable here. I have gained an impression otherwise at times.'

'My dear, I hardly think...'

'Jacob, I'm sure that Helena is perfectly aware of what I'm referring to.'

Helena had also been feeling some resentment

214

at what she felt was discourtesy on Oliver's behalf. It wasn't that he was openly discourteous, but sometimes there had been a barely concealed boredom in his manner. 'Yes of course I do. I'm afraid he always finds it difficult to be away from Graylings.'

Later, before leaving, Helena stood before the large casement windows in the drawing room and gazed out. In one way, Broadway Manor felt so much more like her home than Graylings, and yet she knew she had changed from the light-hearted girl who had left just over twelve months ago. Even then, she had indulged in dreams about Nicholas. Yet now she was beginning to feel resigned about what was, after all, merely a futile fantasy.

Helena had read that in the last months of pregnancy a woman became placid, immersed in the changes in her body, and it would seem to be true. She looked at the empty flowerbeds and stark leafless trees and tried to imagine what the view would be like in the spring, when the showy yellow of daffodils clustered around the trunks and groups of scarlet tulips would bring life into the garden. While at Graylings, she would be giving birth to her own tiny miracle. Please God it would be a boy so that she would provide Oliver's desperately needed heir. Helena turned away from the window feeling a little discon-solate. Sometimes she wondered whether that was his main reason for marrying her.

Chapter Twenty-eight

It was at the beginning of March, three weeks before her due date when Helena felt the dull ache in her lower back. At first, she ignored it, enjoying her early morning sedate stroll on the terrace at Graylings – the weather was unusually mild and she paused to watch the swoop of a falcon in the distance. However, within an hour of returning to the morning room, the ache had become intrusive, heavy and dragging. She felt unsure ... could labour pains begin in the back? Helena went over to the silken bell pull at the side of the fireplace.

The door opened within seconds. 'Crossley, do you know where Mr Faraday is?'

'I believe he went out for a ride, Madam.'

'Then please send a groom to find him. And would you kindly ask Mrs Birley and Miss Forrester to attend me immediately.' She went to sit awkwardly on the sofa and looked up to see the butler's normally impassive expression become one of concern. Helena nodded. 'I am not certain, but Crossley, perhaps if my husband has left any instructions concerning my condition...'

He bent his head in acknowledgement and then once the door had closed behind him, Helena leaned back against the downy cushion, trying to remain calm. Preparations had been made for a premature birth – Aunt Beatrice was supposed to

216

be at Graylings already, only a cold had prevented her arrival. But what about Dr Haverstock, what if he had other commitments he couldn't leave at a moment's notice? What if … panic swept through her … surely he wouldn't send Nicholas in his place? Yet hadn't that been the very reason he had been introduced to them, in case such a situation arose? The very thought of the most intimate part of her body being exposed to those brown expressive eyes made colour flood into her face… Not even her husband had ever seen…

'Mrs Faraday, are you all right?' The housekeeper hurried into the room.

'I think…' Helena winced at a sudden gripping pain.

'I see.' Mrs Birley's tone became one of brisk efficiency. 'There is no need to worry. Mr Crossley has already sent one of the grooms to fetch the master, and a telegram will soon be on its way to London. Miss Forrester and I…' she turned, 'Ah, here she is.'

When Oliver eventually arrived, he found Helena lying on a chaise longue in her room while two maids were busy securing a rubber sheet on the bed. He frowned with distaste and waved a dismissive hand at their startled faces. After they had scuttled out, and still in his riding clothes, his face flushed with exertion, he queried, 'Helena?'

'It has all happened so quickly…'

'You have done nothing to precipitate it?'

She shook her head. 'No, I was just walking on the terrace…'

'Everything will soon be in readiness, Sir,' the housekeeper was hovering just inside the door.

'And I believe the local doctor and midwife have been sent for.'

'It's Dr Haverstock we need.'

'Oliver,' Helena said, 'I'm sure nothing will happen just yet, why don't you go and change and then once the maids have completed their task, Forrester will help me to undress.'

He gazed speculatively at her. She was a shade pale perhaps, but... He gave a nod, and as he left, glanced at the tiny clock at the side of Helena's bed, hoping that the London physician would soon be on his way. The local doctor, the bespectacled impertinent young man who had attended him during his influenza, was taking an unforgiveable time to answer the summons. When eventually he did arrive and later emerged from Helena's bedroom, Oliver snapped, 'Well?'

'I can confirm that your wife is in the first stages of labour. However, there is no urgency, a first confinement is often a lengthy process.'

'But she is three weeks early. You do realise that until Dr Haverstock arrives that my wife's health is your responsibility?'

'As I have told you, there is little I can do at the moment and I have other patients to attend to. However, I am leaving Nurse Robertson here, at least for the moment, although I understand Dr Haverstock will be bringing his own midwife. Good day to you, Mr Faraday.' He swiftly descended the stairs to where Crossley was waiting to usher him out.

Oliver watched him leave with a dislike that bordered on contempt. The man was probably a charlatan.

Would Helena expect him to go in and see her? He would prefer not to have to enter that room again until after the birth was over; even seeing the necessary preparations had been a distasteful experience. However, if it helped to encourage her then he would force himself do so; he must do everything he could to safeguard what was, after all, no ordinary birth.

Although Oliver had been to see her, his stay had been brief and uneasy, and so when later a knock came at the bedroom door, it was with relief that Helena welcomed Molly's familiar and smiling face.

'Cook has sent you some chicken soup, Madam,' she said ,carrying in a tray, 'and she says there's something hot for you, Nurse, if you care to go down. I can stay with Mrs Faraday.'

Once Nurse Robertson had gone, leaving instructions to ring if she was needed, Molly was able to relax into her normal friendly manner. 'My sister was three weeks early, Miss Helena. I remember seeing her all wrapped up in a blanket in the drawer. I must have been about seven at the time.'

Helena looked up in surprise. 'Did you say in a drawer?'

Molly nodded. 'We couldn't afford a cradle. Lots of people used to empty a drawer and use it. You'll be all right, Miss Helena. You don't need to worry until the pains come every five minutes. It can take ages to get going so I'm sure the doctor from London will arrive in time.'

'You're a great comfort to me, Molly. Later,

when you go down could you find out whether any message has been sent to Broadway Manor?'

'Of course I will. It's chaos down in the Servants' Hall. The scullery maids are making sure there's plenty of hot water, and as luck would have it, Mrs Birley only yesterday ordered rooms to be made ready for Dr Haverstock and his nurse, so there's only the fires to be lit. And Cook's got her head in her recipe book, cos she says meals may need to be kept hot as nobody knows what time the baby will be born.'

Helena began to laugh. 'You do cheer me up. But oh dear, I do seem to have caused a great deal of inconvenience.' She pushed away the omelette as she felt another contraction begin.

'It'll all be worth it, Miss Helena. You'll see.'

When Nicholas, in response to the urgent message, arrived at Wimpole Street he found Miss Barnes in a fluster, while Andrew came to greet him with fulsome apologies. 'Thank you for stepping in. At least it's the weekend tomorrow so there are only the remainder of today's appointments to consider.'

'Could there be any mistake with the date?'

Andrew shook his head. 'No, I examined her only ten days ago. But as we know it's not uncommon for a baby to be in a hurry. Nor, might I add, for a false alarm. In any event I should be back in London by Monday, but if not, and anything urgent arises…'

Nicholas smiled at him. 'You can rest assured that I'll deal with it.' He watched the distinguished physician collect his top hat, pick up his medical and overnight bags, and seconds later he was gone. 'So, it's just you and me to hold the fort, Miss Barnes.'

'Yes, Dr Carstairs. I've managed to contact those patients with a telephone, but Lady Trentley is due – it was too late to contact her.'

'Then I'd better straighten my shoulders.'

She laughed, but despite his earlier resolve as he went into his consulting room Nicholas found himself thinking only of Helena. Childbirth was not without its dangers.

By the time Dr Haverstock, accompanied by a hurriedly collected Nurse Parks, arrived, Helena's contractions were coming at increasingly shorter intervals. It was with obvious relief that the village midwife handed over responsibility to the London one, a tall grey-haired woman whose efficient manner and sweet smile must have gladdened the heart of many a mother.

The physician was swift to assess the situation. 'Everything is proceeding as it should, Mrs Faraday. We just need to be patient.'

But two long and exhausting hours later, despite Dr Haverstock administering chloroform to alleviate the pain, Helena was still trying to ride excruciating waves, biting hard on the wad of cloth the midwife had given her and gripping the rods of the brass bedstead. 'You're doing really well.' Nurse Parks was full of encouragement, and then the doctor's brisk voice came. 'The baby's head is crowned. That's excellent. Now when the next contraction comes I want you to push really hard. But when I say stop, cease immediately and

221

take quick short breaths...' With one last supreme effort she managed to find the strength to obey, and within seconds Helena felt a heavy slithering sensation as her body at last expelled its burden. Soon a thin piercing cry was followed by the words, 'You have a daughter, Mrs Faraday.'

Helena's euphoria was crushed. She lay in a listless state, only dimly aware of the physician snipping the umbilical cord and of the midwife taking the baby away. She was lost in a dazed world – and as for Oliver, how could she face him?

'You will be able to see your baby very soon,' Dr Haverstock murmured, as he attended to the afterbirth.

Helena managed to say, 'She isn't too small?'

'I would imagine about five pounds, but we can weigh her properly later.'

The midwife called softly, 'Dr Haverstock?'

Helena turned her head away, unable to prevent weak tears. When he returned his voice was gentle. 'Now then, Mrs Faraday, you're bound to be emotional after all you've been through. Most new mothers are. You'll feel different when you see your baby. But being early it's essential that she's kept warm so Nurse Parks is dressing her first.' He turned and said over his shoulder, 'I think the mittens too, Nurse.'

Several minutes later, sitting propped against her pillows, Helena was at last able to take the tiny bundle in her arms and gaze down at her daughter, marvelling at the pale delicate skin, at the almost transparent veining of her eyelids. The midwife who was standing beside the bed said, 'There, she's opening her eyes, bless her.'

Helena looked down into an unblinking quizzical gaze and she was lost. Joy and wonder swept through her as she whispered, 'She's beautiful.'

'Isn't she? Her eyes may change from blue though.'

Dr Haverstock was now washing his hands and forearms and pulling down his sleeves. Once more in his formal jacket, he came to Helena and said, 'Mother and child, a picture I always like to see.'

'Thank you, both of you, for all your help.'

He smiled at her. 'It's been a pleasure. If I may say so, you've been a model patient, hasn't she, Nurse.'

'I wish all my mothers were as co-operative.'

Helena said, 'My husband…?'

The physician was already moving towards the door. 'I shall go and see him now.'

Oliver was waiting in the library, his impatience mounting as the minutes and hours ticked by with the suspense becoming almost unbearable. At last, the door opened and with eager expectation, he strode across the room. 'Dr Haverstock! Is there news?'

'Indeed there is. May I offer you my congratulations – your wife has been safely delivered of a daughter.'

Oliver could only stare at him wordlessly before sinking on the leather chesterfield to gaze with despair into the crackling log fire. After all his efforts, all these months of hoping and planning…

The doctor came to sit nearby and leaned forward, his hands planted on his portly knees. 'I know you were hoping for an heir, Oliver, but your wife is young and there is no reason why the next child should not be a boy.' Then he paused. 'Although I do have to inform you that there is something…'

Oliver glanced up sharply. 'What is it?'

Dr Haverstock shook his head. 'Might I suggest that we go upstairs? You will be anxious to see your wife and child, and I would prefer to explain then.'

Helena, refreshed, her soiled nightdress changed for a pale blue silk one, lay gazing at the white-lace-frilled bassinet, which was placed carefully out of draughts and near to the fire. Despite wondering why she had only been allowed to hold the baby for such a short time, her main feeling was one of apprehension as she waited for her husband.

And then the door opened, and Oliver came in to walk past the bassinet without a single glance. As he came to the bed and she looked up at him, Helena could see in his eyes such strain, such dismay, that she could only whisper, 'I'm so sorry.'

'There will be another time.'

She longed for some words of affection, a gesture of tenderness. Instead, Oliver nodded towards the bassinet. 'You have seen it?'

'You mean our baby? Oh yes – and, Oliver, she's beautiful.'

'You couldn't see anything wrong?'

She stared up at him. 'How do you mean?'

It was then that Dr Haverstock, who had remained at a discreet distance, came over to join them. 'I apologise for causing you both concern, and repeat again that your daughter is perfectly healthy, but... Nurse, would you bring the baby, please.'

The midwife carried her over and began to loosen the fine blankets in which she was swaddled. As Helena watched with growing apprehension, Nurse Parks lifted first one small hand and then the other, until with the ribbons now untied she gently removed the white lacy mittens.

'I'm afraid,' Dr Haverstock said, 'that as you will see, there is a slight irregularity with her hands.'

Oliver's sharp intake of breath was almost strangled, while Helena stared down in shock and distress at two perfectly formed hands, each with a thumb and not four – but five fingers.

Chapter Twenty-nine

It was Oliver who broke the silence, his voice harsh. 'I want no mention of this. The child must have her hands covered at all times. Dr Haverstock, I trust your nurse is not a gossip?'

'I am a professional midwife, Mr Faraday, not a fishwife!'

'You're impertinent as well!'

'Oliver, I can appreciate that this has been a shock, but...' Andrew's tone was sharp. 'Let me explain. The medical term for this condition is polydactyly. It is quite rare, indeed I have only seen it twice before. Your baby's hands are affected but sometimes it can manifest itself as an additional toe. Fortunately in your case the extra little finger is perfectly formed.'

Helena gazing down in anguish at the tiny fingers now curled into a fist. 'But what causes such a thing?'

'I'm afraid we don't know, although it can sometimes be an inherited condition.'

Oliver had not moved. He was still staring down at his daughter's hands, his expression one of profound revulsion. Then without a glance, or even a word of comfort or reassurance, he turned to Dr Haverstock. 'I shall be obliged if you will join me in the drawing room before dinner. Shall we say in about an hour?'

As he crossed the room to the door, Helena stared after him in bewilderment and disbelief. As the others exchanged glances, into the awkward silence the midwife said, 'Have you decided on a name yet, Mrs Faraday?'

Helena's voice was trembling as she answered. 'I had thought Rosalind Mary, after my husband's late mother and my own.'

'What lovely names.'

Dr Haverstock's tone was one of concern. 'You need to sleep. Nurse will ring for your maid to come and sit with you. There is no need for you to worry about your baby – she's unlikely to wake for some time.'

In the drawing room, Oliver glanced at the French ormolu clock on the mantelpiece. Dinner would have to be served far beyond the usual time, but his dislike of disruption paled into insignificance against his feeling of desolation. This weekend was proving to be the worst of his life. First to be cheated of a son and heir and then to discover that he had fathered that... His mind veered away from the appalling image. He looked up at the gilt-framed portrait of Robert Faraday hanging above the fireplace. Would the man famed for his reserve and arrogance ever have imagined that a grandchild of his would be born so flawed?

Again he glanced at the clock with a frown. His father would not have countenanced dining with a member of the medical profession or indeed any profession, but times were changing, and Oliver had a great respect for this particular man. And then at last Dr Haverstock was ushered in by the butler, but any conversation was constrained until Crossley had performed the ritual of serving their aperitifs.

As soon as he left, Oliver said, 'Do you have any further comments concerning the unfortunate situation upstairs?'

'Only that I understand your double disappointment. Certainly, with regard to your wish for a son, I can only repeat that it is very early days. After all, you have only been married just over a year, and next time...'

'How is one to know that this ... aberration will not happen again?'

'I think that is most unlikely.'

Oliver lowered his glass to stare at him. He said very slowly, 'But you told me this type of malformation can be hereditary.'

'It can be, yes, but it is not always the case.'

Thoughtfully, Oliver took a sip of his vermouth, deciding that any such condition in the Faraday family would have been recorded.

Dr Haverstock said, 'Oliver, I feel I need to talk to you about your earlier instruction concerning your daughter. I really must point out that despite your understandable reticence regarding your private affairs, what you suggest is completely impractical.'

'May I ask why?'

'How are you to conceal the baby's hands? She cannot wear mittens all the time, especially when summer comes. And as the months pass, she will not only become distressed but able to pull them off herself.'

Oliver knew he was speaking the truth. His reaction upstairs had been a shocked instinctive one. And yet how could he allow his family name to become drawing-room or salon tittle-tattle? People would refer to the 'Faraday baby' and the five fingers would become embellished until they became six, seven, or even some other abnormality. Oliver knew only too well the prurient curiosity of the idle and how society loved malicious gossip. But what the doctor was saying made eminent sense. It was idiotic to think that a baby could be so confined, or that tongues could be silenced, no matter how trustworthy and disciplined his staff. It would only take one careless word.

He gazed down into his crystal glass. 'You give sound advice.'

'I try to. And Oliver, you must remember that Mrs Faraday has had a long and difficult labour. What she needs, what you both need, is time to come to terms with all this and then to support each other.'

Oliver gazed at him, the word 'hereditary' preying on his mind. Was there any history of the condition in the Standish family? Intrusive question though it was, he was determined to raise it with Helena's father, whose arrival and that of Beatrice was expected on Monday morning.

The room was cosy with flickering firelight welcoming Helena from a deep and restoring sleep. Her gaze drifted first to the bassinet and then to where Jane was sitting in an armchair, her fingers busy with her needle as she mended a silk stocking. Helena closed her eyes again, feigning sleep, her mind fastening on the earlier scene in the bedroom, the poignant moment when she had seen first seen her baby's hands. And then remembered the horror she had felt on seeing Oliver's revulsion. How could anyone look at their own child, their first-born, in such a terrible way? Rosalind's little hands were not ugly or disfigured – they were just slightly different. When one considered some of the distressing deformities some children were born with... Bitter resentment at her husband's coldness, his lack of interest and tenderness, brought tears to her eyes. Helena raised a hand to brush them away.

Jane, realising she was awake, came over to help her into a comfortable sitting position. 'How do you feel now, Madam?'

'Better, thank you.' Helena glanced anxiously over to the bassinet. 'Is she all right?'

'She's sleeping like an angel, such a beautiful baby. I'd like to offer my congratulations to both you and the master.'

'Thank you, Jane.'

'Would you like something to eat, perhaps an omelette or chicken? I could ask Cook to poach you some fish?'

'Yes, I think I would. Maybe some chicken.'

'I'll just ring for the nurse, and then I'll see to it.'

A few minutes later Nurse Parks returned to check on the baby and to assist Helena with her personal needs. Then she settled herself in the new nursing chair. 'I'm so pleased you had a good sleep, Mrs Faraday. If I may say so, I fully approve that you're going to feed baby yourself. I am afraid I could never understand Queen Victoria thinking that breastfeeding was a "horror". Nor that she could have nine children and nurse not a single one. Fortunately, attitudes are beginning to change and you're not my first society mother to make such a decision.'

'It wasn't easy to persuade my husband,' Helena admitted. In fact Oliver had been appalled at the idea, but she had refused to be swayed. 'I'm afraid I had to compromise and promise to use a wet nurse after the first six weeks.'

'Never mind, it's those first weeks which are the most important.'

'When will…?'

'She'll let us know when she's ready. I'm hoping you can have something to eat first. You will need

230

to keep your strength up.'

And almost as if the baby had heard them, it was not until Jane had been to remove Helena's tray that into the silence drifted an increasingly plaintive wail.

'There we are,' Nurse Parks said. 'Now I must warn you that sometimes it can be difficult the first time.'

'Before you bring her, please would you take her mittens off?' Helena began to undo the silk buttons on the bodice of her nightdress and unsure quite how to proceed waited until she could take the now fretful baby into her arms. Instinctively she guided the small mouth to her breast, wincing at the initial pain, and then her heart softened as she gazed down at the blissful and contented expression on Rosalind's little face. But for the rest of her life, Helena's abiding memory would always be of the moment when her daughter's five tiny fingers first curled around her own.

Chapter Thirty

It was not until the following afternoon when Dr Haverstock had departed for London that Oliver again entered Helena's bedroom, and at his dismissive gesture Nurse Parks rose from beside the fire where she had been knitting. She gave a swift glance towards the bed and then quietly left. Oliver, averting his eyes from the bassinet, walked towards Helena who, sitting propped against the

231

pillows with her hair loose around her shoulders, met his eyes but made no effort to greet him.

He cleared his throat. 'How are you my sweet?'

'I'm recovering well, thank you.' Her voice was cool. 'Don't you want to see Rosalind?'

'I have no wish to disturb her.'

'I am sure that a fond glance from her father will not cause her to wake.'

'I do not take kindly to sarcasm, Helena.'

'Neither does it seem that you take kindly to a baby who has a slight imperfection.'

'I cannot pretend to be overjoyed.'

'Don't you even want to hold her?' Helena's voice had a break in it, but despite the plea in her eyes, Oliver knew that bile would rise in his throat at the slightest contact with those small, malformed hands; even if Helena had given birth to a son, he would have been equally repulsed. He also knew that his revulsion was something she would never be able to understand.

His voice tight, he said, 'Babies are exclusively a female domain. You must surely know that gentlemen rarely involve themselves in nursery matters.'

The short silence that followed was broken by Helena. 'She *is* wearing mittens you know.'

Stung and disturbed by the perception beneath her cutting tone, Oliver turned and went over to the bassinet where his daughter lay sleeping. It was true; both small hands were concealed by white mittens that matched the frilled bonnet. He gazed down at her unable to feel the slightest sense of either pride or tenderness. His only emotion was one of bitter resentment because

232

this baby's arrival, its very existence, meant for Oliver only one thing – that Graylings had been cheated.

He stood back and looked over to his young wife who despite looking pale and tired was still beautiful. It was said that a woman could not conceive while she was breastfeeding so it was fortuitous that he had stipulated a time limit. He forced a smile. 'The child looks well.'

'Yes, the nurse is pleased with her.'

'Then I will bid you good morning, my sweet.'

Helena didn't reply. And as Oliver was leaving he reassured himself that there was no real need for concern. He was a man accustomed to achieving his aims and if all went well, then within twelve months that fussy bassinet would contain a different and much more welcome occupant.

The following Monday, Nicholas arrived at Wimpole Street to the news that Dr Haverstock was expected towards lunchtime. 'I managed to cancel his morning appointments,' Miss Barnes said. 'It's a wonderful invention, the telephone. I've been telling mother about it.'

'One day, Miss Barnes, I think there will be one in most households.'

She smiled at him. 'I hope it happens in my lifetime, then.'

But while Nicholas smiled back at her, his thoughts were elsewhere. During the weekend, even though his mother was visiting from Bath, he had found his thoughts constantly straying to Helena and the situation at Graylings. At least now, he would hear news. But it was much later and not until the last patient had left that Nicholas heard the welcome sound of his colleague's deep voice. When eventually he went into the other consulting room he found Andrew enjoying a pipe while he gazed out of the window. He turned to smile and beckon Nicholas to join him when together they watched a young boy rolling a hoop along the pavement. 'Such carefree days,' Andrew said.

Nicholas gave a nod of agreement. 'I do remember.' He turned to his colleague, 'So, did everything go well in Hertfordshire?'

The two men went to sit in the leather armchairs each side of a walnut coffee table and as Nicholas listened to Andrew's explanation, his heart went out to Helena. It was a shock to any mother to discover that her baby wasn't perfect. 'I have only seen it once,' he said, 'a couple of years ago. In this instance the extra finger, which was also in the postaxial position, was merely a small soft digit. There was no bone so I was able to tie off with sutures. But a perfectly formed one is a different matter.' He paused a moment. 'How have the parents taken it?'

'Mrs Faraday – quite well, she is an admirable young woman. But I'm afraid Oliver, who as you know had hoped for a son, seems to consider it some sort of personal affront that a child of his could be flawed. He views it as a deformity, a slight on his family.'

Nicholas looked down at his own hands, spreading the fingers. He hadn't taken to Helena's husband, but then that might have been the case whoever she had married. 'It's hardly that... I would consider it minor when compared to some.'

Andrew removed his pipe. 'Oliver has been of an obsessive nature since a child. In my own presence, he threw a teddy bear across the room because the ear had come unstitched. Nothing would pacify him, despite his nanny offering to sew it back. It wasn't perfect, you see.'

Nicholas was incredulous as he heard of Oliver's initial wish to hide his newly born baby away from public scrutiny. 'Whatever possessed the man?'

'Family pride I think, to which he is excessively prone. I did manage to persuade him that it was a nonsensical idea, but I doubt whether the child will receive much affection from him, either now or in the future.'

'It doesn't sound as if he will ever be reconciled to the poor little mite,' Nicholas said. 'Well, not poor exactly, but...'

'There's many an unhappy child in a wealthy household,' Andrew commented, 'I think we both know that.'

'There are many not only unhappy but wretched children in London, Andrew. Sometimes the poverty and deprivation makes me feel ashamed.'

'At least by practising medicine we play our part. Come Nicholas, my digestion tells me it is time for lunch. We can continue our philosophy over a good meal.'

'By the way,' Nicholas said as they rose to leave, 'did they name the baby?'

'Rosalind Mary. One can only hope that she has a more fortunate future than those she was named after.'

Helena had been longing to show her daughter to her family, but although she had explained the situation, it was with some apprehension that she watched Jacob and Beatrice stand together to stare into the bassinet.

Jacob was the first to speak. 'How on earth could such a thing happen?'

'I don't know, Papa. But she's still lovely, isn't she?'

He looked across at her. 'Poppet, she's more than lovely, she's a beautiful baby.'

Helena's eyes filled with tears at his use of the childhood endearment. 'I'm sorry I seem to be so emotional at the moment. It is just that Oliver's reaction was otherwise. At first he even wanted to hide her away from everyone, for her to wear mittens all the time.' The hurt in her voice almost broke Jacob's heart. Shocked, he looked down again at his sleeping granddaughter – was Helena telling him that Oliver was ashamed of his own child?

'I do worry how it will affect her as she grows up.'

Jacob frowned. 'Is it possible to have it removed?'

'Dr Haverstock said it could be done, but it would leave an unsightly scar. His advice was to leave well alone.'

Beatrice came over to the bed, and with a rare gesture of affection took her niece's hand in her own. 'Helena she has Standish blood, she will cope with fortitude. After all, what difference does it really make? The only difficulty I can think of is with gloves, but that can easily be remedied – she can simply tape the two little fingers together before she puts them on.'

Helena smiled at her with gratitude. 'You were always practical. Oh I can't tell you how glad I am that you and Papa are here.'

'I shall stay for as long as you need me,' Beatrice said. 'Certainly for the rest of your lying-in period. I take it you have a nanny and an under-nursery maid?'

'Yes, or at least we will have. I'm afraid the baby coming early upset all the arrangements. But the nursery maid is able to come tomorrow – she only lives in the village. And Nurse Parks has promised to remain until the end of the week when the nanny should arrive.' Helena looked up at her aunt. 'I do hope she won't turn out to be bossy, the sort who will want to take complete charge.'

'You must start as you mean to go on, Helena. Remember that Rosalind is your child. I'm afraid sometimes these people need to be reminded of such things.'

Jacob turned at last from the bassinet, and came over to kiss his daughter on the cheek. 'Where is Oliver? We haven't yet seen him.'

'No, he was out with his estate manager when we arrived, which was earlier than expected.' Beatrice went back to the bassinet. 'When is she due for a feed?'

'She will probably wake in about half an hour. I'm sure Oliver will be back shortly.'

'Good. In the meantime, Jacob, shall we go down for tea? And afterwards I shall look forward to holding my great-niece.'

'Ah, but who is going to be first? Remember I am the proud grandfather.'

Helena smiled at their familiar banter and once alone glanced around her large and luxurious boudoir. Why was it that she often longed to be back in her own cosy bedroom at Broadway Manor? Sometimes she wondered whether Graylings would ever feel like her real home.

Jacob, who was seated opposite his son-in-law as they dined that evening, found it impossible to forget his daughter's disturbing admission. With new and worrying insight he recalled how he and Beatrice had previously discussed the absence of any dogs at Graylings and the almost eerie plethora of good-looking staff. And now it would seem that he had rejected his own baby. Was Oliver such a perfectionist that it bordered on paranoia? What other explanation could there be for such an outrageous suggestion. And Beatrice must have similar concerns because although she contributed to the conversation, Jacob noticed that apart from her initial congratulations she didn't once mention Rosalind.

However, later, once the two men were alone with their brandy and cigars, Oliver himself raised the subject. 'It is unfortunate about the child's hands.'

Jacob was wary. 'Indeed, but children are born with far worse.'

'Dr Haverstock,' Oliver said, 'who by the way is an excellent physician should you ever need one, told me that the condition was often hereditary.

As I am not aware of any such history in the Faraday family, I wondered whether you could throw any light on the situation.'

So that was it, Jacob thought. The man is trying to apportion blame. He managed an even tone. 'I can assure you that I can't. Certainly I have never heard of it in the Standish family.'

'I see.'

'You say he used the word "often", so I take it that he didn't mean always?'

'Yes, but...'

'Then I suggest, Oliver, that you put the possibility out of your mind. Otherwise...' Jacob's voice trailed away.

'We will know when Helena has another child, won't we?'

Jacob disliked his tone. He had not expected to journey to Graylings and find on his arrival a young mother and baby lacking the love and support they deserved. At the end of the evening when he made his excuses to retire early, his thoughts were not easy ones. He may have encouraged this marriage, but now disturbingly he was beginning to wonder whether he could have made a serious error of judgment.

Chapter Thirty-one

In London, Cora was becoming not only restless but also increasingly bored. During the first weeks and months of living in St John's Wood, she had found the novelty of having an apartment of her own more than compensated for what became largely a solitary existence. With the luxury of space and privacy and the satisfaction of earning more money with time to pursue any hobby she wished, she had told herself she was in clover. It had taken some time for her to realise why she couldn't really settle. She didn't like the silence.

Cora had been surrounded by noise all her life. As a child in the workhouse, even in the night there would be the sound of weeping, snoring or the scream of someone having a nightmare. Then as a young girl helping Sid on his flower stall, when she'd sat on the bucket behind it practising her letters, she'd had to try and shut out the shouts of the other stallholders. At Belle's there may have been screeching, jealousy and quarrelling, but there had also been gossip and laughter. And she missed it.

On this particular morning, Cora stood by the window and gazed out at the quiet street. Everyone here was so toffee-nosed. She looked down at her new skirt, not a single flounce or frill, and in a quiet, dignified grey. She would never have bought that in the old days; even the woman on the market stall had been surprised at her choice. But she didn't go out any more in her normal clothes, the ones that Johnnie liked her in. People only thought she was 'tarty', she could tell. Funny that, she'd never minded before, in fact she'd gloried in it. If you've got it, flaunt it, had been her motto. Now even Sybil had noticed the difference in her.

Not that Cora was the only 'fancy bit' in this street, she'd seen another one – Cora could recognise the type anywhere. But Johnnie didn't want her to make any friends, not locally anyway. Yet his infrequent visits left days and evenings when the hours stretched ahead, long and empty. She might see Sybil sometimes, but it was loneliness she came home to.

Cora knew the dangers for a girl like her. Not a bottle of gin would she have in the place, even though she could afford it. Instead, she held fast to her ambition, stashing her allowance away and the growing amount in the cash box she had bought and hidden in her wardrobe was the one thing that cheered her up, and the rooms were clean and nicely furnished, she couldn't complain about that.

Cora turned and went to sit at the small table and, pulling towards her a sketchbook, looked down at a watercolour she was struggling with of a small house with its own gate and a path leading to a door with roses climbing beside it. She had seen similar scenes on chocolate boxes. But she wanted to paint from her imagination, not to simply copy. Cora leafed through the previous pages. All of her previous efforts had been of flowers but a house was different, it was much more difficult.

She wondered whether someone like her would be allowed to join the public library. Maybe a book in there could help her. Well, it said 'public' didn't it? And she could look as respectable as anyone, especially if she went dressed like this and didn't paint her face.

That same weekend Graylings was the scene of a house party; the first in the three months following Rosalind's birth. Helena was desperate for the distraction. Regardless of her love and joy in her child, the tensions of these past weeks had clouded any enjoyment of life beyond the nursery. She found Oliver's constant avoidance of contact with their baby profoundly hurtful and her resentment was such that lately she could hardly bear to be in his presence. Fortunately, he was often out riding with his estate manager, or spending long periods of time in his study. He also made not infrequent visits to London. When they dined together their conversation was polite and desultory, and afterwards it was rare now that after dinner Oliver joined her in the drawing room. Helena was not only glad to escape to the nursery but every night as she finished her bed-side reading, she was vastly relieved that so far the inter-connecting door between Oliver's room and her own remained closed.

But now, her voice was light as she stood in the drawing-room on Saturday evening, enjoying her aperitif while she chatted to a smiling Johnnie.

And he didn't disappoint her, his uplifting tone and light-hearted outlook as amusing as ever.

'Not a single filly did I fancy,' he told her. 'I went to every wretched party, every white-tie ball. But not one of this season's debs was a patch on you.'

'You always were a flatterer.' She laughed up at him. 'I hope you realise you're talking to someone who's now a mother.'

'And it suits you. Lovelier than ever, isn't she, Hugh?'

Dorothy's brother had come to join them. 'Wouldn't take me on though, Johnnie, no matter how many times I offered.'

'You know if you two want a young lady to take you seriously, you need to try and appear aloof and intriguing.'

'I've told you about reading all those romantic novels,' Dorothy commented as she joined them. 'Although even I felt a frisson for Jane Austen's Mr Darcy and he fits that description perfectly.'

'And how do I compare?' Peregrine appeared at her shoulder, and she laughed up at him.

It was obvious that they were in love, Helena thought, and she was delighted, although a little envious of their easy way with each other. Why did Oliver have to be so complicated, so difficult?

With a smile, she excused herself and went to circulate among her other guests. Jacob was listening earnestly to Angela Shirley, the same sweet-faced widow whom he had met at Graylings several months before. He smiled at Helena as she went by. Aunt Beatrice too was playing the part of a listener, although in her case it was to the wife of a local magistrate, a woman Helena considered both a snob and a bore. Seeing the strain in her aunt's expression, she went over. 'Mrs Spencer, I can't allow my aunt to monopolise you completely. I thought you might like to meet one of my husband's friends. You may be acquainted with his mother, Mrs Camilla Horton?' Johnnie's look of horror as they approached was delicious, and it was with some amusement that she saw Hugh was already sidling away.

It was not until after dinner when everyone gathered in the drawing room that Oliver had the chance to talk undisturbed to Johnnie. Elsewhere cards were played, some people had gathered in small groups to converse, while Jacob and a country squire were absorbed in a game of chess. Oliver noticed his wife's absence and his lips tightened. No doubt she was neglecting their guests to go up to the nursery. He would never understand Helena's obsession with the child. In a well-ordered household, a baby should not cause the slightest disruption.

Johnnie said, 'When am I going to see the sprog, then?'

'I believe she will be brought to the morning room tomorrow.' Helena had insisted that their guests would expect it. However, in this instance she had agreed that Rosalind would wear mittens. 'I have no wish for her to be a public exhibition.'

'It's a blasted shame,' Johnnie said, 'You know, about her hands.'

'I don't need sympathy, from you or anyone else.'

'There's no need to be so testy. And if you don't

244

mind my saying so old boy, you do seem rather tense. Don't tell me that life with the heavenly Helena isn't quite so...'

'Mind your own business.'

Johnnie just grinned at him. 'Tricky sex, aren't they. I'm having problems myself, well sort of.'

Oliver, guessing that he was referring to Cora, recalled telling Johnnie on a previous occasion that Graylings was hardly the setting in which to raise such matters. But now he felt curious. He touched the younger man's arm. 'Let's walk on the terrace for a short time, I need a cigarette.'

A few minutes later, after inhaling and releasing a stream of smoke, Oliver leaned back against the ancient stone balustrade, his eyes narrowing. 'Don't tell me that doxy is touching you for yet more cash?'

He shook his head. 'No, but she's changed, Oliver, quietened down somehow. We used to have a smashing time together at Belle's, but she's not nearly so much fun lately.'

Oliver felt irritated. 'Then get rid of her.'

Johnnie looked down and scuffed his feet. 'I can't bring myself to do that, at least not yet. Anyway, I'm fond of her. But I do miss Belle's – raised the old spirits, you know, seeing all that comely flesh on offer. Now it all feels a bit domesticated.'

'She'll have to go sooner or later, Johnnie. After all, if you feel like this after a few months...'

'You're probably right. I am becoming a tad bored.'

'And I told you she was a mercenary little bitch. I should watch your wallet if I were you.'

Johnnie shook his head. 'No, she's not that sort

245

of girl.'

Oliver finished his cigarette and flung the stub on to the garden below. 'You have a lot to learn, Johnnie. These types of girls are as hard as nails. They'd sell their grandmothers to get what they want.'

As the two men began to stroll back, Oliver saw Helena return to the drawing room. She was looking utterly desirable in an emerald green shot silk gown, her beauty a shining light in a mainly middle-aged gathering. Yet Oliver feared to go to her bed that night, just as he had refrained from doing during the past two months. And he was convinced that the cause was the constant presence of that wretched defective baby. Despite his desperation for a son and heir, the spectre of those hands, the horror of it happening again was preying on his mind to such an extent that he now dreaded even trying to make love to his wife. Such mental turmoil could threaten a man's performance, might even render him impotent. Oliver refused to risk that ultimate humiliation. He watched Helena move gracefully among their guests, knowing that although he might be the envy of several men in the room his marriage was at an impasse. He also knew that after being celibate for over a year, a man could only wait so long.

Chapter Thirty-two

Below stairs, Molly was wondering if anyone else had noticed that there was something going on between Miss Forrester and Mr Hines. Not that she would ever say a word, even if it would be to her advantage. Then one afternoon she was about to descend the stairs from the third floor when over the banister she could see Susan loitering around a corner on the first landing. Suspicious, Molly paused. The door of Mr Faraday's room opened and his valet came out and almost at the same time, Jane Forrester emerged from Mrs Faraday's adjoining room. Susan, just out of sight, crept nearer, her obvious intention to eavesdrop.

Outraged, Molly leaned over the bannister to flap her feather duster and managing to attract Jane's attention, made wild gestures to go back. Startled, Jane obeyed. Jack Hines glanced up and seeing Molly, made his way casually downstairs.

Later that evening, he drew her aside. 'Thank you for that,' he said quietly. 'I'm not sure exactly what was going on...'

Molly explained. 'Luckily she couldn't see me, but you'd better watch Susan, Mr Hines. She's poison.'

But it was Miss Helena who was mostly on her mind. Because there was no doubt about it, the master took not a whit of notice of that little baby. She had even seen him walk out of a room if the nanny brought in Miss Rosalind. And she was a lovely little thing; besides, once you got used to her hands you hardly noticed there was anything wrong with them.

Helena didn't have time for an anti-climax once everyone had left, because the post that arrived the following morning brought forth from Oliver a spluttered expletive. 'I'm sorry, Helena, but of all the...'

'What is it?'

He held up a stiff gold-edged card. 'That blighter Selwyn is getting married.' He glanced down at the invitation. 'I had no idea he was even engaged. Who on earth is Caroline Vasey?'

Helena dabbed her lips with her napkin and placed it at the side of her plate. 'Oh dear, your cousin could have made a better choice.'

'You actually know her?'

She calmly poured herself more coffee. 'No, she came out about three years before me. But Dorothy did repeat scandal she had heard at a Hunt Ball.'

'So it seems we have a bounder marrying a slut. And as I don't recall seeing an announcement of the engagement, he's obviously being forced into it.' Oliver frowned. 'Is this Caroline an only child?'

'I have no idea. When and where is this wedding taking place?'

He glanced down. 'In about three weeks, in London. Naturally, we shall have to accept.' He sat back in his chair and thoughtfully surveyed her. 'You know, I can't help thinking that this has come at an opportune time? A few weeks in

London, what with Wimbledon and the Henley Regatta, will be a pleasant distraction for you.'

'It does sound appealing. Of course I shall need to ensure that nursery provision at Faraday House is organised.' She glanced up to see Oliver gazing at her rather strangely. 'What's the matter?'

'I hope you are not suggesting that the child comes too.'

'But of course. I have no intention of being separated from Rosalind for such a long time.'

Oliver's lips tightened. 'You are being ridiculous.'

'I don't understand your objection.'

'I would simply prefer that she stays here at Graylings.'

'And I am her mother and I prefer that she comes with us to London.'

His voice was heavy with exasperation. 'To do what you suggest would cause a great deal of inconvenience.'

'There would be nothing that need cause you the least discomfort. I'm sorry, Oliver, but I won't change my mind.' Her gaze was unflinching.

'Then if you insist.' Oliver rose and stalked out of the room. He was furious. This wedding would have offered the ideal scenario, because in London, without the presence of that wretched baby...

Later, with a cool breeze against him and the feel of his mount's strong muscles beneath his knees, Oliver tried to gallop out his increasingly dark and depressive thoughts. Eventually reaching a hillock, he reined in to gaze down at Graylings in its peaceful setting below. With its grandeur and history it had been the one consuming passion in his life, he had even married to give it security. He sat with his hands resting on the pommel, while his black stallion Salem lowered his head to crop contentedly at the grass. Helena would never be prised from that child, he knew that now. And yet this irrational fear he had of ugliness, something he had never confessed to living soul, had been part of his nature for as long as he could remember; a trait he had fought hard against and tried to conceal by means of avoidance. But he had to accept the unpalatable truth. It was not only causing problems within his marriage, it was threatening to endanger the future of his beloved home.

'Who's getting married?' At Broadway Manor, Cook leaned her elbows on the kitchen table.

'Mr Faraday's cousin,' Enid Hewson told her, 'but I don't think they can be close because Miss Beatrice has only met him once, at Miss Helena's wedding. Mind you, it's a bit short notice, I mean only three weeks...'

'Shotgun, I expect,' Charlotte said with a sheepish grin. 'They do say that these things can happen in the best of families, though my mum would kill me if I got into trouble.'

'I don't think my mum will ever get the chance.'

Hearing Annie's tone, Enid glanced at her set face and hurriedly changed the subject. 'Well, Miss Beatrice is planning to go two weeks before, and then to stay two weeks after. I do like Carlton House Terrace; it's in the best part of London you know, near Buckingham Palace and everything. I hope Miss Helena brings the baby, I'm dying to see her again.'

'Poor little thing,' Charlotte said. 'I couldn't believe it when you told us about her hands.'

'She'll learn to live with it,' Annie snapped. 'At least she'll be able to conceal her problem.'

'I've never met Mr Faraday.' The dark, serious girl who had replaced the miserable parlourmaid was, unlike her predecessor, popular with everyone.

'You've not missed much.' Annie's tone was bitter.

Cook gazed at her. 'Annie, love, you do seem to be down a bit these days. Is it getting to you, you know, more than usual?'

Annie flushed, the heat making the disfigurement even worse. 'I suppose it is. I'm sorry, I don't mean to be a misery guts.'

But later it was Charlotte who told the cook that Annie was sweet on one of the soldiers she met when she visited Ida. 'She knows it's hopeless, but you can't help your feelings can you? And seeing Ida so happy, being pregnant and all, that doesn't help either.'

'There are worse fates than being a spinster. I'd rather that than spend my life being married to some men. I could tell you stories about my poor sister that would make your hair curl.'

Charlotte looked troubled. 'Yes, but how do you know beforehand, what they're going to be like I mean?'

'Don't ask me. I gave up long ago trying to understand men; some women too for that matter.' She heaved herself up. 'I'd better get on with those apple dumplings for luncheon. Where's Daisy?'

'I'm here, Cook.' The young girl popped her head out of the scullery. 'I've just finished washing the carrots.'

'Good. Well you can peel those Bramleys in the basket.' She smiled at her. 'You're a good worker, even as good as Annie used to be.' And as she told the butler later, the smile on that girl's face could light up a Christmas tree.

A few days later, Helena sat opposite Oliver during breakfast and discussed with him the dates for their visit to London. 'I thought perhaps we could time our plans to coincide with those of Aunt Beatrice.'

'Yes, of course.'

She looked across at him. 'It was really kind of you to offer Papa the use of Faraday House when he needed to attend Parliament. I don't think I ever thanked you for that.'

'It was my pleasure. I prefer the staff to be busy otherwise they can become lax in their duties.'

Helena forked a small portion of her scrambled eggs, wishing he could be as amenable in his attitude to Rosalind. Otherwise she could see this impasse between them lasting forever. And it disturbed her that he had been so vehement she should be left behind when they went to London. Tempted at first to dismiss it as another of her husband's peculiarities, lately Helena had begun to wonder whether there was a more sinister reason. For instance, exactly why did Oliver wish those portraits hung in a rarely used room? Was it just so that he had no need to gaze on the facial deformities, or so that he could forget their very presence? Was her husband so paranoid that he wished he could do the same with his own child?

Chapter Thirty-three

It was a week later when Oliver came across the isolated perambulator. Left alone beneath the shade of a tree beside one of the sweeping lawns, he could only assume that the buxom and conscientious Nanny Harris would not be far away. Helena was stringent in her rules regarding Rosalind. And the discovery presented him with a rare chance to stroll closer and to stare unobserved at the sleeping baby. In the warm sunshine, she lay in a relaxed position, her legs and dimpled knees apart, and it was only then that for the first time Oliver saw her uncovered head. Staring in stunned disbelief, he thought of Helena's honey-gold hair and raising his hand studied the fair ones where his wrist was visible beneath the white gold-linked cuff of his shirt. Into his mind came an image of his father whose moustache had been blond like his own, and then slowly he looked down again at the small head with its fine dusting of black hair. As the nanny approached across the grass, clutching a white sunbonnet, Oliver was already turning, his mind and emotions in indescribable chaos. Blindly, he strode away across the grass walking on and on deeper into the grounds, not even reducing his pace as he reached a spinney, regardless of over-hanging branches, of rabbits scattering before him. Then he suddenly came to a halt, to lean his forehead against the trunk of an ancient oak.

He tried to think in a logical, reasoned manner, but to no avail. Jacob's hair and beard were light brown in colour. Beatrice was nondescript, mousy. Before him came the image of that shocking scene he had encountered in the music room. The black hair of the music tutor, Helena's crimson face ... she had been the picture of guilt – the sickening evidence was lying in that perambulator. There *had* been intimacy, she *had* betrayed him. Why had he been such a gullible fool? Why had he listened to her denials, her protestations of innocence? And was it coincidence or a deliberate concealment that during all these months he had never before seen the baby without a bonnet?

He turned to lean back against the tree, but even the warmth of the dappled sunlight through the leafy branches failed to calm him. Through his anger, his fury, there came the memory of that similar oak tree at Broadway Manor, where for the first time he had kissed her. How soft and trusting her lips had been and yet within a year she had turned him into a cuckold. But he was determined that now he was in possession of the truth, knowing that there was no correlation be-tween the Faraday bloodline and those deformed hands, he'd soon be ensuring that his young and unfaithful wife fulfilled her purpose.

Eventually Oliver began to make his way back to the house, and once out of the spinney, he could see in the distance the perambulator still standing in the shade, while beside it the nanny was sitting in a garden chair absorbed in a book. But the hour he had spent in the spinney had not been wasted, nor would he meekly accept the situation, because already a germ of a plan was growing. It was devious, even dangerous but if it succeeded then Graylings would not be contaminated for very much longer by the presence of Longford's bastard.

'Two months? You're going to Italy for two whole months?' Cora stared at Johnnie in horror and disbelief.

'Sorry, old girl.' They were both enjoying a cigarette after an even more enjoyable pastime. 'It's a family obligation. Some cousins of ours have taken a taken a villa in Tuscany and invited the whole family. Even Pater has agreed to go. The plan is to spend one month there and another with a maiden aunt in Florence. She's pretty ancient so it might be the last time we'll see her.'

These people lived in a different world, she thought. And it was odds on his family were looking after their inheritance. But two whole months! Whatever would she do with herself for eight weeks stuck in this place with no company and not even the hope of seeing Johnnie?

'Don't look so downcast, sweetheart, the time will soon go. I can always send you a postcard?'

Her laugh was mocking. 'Lovely.' Cora was beginning to think that if it wasn't for her steadily mounting nest egg, she'd regret the whole arrangement. It had got to the stage when her boredom was such – and this was something that Sybil would never understand – that Cora even missed the punters. Not all of them of course, even Belle hadn't been able to weed out every rotter, but Cora had known how to deal with them. A kid growing up in the workhouse soon learned how to defend itself.

But she couldn't face the thought of two months of long and empty days and even longer nights. At least she'd felt alive at the brothel, not shut away from the world.

'Johnnie,' Cora went over to sit on his knee. 'If you're going to be away all that time, how about if I get meself a bit of fun in the evenings. You know go out sometimes, have a few drinks and a laugh?'

'I don't know about that, Cora. The men would be round you like a honey pot. And I'm not paying for other people's pleasure.'

'You wouldn't 'ave to worry about that, Johnnie, I give you my word. And you've always said I'm as straight as a die.'

'I know, but…'

'Please … it's going to be so lonely here on my own, and you'll be in Italy in all that sunshine, having a wonderful time.'

Johnnie hesitated.

'You did say I wouldn't be a prisoner, when we first fixed all this up. And I've been ever so good. You know I never go out after six, just in case you come.'

'I suppose I am being a bit selfish.'

Cora flung her arms around his neck. 'You won't regret it, I promise.' She had meant what she said. A bargain was a bargain as far as she was concerned. But to be free on the long summer evenings to wander around the East End, have a drop of port or gin in a pub, perhaps with a good old Cockney knees-up, even see the occasional fight. Well, that was the real world.

London in June was not the most comfortable place to be. Summer heat in the capital always seemed more oppressive than in the country, and Helena instructed Nanny Harris to take the greatest care of Rosalind when she wheeled her out in nearby St James's Park. But there was a definite stimulation to be found in the city, and although she had been expecting it – Peregrine had recently been a frequent visitor to Dorothy's home – it had given her enormous pleasure to see their engagement announced in *The Times* that morning.

Jacob and Beatrice had been at Faraday House for several days before they raised their concern. One afternoon when they were taking tea in the drawing room Jacob said, 'Helena, my dear, Oliver seems to take so very little interest in Rosalind. You did tell us something soon after her birth that disturbed us. Surely after all this time it can't be that he still hasn't accustomed himself to her problem.'

Helena replaced her cup on its fluted saucer. Her voice was quiet. 'I am fearful that he never will.'

While Beatrice stared at her with shocked eyes, Helena could see startled anger in those of her father. 'I don't think it is wholly his fault. He

257

seems to have a sort of phobia about, oh I don't know, any sort of ugliness I suppose.' Slowly she confided to them the hidden away portraits, before going on describe his appalled reaction on seeing Annie's scarred face. 'I felt awful,' Helena said. 'She must have been so upset by it.'

'So you were aware of this trait in his character when you agreed to marry him?' Jacob's tone was sharper than he intended and he regretted it when he saw distress in his daughter's eyes.

'I just thought it was an isolated instance. And he was very persuasive.' Her cheeks flamed as she remembered that evening in the dining room, his lips on her bare shoulders, the way he had stirred her emotions.

Jacob drummed his fingers on the arm of his chair. The girl had been too young, too inexperienced, she would have been an easy prey to an attractive older man. He should have been more cautious, more perceptive, and certainly not have allowed his political ambitions to influence his judgement.

Beatrice leaned forward. 'But you are happy, my dear?'

Helena couldn't bear to see the anxiety in her aunt's eyes, nor the deep concern in her father's. She had thought she had overcome the shadow of that disastrous wedding night, but Oliver's hurtful rejection of their child had only confirmed the cruelty of which he was capable. How could she be happy with such a man? And during the long nights spent alone she had come to the conclusion that she had no choice but to accept the arid future stretching before her. After all, what choice did she have? She would play the part of a dutiful wife, the mistress of Graylings, a society hostess, but she doubted there would be any true joy and love in her life, except towards and from her children. Helena had no doubt that despite the coldness between them Oliver would wish to lie with her again. His desire for a son and heir would ensure that. Yet recently she had been feeling uneasy, puzzled by Oliver's behaviour, his rather strange attitude towards her. But what would be the point of transferring her unhappiness and pain to these two beloved people. Helena gazed back at her aunt and managed to smile. 'But of course.'

It was later as she went upstairs to the nursery that Helena found herself thinking of Nicholas. Perhaps it was because she was in London but she was finding it more difficult to suppress the memories; in the past weeks, concern for her baby had done much to alleviate her regret for what might have been. Now, there were still moments when the image of his warm brown eyes and the message that had passed silently between them seemed just as vivid, as fresh. Yet it was months since that meeting in Wimpole Street. However, she thought as she entered the room where her baby lay sleeping, it was doubtful whether their paths would cross; his busy and useful life would hardly coincide with Oliver's plans for their own entertainment.

Chapter Thirty-four

It was during tea the following day that Beatrice first complained of a headache. Jacob, enjoying a slice of plum cake, glanced across at her. 'You probably lingered too long in Bond Street. I still don't see why your usual milliner couldn't have looked after you.'

Helena looked at him with indulgence, wondering why it was that men had so little understanding of such things. 'Papa, we wanted to consult Madame Delancy, her designs are so much the vogue this year.'

'But perhaps you are right,' Beatrice conceded. 'I did try on an inordinate number of hats.'

Helena laughed. 'So did I, we had a lovely time and have bought delicious confections to wear at the wedding.'

'You certainly look glowing.' Oliver gave her another of those strange looks. Since their marriage, she had come to recognise most of his moods, but lately he was mystifying her, he seemed so distant and brooding. She was only thankful that there had been no suggestion that they might become intimate again, although she knew it was only a matter of time. Her husband's priority would always be the security of Graylings. Now, as he and Jacob continued to discuss their plans for the following day, she smiled with sympathy at her aunt as Beatrice excused herself to go and rest,

260

only later to send a message that she would not be coming down for dinner.

It wasn't until Jane was peering at an intricate clasp on a rope of pearls and murmured that Hewson was worried, that Helena began to feel concerned. 'Apparently,' Jane said, 'Miss Beatrice told her that it's the worst migraine she's ever had.'

Helena paused from her task of selecting which ring to wear, knowing how her aunt hated the term and rarely used it, considering it gave her headaches the status of an illness. 'I'll call and see her before I go down, Jane. The problem is that as you know, my aunt does hate anyone fussing.'

A few minutes later she went into a familiar scene, one of a still fully dressed Beatrice prostrate on the eiderdown, a folded flannel placed on her forehead that Helena knew that Hewson would have soaked in vinegar and water. Going over to the bed, she said gently, 'How are you?'

Beatrice's voice was weak, even trembling. 'I'm not at all well. And my left side – I cannot seem to move it, there is no feeling there. Helena, the pain in my head is dreadful.'

Helena was shocked to see how gaunt she looked. 'I shall ask Oliver to send for a doctor. I'm sure it's nothing to worry about, Aunt Beatrice, but it's best to be sure.'

Her heart pounding she lifted her skirt to hurry out of the room, down the staircase and across the wide hall to the drawing room where as she expected Oliver and her father were enjoying their aperitifs on the terrace and deep in conversation. Helena interrupted them, 'Excuse me, but

Papa, I come from Aunt Beatrice's bedroom. I think we should send urgently for a doctor.'

He stared at her. 'What is it? What is wrong?'

'I'm not sure,' Helena found her voice shaking. 'But she thinks her left side has become paralysed and she's suffering terribly with her head.'

Oliver turned away. 'I shall telephone Dr Haverstock.'

Jacob put his glass down on a side table as Helena said, 'Papa, I am returning to her, and I think you should come too.'

With alarm and anxiety, he followed his daughter upstairs and into his sister's bedroom, where she stared up at him, her face drawn. 'I'm sorry ... I cannot withstand the pain and my left side...' There was a catch in her voice and he felt a leap of apprehension, even fear. Bending down he gently took her hand. 'Oliver is even now telephoning the doctor. Is there anything further we can do for you, my dear, anything you need? You did bring your preparation?'

'Yes of course...'

'Then you must remain quiet and rest.'

Helena was hovering behind her father. 'I'll stay with you, Aunt Beatrice.'

'Thank you.' Her whisper trailed away as she closed her eyes.

Jacob turned to Helena, and she could see in his expression a reflection of her own unsaid fear. He muttered, 'I'll go and see what's happening about the doctor.'

'Is there anything I can do, Miss Helena?' Enid Hewson's eyes were wide with panic.

Helena looked helplessly at her. 'Perhaps you

262

could try dabbing her temples with lavender?'

That same evening Nicholas was settling into his armchair with a glass of whisky and stretching out his legs in an effort to relax. With Andrew away on vacation in Scotland, the past few days had been hectic. He had been called out today from his own practice too. Nicholas frowned. His list of patients at Wimpole Street was growing, and it had always been his intention that the more affluent practice would not affect the other. Like all great cities, London had two faces: one of privilege, success, and splendid architecture, the other of poverty, hunger, and slums. Always an observer of human nature his profession provided insight into both worlds, but while he had often felt humbled by the courage and dignity he found among the poor, that didn't mean he didn't despair at times of the mean brutality he found there. There was also corruption among the upper classes, but they knew how to conceal it beneath a veneer of civilised behaviour. Musing on the ways of the world, Nicholas took an appreciative sip of his single malt only to swear under his breath when the shrill peal of the telephone shattered his tranquillity. He half moved to rise and then heard the pattering footsteps of his housekeeper as she hurried to answer it. The widowed Mrs Miles, thin, sharp-featured and a devout Methodist, had been terrified of what she called 'this new-fangled invention' at first. Then he found to his amusement that it had not only given her a sense of self-importance, she had adopted what she considered a 'genteel voice' especially for it. He waited with resignation until she came into the book-lined room that doubled as both drawing room and library. 'It's a Mr Faraday, doctor.'

Startled, Nicholas's first thought was of Helena, but on listening to the clipped voice of Oliver Faraday, felt relieved to learn that the patient was a Miss Standish and also thankful that the Faradays were in London rather than Hertfordshire.

'You haven't got to go out again, doctor?'

'I'm afraid so, Mrs Miles.' He was already moving away. 'But at least I shall be travelling in comfort, because Mr Faraday is sending his motor car.'

'Noisy dratted things. They ain't natural, that's what I say. I'm just thankful you've managed to eat your supper.'

'And an excellent pie it was, Mrs Miles, thank you.' He smiled at her before going to check his medical bag. Faraday had mentioned the possibility of a stroke and Nicholas could only hope that he was mistaken; in his opinion, strokes were one of the worst afflictions anyone should have to bear. Once satisfied that he had everything he might need, he went upstairs to his room to freshen and to change his linen. He told himself that he would have done so anyway on visiting such a prestigious client, but deep down Nicholas knew the true reason. If her aunt was at the London house, then Helena might also be there. He fumbled first to remove a stiff collar and then to fasten a stud in a new one, all the time feeling both anger at his weakness and a rush of adrenalin at even the thought of seeing her again.

When her father returned to the bedroom Helena rose with impatience from her chair beside the bed and went to meet him. 'Is he coming?'

Jacob nodded. 'Yes, the motor car has been sent. But unfortunately Dr Haverstock is away in Scotland, so it will be his colleague, Dr Carstairs.'

Helena's breath caught in her throat. Nicholas? With a struggle, she managed to keep her features composed, her voice even. 'I have met him, Papa, and thought he seemed most capable.'

'I certainly hope so. How is she?'

'About the same, but at least she isn't any worse.'

Jacob glanced over to the bed where a pale-faced Beatrice was lying with her eyes closed. 'Perhaps you will let her know what is happening while I go and await his arrival.'

'Yes, of course.' Helena knew her colour had heightened, and saw the maid give her a curious glance. Hurriedly she said, 'You must be in need of a rest and some refreshment, Hewson. Would you like to go downstairs for a while? I promise to ring down once the doctor has been.'

'Thank you, Madam. Would you like me to arrange for a tray to be sent up?'

Helena shook her head. 'Not yet. I will ring down later.'

In the now silent room Helena tried to remain calm, aware that she should be thinking only of her aunt, but finding it impossible to suppress her rising sense of excitement. She put a hand to her hair, glad that she was wearing one of her most becoming gowns in a soft coral trimmed with cream. And then guilt at her vain and selfish thoughts made her return to the bed.

Beatrice opened her eyes. 'Did I hear Jacob's voice?'

Helena gave her the message. 'Is the headache as bad?'

'It's lessening slightly, and although still severe, is no different than usual,' her voice wavered, 'but what worries me is that I still can't...'

Hating to see her aunt so ill and frightened, Helena held her hand. 'The doctor won't be long now.'

It seemed an eternity until at last, there came a tap at the door and Helena's heart missed a beat as Jacob ushered in the tall, clean-shaven doctor and brought him over to the bed, murmuring, 'I think you have already met my daughter, Mrs Faraday.'

Nicholas said quietly, 'Yes. Good evening, Mrs Faraday.'

'Good evening.'

Jacob said, 'I shall leave you in the doctor's capable hands, Beatrice.'

'Would you like me to leave too, Dr Carstairs?'

Beatrice's feeble voice came, 'No, please stay, Helena.'

After Jacob quietly closed the door, Helena hovered at a discreet distance, watching as Nicholas bent over the bed, seeing his expression soften as he looked down at his patient. 'Miss Standish, you are suffering, aren't you? Tell me, have you had these headaches for very long?'

'About ten years.'

'And how often do they occur?'

'Two or three times a month.'

'But this one is the worst?'

'Yes.'

'And you have never had this numbness before?'

'No.' Her voice wavered, 'I can't feel my left side at all.'

'Have you noticed any difficulty with your speech?'

'Only that my brain feels a little slow.'

With Beatrice's permission, Nicholas examined her, while all the time Helena watched his deft hands, his gentle professional manner, hardly able to believe his presence, that he was only a few feet away.

At last, he straightened up and removed his stethoscope. Helena went to help adjust her aunt's clothes and to make her comfortable then drew back.

Nicholas smiled. 'Miss Standish, I can assure you that you have not suffered a stroke. What you have is an attack of hemiplegic migraine, a condition very similar to a mild stroke and it can be rather frightening the first time. I promise that you will make a complete recovery. Now I want you to take the sleeping draught I will leave, and hopefully when I come and see you tomorrow morning, you will be much improved.' Seconds later, closing the clasp of his leather bag, he added with a reassuring smile, 'Of course if you become worse or concerned in any way, please don't hesitate to send for me.'

Helena saw her aunt's eyes glisten and bent to touch her hand. 'Isn't that wonderful news, Aunt

Beatrice? I will just take Dr Carstairs down to Papa, I won't be long.'

He followed her out of the room and it was not until they stood on the wide landing together that at last she was able to raise her eyes to his. Her words were merely, 'Thank you,' but her gaze was searching for ... and she found it in those now familiar brown eyes. Fleeting, intense, but heartbreakingly brief as at a sound below in the hall she was forced to look away, to turn and then Nicholas stood aside so that she could precede him down the curved staircase and into the hall.

Helena's voice was now cool, brisk as she saw a footman. 'Perkins, please would you take the doctor to the drawing room to Mr Faraday and my father. I shall see you tomorrow, Dr Carstairs.'

Congratulating herself that not even the actress Sarah Bernhardt could have put on a better performance, Helena began to go back upstairs, hugging to herself the fact that tomorrow was only hours away.

Chapter Thirty-five

The following morning, expressing their regret that Beatrice and Helena were unable to join them, Oliver and Jacob departed for Wimbledon Lawn Tennis Club.

Meanwhile Beatrice was fretting at having to remain in bed. 'Exactly what time do you think

Dr Carstairs will come? I so dislike inactivity.'

'He didn't say.' Deciding to leave her to be querulous with Hewson, Helena went downstairs to wander restlessly around, conscious of every sonorous chime of the grandfather clock in the hall. Again and again, she went over to the casement window in the drawing room to gaze out over St James' Park, and then at last she saw him, walking along the pavement in the summer sunshine. The scene so reminded her of her debutante days in Cadogan Square – how young and innocent she had been. So much had happened since then: her engagement, her marriage, Graylings, the birth of Rosalind. And yet, the feelings that rose within her at the sight of him, the breathlessness, the anticipation, hadn't changed at all. As he grew nearer she could see once more that same intelligent, sensitive face, and remembered the rush of shock and joy she had felt last night on seeing him enter the bedroom at the side of her father. How skilled he was, how compassionate his bedside manner. She felt so much respect for the useful life he led. Helena willed him to glance up at the window, not caring that it was unseemly for her to feel like this, to act like this. She needed that reassurance, needed to know that he too remembered.

Nicholas had not slept well. When he had arrived home the previous evening, he had felt not only weary after the long day but seeing Helena's poise, her confident role as the mistress of a fine London house, had only served to emphasise the wide social gap between them. And this morning, having followed his usual policy of asking the cab driver to stop some distance before his destination – the chance of exercise was far too rare – the scene before him was a poignant reminder. The houses, tall and with casement windows, were of a similar architecture to those in Cadogan Square and as he drew nearer to the Faraday house, illogical though it was, he glanced up. And there she was, just as before, outlined against the glass. Was it vanity to think that she might have been waiting for him? Nicholas made a movement with his hand and she returned the gesture, then with a smile, she turned away.

Yet Helena's expression as the butler ushered him into the room was a mask of politeness. 'Good morning, Dr Carstairs.'

'Good morning, Mrs Faraday.'

'Thank you so much for coming and I am pleased to say that my aunt is much improved. I will take you up to her.'

And so the following fifteen minutes passed with Nicholas examining his patient with his usual professional calm, after which he agreed that she might get up, but only if she took care over the rest of the day.

'Yes I do feel tired,' she admitted, 'but so relieved that I no longer feel numb.'

He smiled down at her and glanced at a bottle by the side of the bed. 'I see you take ergot. Do you find it helps?'

'Yes I do, at least to some extent. Thank you, Dr Carstairs.'

'You are extremely welcome, Miss Standish.'

Out on the landing, Helena said, 'Are you sure there is no need for further concern?'

Nicholas shook his head. 'No, I can reassure you of that. I just wish we could find a way of preventing these attacks, they can be so debilitating.'

A few seconds later Nicholas followed Helena down the staircase, his gaze lingering on the softness of her honey-gold hair, wondering how it would look free and loose around her shoulders. But that was a pleasure he would never know. As they reached the hall where a footman was waiting to usher him out, Helena turned, saying, 'May I offer you some refreshment, Dr Carstairs? Do you have time to join me for coffee?'

He didn't hesitate. 'That would be most welcome, Mrs Faraday.'

'We will take it in the morning room please, Perkins.'

His pulse quickening, Nicholas followed her into a spacious room, the antique furniture gleaming with the patina that only age can give. He wondered what it must be like to be accustomed from birth to such graceful and civilised surroundings. His background could never be described as deprived, in fact the reverse when compared with many, but wealth such as this could only ever be inherited.

As he sat opposite her on a velvet button-backed armchair, they embarked on a dance of restrained and trivial conversation. She told him that her husband and father were at Wimbledon, they commented on the weather, talked of London; Nicholas told her that Dr Haverstock took an annual vacation in Scotland as he had been born in Edinburgh, and all the time between them was a raw emotional tension. It was a relief when there came a tap at the door and a young parlourmaid carried in a laden tray.

'Thank you, I will pour myself.' She was, he thought, the epitome of the perfect hostess. He watched Helena busy herself with the silver coffee pot, china, cream and biscuits, all the time aware of the slimness of her hands and wrists, the curve of her shoulder, the softness of her throat.

Helena's heart was pounding, her mouth dry. Surely, they should be safe now, away from curious eyes and ears. Had Nicholas realised why she had been so distant, so cool? As she passed over his coffee, she said quietly, 'It is unlikely now that we will be disturbed.'

He glanced sharply up and across at her, and with relief she saw understanding dawn.

'Nicholas, I am sorry if I have appeared...'

He gazed across at her, his eyes searching, questioning, and in her own he must have seen the answer he sought. 'Are you as bewildered as I am?'

She nodded.

His voice was intense. 'I have been haunted by you from the very first moment.'

'It has been like that for me too.'

Nicholas was slowly shaking his head. 'I can't explain it.'

'I have thought of you so many times,' she said, 'wondered whether you were perhaps engaged or...'

She couldn't stop looking at him, at tiny lines at the corner of his eyes, an endearing imperfection in one of his eyebrows. To be alone with him, how often had she dreamed of it?

'I was there, you know, among the crowd outside St Margaret's Church.'

She was startled. 'You mean you actually came to see me married?'

He nodded. 'I had the vain hope that the bride wouldn't be you, that it would be a different Helena.'

'Oh Nicholas, I'm so sorry.' Her voice was a whisper.

He wondered if it were true that some were born soul mates. She was so lovely – his gaze lingered on her throat, the slight swell of her breasts, her soft lips, how he longed to take her in his arms – but this was another man's wife and he was in that man's house. He also knew that a butler had the right to enter any room except bedrooms without knocking. Sadly, he sipped his coffee. The silence was poignant, disturbed by the sound of the clock softly chiming the hour, a reminder of time passing. With dismay, Nicholas knew that it would be inappropriate for him to remain very much longer. He leaned forward and asked gently, 'Are you happy, Helena?'

Her hesitation tore at his heart before she said in a low voice, 'Let us say that in many ways I am fortunate. Nicholas,' she raised her eyes to his, 'I can't help wondering whether we will ever see each other again.'

His eyes must have revealed the truth because she said in a small voice, 'You think it best not to, don't you?'

He tried to not to make his tone harsh. 'Helena, what would be the point? I think we are both too honourable to indulge in an illicit affair.'

Helena gazed at him, wondering if he knew how for her those words brought with them such a delicious image.

Feeling the colour rise in her cheeks, she said quietly, 'You are of course right. I feel guilty even talking to you like this. But I'm still glad to have had the chance to...'

'And so am I. I shall never forget today, Helena, never. I'm afraid I really must leave, but...' he took out his wallet and extracted a card, 'please promise to keep this – just in case you ever have need of me – and I don't mean as a doctor. Heaven forbid that you should ever be one of my patients.'

As they both stood up, Helena said, 'I would have liked you to see Rosalind, but Nanny's strict routine includes a morning airing in the park.' She attempted a smile. 'Poor child, she is taken out rain or shine.'

'It will do her no harm. And Helena, Dr Haverstock told me about her hands. I am truly sorry.'

'That is kind of you.' Slowly Helena walked across to the fireplace, only to turn before she reached for the silken bell pull. Nicholas knew that was how he would always remember her, gazing at him with pain and sadness, both of them aware that it could be for the last time.

Chapter Thirty-six

When Oliver and Jacob returned from Wimbledon relieved to find Beatrice almost completely recovered, they were full of the news that the winner of the men's final had been Norman Brookes from Australia.

'It's the first time an international player has won the tournament,' Jacob said. 'You both missed an excellent match.'

Helena was too distracted to join in the conversation. Her thoughts were full of Nicholas and their morning together in the morning room. She did sense Oliver's brooding gaze rest on her a few times, and later during dinner, she gradually became aware of a heightened tension when their eyes met. Instinctively she knew that her husband had more on his mind than praising the quality of the seven-course meal. Helena's stomach twisted in knots. After all these weeks, was Oliver going to choose tonight, when her mind and heart were full of her feelings for Nicholas? Later as Jacob and Beatrice drifted out on to the terrace to enjoy the warm evening air, she wanted to flee the room as she saw Oliver stroll across to sit beside her on the deeply cushioned sofa.

'If I may say so, my sweet,' his voice was low, his smile full of charm. 'You look especially enchanting tonight, emerald green suits you. Perhaps I should buy you a pendant to complement that dress.

'You are too kind.' Her tone was gentle but his assumption that buying her jewellery would soften her resentment towards him she found insulting. 'I think Rosalind is cutting her first tooth. I do wish, Oliver, that you would pay her a little more attention.'

'Nonsense my dear, babies are a female domain.' He paused, 'And that subject brings me to ... I wondered...'

Her reply was swift. 'I am sorry, Oliver, I'm afraid I am indisposed.'

He drew slightly back. 'That is rather unfortunate.' His eyes narrowed as he gazed at her. 'Perhaps you would be good enough to keep me informed?'

'But of course.' Helena had no qualms about her lie, nor did she have any fears that her husband would discover it. Her cycle was somewhat unsettled since her confinement. She stared down at her hands, twisting on her finger the beautiful engagement ring and slim gold band. Her lie may have given her a respite, but she knew it would only be short. There was no escaping the fact that within days, Oliver would come through the interconnecting door and she would have no alternative but to submit to him. Helena really wasn't sure whether she would be able to bear it.

The following morning, Oliver was full of adrenalin. A strategy to rid Graylings of the child he regarded as the 'cuckoo in the nest', had eluded him at first, but despite his hatred of the man,

Selwyn's wedding invitation proved opportune. Not only had it brought them all to London, but Johnnie's careless chatter prior to his departure for Italy had provided Oliver with the inspiration he needed. And today he intended to embark on the first stage of his plan.

The necessity of visiting a public market had not been an appealing one. However, the reality appalled him. Forcing himself to stare into pock-marked faces and jostled by rough shoulders, to inhale stale sweat and rank breath, Oliver immersed himself in the throng of common people. The noise was raucous, from laughter to the stall-holders yelling their wares and quarrels, shouting and cursing around him. Conscious of curious and calculating glances, he guarded his wallet and resisted the temptation to put a silk handkerchief to his nostrils. At first he had difficulty locating the type of stall he sought; there were many fruit and vegetable ones, others stinking of fish or displaying odorous looking meat, but eventually he found some that sold second-hand clothes and one that seemed suitable. Thankful of the protection of his kid gloves, he began with wariness and distaste to rummage through the garments until he found what he needed in a reasonably clean condition.

The bulbous-nosed stallholder grinned through fag-hung lips. 'Fancy dress is it, guv?'

Oliver nodded, paid for his purchases and after threading his way brusquely through other shoppers, within minutes was instructing a cab driver to take him to Smythson's in Bond Street. What the shop assistants would think of his crumpled brown paper parcel he neither knew nor cared, but he was confident that his arrival at Carlton House Terrace with an expensive leather week-end bag would cause no comment at all.

That same evening, having studied in detail a map of London, Oliver was ostensibly dining at his Club but in reality only partaking of an early cold supper before leaving for the area he had chosen. And it didn't disappoint. After walking along the streets for several minutes he found a short back street where one of the seedy early Victorian houses had misnamed itself as a private hotel; its air of general decay and flaking paint no doubt the reason for the sign declaring 'Vacancies'. Oliver stood outside for a moment, the only movement nearby from a mongrel relieving itself against a lamp-post. This, he decided, would suit him perfectly.

In the cramped reception area, the stubble-bearded man slumped behind the desk didn't even bother to glance up.

'I need a room, my man.'

In shirtsleeves and braces, he straightened up, his beetle-browed eyes narrowing at the tone, and then widening as he took in Oliver's immaculate appearance. 'Did yer say a room?'

'Yes, a room. Not to sleep in you understand. One I can use when needed.' Oliver put a hand inside his jacket where he had secreted money in an inside pocket and flung down a guinea.

There came a knowing look in the man's eyes. ''Ow long do yer want it for?'

'Possibly a few days.' Oliver held out another. 'And no questions asked.'

The money disappeared swiftly into nicotine-stained fingers and he gave a shrug before turning to a board behind him to take a key off its hook. 'No problem to me, guv! Here – number three, top of the stairs and third left.'

It was worse than Oliver could have imagined; its squalor compounded by an unpleasant fusty smell, the cheap flocked wallpaper spotted with damp. A single bed with its sagging mattress and none too clean eiderdown stood on grimy linoleum; the only furniture a scuffed chest of drawers while a limp curtain across one corner of the room served as a wardrobe. Lifting the weekend bag on to the bed and taking out the brown paper parcel, he untied its string and began to change his clothes. The material of the shirt was coarse but at least it seemed to have been recently laundered. The rough textured jacket held a slight odour and was tight across his shoulders but he doubted that a working man would be familiar with a tailor. He examined the trousers for lice, trying not to think that the material had previously touched another man's skin, and tried them on. They were slightly short and the brown well-worn shoes felt heavy, but at least they didn't pinch. He peered into a cracked mirror on the wall, but then shrugged and began to put his own clothes into the bag before locking and placing it behind the curtain. The cheap cap he kept in his hand.

With the room key safely in his pocket he went downstairs and out of the now deserted lobby to find a cab, and was at last dropped at a point a little distance from his destination. Slowly he walked along the pavements until he came to the familiar road, the one where the apartment was situated and now leased by Johnnie, and where previously Oliver had enjoyed many decadent hours in the company of the sensual Sybil. He stared up at the window for a moment, wondering for the first time what had become of her, and then after one or two abortive attempts, he managed to find a little further away and on the opposite side, an inconspicuous vantage point.

Fortunately there were few people about, but even so he was forced to employ at times such subterfuges as bending to tie a shoelace, turning to gaze at doors as if searching for an address, or walking on only to later retrace his steps. But as far as he could ascertain, and his attention was acute, so far the only person to emerge from the apartment building had been an elderly woman wearing widow's weeds. He checked his pocket watch, the glint of the gold making him curse his mistake in not having bought a cheap one.

Then after an hour, his patience was rewarded. When the glass fronted entrance door opened and a flame-haired young woman came out and began to walk along the pavement, Oliver narrowed his eyes. She was the right age and her curvaceous figure and hennaed hair certainly fitted Johnnie's description. He smiled with satisfaction. It was all in the swing of the hips; one could always tell a whore.

Oliver waited in his shadowy position until she was a short distance away. Then putting the cap on, he followed her.

Chapter Thirty-seven

Cora's spirits were high as she set off for what was quite a long walk, but which led to the pub that was becoming her favourite. She was already becoming known there and greeted with cheeky banter; but she was being true to her promise, a bit of flirting and horseplay she both allowed and encouraged, but no man would have what she gave Johnnie. After all, as she kept reminding herself, his money put clothes on her back and food in her belly. The evening in the cosy bar began like any other as she sat with Ruby who used to work there as a barmaid, until she had the bad luck to develop varicose veins.

'It was the standing,' she'd told Cora when they first met. 'I was in agony by closing-time.'

She and Cora had forged a friendship based mainly on Ruby's wicked sense of humour. Cora hadn't laughed so much since she'd left Belle's and yet again she thought how restricted and quiet her life had been since she'd taken up with Johnnie.

'I'm orf,' Ruby said eventually, heaving her bulk off the stool. 'I've got to get me old Ma to bed. Our Cissie can't do it cos she's got the 'flu.'

'See you tomorrow night, then?'

'Not if I see yer first!'

Cora laughed and watched her jostle her way through the crowd. And it was then that she noticed the tall, good-looking man in a brown suit standing just inside the door. As Ruby pushed past he glanced over towards the corner where Cora was sitting and she tilted her head and smiled, hoping to get a free drink. Slowly he began to make his way over and on reaching her small mahogany table removed his cap and said, 'Good evening, may I...?'

She shrugged. 'It's a free country.'

'Would you care for a drink?'

'I'll 'ave a port and lemon, thanks.' She spluttered as she saw him raise a hand to summon someone. 'Er. You'll 'ave to go to the bar, ducks.'

As he turned away, Cora watched him. If there was one thing she prided herself on, it was summing up men. And her waters were telling her to be on her guard, there was definitely something funny about this bloke. He didn't have an accent for a start, in fact if it wasn't for that cheap suit she would have taken him for one of the gentry. When later he returned with a port and lemon and another small glass Cora felt even more suspicious. 'Crikey, it isn't often I see a bloke with a short!'

'A short?'

'Your drink.' Was he stupid or what? She peered at it. 'What is it, anyway?'

'Vodka. I asked for vermouth but they didn't have it.'

Cora stared at him. 'What are you doing, slummin' or something?'

She saw his expression change. 'What makes you say that?'

'Look, ducks, I've never known a working man

282

order a poncy drink like that!'

He smiled across at her. 'Let's just say that I like to be different. By the way, my name is Edward but most people call me Ned. And yours is?'

'Cora. Cora Bates.'

'It's nice to meet you, Cora.'

'You're not the usual type what comes in here, I know that.' She took a sip of her drink. 'You don't fool me, few men do.'

'Now why would I want to fool you?'

'Mebbe you do, mebbe you don't.'

'Let's just say that there was someone I needed to see.'

'Looking for Ron, are you? It's a fool's game. I've never met a poor bookie, and I should know cos I've had plenty as punters. And don't pretend to be startled, I bet you'd guessed what I am. I'm not ashamed of it either. But I'm spoken for, so don't go getting any ideas.'

'There's no reason we shouldn't enjoy each other's company, is there?'

'I suppose not.' She watched as he picked up his glass. Whatever he did, it wasn't labouring, not with those hands and finger nails. 'What do you do?'

'Do?'

'For a job. I take it you do 'ave one.'

'Oh I see. I'm a clerk.'

Well, Cora thought, that could explain his soft hands and perhaps even the way he talked. 'So you're clever, then.'

He smiled at her and she felt her pulse quicken. He was a charmer and no mistake.

'Oh yes,' he said softly. 'I can assure you that I have a brain.'

'Well, don't think you're the only one. I never had no education, that's all.'

'And if you had, what would your ambition have been? For instance, if you could choose, what would you want to do with your life?'

She stared at him. He didn't seem to be the usual type who wanted to 'rescue' her from a life of sin. They usually wore a dog collar.

'I want to have me own flower shop.' The words came out sharp, challenging.

'You want to open a flower shop?'

'Yes, that's what I said – I want a flower shop. Nothing wrong with that, is there?'

He shook his head. 'It would take a fair bit of money, though.'

Her reply was short. 'I'm saving up.'

He nodded to her almost empty glass. 'Would you like another?'

'I'll 'ave the same again, seeing as you're asking.'

Cora frowned as she watched him make his way to the bar, almost seeming to hold himself apart from other people. He was a strange one and no mistake. She was not only enjoying herself, she was curious. Now what could this bloke be after, cos she'd bet a pound to a penny he wasn't in this pub by accident. If it hadn't been to find Ron or any of the other customers, then he'd come looking for something or someone else and she had a feeling it was her. And she was proved right, because as soon as soon as he returned with the drinks he said, 'You interest me, Cora. In fact I'd like to make you a proposition.'

She looked at him warily. 'I've told you, I'm not available.'

He shook his head. 'I don't mean that.' He paused, drumming his fingers on the table. 'I take it you were intending to find some premises to rent, for your flower shop I mean.'

Cora narrowed her eyes; he didn't half talk in a posh way. 'That was me idea.'

He cast a glance over his shoulder even though the cramped corner where they were sitting was reasonably private. 'How would you like the cash to buy one outright? You'd make a lot more profit and it would be cast-iron security for you.'

'I'd like to be the King's mistress, but I don't suppose I will. Where would I get that sort of money?'

Slowly he downed the rest of his drink. 'I would give it to you.'

Taken aback, she could only stare at him. Then with a grin Cora said, 'Oh yes, pull the other one.'

'You know, Cora, it never does to judge a book by its cover. Or in my case,' he said, glancing down at his suit, 'by what a man is wearing.'

Cora stared at him. 'You know you're a right mystery, you are.'

He smiled. 'Good. Let's keep it that way. But I'm serious. You help me out in a little matter, and I'll pay you...' he paused then leaned closer, 'the princely sum of one hundred pounds.'

Cora burst out laughing. 'Aw come off it, where would you get a flaming fortune like that? Look, ducks, I wasn't born yesterday.'

'I mean it. In fact I'll make it guineas.'

His tone was sharp, and no matter how Cora searched his eyes bewilderment, all she could see was steely determination. 'You can't mean that you could actually put your hands on...'

'Keep your voice down. Yes, without a doubt.'

Her mind began to race. Was this bloke an out and out nutter? Or – and she hardly dared to believe it – could he be on the level? She studied him, noting his well-cut hair and expertly trimmed moustache. Yet that suit was terrible. Cora glanced down at his shoes – they weren't much cop either. She looked across at him and held his gaze.

'Go on then, convince me.'

'Would it help if I promised to give you half of the money first and the rest once the matter is attended to?'

She stared at him in disbelief. 'Are you saying you'd give me over a hundred quid just like that?'

'Not exactly, I'm not a fool. You'd have to agree to my plan and convince me you could carry it out.'

'I see. What exactly is "this little matter"? Cos if it's robbery or some other hare-brained idea, you can forget it, money or no money.'

He shook his head. 'It's nothing like that. But I have no intention of telling you now. I'm going to give you some time to think about it. But I warn you Cora,' his eyes bored into hers and she realised that this was not a man to mess about. 'Say a word to a living soul and the deal's off.' He got up from the table. 'Remember, a chance like this comes only once in a lifetime. Do you know

St John's Church gardens?'

'Yes, of course I do.'

'I'll meet you there tomorrow at midnight.' He turned to pick up his cap. 'And don't be late.'

Stunned, Cora stared after his retreating figure certain now that she'd been the one he'd come looking for, and that was a mystery in itself. But he must be off his rocker to think she'd meet a stranger in the dark at a creepy spot like that. After all, they never did catch Jack the Ripper! Then she told herself that she was being daft, this bloke was much too young to be *him*. However, later, after she had made her way in excited confusion back to the apartment, Cora found it impossible to sleep, instead pacing the rooms in an effort to control her fevered imagination, seeing in her mind a lovely pile of golden coins, despite all her misgivings wondering what a hundred guineas would actually look like.

Chapter Thirty-eight

It had been after midnight when Helena, who was finding it difficult to sleep, heard the faint click of Oliver's bedroom door closing. He had probably been to one of the gambling clubs, but knowing that he would never risk losing Graylings, she had no fears that he might follow his cousin's example. Perhaps once Selwyn was married, even he would become more responsible, although from what Helena had heard of his future bride, Caroline

Vasey, she doubted it.

After breakfast the following morning, Oliver immersed himself behind the *Financial Times*, while Jacob declared his intention to go into the City. Beatrice, now fully recovered, with resignation went to catch up with her correspondence, and Helena followed her normal routine of going up to the top floor. The nursery had been completely refurbished, with pink and white striped wallpaper, tiny pink rosebuds edging the plain curtains, a rocking horse in one corner, and already a larger cot in readiness for when it would be needed. Nanny Evans, having travelled from Graylings accompanied by Betsy the young nursery maid, had settled in comfortably and as the door opened, glanced up from the nursing chair.

Helena smiled at her. 'Good morning, Nanny. Did she have a good night?'

'Good morning, Mrs Faraday. Yes, bless the little soul, she slept straight through.'

'That's wonderful. And she is still taking the powdered milk well?' Helena had been disappointed to cease breastfeeding so soon. She had intended to do so far longer than Oliver had insisted upon, but nature had decreed otherwise.

'There are no problems at all, Mrs Faraday.'

Helena went over to the crib. 'Hello, sweetheart,' she said softly, looking down into the blue eyes that met her own. 'Are you going to come to Mummy, then?' Lifting her little daughter into her arms, she turned. 'Perhaps you both might care to give me a little time alone with her?'

Nanny, who was forthright in her views about

spoiling children, gave a heavy sigh and rose, while Betsy, who was both excited and over-awed at being in the great city of London, scuttled after her.

Alone, Helena was able to indulge both herself and her child; to enjoy the warmth of the small body in her arms as she strolled to the window to show her baby the blue sky and the world outside, loving the scent of her, whispering how much she was loved. She paused after a few moments to gaze down at the tiny extra fingers, wondering yet again whether they would be limiting. Even if Rosalind had some talent for music, Helena was uncertain whether she would be able to master the piano. Certainly, she would have difficulty with the 'five-finger' exercises Helena had needed to practise. Would a stringed instrument be possible? 'We have so much to learn, little one,' Helena murmured as the small head nestled against her shoulder. The dusting of hair was still dark, but Nanny seemed to think it would soon change, forecasting that Rosalind would grow up to be a true English rose.

And it was then, as she nursed her child, that Helena finally faced the truth. She had to accept what she had long suspected, that her marriage had been a mistake. Swept along by girlish infatuation and a desire to please her father, Oliver had appeared so charming, had been so eligible. But Helena knew now that she didn't love him, had never really loved him; despite being the father of her child, there was something in Oliver's nature that chilled her. Yet as she looked down at her now sleeping baby, she knew that whatever happened in the future, she would never regret having Rosalind.

That evening Jacob frowned when he realised that Oliver once again planned to dine at his club. That probably meant that he would be out until all hours again, gaming. Didn't the man realise that he was now married and with a family? Raffish company and the sowing of wild oats – not that he suspected his son-in-law of the latter – was a pastime for bachelors. He himself had never had any interest in risking hard-earned money in the pursuit of such shallow pleasures. 'Rather hard luck on the ladies,' he said, 'having to put up with just my company again.'

'What's this?' Beatrice swept into the room wearing the dark green dress that did little for her sallow complexion. 'Deserting us again, Oliver?'

'I'm afraid so.' Oliver turned as Helena came in to join them and waited until the butler had poured her a glass of sherry before he said, 'Your father is right, my dear. We all need a little more stimulation. What do you think of having a dinner party?'

She smiled. 'But of course.'

Jacob rubbed his hands together. 'Now that is an excellent idea. With your approval, Oliver, there are a couple of parliamentary members I would rather like to invite, naturally in the company of their wives.'

'I did hear that Mrs Shirley is in town, staying with her sister,' Beatrice said. 'Do you remember her, Jacob. We met her at Graylings?'

'I do indeed, a delightful woman.'

'And could I suggest that nice young doctor who came?'

They all stared at Beatrice in astonishment.

'Don't look at me like that,' she said. 'If I remember correctly, Oliver, Dr Haverstock dined with you at Graylings.'

'That is true, but it was unavoidable.'

'And did he eat peas from his knife?'

Jacob exploded into laughter. 'Beatrice, I do believe you're becoming a Socialist.'

She glared at him. 'Heaven forbid. I just thought that Dr Carstairs was an excellent young man.'

'That may be so,' Oliver's voice was firm. 'But I think not, Beatrice.'

Helena, who had listened to the conversation with growing horror, felt almost giddy with relief. No matter how she longed to see Nicholas again, the prospect of being in the same room, dining at the same table, all the time conscious of Oliver's scrutiny and her father and aunt's perceptiveness – she could never have kept up such a pretence.

'And you, my sweet, do you have anyone in mind?'

'I'm wondering if Peregrine is in London. Why don't I invite Dorothy to spend a few days with us?'

'There,' Oliver said, 'we are already compiling a list of guests. So shall we agree on a date?'

Cora had decided to go. Hadn't she struggled to save every penny these past years, concealing her hoard of coins behind that loose brick in her bedroom at Belle's? Only the week before she had discovered in the library a book called *Starting your*

291

own Business. Cora had not only learned about such terms as cash flow and overheads; there had been a whole chapter devoted to the dangers of venturing into business with too little capital. And she knew that the sum she had – she knew the amount to the last farthing – fell far short of what would be needed. Cora had no illusions about men like Johnnie. He was a decent sort and she was fond of him, but she knew that he would tire of her after a while and then it would be back to Belle's. She was well aware what her future held. The 'mirror dread' would begin. All the girls suffered from it. Every year laid its stamp on the complexion, and soon a body would begin to thicken, its breasts sag. Belle was strict about standards. What would follow could be the streets and Cora was determined that would never happen. So, she had decided. St John's Church gardens it would be. But she was wary enough to secrete a sharp pair of scissors in the pocket of one of her 'sensible' skirts. A girl could do a lot of damage with a pair of scissors.

She could see him in the distance, standing before the railings. There was no one else around and as she walked towards him, a match flared in his fingers as he lit a cigarette. 'I thought you would come.'

'You've been proved right, then.'

'You haven't talked to anyone?'

She shook her head.

'Good. So I take it that you're interested in my proposition?'

Cora squared her shoulders. 'I don't know what it is yet. But before you tell me, I want to know why you came looking for me. And don't deny it either.'

'I have no intention of doing so. I knew you were ambitious. However, it would betray a confidence to explain further.'

Cora decided that it could easily have been one of her punters. A couple of glasses of bubbly did sometimes make her careless. She held out her hand. 'Show me, then.'

'What do you mean?'

'Show me the guineas. Prove to me you're telling the truth.'

'Really, Cora, you have very little trust in people.'

Her voice was quiet, determined. 'Show me.'

She stepped back as he put a hand into his inside pocket, her own closing around the scissors. Cora stared down at the golden coins in his hand.

'Satisfied?'

She nodded.

'So now I want you to listen. And don't either interrupt or argue.'

They stood a few feet from each other beneath the branches of an overhanging tree. His words were steady, his explanation clear. Cora was under no illusion about what he planned to do. 'A hundred guineas,' he said. 'Think of it, Cora. Think how it would change your life.'

She took a shaky breath. 'But...'

He held up a hand. 'I have done my research, the plan is foolproof. But you can see now why I need your help. A few hours of your time, Cora, that is all I ask.' He moved closer to her. 'Now you wouldn't ever think of going to the police, would you?'

'I'd cut me wrists before I'd get involved with *them*.'

'Good. Now I want you to think about it very carefully, especially your part in the plan. When you describe to me what you've concocted, I will give you the first half of the money.' He began to turn away, saying over his shoulder, 'I'll be here for your answer at the same time two days from now.'

Cora, shaken by what she had just heard, closed her eyes as she leaned back against the railings. In a silence broken only by the hoot of an owl, she knew to her shame that she was tempted. Into her mind came the phrase 'thirty pieces of silver', thundered from the pulpit on the one and only time when out of curiosity, she had gone to a church service. Cora was often devious and many times in her life, she had used cunning, but she had never done anything remotely like this. Yet even as she began to make her way back to the apartment, her feelings of shock was lessening. Cora's conscience might be troubled, she might even be afraid, but this daring scheme held the key not only to realising her dream, but to securing her future.

And almost to her horror, by the time that the light of dawn came filtering through the curtains, she had made her decision.

Chapter Thirty-nine

'Why have we come to this dump?' Sybil wrinkled her nose in distaste as she saw the cracked oilcloth on the tables and the peeling green paint on the walls.

'Because it's half-empty.' Cora led the way to a corner and sat with her back to the few other customers. She couldn't afford to take any chances; it wouldn't be the first time a nosy type had tried to eavesdrop by lip-reading.

'I'm not surprised, a bit of soap and water wouldn't go amiss.' Sybil took the chair opposite and after a disdainful glance at the floor kept her handbag on her lap. 'I suppose you must have a reason for coming in here, but I can't think what.'

'I need to talk to you – in private.' She turned as a slovenly waitress shuffled up, 'Two teas, love.' Cora waited until she'd left and then said, 'But we'll keep our voices down.'

'I do like a mystery. Go on, girl.'

Cora gazed across at her – the shadows beneath Sybil's eyes were more marked every time they met. 'First of all, do you still want to get out of Belle's?'

'I'd give me eye teeth for it.'

'Maybe, but would you be willing to take a risk, do something against the law?'

Sybil frowned. 'How do yer mean?'

Cora leaned forward. 'I've had a proposition.'

'I thought you were well set up with Johnnie.'

'Not that sort you daft cow.'

'What then?'

Cora bit her lip. She didn't know how she was going to put this. 'The other night I met this bloke in the pub...' Lowering her voice even further she began to talk, all the time aware of the growing shock in her friend's eyes. And she had to admit that when she was forced to put it into words...

Sybil's reaction was instant. 'Come off it, he offered to give you that much money? It's a bleedin fortune! You must 'ave been three sheets to the wind.'

'I'm telling you. It's God's honest truth. Ssh...'

They drew back as the waitress slopped in front of them two earthenware beakers. Cora began to spoon sugar into hers and looked at her friend. 'Sybil, he's on the level. He showed me some of the guineas.'

'What, in the pub?'

'He's not that daft.' She told her about meeting Ned again at St John's Church gardens.

'You stupid bugger, you weren't 'alf taking a risk.' Sybil sipped at her tea and pulled a face. 'Stewed, didn't I warn you this was a dump?' She put the beaker down. 'So, did he give you any more details? About what he wanted you to do? Not that I don't find it all a bit much to take in. But you're nobody's fool, Cora, so he's either a damn good actor or as you said, he's on the level.'

'Oh yes, he told me. And it knocked me for six, I can tell you. In fact I nearly told him where to go, but he gave me time to think about it – clever devil. Can you just imagine, Syb, what it would be like, not having to be beholden to anyone, knowing your future's secure?'

Sybil looked wistful. 'I can certainly understand you being tempted.'

'Well, anyway, I went to meet him again and said I'd do it.'

'You haven't told me what it is yet.'

'I will in a minute. The thing is I need someone to help me, someone I can trust. And that's where you come in. I'd make it worth your while, Syb. I'd pay you half – forty guineas.' Cora had told Sybil that Ned had offered eighty guineas. Not that she had any qualms about that. After all, she'd been the one Ned had come looking for, and she was going to be the brains behind the venture.

Sybil was staring at her in disbelief. 'Forty guineas, you'd give me forty guineas?'

Cora took a sip of her tea. 'It'd be more than enough for you to leave Belle's. Besides, I've been saving up for years. I've got a bit put away, and with what Ned gives me I'm goin' to get a flower shop and live on the premises. You could share if you like, we could even work together.'

'But I don't know nuthin' about flowers.'

'I do, I used to work on a flower stall.'

'I can't believe it,' Sybil brushed away tears. 'I never thought I'd ever get the chance ter... I'm sick of men and their mucky ways.'

Cora leaned over and touched her hand. 'Honestly, Syb, I really do think we could do this.'

'But you still 'aven't told me what it is. It ain't anything violent, is it? I've known folk murdered

297

for less. If so, I'm having no part of it, money or no money.'

'What do you take me for?'

'What is it, then?'

'First of all, are you interested?'

Sybil straightened her shoulders. 'I'm interested all right. But I'm still waiting to hear what I'd 'ave to do.'

Cora looked at the other girl's crimson dress with its plunging neckline, at her hat with gaudy feathers. 'Wear something different for a start, and now – promise on yer mother's deathbed not to breathe a word to anyone...'

The following morning, the two young women walked with some trepidation along The Mall, and eventually paused outside the large ornate gates to St James's Park.

Sybil glanced nervously over her shoulder. 'Are you sure this is the right place?'

'St James's Park, that's what he said.'

'It's a flaming posh area.'

Cora took her arm. 'Come on, we can't stand outside all day.' Even she felt some trepidation as they went through the entrance and saw the stretches of closely-cut grass, glorious flowerbeds and the glint of water from the lake in the distance. 'Now this is what I call a park.'

'Not for the likes of us, though.'

Cora glanced first at Sybil's lilac skirt and blouse bought yesterday from the market, and then down at her own navy skirt and high-necked white blouse. 'Dress subdued, Ned said, though these other women look like fashion plates. At least we look respectable, and that's what he wanted. I suppose his boss must live close by.'

'He won't be short of a bob or two, then,' Sybil said. 'Which way do you think we should go?'

Cora considered and then decided to head towards the lake. 'Poor sod, Ned's boss I mean. Fancy finding out your kid is somebody else's. Ever likely he wants rid.'

Sybil shuddered. 'It sounds awful when you put it like that. Are you sure we should be doing this, Cora?'

'Don't start that again,' Cora said. 'I've told you, I'll ask Ned the question tonight, I promise. I want to know the answer as much as you do. But what we need to do now is to spy out the land. So we'll just stroll along like two respectable married women.'

Sybil held out her left hand. 'At first glance you can't tell this is just a curtain ring.'

'You'd soon find out if you wore it a lot and your finger went green. Now remember, we're looking for a middle-aged nanny in a grey uniform, pushing a navy Silver Cross pram. He said there's likely to be other nannies out walking, but the one we want is plump and she always comes just after eleven o'clock. Oh and she wears a flower in her lapel, apparently the mother likes the baby to look up at nice things.'

Sybil came to a stop. 'Aw Cora, I don't like the sound of it.'

'Look, you were brought up in a place not too different from where we're supposed to take the kid to. I was brought up in the workhouse. We survived, didn't we?' Cora was looking around her as they walked further into the park. 'What we're looking for is somewhere I can't be seen from the path, somewhere near an entrance.'

'And all I'll have to do after is slip away?'

'That's the plan. I reckon the nanny will be too busy squawkin ter notice.'

Sybil's face was mutinous. 'I still feel sorry for the mother.'

Cora's reply was short. 'Maybe, but I bet she's never done a day's work in her life, and she can 'ave other kids. We'll never get another chance like this.' She glanced sharply at her friend. 'You're not getting cold feet?'

She shook her head. 'No, I won't let you down, not now I've given me word. But you're to ask him, you know, what we talked about?'

'Don't worry, I will.' Cora nudged her. 'Hey look over there on that island. They're pelicans aren't they? I've only ever seen pictures of them in a book.'

Sybil shielded her eyes against the sun. 'Fancy that. It's really beautiful 'ere, Cora.'

'Yes, well we haven't come to admire the scenery. Hang on, I think that's her, coming straight towards us.' She glanced at the fob watch Johnnie had bought her. 'And she's dead on time.'

The buxom nanny, her stride slow but steady, glanced over to them as the two young women passed by, and as she gave a slight nod of acknowledgement, Cora smiled and inclined her head. Once they had strolled on, she whispered, 'Would you recognise her again, even without the flower?'

Sybil nodded. 'I'll know her. She reminds me of

that landlady I had, the one I reckon pinched my stuff.'

'Right, let's turn round.'

They followed at a discreet distance as the nanny walked for at least twenty minutes. Although she gave a nod to a few other nannies she passed, Cora noted that not once did she stop to chat.

'Do you think she always takes the same route?'

'That's what we'll need to find out, Syb. Depending on what Ned says tonight, we'll come back tomorrow and the next day. Remember – no paint or powder, and iron your blouse and skirt before you come.'

'Belle's goin to wonder what I'm up to.'

'Tell 'er you're off to visit a sick friend.' Cora slowed down. 'Look out, she's leaving.'

They waited until the nanny had disappeared and after a few minutes went out of the gates and began the long walk back to the nearest tram stop. Sybil was quiet on the journey, and Cora too felt thoughtful. When the time came to part and to make arrangements to meet the following day, she said, 'Don't worry, Syb. I'll ask him the question.'

She watched her friend walk away, aware of how reluctant Sybil was to face the night's work at Belle's, and of how fierce her hope of escape. And so is my hope of achieving my dream, she thought. But there is a limit as to what even I would do for money. This morning, actually being in the park, had made the whole venture seem far more real, and she felt her first flicker of fear. What if it all went wrong...?

301

Chapter Forty

That same day at Faraday House, luncheon had been a family affair. Oliver had gone out immediately after breakfast and with Parliament now in recess, Jacob was able to enjoy some relaxation. Yet afterwards when they were taking their coffee in the drawing room, his expression was so serious and thoughtful that Helena glanced across at him with concern.

'You look worried, Papa. Are there problems at Broadway Manor or with your business?'

'No, it's nothing of that sort.' Jacob hesitated. 'I was just thinking that perhaps this is an ideal opportunity – while there are just the three of us – for me to raise a certain matter, one that has been much on my mind.'

Beatrice replaced her cup and saucer on the coffee table and gazed across at him. 'We're listening, Jacob.' She smiled reassuringly at him.

He looked at Helena who was sitting opposite. 'My dear, I don't think you will be surprised at my confessing that I have lately been feeling rather concerned about your marriage. I was the one who encouraged the match and from my own observations, plus what you have told me, it now appears that Oliver has characteristics that are, how shall we say, rather unfortunate?'

'There's no need to worry, Papa, truly.'

'That may be so, at least to some extent. But I

do find it difficult, as I am sure you do, to tolerate his coldness towards little Rosalind.' There was a pause. 'One of my fellow members was a physician before he entered the House and I took the liberty of consulting him – in a non-professional way, of course. I merely mentioned being puzzled about a friend of mine.' Then in a quiet but steady voice he said, 'Tell me, have either of you heard of the term, "cacaphobia"?'

Feeling somewhat bewildered, Helena shook her head.

Beatrice frowned. 'No, I don't think I have ever come across it. What does it mean?'

'Let me just say that when I explained this so-called friend's aversion to any type of disfigurement, how he surrounded himself only with good looking servants, that even paintings of his ancestors were concealed if their faces had the slightest blemish, there was no hesitation.' Jacob's expression was sad but resigned as he turned to his daughter. 'It would seem that we, certainly in the case of your aunt and I, have been somewhat judgmental. The truth is that Oliver could be suffering from cacaphobia, a recognised medical condition. The name stems from the Greek word *kakos*.'

Beatrice looked puzzled. 'And exactly what does *kakos* mean?'

Jacob's answer was short. 'It translates as ugliness, and so cacaphobia is...'

'A phobia,' Helena said slowly, 'a fear of ugliness.' Shaken, she stared at him. 'You mean – that his unreasonable behaviour is something he cannot help, that it is a form of illness?'

'I wouldn't call it an illness exactly, more of a severe phobia.'

She was still feeling stunned. 'And yet he has never mentioned it.'

'A man is loath to admit to a weakness, Helena. It could even be that he isn't aware that it *is* a medical condition.'

'I have certainly never heard of such a thing,' Beatrice admitted.

'I imagine that not many people have.'

'And is there any treatment or cure for it?' Helena's voice was tense. If only Oliver could see beyond Rosalind's flawed hands.

But Jacob was shaking his head. 'Apparently not, at least at present. But I'm told that in medical circles, not least because of Dr Sigmund Freud's writings, that there is an increasing interest in psychology. So perhaps one day in the future...'

'Oliver would never admit to it,' Helena was adamant. 'He would not countenance any discussion whatsoever.'

Jacob gave a heavy sigh. 'I fear I have to agree with you.'

Beatrice said with dismay, 'Do you think Dr Haverstock knows of it?'

Jacob stroked his beard and frowned. 'Possibly not, after all it was several instances that aroused my suspicions, and he would not have the advantage of those.'

There was a short silence before Helena said, 'I suppose I ought to have felt some sympathy for his attitude rather than resentment.'

Jacob shook his head. 'You have nothing to

blame yourself for, Helena. How could you have known?'

Helena refused to regard Rosalind's tiny hands as any form of ugliness but as several minutes later she went upstairs to the nursery, she did wonder whether this new knowledge might help her to understand her husband more. She might never know the joy of sharing her life with Nicholas, but maybe if she could persuade Oliver to be a loving father... But as she crossed the landing and glanced towards her husband's bedroom, Helena couldn't help feeling that same familiar dread...

Cora had spent the evening at home. Tired after returning from St James's Park, she wanted time to recover her energy before she ventured out to meet Ned. And as in the darkness she walked along the pavement to the deserted St John's Church gardens, she could see him standing before the railings, the end of his cigarette smouldering. As she drew near, he stubbed it out with the toe of his shoe. 'You're late.'

'Not much – only about five minutes.'

He frowned. 'Timing is of the utmost importance, Cora. Tell me, the accomplice we discussed, you have found one?'

'Yes, and she can be trusted.'

'You have kept your word, she hasn't come with you?' He moved further out on the pavement and looked both ways up the road.

'You don't need to worry. I'm on my own. And while we're on the subject,' Cora lifted her chin with defiance. 'That night in the pub you promised to give me one hundred guineas. You didn't mention I'd 'ave to fork out to pay somebody else.'

She saw his eyes narrow. 'How much are you going to be out of pocket?'

Cora thought swiftly. This bloke wasn't one to try and fool but she could risk adding on another ten. 'I promised her fifty guineas.'

After a pause he said, 'Then I suppose I shall have to reimburse you.'

'I've got a question to ask you.' Cora's tone became hard. 'We want – my friend and me, ter know more about it.'

He drew back slightly. 'What do you mean?'

'Where I'm to take the kid; if it's the sort of place those two women ran in East Finchley – you know that Amelia Sachs and her pal Annie Walters – well, hanging was too good for 'em. And I'm telling you now, I'll 'ave no part in baby killing.'

Oliver stared down at her in indescribable horror. That such a creature as Cora could believe him capable of being involved in murder. His plan might be an appalling one, but never could it be compared to that.

His voice was harsh. 'What sort of monster do you take me for?'

'You're doing what your boss wants, and getting paid a fair sum for it I'll be bound. He could be a right bad lot for all I know. I'm just saying,' Cora said with stubbornness. 'I want a few more details.'

'All right, I'll tell you. You'll be taking the baby to a house in Wandsworth – one with an excellent reputation. You can rest assured that she will be well cared for and eventually placed in recommended and respectable service.'

'So it's a girl, then?'

Oliver nodded and watched Cora turn over the information in her mind. He saw no reason to mention that Rosalind would almost immediately be taken out of the country. Even he had been surprised at the ease with which a few discreet enquiries at his Club had elicited the information he needed.

'All right, then,' Cora gave a brisk nod. 'I'll do it.'

He had never doubted that she would. 'Excellent. Now did you identify the nanny?'

'Yes, we picked her out early.'

'So carry on checking her route and meet me here again on Saturday night. I shall then give you the first half of the money, fifty guineas for you and twenty-five for your friend.'

'And we'll want it all in coins. Notes get more noticed, they'd draw attention.'

'I had anticipated that.' He paused. 'I want you to make your first try on Monday. Be sure to wait for the right opportunity, though. We can't risk other people being around.'

'You needn't worry, I'll be careful.'

He remained by the railings watching until Cora was out of sight, then twenty minutes later using his late-night key he entered the empty and now familiar hotel lobby and went up to his room to change, welcoming the coolness of his own fine lawn shirt. Then he paused and stared into the cracked mirror. No, he was not a monster. Helena had been guilty of betrayal, of trying to foist her black-haired bastard on him. No man of honour could be expected to accept such a slur. Yet as he stood in the shabby room, even he had qualms now that the actual time was approaching. Then he hardened his heart. Yes, she would be devastated at first, but once he had impregnated her, once his young wife had another child and this time a perfect one, she would soon forget the first. With a shrug Oliver completed dressing, packed the second-hand clothes away and placed the leather bag behind the curtain, then turning to leave the dingy room, paused at the door and glanced back. It was his profound hope that soon he would be making his final visit and this whole necessary but unpleasant episode would be over.

Chapter Forty-one

Dorothy arrived at Faraday House the day before the dinner party but brought with her news that because her mother was unwell, her stay would of necessity need to be short.

'In all honesty,' she said to Helena as they relaxed over tea, 'Papa is useless in the sick room. He hovers in the doorway for a couple of seconds and cannot escape quickly enough. Truly, he's much better with dogs than he is with people.'

'But your mother's illness is not serious, I hope?'

Dorothy shook her head. 'Not life-threatening, thank goodness. As you know, she was weakened by scarlet fever as a child and sometimes has these episodes of ill-health.'

'At least you'll be seeing Peregrine tomorrow.' Helena smiled at her friend. 'I still can't believe you're actually engaged.'

Dorothy held out her left hand, admiring the sparkling emerald. 'Yes and there was I, the veritable bluestocking. But we're terribly well suited, Helena, and he's completely supportive of my work for the WSPU.'

'What about Hugh, has he found a suitable wife yet?'

'My dear brother has never recovered from his dashed hopes concerning you.'

Helena smiled. 'You do talk tosh. But let us go up to the nursery so that I can show you Rosalind.'

The following morning after persuading Beatrice not to wear her favourite green dress that evening, Helena went up to the nursery to examine the pile of outgrown baby clothes she had instructed Nanny to lay out. Betsy greeted her with a shy curtsey.

'I thought,' Helena said, 'that while Nanny is out at the park, you and I could decide which of these Ida would find useful. I know you have never met her, but she was parlourmaid at Broadway Manor for years before she married a soldier from the nearby barracks. Her first baby is due next month.' She was hoping to build Betsy's confidence, which tended to be swamped by Nanny's stronger personality.

The young girl's face flushed with pleasure at

having her opinion sought.

'And afterwards,' Helena said, 'perhaps you could make up the parcel and take it to Miss Beatrice's maid. And could you ask her to pass on a message?'

'Yes, of course, Madam.'

'Please could you say that I intend before the end of the summer to come to Broadway Manor for a few weeks. And that I'm looking forward to showing Rosalind to everyone.'

The dinner party was a resounding success. Jacob's two colleagues at the House proved to be good conversationalists and Angela Shirley discovered an earlier acquaintance with one of their wives. Peregrine's easy charm always added to any occasion, and afterwards taking a seat beside Dorothy on one of the deep-cushioned sofas in the drawing room, Helena decided that she was now free to relax.

'I find the custom of "ladies withdrawing" extremely irritating,' Dorothy complained. 'Why should it be assumed that serious topics are of no interest to us?'

'And what serious topic would you raise?' Helena said, smiling at her friend.

'Women's suffrage of course – did I tell you that I'm going to hear Mrs Pankhurst speak tomorrow morning? There are four MPs in that dining room smoking cigars and drinking port, yet I have to sit here with the women. And of course the rule is no politics over dinner. You do know the reason given for depriving us of our right to vote – that as women we would be unable to understand how Parliament works!'

'They can't really believe that, it's ridiculous.'

'I suspect the reality is a fear of their wives' intelligence. If it were to appear superior to their own, where would be the deference they demand?'

Helena glanced across the room to see one of the parliamentary wives stiffen. 'Dorothy, I think you're ruffling someone's feathers.'

'I don't care, to be honest. What ruffles mine is that some *women* oppose our fight. Can you believe that?'

Helena bit her lip. 'I know. Even Aunt Beatrice feels that giving women the vote will change the fabric of society.'

'And how do you feel? I know you support us, but...'

'They should never have inflicted prison on Annie Kenney for nothing more than trying to stand up for women's rights. Even I can understand why some are reluctant to be militant, but I fiercely defend their right to have that freedom.'

Oliver was finding the evening a welcome distraction. The seedy hotel, the furtive meetings at St John's Church gardens seemed a world away from this civilised gathering of well-dressed men and stylish women. Even Beatrice seemed to have made an effort and looked almost passable in a pink-coloured gown. Now, as he entered a drawing room alive with the murmur of conversation and the sound of laughter, he saw that Helena was leaving Dorothy's side and going to converse with Mrs Shirley. It was then as he saw

Jacob stroll over to join his daughter that Oliver realised how much he missed Johnnie's artless chatter. His last postcard from Tuscany had mentioned 'the delightful Selina', and Oliver was hoping that at last his friend might cease hankering after Cora. Once he had paid her off, Oliver was hoping neither to see her, nor hear her name mentioned ever again.

As he stood leaning nonchalantly against the mantelpiece he returned his attention to his young wife. In shimmering blue silk with a revealing décolletage, she would be a temptation to any red-blooded man. As she had been to the music tutor – it had not been difficult to use his influence to make the fellow's life untenable; the man would never return to England. And if all went well, very shortly neither would his bastard. No, that regrettable episode could now be relegated to the past; not that Oliver would not find some subtle way of causing Helena to regret it.

It was then that she turned and saw him staring at her. For one moment she hesitated, and then gave a small smile. Oliver inclined his head, aware with satisfaction of a definite thaw in her coolness towards him. However, it was true what they said – revenge was better cold. When stricken with grief she turned to him for comfort and affection – then he would take her.

Chapter Forty-two

On that same evening, Nicholas was also enjoying a dinner party where he found himself the centre of attention of not only one, but two attractive young ladies. The whole scene was being watched with considerable amusement by Andrew Haverstock, whose motive behind the invitation to dinner had, Nicholas now realised, been far from an innocent one.

Elspeth and Louise Murray were the twenty-year old daughters of Mrs Haverstock's cousin who together with her husband, a professor at Aberdeen University, were spending the summer in London. Nicholas supposed that as he was a bachelor becoming established in his profession, he would naturally be regarded as a possible and eligible husband. And even he had to admit that the light-hearted repartee and flirtatious teasing being directed at him was rather a pleasurable experience.

So in the drawing room while the two cousins indulged in gossip, Andrew and the professor settled down to concentrate on the Oriental ebony chess set that had belonged to Andrew's father. Nicholas, seated between the two girls, was forced to indulge in the type of conversation he had always considered vacuous socialising.

'Tell me, Dr Carstairs, do you think we are alike?' Elspeth smiled at him, her lips curving in a way that hinted at humour.

'If you mean would I describe you as identical twins, then I have to admit that I wouldn't.'

'So,' now it was Louise leaning forward, 'please do describe to us what you see as our differences?'

Nicholas glanced helplessly at his nearby colleague, but Andrew merely stroked his beard and moved his knight to a threatening position.

Louise said, 'Don't you think that my profile is more appealing?' She turned her head sideways.

Nicholas laughed and decided to join in the spirit of the thing.

'I'm not sure. Perhaps Miss Elspeth would care to adopt the same pose?'

She promptly obeyed.

'No,' he said, 'I think you are both equally perfect.'

Elspeth raised a perfectly arched eyebrow. 'But as you don't consider us identical there must be something you consider different.'

Nicholas smiled at her and then studied them, thankful that they were not dressed alike, a practice he thought ludicrous in adults. 'I think it's more a matter of character.'

They spoke simultaneously. 'Oh, please do explain.'

Nicholas turned to see both the professor and Andrew grinning at him. Then he looked at Elspeth and Louise and saw that their flirtatious manner belied two pairs of rather fine eyes. 'Would you like me to be completely truthful?'

They both nodded. Nicholas looked first at Elspeth who he considered the more handsome of the two, seeing a determination in the set of her mouth, a tilt to her head. 'I think you are a young lady of perhaps strong opinions and even a little temperamental?'

Louise said eagerly, 'But that's exactly right! Now Dr Carstairs, please describe the way you see me.'

Nicholas regarded the candour in her gaze, the way her hands were folded neatly on her lap, 'And you, Miss Louise, I feel would be rather a tranquil person to be with.'

'And that is true too,' Elspeth said. 'Really, Dr Carstairs, you are quite brilliant.' As she smiled at him, something in her manner reminded him of Helena. Elspeth's hair might be auburn rather than honey-gold, she might have a scattering of light freckles, but he could sense that same underlying strength.

Andrew, in triumphant mood from having achieved a rapid checkmate, was now rising from his chair. 'I think, my dears, that you have monopolised my colleague quite enough. Would you care to equal my performance, Nicholas? Although the professor will now be on his mettle?'

'That is a challenge I cannot resist.' As Nicholas got up to move to the low chess table, he found his gaze lingering on the two young women. And later that evening, as he sat in a cab listening to the rhythmic sound of trotting hooves, Nicholas stared out of the window at the passing London streets and thought that perhaps there came a time in a man's life when comfort and clean laundry were not enough. He had never felt like this before, always there had been his work to occupy his mind, his ambitions to realise. And during these past eighteen months, in fact from the first moment he had seen Helena, he had never had any inclination to seek other feminine company. Surely now the time had come to abandon what had always been a futile dream.

It was with a jolt that he realised the driver had drawn to a halt, and after paying him, Nicholas inserted his key in the heavy door, glanced at the one on the other side of the wide hall that belonged to a reclusive writer and went into his own silent rooms. Perhaps it was because of those tender moments he had spent with Helena, the wonderful sense of closeness and warmth he had felt, that the old saying 'man is not meant to live alone' suddenly seemed a poignant one.

When on Saturday night Cora left Ned outside St John's Church gardens, she kept close to hedges and walls as she began to make her way back along the deserted road. The guineas were heavy in the small hessian sack she'd hidden in the carpet bag she was clutching to her chest. Part of a soiled blouse protruded from the top and it was her hope that it would look as if she was carrying dirty laundry. London born and bred, and used to living in what many would consider risky areas, she had long overcome any tendency to feel nervous when walking its streets; but tonight her heart pounded with apprehension. Forcing herself not to hurry or to lower her head in a furtive or timid way, nevertheless her gaze was wary, her shoulders hunched. And up one sleeve, easily accessible, Cora had secreted a knife.

But she received few curious glances, dressed as she was in her sober skirt and her face devoid of paint, and with profound relief she reached her apartment building safely and seconds later was inside her own door. She secured the apartment and only then took out the hessian bag, carefully tipping out the golden stream of guineas on to the square mahogany table. Some rolled and some scattered, but most lay in a gleaming pile. She picked one up and putting between her front teeth, bit hard. Then she began counting. The amount was exactly as Ned had promised. Fifty guineas for her, and twenty-five – Cora would give her twenty – for Sybil.

Cora took a deep breath and went over to the sideboard where a decanter and glasses stood in readiness for whenever Johnnie decided to return. She didn't care much for brandy, but tonight she welcomed the burning sensation in her throat of the golden liquid, hoping it would steady her nerves. Now desperate for sleep, she needed the unwanted thoughts to stop circling in her mind. Tomorrow she would meet Sybil and pass over her share of the money, because her friend's conscience might be more fragile, but once she had taken the guineas then there could be no going back.

Oliver hadn't walked away from St John's Church gardens immediately. He had watched Cora make her way along the pavement, remembering the glitter of avarice in her eyes when he had, as she demanded, allowed her to look inside the hessian bag. He had no fears that she would not reach her apartment in safety; Johnnie's paramour was a young woman who knew how to look after herself. He had agreed to her demand that the final payment should be made immediately she had fulfilled her part of the bargain. There would be only one brief time he would stand outside these gardens, one more time he would have to wear these disgusting clothes. Oliver knew that he had been fortunate at the hotel, the late hour of his arrival and departure had so far meant that he had never encountered any other guest. All he would need to do was to change into his own clothes, settle his final bill and take with him the leather weekend bag, which together with its contents he would dispose of with stealth. He could foresee no problems. At least not here, he thought with grim trepidation. But within a few days from now Faraday House would be in turmoil.

Chapter Forty-three

When on Monday morning the blue brocade curtains were drawn back, Helena shielded her eyes from the early sun. 'Good morning, Jane, it looks a lovely day.'

'Indeed it is, Madam.'

But as her maid brought over the bed-tray with its china pot of hot chocolate, Helena sensed that she was distracted and guessed that the subject of her thoughts was Oliver's valet. The romance that had begun fifteen months ago in Italy had never

318

wavered, but although both were circumspect, Helena knew that her husband would never tolerate a married couple on his staff. Tempted to probe, she resisted, knowing that Jane would confide in her when she felt the need to. Instead, taking an appreciative sip of her sweet chocolate, Helena said, 'I shall be sorry to see Miss Dorothy leave this afternoon. I've so enjoyed having her here.'

'According to her maid, she will be loath to go.'

Later when Helena went down to the breakfast room she found that everyone else was already there. Oliver glanced up. 'Good morning, my sweet. I can recommend the kidneys.'

'You know I never eat them. Good morning everyone, I am sorry I'm a little late.' She went to the sideboard and after surveying the array of dishes, helped herself to crispy bacon, scrambled eggs and grilled tomatoes. Carrying them to the table, she said, 'It's such a lovely morning, Dorothy. I thought that perhaps you and I could take Rosalind for her airing in the park this morning, instead of Nanny. You know she takes her rain or shine, at eleven o'clock precisely.'

Dorothy looked up with eagerness. 'Yes of course. I've never actually pushed a perambulator.'

Helena laughed. 'Oh, I don't think you need special training. In fact, I think I might decide to do so every day from now on. I would find it most enjoyable.'

Oliver was stunned. Of all eventualities that might interfere with his plan, he had not foreseen this one. Shock and desperation froze his mind

319

and then inadvertently Beatrice came to his rescue.

'Helena, my dear, the notion is most unsuitable. May I remind you that Mrs Shirley is calling this morning? As for your suggestion that you should wheel out Rosalind yourself on a regular basis, have you thought that you would be depriving Nanny? Here in London she is restricted in fresh air and exercise.'

Oliver held his breath, his gaze lowered to his plate.

'Oh I'm sorry, Aunt Beatrice,. Helena was penitent. 'I had forgotten about Mrs Shirley. And you are right of course about Nanny. Never mind, it was a nice idea but as you say, hardly practicable.'

Monday morning dawned for Cora with sickening reality. She opened her eyes to stare at the wardrobe that dominated one corner of the room. Secreted inside the crown of a hat and buried beneath layers of tissue paper, lay the hessian bag of guineas. Its presence seemed almost threatening although Ned had minimised the risks of the 'enterprise', insisting that if she took the precautions he'd specified it was unlikely that anything would go wrong. But Cora wasn't so sure. And he wouldn't be the one going to prison.

But it was too late now to give in to doubts. Cora forced herself to eat buttered toast and to drink a small cup of tea, wishing she was a smoker. People did say that it calmed the nerves. She could only hope that the whole flaming business could be finished with this morning, otherwise she would have to face waking up yet again with this awful dread in the pit of her stomach. She washed up the dishes and, knowing that she could postpone things no longer, went to get ready. Half an hour later, the mirror told her that not even Johnnie would recognise her. In second-hand rimless spectacles and a mousy wig, she looked positively plain, while her dull grey clothes and prim velour hat would attract no-one's attention.

When she went to meet Sybil, Cora saw that she too had made a success of her disguise. The wig beneath her hat was pale ginger – pepper and salt really with its flecks of grey – but distinctive enough to throw suspicion in a different direction. Her clothes, like Cora's, were almost colourless, neither wearing what they had worn on previous visits to St James's Park. Luckily, they had both managed to find all of the items cheaply in the market, regarding them with reluctance as a necessary expense.

'It's arrived then,' was Sybil's greeting.

Cora nodded. 'You've got it all in yer head?'

'Thought of nothing else all weekend.'

The two young women boarded a tram and sat in silence on the journey. Cora's stomach was twisted in knots and she guessed that her friend's was the same. But they couldn't risk talking, not even a whisper of what they planned to do. It was wisest to keep calm, quiet, like soldiers before a battle; Cora doubted that when they were preparing to charge they talked much either.

Their arrival at the park was an early one. Cora wanted to seize the chance to explore the perfect spot to hide in the bushes near the previously chosen entrance. And she needed to do so before the 'nanny brigade' turned out. And so while Sybil paused to watch the squirrels, Cora slipped away, returning almost immediately to take Sybil's arm. 'I found the ideal place. And it's where I can be straight out of the gates.'

'You've got the shawl?'

Cora nodded.

'I won't half be glad when it's all over.'

'Let's hope we're lucky first time.' Cora glanced at her small fob watch. 'It's ten to eleven so we'd better go out of the park and come in again.'

As they walked along the pavement, they saw one nanny enter the gates, and a few seconds later another who greeted her with a smile and they set off together chatting while they pushed their perambulators. Then a few minutes later, Cora nudged Sybil. It was exactly five minutes past eleven. 'There she is, with a yellow rose in her lapel.'

The two young women followed through the park gates. In the vicinity there was only a man pushing a bathchair, and two elderly women with walking sticks. To Cora's relief the small group began to head in a different direction, leaving a broad empty path where the nanny would soon pass the vital entrance. The situation was perfect.

'It's now, Syb. You begin to walk faster so you can just pass her. I'll nip into the bushes.'

Within seconds, Cora was out of sight, hidden by branches yet with a clear view of the crucial stretch of path. With feverish anxiety, she watched Sybil glance over her shoulder, quicken her step and begin to overtake the perambulator.

322

Once safely past and several yards ahead, she faltered, then with a weak cry clutched at her head and slowly sank to the ground.

As the nanny hurriedly put the brake on the pram and rushed forward in alarm, Cora left her hiding place, her steps light and silent. The sleeping baby was lying beneath the sunshade and barely stirred when lifted out. Within seconds, Cora was out of sight in the bushes and moments later she was not only safely away from the park, but also as befit a mother weary from carrying a child, she was hailing a passing hansom cab.

Chapter Forty-four

Once Nanny had left, today wearing in her lapel a small yellow rose, Helena went into the morning room to watch her walk along the leafy road. It had irked her at breakfast to have her wishes so dismissed. Wealth comes with so many petty restrictions, she thought, and most of them make little sense. It would have been so enjoyable for Dorothy and herself to stroll and chat in the park with little Rosalind gazing up at them. But her aunt had made a valid point about depriving Nanny Evans of her daily dose of fresh air.

And as always when she stood in this casement window, Helena found her thoughts turning to Nicholas, of the morning when she had seen him walking along the pavement on his way to visit Aunt Beatrice. She remembered the somersault of her heart when he had glanced up and the later so precious hour they had spent alone. Even now, she could never sit in that same chair without remembering how he had sat opposite, the warmth of his eyes and the tenderness of his smile. She wondered where he was now. Was he listening with patience to the sick, prescribing remedies, reassuring their loved ones? Was he studying articles, endeavouring to learn more about medicine? He could even be bringing a new life into the world. Yet her own time was going to be spent in entertaining the softly spoken Mrs Shirley. Helena could understand so well Dorothy's frustration with what she saw as her shallow life of social niceties. But that would change once she and Peregrine were married. And at least I have Rosalind, Helena thought, and turning, smiled at her friend as she came to join her at the window.

'This is such a lovely part of London,' Dorothy said. 'What a stark and empty world it would be without the beauty of trees.'

'I know. I do love the city, but once the wedding is over, I shall be glad to return to Graylings. Blaze is due to foal, you know, and I'd hate to miss those early days.'

They turned to go and sit on the large and comfy sofa, Helena idly picking up a copy of Vogue. Dorothy frowned. 'You really enjoy reading that?'

Helena smiled at her. 'Now Dorothy, you are not uninterested in fashion. You were quite envious of my new hat...' she broke off at the clamorous jangle of the doorbell, pulled repeatedly with an urgency that brought both of the young women to their feet and to rush out of the room where they saw the butler open the door to a distraught Nanny Evans. Gasping for breath, she stumbled into the hall. 'Baby's been taken!' Her face red with perspiration, tears were pouring down her face. 'In the park...' her chest was heaving, her breath coming in gasps, 'a woman collapsed...' she stared at them wild-eyed... 'I'm so sorry, so terribly sorry.'

Helena rushed to the door and screamed on seeing the empty perambulator at the bottom of the steps. In panic, she ran into the road to look in both directions while Jacob, still in his shirt-sleeves, was already coming to join her.

As Beatrice hurried down the staircase, Dorothy said, 'It's the baby,' she said. 'It seems she's been stolen.'

The door to Oliver's study was flung open, and he hurried out. 'What on earth is going on...?'

While Dorothy told him, Jacob, now holding Helena's arm, was leading her into the house.

Oliver was glaring down at Nanny Evans and shaking her. 'Tell us what happened, woman!'

Terrified, she could only sob even more.

Jacob said, 'We must send for the police.'

Oliver turned away from the nanny. 'I'll do it.' He instantly headed for his study.

'Papa...' Helena said brokenly.

'I'm going to the park.' He called over his shoulder, 'Someone send the footmen to follow me.'

Frantic and now almost hysterical, Helena confronted the crying woman. 'Nanny, you must pull yourself together. Now think clearly, tell us exactly...'

A parlourmaid came forward with a chair, saying to Beatrice, 'Shall I fetch a drop of brandy, Madam?'

Beatrice, her face ashen, nodded.

A few seconds later, Nanny sipped at the brandy and dabbing at her eyes with a sodden hanky mumbled, 'All I did was to put the brake on and go to try and help her.' In distress, she stared up at the circle of faces. 'I was only a few yards away.'

'Who, Nanny, who are you talking about?' Helena's voice was harsh.

'This woman in the park. She fell to the ground you see, in front of me. She just lay there, I couldn't rouse her, and when I turned round...' her sobs became a wail. 'The pram was empty. I didn't know what to do – I began to scream for help and ran back along the path towards some people.' Her voice sank to a whisper. 'When I went back...' she gazed at them all in bewilderment, 'the woman had vanished.'

Dorothy turned to Oliver who had some seconds before returned to the hall. 'Surely it's obvious. She was an accomplice, a decoy.'

'I think I was capable of working that out.' Oliver glared down at Nanny Evans. 'And these people? Where are they, they could be witnesses.'

Helena bent to take her hands. 'Yes, think Nanny.'

Slowly shaking her head, she said, 'I don't know, I don't know. They said they hadn't seen anything.' She gazed up at Helena. 'And they wouldn't have, Mrs Faraday, because there's a bend in the path.'

Beatrice demanded of Oliver, 'What did the

police say? Are they coming?'

'I didn't telephone them.' At the gasps of disbelief, he held up a hand. 'We need to be extremely careful. If we go to the police, the kidnappers might harm the child.'

At those terrible words, Helena gasped. 'You don't mean ... you can't mean...?'

'I had to take that decision. We just can't afford to take the risk.' He turned to the butler who was struggling to maintain his composure. 'Not a whisper of this must leave the house. No-one is to leave and I want you to gather all of the staff in the servants' dining hall. I shall be down directly to address them.'

'Mr Standish requested that the footmen should go to help him search, Sir.'

'Then let me know as soon as they return.'

Helena was battling crushing horror, hot tears of fear and desperation coursing down her cheeks. Seeing her beginning to tremble, Dorothy put an arm around her and guided her into the morning room. 'You need to come and sit down.'

Beatrice turned to where Nanny Evans was still slumped on the hall chair. 'Go up to the nursery and send Betsy down to the Servants' Hall. Then, I think you had better lie down. There is nothing more you can do here.' She went to her niece. 'I wish I could say something that might help you my love. I can't believe such a thing could happen – in broad daylight as well.'

Dorothy reached out and took her friend's cold hand into her own. Gently she began to rub it. 'Helena, as Oliver has suggested, Rosalind may have been kidnapped for some sort of ransom.

Or it could be that some poor woman who has lost her own baby is so crazed with grief that she has taken yours. It really is unlikely that Rosalind would have been harmed.'

Helena gazed at her, knowing that what she said made sense, but wave after wave of nausea was sweeping over her, despite the deep breaths she kept taking. This was a living nightmare. There was such evil in the world and her baby was out there at the mercy of strangers! She released her hand from Dorothy's and going over to the window, opened it wide, leaning out as far as she could. 'I can't see any sign of them, either Papa or the footmen.' She turned and began to hurry across the room. 'I'm going out to search myself, I've got to. I can't just stay here and do nothing.'

Beatrice hurried to her. 'No, Helena, let the men do it. You'd be better here just in case someone brings Rosalind back.'

With tears pouring down her face, Helena said, 'But what if they don't. What if I never see her again?'

Beatrice held her close. 'Now don't even think of such a thing. We must remain positive, strong. Otherwise...' she broke off as Oliver came into the room.

'I think the staff will keep our confidence,' he told them. 'They are certainly under no illusion of the consequences if even a hint escapes outside this house.'

Helena raised her head to look despairingly at him and he had to steel himself against the stark anguish in her brimming eyes. But a few minutes later, having declared his intention to join the others in searching St James's Park, Oliver was striding along the pavement, his spirits rising in triumph. It had all gone exactly to plan, and all he needed to do now was convince Jacob of the need for delay before contacting the police. A time span was essential if that bastard was to be spirited out of the country before any alarm was raised. If the Faraday name was dragged through the press then so be it. Most of the people who mattered – his own social circle – were already aware of the baby's deformity – and Oliver cared little about the great unwashed.

Chapter Forty-five

Cora was now in her third hansom cab in a ploy to evade any possible detection. The jolting of the journey was doing little to steady her nerves and she was desperately hoping that Sybil was safely on her way back to Belle's by now.

It had been impossible not to look down at the small body nestling in her arms; she was a beautiful baby, her eyelashes spread like fans against her rose-tinted skin. She had been good too, sleeping through the entire episode, although it would matter little now if she cried and drew attention because Cora guessed that they were nearing their destination. She looked out of the window, impressed by the cleanliness of the tall three-story houses and the respectability of the tree-lined roads. Ned had been telling the truth, this was no furtive hiding place, no 'baby-farm'. As for the kid going eventually into service, Cora would have liked to have had the chance; but her particular workhouse was deemed too 'rough', its reputation too tarnished to provide the standard of girl that most wealthy households insisted upon. And she'd had no intention of being some jumped up woman's skivvy. It had been Sid and the market for Cora, even if it did mean sleeping on a mattress on an attic floor. After his death, she had drifted into the life at Belle's. But she'd survived, hadn't she? She had never been homeless and now thanks to this bundle she was holding, she never would. Cora looked down again, startled to see a pair of trusting blue eyes gazing up at her. Instinctively she smiled and in return was rewarded with one so sweet that she caught her breath. She remembered the younger children in the workhouse, their pinched faces and hopeless eyes and how cold the winters had been, how harsh the treatment, disgusting the food. But Ned had promised that this baby would be well cared for. As for its mother, even if Sybil had felt guilty about the mother's feelings, Cora found that difficult. She may have slept with so many men that she could hardly remember one from another, but she would never have cheated on Johnnie nor tried to foist another man's kid on him. Cora closed her mind to the unwelcome image of a faceless weeping woman and instead peered out of the window, feeling relieved when she heard the slowing clop of hooves.

It was when she moved in readiness to leave the

cab that the baby began to whimper, struggling to be loose from the confines of the shawl. Seeing one of her mittens had become loose, Cora put her down on the seat and began to retie the white ribbon. It was ridiculous for the kid to wear mittens in this warm weather, but she couldn't risk leaving even the slightest evidence behind.

When a few minutes later Cora watched the cab move away and looked up at the silent house before her, suddenly the enormity of her actions, of what she had done in the park, of what she was now going to do, seemed overwhelming. No matter that the steps were well-scrubbed and the front door boasted glossy black paint, nothing could change the fact she was handing this baby over to total strangers. Cora found herself hesitating, feeling unsure. Then she told herself that she was being weak, even stupid. Weren't there freshly laundered net curtains at the window? Ned had been right – this was a respectable place.

On the first peal of the bell, the door partially opened. Then a woman's voice, quiet and authoritative, said, 'Who sent you?'

Cora's throat was dry. 'Ned did.'

'I shall move away from the door and open it further. Put her down on the floor.'

Cora obeyed and as she gently put the now crying baby on the hard tiled floor, two long arms in black sleeves reached down and gathered her up. The cries swiftly became screams. Within a few seconds, the arms emerged again, holding the cheap shawl that Cora had bought from the market. 'Dispose of it.' The door closed and it was over.

At first taken aback by the curt dismissal, Cora then saw the sense of it. Neither she nor the woman behind the door would ever recognise each other. Ned was a flaming genius, he had thought of everything. But as she stuffed the shawl into her bag, descended the steps and began to walk away, her legs were heavy, her forehead clammy with sweat. She had never expected to feel this shame, this terrible guilt. Several minutes later Cora hovered in confusion on the kerb of a busy corner. Ahead she could see a horse-tram waiting but she seemed unable to move forward, standing in a daze as people brushed by, her mind feverish. Even if she returned to the house and demanded the return of the baby, they'd never give her back, not when they'd been paid good money for her. Suppose by some miracle they did, what would she do then? She could hardly take her back to St James's Park, by now the police would be crawling all over it. And if she left her somewhere else anybody could pinch her.

It was then that with a sickening jolt, Cora saw the police officer. He was walking stolidly past a flower shop with its door open to the sunshine, carnations and clusters of sweet peas spilling out of galvanised buckets in front of the plate-glass window. As she stared at her future, one terrifying, the other her long-held dream, Cora's strong instinct of self-preservation rose to the surface. With shoulders squared, back straight and hardly daring to breathe, she moved safely past him, and seconds later was paying her tram fare.

When Jacob, desperate with the failure of his

search, returned to Faraday House and went to the morning room, it was to be confronted by a white-faced anguished daughter, a sister who was pacing the room, and a concerned Dorothy. As three pairs of agonised eyes met his own, he shook his head. 'There's no sign of her. Where is Oliver, where are the police?'

'He has gone over to the Park,' Dorothy said. 'It's a wonder you didn't see him.' She glanced at the others. 'He didn't telephone the police.'

Beatrice was twisting her handkerchief into a ball. 'He seems fearful of Rosalind being harmed if he contacts the police. He thinks she's been kidnapped.'

Jacob's eyebrows shot up. 'We can't be sure of that. It could be some deranged woman...'

Helena was bordering on hysterical, her eyes wide with fear. 'But Papa, we can't take the risk. We must do nothing that will endanger Rosalind– I couldn't bear it if...'

Jacob, still in his shirtsleeves and perspiring from the heat and effort of searching the park, sank on to one of the armchairs. 'I can't believe I'm hearing this. Are you telling me that Oliver wants to wait for a ransom demand? That child is out there with God knows who, and her father hasn't even called the police? How long does he intend to wait?'

Dorothy said, 'He didn't say. But he has sworn all the staff to secrecy.'

Jacob looked at them all with helpless rage. 'Where is the nanny?'

'It's no use, Jacob, she can't help at all.' Beatrice told him everything they knew.

Dorothy turned to Helena. 'If you think my presence will help in the slightest way, I could stay.'

Helena put a hand out to touch hers. 'Bless you, but we both know that your first duty must be to your mother.'

Jacob said, 'Dorothy please, not a word, not to your parents, or even to Peregrine. I'm sorry but...'

'I understand, Mr Standish.'

It was then that Oliver returned. He shook his head.

Jacob got up. 'Are you sure you have made the right decision? Not to bring in the police?'

'I think Helena will agree with me that our first priority must be the safety of our child.'

Jacob glanced at his daughter, at her tormented eyes and then back to his son-in-law. 'And if there *should* happen to be a ransom demand, surely you are not going to give in to the blackguards? What sort of a country would we have if people think they can steal children and not be brought to account?'

'I'm sorry, Jacob, but you are thinking like a politician.'

Jacob's expression hardened. 'I am the child's grandfather and I say that valuable time is being wasted.'

'And as her father, I insist that the decision must be mine.'

'Then I only hope that it is not one you will regret.'

Helena gazed at them, hating their conflict, her arms aching to feel her baby's warm little body, to hold her safe against her. If Oliver was right, then their wealth and privilege instead of protecting her had instead put her in danger. But if he was wrong, then her father was right – they were wasting vital time.

Oliver walked silently over to the window and gazed down into the street, his mind dissecting, planning. Soon life would return to normal, and hopefully by next summer his heir would have been born. Once Rosalind was safely out of the country, it was unlikely that the police would be able to trace her. And he doubted whether they would uncover the slightest evidence that would lead them to Cora and her friend. There was, of course, the danger that as one of the grieving parents, the newspapers might print his photograph, but Cora would never dare to unmask him. She would fear her own discovery too much. There was little likelihood that a whore's word would be taken against that of a gentleman, and one whose father-in-law was a Member of Parliament. No, Oliver foresaw no problems, not even from the man at that disreputable hotel; a rogue like that was unlikely to invite the law to pry into his shady affairs.

Helena's voice, shrill and accusing, disturbed his thoughts. 'If Dorothy and I had taken her out this morning, this wouldn't have happened. With two of us there, no-one would have dared to take her.'

'No-one was to blame,' Jacob said sharply, seeing his sister's distress. 'None of us could have foreseen this.'

Oliver went over to take Helena's hands and

drew her gently into his arms. Gazing down into her haunted, frantic eyes, he said, 'My sweet, trust me. I promise that we will soon have Rosalind safely back.'

But Helena felt desperate to take positive action and looked over his shoulder into her father's blazingly angry eyes. 'Oliver, I can only pray that you are right.'

Chapter Forty-six

When late that evening Cora left her apartment building and began to walk along the silent pavements to make her way to St John's Church gardens, she only knew that she wanted this dreadful day to end. She tried to console herself that at least when she saw Ned she would find out whether Sybil got away safely. One of the girls at Belle's used to talk of something called mortal sin; Cora had never had much truck with religion but she knew that she had committed a wicked and unforgiveable deed. It hadn't seemed so bad when the plan had just been talk, but once she'd held that kid in her arms... If Sid had been alive, the stall-holder would have despised what her ambition and greed had brought her to. But then, they did say that everyone had a dark side.

When she reached the corner and walked along to stand beneath the trees to wait in the usual meeting place, Cora glanced up to see dark shadows as bats flitted among the branches and she shivered despite the warm night air. Was this how Judas had felt? There had been Bible readings during every meagre meal at the workhouse, so she knew all about the disciple's betrayal. And wasn't that what she had done – betrayed that little baby?

At Faraday House, Oliver had been forced to wait until the entire household had retired for the night. It would have been crass to announce that he was going to his club, and would without doubt have provoked outrage from Jacob. So Oliver knew that he needed caution, and it was quite late when he went into his dressing room and unlocked a small cupboard. It was one that only he had the key to, not even Hines had ever seen inside. Oliver withdrew the satchel containing the remainder of the guineas and a few seconds later closed his bedroom door quietly behind him. Gingerly he descended the staircase, and with a feeling of relief, eased back the bolts on the front door.

Within half an hour he was at the hotel where again he encountered not a single soul. Oliver had decided that the lout at the desk was seemingly as fond of his bed as he was of his whisky bottle.

When later he turned into the now familiar quiet road, Cora was waiting outside the church gardens. He might have expected the avaricious little bitch to be early. She had served her purpose but now he had an intense desire to be rid of her.

He didn't bother with formality. 'So everything

went well.'

Cora nodded.

He opened the satchel and handed over the hessian bag. Cora took it, glanced inside and then put it into a cheap carpet bag she had brought with her. Then she stared into his eyes, her own as cold as his. 'I'm not proud of what I've done, Ned.'

'Maybe not, but you've been well paid for it.'

'Yes, I know.'

'So Cora, all that remains is for me to thank you and bid you farewell.'

'Goodbye, Ned.' She looked up at him. 'Yer won't come looking for me again, will you?'

He shook his head. 'There's not the slightest chance.'

Oliver watched her go. Only yesterday, a letter from Johnnie had again been full of Selena's charms and as the daughter of a respected land-owner she would be an excellent match for him. Cora's days as Johnnie's mistress were coming to an end and when they did so would her last tenuous link with himself.

He turned and as he began to walk briskly back along the road, before him rose an image of Helena, not as he had last seen her – white-faced and tearful – but smiling in the sunshine. He planned to take her on holiday at the beginning of winter, perhaps to Madeira. Foreign climes always provided a tonic and there was no reason why there in the soft and balmy air she should not conceive again.

His thoughts racing ahead, he soon reached the shabby hotel, inserted in the entrance door his late-night key and went swiftly up the narrow stairs. He met no-one; sometimes he wondered if he was the only guest.

Once in his room Oliver divested himself of the hated trousers, jacket and the soiled shirt and tossed them on to the counterpane. The heavy shoes he put aside. Once dressed in his own well-fitting clothes, he retrieved the leather weekend bag from behind the curtain and packed everything in it including the satchel, before snapping shut the clasp. Feeling complacent, he glanced in the cracked mirror to smooth his fair hair and moustache, and it took one glance around the dingy room to check that he had left nothing behind.

Going down to the lobby and despite having paid his bill in advance, he placed an envelope containing a generous sum in a drawer of the desk. Silence could always be bought. His room key he placed on top.

Then as always he waited until he was some distance away before flagging down a hansom cab.

The driver's voice was gruff and tired as he queried Oliver's call. 'Where on the Embankment, Guvnor?'

'It doesn't matter. Anywhere will do.'

The leather upholstery smelt of tobacco, the horse went at a spanking trot along the almost deserted roads and Oliver felt an almost un-natural sense of calm. When later he began to walk along beside the Thames there were few people about, the only noise coming from the river's water traffic. Once certain that he was unobserved, he opened the leather bag. The boots were first to be flung over the parapet and despite the steep drop he heard a satisfying plop. Taking great care with his aim, he followed with the shirt and jacket. Then a few minutes later having walked further along, into the flow of dank water went the trousers.

Oliver continued on his way, giving a courteous nod to the few people he passed. He was thoughtful. An odd item of sodden clothing would be a common sight, but if the leather bag didn't sink, it would attract attention. Inside was the satchel, but something heavier? Distracted and conscious of time passing, Oliver took out his watch, its gold casing glinting beneath a streetlamp as he gazed down. The hour was later than he had thought; he should be returning to Faraday House. He moved nearer to the grass verge, his gaze searching beneath the trees for stones. And it was then that he heard soft footfalls behind him.

He tensed but the shadow was already looming, bringing with it a crawling fear. Oliver swung round but the first blow came swift and vicious as a fist smashed into his face. A second came to his chest and then he felt the coldness of steel, piercing and cruel as the sharp blade twisted beneath his ribs. Gasping in pain, he collapsed, only for hands to tear the leather bag from his grasp, to invade his body; snatching his watch, his wallet, his rings. There came the sound of running footsteps retreating and, left in a crumpled heap, Oliver lay in agony, a warm and heavy stickiness seeping through his clothes, a frightening weakness in his limbs. Into his mouth came the desolate and acrid taste of failure. He would leave behind no son, no heir. Faint voices came in the distance, growing nearer, but he knew it was too late, already he could feel his life blood ebbing away.

Chapter Forty-seven

When at last alone in the privacy of her room, Helena sat in the bedside chair, rocking to and fro, weeping with grief, her fear and longing for her baby a physical pain. It was not only worry for Rosalind's safety – an unfamiliar formula could make her ill, she had a nappy rash that needed zinc and castor oil cream, and unused to strangers she would be so bewildered and frightened. Repeatedly, as the dark hours lightened into dawn, she paced the room and stared out of the window at the empty street. How could anyone be so cruel as to steal a child?

Jacob too had slept badly, convinced that Oliver was wrong, that his decision was hazardous. Had he no conception of what evil men were capable? In fact, Jacob's hope was that some poor woman had taken the baby as a replacement for her own; at least she would be less likely to harm her. The night seemed endless and his valet's ministrations in the morning more welcome than usual. Jacob was a great believer in the restorative powers of a shave and hot towel. Later, as he descended the staircase his desperate hope was that the morning post would at least bring some some information – even if it was a ransom demand. However, as soon as he reached the hall the butler came forward. 'Good morning, Mr Standish. Might I have a word, Sir?'

'Do you have news?'

'I'm afraid not.' He hesitated. 'It's just that Hines informs me that Mr Faraday's bed hasn't been slept in.'

Jacob stared at him. Was that so unusual? Oliver could simply have slept in his wife's room. He frowned. 'You mean that he is not in the house?'

'Yes, Sir.'

'Did he leave the house last night?'

'Hines was not aware of it – a most unusual occurrence.'

'Mr Faraday could have gone to his club I suppose, although I can hardly believe that after the happenings of yesterday...'

'Hines would normally wait up for his return, Sir. Mr Faraday always informed him of his intentions and whether further service would be required.'

'Thank you, Gray.' Jacob went into the dining room only to find that the post contained a letter for Oliver from his stockbroker, a couple for himself from his constituency office, and the other addressed to Beatrice in handwriting he recognised. There was no cheap envelope with badly spelt words, or even those cut from a newspaper, or did that only happen in fiction? Slowly he walked over to the sideboard, only half concentrating as he helped himself to his usual breakfast, wondering once again whether all was well in his daughter's marriage. For the staff to be concerned that a married man's bed had not been slept in did seem a little odd.

'Good morning, Jacob.' A pale and tired-looking Beatrice joined him at the table. 'I haven't had a wink of sleep. I have just been in to see Helena. She is still not dressed and I'm terribly worried about her, she looks dreadful.'

'Good morning, my dear. Yes, I too found sleep difficult. May I ask – was Oliver with Helena?'

'Jacob, I would hardly enter her room if he were.'

'But how would you know? I'm sorry Beatrice, I'm not asking out of idle curiosity.'

She looked at him in surprise. 'Oliver always rises much earlier.'

'Would you mind my dear, going to ask whether she knows where Oliver is? Apparently his bed has not been slept in.'

Jacob was becoming fidgety and after a few minutes he went into the hall to gaze up the staircase, only to see that Beatrice was already on her way down.

She shook her head. 'She is as mystified as we are.'

As they sat on opposite sides of the table, Jacob was so on edge that the even the sound of Beatrice scraping butter on her toast irritated him. Where, in God's name had Oliver got to? His newspaper still folded and unread at the side of his plate, he gazed across at her, his fingers drumming on the tablecloth. 'You know I haven't changed my mind. I think Oliver is badly mistaken in not involving the police.'

'It's very difficult for you, I can see that.'

They both turned as a dishevelled Helena came hurrying into the room. 'Papa, what is this about Oliver? Aunt Beatrice tells me that his bed has not been slept in.'

Distressed by the shadows beneath her eyes, Jacob said, 'It appears not, and he hasn't been seen this morning.'

'I heard his door close about an hour after I went to bed... I thought he was unable to rest, that perhaps he had gone down to his study.' Her voice wavered, 'Papa, the kidnappers may have contacted him – he could have gone to meet them.'

He shook his head. 'He would have told us – certainly me. And it wouldn't make any sense, not without the means of paying a ransom. And for that he would need to wait for the bank to open.'

But Helena had agonised all night and burst out, 'I don't know *where* Oliver is! It is Rosalind who concerns me. I cannot bear this waiting, this worrying, this inaction! It was Oliver's decision not to involve the police, but he isn't here...'

'You are prepared to go against his wishes?' Beatrice spoke sharply.

'I would do anything to bring Rosalind back.'

Then Jacob said, 'I cannot believe that Oliver would be so selfish as to deliberately cause us further anxiety. I shall go to Scotland Yard and make discreet enquiries.'

Helena said swiftly, 'You will tell them about Rosalind?'

'I intend to make that judgment at the time.' Jacob rose from the table. 'Helena, do take breakfast, you need to keep up your strength.'

She went wearily to the sideboard but even the sight of kidneys and sausages turned her stomach.

'Just settle for toast and coffee as I have, dear.' Beatrice gave a long sigh. 'It is going to be a very difficult morning.'

The New Scotland Yard building was on the Victoria Embankment and although familiar to Jacob, he had never before actually entered its premises. Walking briskly, he went through the entrance to where at the Enquiry Desk the station sergeant was looking down at some papers. Jacob stood before him. The man's voice was laconic. 'Yes?'

'Good morning,' Jacob said. 'My name is Jacob Standish and I am a member of His Majesty's Government. I wish to make some enquiries.'

The sergeant's head shot up, his face reddening above his handlebar moustache, but already on hearing Jacob's commanding tone, another officer was coming forward to replace him. 'I am the senior station sergeant, Sir. I will detain you only a moment.'

As he waited, Jacob glanced around at some of the posters on the walls, mostly warning of penalties, with Helena's word 'inaction' still ringing in his mind. *Could* Oliver have gone to meet the kidnappers? He would not like to think that by coming here to report his disappearance, that he was putting any arrangement in jeopardy. But Jacob still felt that 'kow-towing' to criminals was beyond the pale. That was not the English way at all.

Then almost immediately he was ushered along a corridor and into the presence of a hawk-nosed man with silvering temples. He was not in uniform.

'Mr Standish? My name is Chief Inspector Morris and I am with the CID. Please,' he indicated a chair opposite his cluttered desk. Jacob took a seat and leaned forward, both hands resting on his silver-topped cane.

'So Mr Standish, how can we be of help?'

'May I speak in confidence?'

'You have my word on it.'

Jacob hesitated, unsure of exactly how much to reveal at this stage. 'I am concerned that a gentleman of good character has failed to return home.' He saw the man opposite frown.

'It is merely that he has been missing overnight?'

Jacob nodded. 'Yes. But there are particular circumstances that would rule out any of the normal, er...'

'I see. Well, there are two possibilities. An accident or illness in which case we can check the hospitals for you, and also...' He pressed a buzzer on an intercom on his desk and spoke into it. 'Please bring in a list of any incidents reported since...' he glanced at Jacob for confirmation, 'shall we say ten o'clock last night?'

Jacob nodded.

'The gentleman you speak of, you have not yet furnished me with his name.'

'May I beg your forbearance, Chief Inspector?

346

At least for the moment.'

He turned at a light tap at the door, and watched as a manila folder was handed over. The detective opened it and began to run his finger down a typewritten list, its length confirming Jacob's opinion that the less salubrious areas of London abounded with criminals and ruffians. The finger paused. 'Mr Standish, might I have a description of the person you are worried about?'

Jacob's answer was swift. 'About six feet tall, aged around thirty, fair-haired. And clean shaven apart from a moustache.'

There was a moment's silence, and Jacob's fingers tightened on the knob of his cane. Then the Chief Inspector said, 'There is a report of a serious incident that took place last night on the Embankment. Now we have no reason to suspect that the victim is the person you are concerned about but...'

'The description?'

'It is not dissimilar.'

Jacob felt a cold dread in the pit of his stomach. 'You say a serious incident...'

'A man was robbed and stabbed.' His gaze was steady. 'I am afraid it is a case of murder.'

After the warm sunshine outside, the chill in the airless room seeped into Jacob's tense bones as they stood waiting in one of the city's mortuaries. Then at last a trolley was wheeled in carrying a shrouded still form. At a nod from the Chief Inspector, the mortuary attendant partly drew back the white sheet. Jacob's gaze, at first fearful and then appalled, fixed on the grey and waxen features of the battered face of his son-in-law. Slowly he turned his head away and lowered it in assent.

'Might I ask his name, Sir?'

Jacob's voice was hoarse. 'Mr Oliver Faraday.'

'My commiserations, Mr Standish. Might I ask how he is known to you?'

'He is my son-in-law.'

'And so the victim's next-of-kin would be your daughter.'

Jacob stared at him, suddenly shocked out of his stunned state. What if whoever had done this... If it was connected with Rosalind, she could be in mortal danger... He was already moving away, heading towards the door. 'She must not be contacted, not until you have heard what I have to tell you. Chief Inspector we must return to Scotland Yard immediately. Hurry, man!'

At Faraday House, as her father had dismissed the notion of Oliver having gone to meet the kidnappers Helena scarcely gave her husband another thought. She was feeling physically sick, her mind so wild with fear for Rosalind that she felt she would go mad, and her continual pacing around the drawing room caused Beatrice to snap, 'For heaven's sake sit down, I'm beginning to get a headache.'

Helena swung round. 'Then you'd better go and lie down before it turns into a migraine!'

Pale-faced, her aunt left the room and Helena went back into her own desperate thoughts, fighting a need to go up to the nursery, to bury her face in Rosalind's soft blanket, longing to breathe in the sweet baby scent of her. But to do that she would have to face the woman whose carelessness... And Helena didn't trust herself, not yet.

Then at last there came the sound of the motor car and hurrying to the window, she saw it draw up only to be closely followed by another. Had her father any news? Had he told Scotland Yard about Rosalind? Anxiously she watched their chauffeur stand aside for Jacob to alight and two men climbed out of the other vehicle. One was tall with greying hair, the other portly with a beard; both had an air of authority. Her father's expression was grave and it was with growing dread that Helena went to wait before the fireplace. She could hear the sound of hats and canes being received and the heavy tread of footsteps on the tiled floor, and when they paused, she heard Jacob's deep voice, 'If you would be so kind as to give me a few moments, Chief Inspector.'

Her gaze fixed on the door and as it opened Helena's eyes were wide with apprehension.

'My dear...'

She felt suddenly cold as her father came to take her hands in his. 'Please, come with me.' He led her to the sofa.

As she sat beside him, her whisper was one of terror. 'Is it Rosalind?'

He shook his head and she felt sick with relief. But then her gaze searched his face only to see in his eyes a profound sympathy. 'I'm afraid, my darling, that it's Oliver.'

Her throat closing in horror, she listened to his

strained voice, to the terrible and shocking words. She looked at him, her voice shaking as she said, 'Surely there must be some mistake. There must be.'

His eyes were full of sadness. 'Helena, I have been to the mortuary myself, there is no mistake.'

'But I don't understand,' her voice was shaking. 'On the Embankment – at that time of night? Whatever would he be doing there?'

'I don't know, sweetheart.'

'Do you think...' she clutched at his sleeve. 'Do you think he could have heard from the kidnappers, gone to meet them?'

'Helena, how can we assume that? In any case, it is all out of our hands now. The police know about Rosalind. There is a Chief Inspector and a Detective Sergeant here to interview Nanny Evans.'

She closed her eyes. 'Thank God.'

'I will fetch Beatrice to be with you.'

'No, Papa, she has one of her heads.'

'But...'

'Please, I'd rather be on my own for a while.'

'I understand.'

Helena sat alone in the quiet room and despite the sunshine streaming in through the windows, wrapped her arms around her chilled body. He had not deserved to die so young, not in such a cruel and senseless way, no-one did. She closed her eyes trying to shut out the ugly image of him being attacked, of suffering violence, praying that his end had been mercifully swift. And then, the slow tears came, because whatever Oliver's faults he had not only been her husband, he had given her the precious gift of Rosalind. And yet, she would never see him again, never face him each morning across the breakfast table. And it was only several minutes later that to her shame the unworthy thought flooded into her mind; never for the rest of her life would she have to dread the handle being turned on that inter-connecting door.

Jacob had delegated the use of Oliver's study for the detectives. He himself had been rebuked for failing to report earlier the fact of Rosalind's kidnapping, and told that the delay would seriously hinder the police investigations.

'Will the police officers require refreshment, Sir?'

Jacob turned to the butler. 'Yes, of course, once they have interviewed Nanny Evans. Perhaps some coffee and sandwiches? And for me too, but I will take mine in the dining room.' He had decided to relay the bad news to Beatrice once she was feeling well. Later, once all of the staff had been interviewed, he went to see the police.

The Chief Inspector twisted a pencil between his fingers, a frown between his eyes. 'Yes, Mr Standish, I understand your concern. There is no evidence yet to link the two cases. However, at this stage we are not ruling anything out, which is why we have no plans at present to release any details of the kidnapping. Our hope is that any police presence here will be assumed to be connected with the death of Mr Faraday.'

'Is it not,' Jacob said, 'becoming a little late for a ransom demand?'

The detective shook his head. 'There have been reported instances – especially in America – of two or three days passing before any contact is made.'

'And if not?'

'Then there will be a blaze of publicity. If it does transpire that the culprit is a woman who has lost her own baby, then someone out there must have seen...'

Jacob finished his sentence, 'A baby with five fingers instead of four.'

'Quite.'

'Tell me, Chief Inspector. Is it your opinion that there is a reasonable chance of recovering my granddaughter, of her being unharmed?'

'I don't have a crystal ball, Sir. I can only assure you of our utmost support and assistance. Now I know it is a lot to ask when she must be in a state of shock, but do you think that we could have a few words with Mrs Faraday?'

Helena was sitting listlessly in an armchair, her head resting on a cushion, her hands holding a damp handkerchief when the three men came into the drawing room. But as Jacob had already told the detectives, there was little she could tell them. 'I'm sorry, I had no idea he was out, let alone why he should have been on the Embankment so late at night. And I am certainly not aware that he had any enemies.' She rose to face both detectives, gazing with frantic eyes first at one and at then the other. 'You will do all you can to find my baby?'

The Chief Inspector's eyes were full of compassion. 'We are both family men, Mrs Faraday.

You need have no fears on that score.'

Once they were alone Jacob said with a frown, 'Oliver's death is bound to be reported in the newspapers, Helena. We must not allow the staff at Graylings and Broadway Manor to learn of it in such a way.'

'And I fear, Papa, that we can't delay much longer before telling Aunt Beatrice.'

But later Beatrice, after her initial shock, proved to be of stronger mettle than Helena could have imagined. Still pale after her migraine attack, nevertheless she rallied herself to practicalities. 'Has anyone notified Selwyn?'

Jacob slumped in an armchair and ran his fingers through his hair. 'I hadn't given the man a single thought.'

'And then there is the wedding on Thursday ... he may wish to postpone it. We shall be unable to attend whatever he decides.'

'I would expect him to be already in London,' Jacob said.

Helena rose. 'Oliver will have a note of the number in his study.'

Beatrice watched her leave and turned to her brother. 'She is being so brave.'

'Yes, I feel very proud of her.'

Helena hesitated outside the door to Oliver's study. It wasn't a room that she often went into but when she entered, the detectives' lingering fug of unfamiliar tobacco already gave it a different atmosphere. She gazed at the bookshelves, at Oliver's button-backed swivel chair, thinking that never again would he sit there to attend to his correspondence, or to business matters. Then she frowned; the desk had been cleared of papers, even the address book was missing. Realising that the police must have removed Oliver's personal effects, Helena knew that he would have been furious at such an intrusion and went to slump in misery and confusion on the leather wing armchair.

Why could she not have loved him more? She had felt so happy on their wedding day, so full of hope. Yet after the brutal way he had used her on their wedding night no matter how she had tried, she had never been able to feel the same about him. She stared into the fireplace. Had he ever really loved her? He hadn't even loved their baby. And yet only last night he had told her to trust him, had promised to bring her home and now... She raised her head. He *must* have gone out to find her, no matter what Papa thought. Why else would he have been on the Embankment at that unearthly hour? Nothing else made sense. And it was then that she rose on trembling legs and began to walk towards the door. Helena had never felt so frightened in her life, because if she was right – and Oliver *had* been killed by the same person who had kidnapped Rosalind, then even now, her baby's trusting blue eyes could be gazing up into the face of a murderer.

Chapter Forty-eight

At Broadway Manor the staff had gathered in the Servants' Hall for afternoon tea, when they heard the peal of the doorbell. Henry Bostock, who had removed his jacket and settled in his customary place at the head of the table, asked one of the footmen to answer it. 'It's not likely to be anyone important, not with the family away.'

'It's a telegram, Mr Bostock!'

They all turned to stare at the young footman as he came back down the stairs. The butler turned to take it from him and removed his reading glasses from his top pocket.

'I hope it's not bad news.' Cook put down her knife just as the clock on the wall struck the hour. 'I never did like those dratted things.'

'It doesn't have to be,' Annie said. 'Maybe Mr Standish and Miss Beatrice are coming back early, that's all. Her little dog'll be pleased that's for sure.'

'Be quiet all of you!'

'What's wrong?' Mrs Kemp leaned forward in alarm.

'I am afraid it *is* bad news. The telegram is from Mr Standish. I shall read you exactly what it says. *'Regret to inform you of death by a violent crime of Mr Oliver Faraday.'*

Mrs Kemp's gasp rose above the others. 'Oh, my good Lord!'

355

'Our poor Miss Helena.' Annie's voice was a whisper.

Charlotte, wide-eyed, crossed herself.

'Oh, that such a terrible thing should happen,' Mrs Kemp lifted a corner of her white apron and dabbed at her eyes. 'And him so young an 'all.'

'When I think how lovely she looked,' Annie said, 'that day when she stood on the staircase in her wedding dress and now she's already a widow. It's a cruel world, it really is.'

'What will happen, Mr Bostock?' Mrs Kemp turned to him. 'Will Miss Helena have to leave Graylings?'

'Almost certainly. I believe a cousin will inherit as Miss Rosalind wasn't a boy.'

'It shouldn't make any difference if you ask me,' Annie said.

'Men rule the world, they always have, they always will,' Mrs Kemp said. 'I don't suppose it will ever change.'

There was a moment's thoughtful silence as they all took a few sips of their tea, and then Annie said, 'Well, I know it's terrible – him dyin' an all – but I for one hope Miss Helena comes back to Broadway Manor.'

At Graylings, Molly had still not heard the news. The housekeeper was taking advantage of the family's absence by delegating the 'turning out' of rarely used rooms. Therefore Molly was in what she always thought of as the 'creepy one', dusting the family portraits that for some reason the master kept shut away. She stood back to gaze at the image of a young woman. It may have been the fashion then to have such low-cut bodices, but in Molly's opinion it was a wonder the women didn't catch their death of cold, although so much flesh on show did divert attention from a homely face, and certainly this girl could never be called pretty. She shrugged and turned her attention to polishing the window and dusting the pelmet and skirting boards.

Relieved to finish her task, she closed the door behind her and, struggling with her mop, dusters and polish went awkwardly down the back stairs to the kitchen, only to be summoned to join the rest of the staff in the Servants' Hall. It was whispered that it was something to do with a telegram.

In London, Helena and Beatrice were sitting desolate in the drawing room when Jacob came to join them. 'As I thought,' he said, 'Oliver had a note of Selwyn's number in his study at Graylings. Crossley has received my telegram and has conveyed the sincere condolences of the staff. They are all extremely shocked by the sad news.'

'Thank you.' Helena's tone was vague, she was yet again pacing the room, dark circles beneath her eyes, her pallor so marked that Jacob exchanged further worried glances with Beatrice.

'I am afraid Selwyn insisted on coming immediately to Faraday House,' he went on. 'I judged it best to make no mention of Rosalind.'

Helena swung round to face him. 'Papa, how do we know that the police are out there looking for her, that they are doing everything possible?'

'My dear, I'm sure the Chief Inspector is doing

all he can.' Beatrice's words sounded as weary as her platitude, and the silence in the room grew so heavy with their hopeless frustration that it was almost a relief when the doorbell eventually rang.

The butler ushered in the man who, despite being his cousin, Oliver had detested.

Selwyn's florid face above its fair beard was composed in a pious expression, but his pale blue eyes were gleaming with satisfaction. His tone was, in Helena's opinion, one of pure cant. 'My dear cousin-in-law, what can I say to comfort you. Oliver will be a grievous loss to us all. He was held in the highest regard by everyone who knew him and I shall miss him greatly.'

'Thank you, Selwyn.'

'Please accept my deepest sympathy.' He gave a discreet cough. 'I shall of course allow you the utmost latitude. In the matter of vacating the houses, I mean. Shall we say one month?'

Jacob moved protectively before his daughter. 'For heaven's sake man, have you no decency!'

'Yes of course, but I shall be abroad for a few weeks don't you know. I thought it best to…'

'You are acquainted with the firm of McPherson and McPherson I assume, the lawyers who handle the Faraday affairs?' Jacob's voice was harsh. 'Mr Finlay McPherson will no doubt be in contact with you at the apposite time, namely after your cousin's funeral. Am I to take it that you will not be attending the service and that the wedding will go ahead?'

'Regretfully that is correct Mr Standish. I do have to consider my future wife.'

'Then I must bid you good day, Mr Faraday.'

He went over to the bell pull. 'I offer our apologies, but under the circumstances we will not be able to attend your nuptials. We do of course wish you well.'

Seconds later, he turned to a silent Helena and an irate Beatrice. 'That man,' he said through gritted teeth, 'is not a gentleman.'

Helena's frustration was reaching fever pitch; it had been a shock to hear Selwyn refer to 'houses'; she had never once thought of having to leave Faraday House. Whether he came to the funeral or not was of no consequence, her only concern was for Rosalind. If only they could hear *something!* No matter how high the ransom was... And then suddenly she was panic-stricken. 'Papa? When the kidnappers contact us ... will the bank give me access to Oliver's money?'

He shook his head. 'A large sum could present a problem – at least until the estate is settled. But my dear, I am not without funds.'

Beatrice said quietly, 'And I have my own savings.'

Helena gazed at the two dear people before her. 'What ever would I do without you both?' And it was then that she broke down. 'I can't bear it, I really can't. The thought that someone could even now be hurting Rosalind is tearing me apart.'

Chapter Forty-nine

'Well, ain't you a sight for sore eyes!' Belle stood aside and waved a hand for her visitor to come in. 'Any chance of yer coming back, Cora? Some of yer regulars are still asking.'

Cora wrinkled her nose at the stale air still thick with cigar smoke from the night before and glanced at the pink velveteen sofas and heavily fringed cushions. 'Sorry, Belle, no chance. Is Sybil about?'

'I expect she's up, with a face like a drainpipe as usual. I'm tellin' you, Cora, if she doesn't buck her ideas up she's out of 'ere. A bloke don't want ter pay good money to lie on top of a stuffed mattress. He can do that at 'ome. Sybil!'

As always, Belle's screech nearly burst the eardrums, but it had the desired effect, bringing Sybil to peer over the landing, her face blanching as she saw Cora.

'I'll leave yer to it, I need to sort out the laundress.'

'Good to see you, Belle.' Then Cora hissed up the stairs. 'Syb, get yer hat and coat!'

'I thought you said we weren't to meet up for a week.' Sybil's face was panic stricken as a few minutes later she closed the front door behind them.

'I know, but something's come up. Not the rozzers, so don't look so scared, but I need to talk

360

to you in private.'

'Fancy pie and mash? There's that dark corner in Fat Sam's?'

Cora shook her head as they began to hurry along the road. 'I need a bit of daylight for this. How about Charlie's?'

'Suits me.'

Ten minutes later, they went into the small stuffy cafe and found an empty table by the window. Once they were sitting opposite each other Cora glanced warily over her shoulder, but sitting behind her was only an old crone bent over her dinner plate, while the table behind Sybil was unoccupied. She waited until they had given their order then took a newspaper out of her bag. 'I went to buy this to look at the adverts, and got the shock of me life when I saw the front page. The name might be different but as God's my witness, Sybil, this chap that's bin murdered on the Embankment, it's Ned. Not only that but it must have happened not long after he left me.'

'What? Here, let me look...'

Cora pushed the newpaper across to her. 'I only saw him once without his cap on, but it's him all right, I'd swear to it.' Then her voice trailed away as she saw the other girl's eyes widen, her face grow pale. 'What's up?'

'Cora, he may have called himself Ned to you, but I knew him as Gerald.'

'Gerald?' Cora stared at her. 'You mean that bloke who dumped you, left you homeless?'

Sybil nodded. 'It's him all right. I told you he was a toff.'

'Well, I'll be blowed. Here, pass that paper

back.' Cora read the whole article again, more carefully this time. This chap had set up Sybil in an apartment in St John's Wood, and hang on a minute, what did it say here – Mr Oliver Faraday had married a Miss Helena Standish of Lichfield in Staffordshire. Cora raised her head and stared out of the grimy window. Staffordshire, now where had she heard of that before? She frowned as her glance fell on a used cup and saucer left on the table by a previous occupant. That was it – Johnnie had gone to a weekend house party up there, she remembered him teasing her about the Potteries. Now either it was just a coincidence or...

She leaned back as the blowsy waitress brought two steaming plates of food. Then Cora folded the newspaper, replaced it in her bag and before picking up her knife and fork, leaned forward. 'Syb, what was the exact address of that apartment, the one he set you up in?'

An hour an a half later, they were both in St John's Wood, with Sybil wandering around the apartment that had been her home for just over two years. She was not only full of nostalgia, but even becoming tearful. 'I can't believe it, Cora, that all this time you've been living here, where I'd been so happy. I'm really sorry he's dead you know, I got right fond of him.'

'He used you. They all use us. I suppose we use them if the truth's known.' Cora had no patience with sentiment. 'And I couldn't tell you where I was, I told you – it was one of Johnnie's conditions that I told nobody.' She was leafing through her journal and frowning in concentration. 'Here it is. I was right. "*Johnnie – last weekend – country estate near Lichfield.*" I remember him telling me it was in Staffordshire, and look at the date. It all ties in Syb.'

'You mean Gerald – as I knew him anyway – passed on this apartment to Johnnie?'

'Not only the apartment either. I bet a pound to a penny he told this Oliver how ambitious I was. So when he wanted someone to do his dirty work... I bet he watched me, knew which pub I went to. And my, he couldn't half spin a tale. What I'm wondering is, whether anything he said was the truth.'

'What do you mean?'

'That story he told us, about his boss not being the kid's father. Well, he didn't have a boss, that's obvious. So, whose baby was it?'

'It must have bin his own.'

'So why did he want rid?'

'Same reason I suppose, but he'd have bin too proud to admit it.'

Cora shook her head. 'I dunno, Syb. I mean, how can we believe any of it? He was a damn good liar, I can tell you that.' She glanced across at her friend. 'I didn't tell you, did I? What happened after I left you at the park?'

A few seconds later, Sybil was staring at her with horror. 'Yer never put that baby down on a cold tiled floor!'

'Don't look at me like that! What choice did I have?'

'Oh Cora, whatever have we done?'

'I know what we're going to do. We're going to

do some thinking, but I need a bit of Dutch cour-age.' She got up and went over to the sideboard. 'Brandy all right?'

Sybil shook her head. 'It's a bit early for me. I've only been up three hours.'

Cora's brandy glass was almost empty before she reached her final decision. 'We're getting out of here. Kidnapping and murder? I don't know what's bin going on but we're better out of it. We can set up a flower shop anywhere, it doesn't have to be in London.'

'Move right away, you mean?'

'I think we'd be safer somewhere we're not known.'

Sybil's face lit up. 'Do you think we could go to the seaside?'

'Why not? Nowhere too quiet though. How about Brighton, that's supposed to be all right. But listen, Syb. Until we can leave, you've got to get your act together at Belle's.'

'Why, what's she bin saying?'

'Nothing you don't already know. But if she gives you the push before then, where are you going to go? You can't come here, 'cos Johnnie's bound to come back for the funeral. And you can't go wasting your guineas on lodgings, we're going to need them. Which reminds me, they'll be safer here than at Belle's.'

Sybil nodded. 'All right. When do you think we'll be able to go?'

Cora gazed at her. 'Once I've seen Johnnie. I owe him that much.' She got up and went to the kitchen to rinse out the two brandy glasses. For all she knew Johnnie might have already heard the news, he may even be on his way back to England and there was no sense in taking any chances.

She went back into the sitting room. 'You'd better go and get glammed up for tonight. Remember what I said. Put a smile on yer face from now on.'

As she closed the door behind her friend, Cora's expression was not only thoughtful but inside her was a growing fear, because the idea that had been niggling at the back of her mind was growing stronger with every second that passed.

Chapter Fifty

That same morning as was his habit during the summer months, Nicholas had travelled by hansom cab to a certain point and then walked the rest of the way to Wimpole Street. He was a great believer in the benefits of fresh air and exercise, and it was being in this exclusive area of London after the poverty-stricken one of the previous afternoon that led him to muse on the vagaries of life.

Then in the East End of London in the sweltering heat, he had been helpless to prevent a fair-haired little girl in a grubby vest, her throat strangled by diphtheria, lose her struggle for life. The contagious disease had also taken her two-year-old brother a few days earlier. Her mother was in the early stages of tuberculosis, and Nicholas could only guess at the sparse diet that the remaining four children survived on. Yet today he would spend tending to the ills both real and imaginary of people whose lives were a constant round of ease and pleasure. Even for himself, due to a mild indisposition of Mrs Haverstock, last night had brought the contrast of an impromptu theatre invitation, and a delightful evening it had proved to be, with once more the company of the Murray family, and the twin daughters in high spirits.

It was with an image of Miss Elspeth lingering in his thoughts that he went up the steps and into the practice to bestow a warm smile on Miss Barnes. 'What a lovely morning.'

As always, her colour rose as she looked up at him. 'Good morning, Dr Carstairs, and indeed it is. Dr Haverstock expressed a wish to see you immediately you arrived.'

Nicholas frowned and after a light tap on Andrew's door found him standing before the window with a copy of *The Times* in his hand. He turned, his expression grave. 'Nicholas, what a dreadful business.'

'I'm sorry?'

'You haven't seen this morning's newspaper?'

Nicholas shook his head. 'I seem to have a problem with my delivery lately; my housekeeper is looking into it.'

Silently Andrew held out the paper and Nicholas stared down at the front page. Below the main news item was a headline, '*Prominent man murdered on Embankment*' and beside it a photograph of Oliver Faraday. Nicholas caught his breath, his eyes widening in shock as he read the report in growing disbelief. Oliver dead? He'd been murdered? Stunned, he looked across at Andrew. 'As you say, this is dreadful.'

'It's outrageous that a man isn't safe in his own city!' Andrew's burr was even more pronounced than usual.

Nicholas shook his head, looking down again at the article. 'But why, how?'

'No details are given, nor exactly where he was on the Embankment. Whoever did it needs hanging – it's damn well nothing but thuggery. I spent some time in India, Nicholas, and could tell you things...' Andrew shook his head. 'This has shaken me, I can't deny it. I knew Oliver from a child, as I did his parents.'

Nicholas nodded, but his own thoughts were flying in desperation to Helena. She must be devastated...

'As Mrs Faraday is my patient, I must send my condolences. I shall ask Miss Barnes to arrange for a note to be sent round.'

Nicholas thought swiftly. 'I think I can help you there. Miss Standish too must be in shock. If you recall I treated her for hemiplegic migraine and a sleeping draught might be advisable. My appointments are light today, I could easily call at Faraday House later this afternoon and take a prescription for her and your note at the same time.'

'Excellent. And I shall prescribe a sedative for Mrs Faraday too, just in case she might find it

367

helpful. Thank you, Nicholas.'

Nicholas turned at the sound of an imperious voice outside.

'That will be Lady Trentley,' Andrew said, 'and she doesn't like to be kept waiting. Are you able to join me for lunch?'

'Yes of course.' Once inside his own room, relieved that his first patient was not due for another half hour, Nicholas sat thoughtfully in his leather armchair. Like Andrew, the news had shaken him. He may not have held Oliver Faraday in high esteem but he had been Helena's husband, the father of her child, and no man deserved such an untimely and violent end. Into his mind came her lovely image, followed by a thought that later shamed him. Once time had passed, when her mourning period was over ... could it be possible ... and then he smote one fist with the other. God in heaven, the man was not yet in his grave.

What he should be doing was to think of Helena's needs, of her distress. Even if he could only see her for a few moments, it might be that she could find some comfort in his presence, however fleeting. At least he had the reassurance of knowing that she had her baby to hold in her arms, Nicholas had seen many times what comfort that could bring to a young mother.

It was after lunch that Helena, having discovered that Nanny Evans was remaining in isolation, knew that she could no longer evade her duty. As she climbed the stairs to the third floor her conscience was heavy, knowing that she had been so immersed in her own misery and pain that she had given little thought to that of anyone else. However, she still had to force herself to enter the prettily decorated nursery where in the sunlight Betsy was sitting by the fireplace sewing. Seeing her visitor, she hurriedly put the pillowcase aside and jumped up. 'Good afternoon, Madam.'

'Good afternoon, Betsy. Where is Nanny?'

'She's in her room, Mrs Faraday. Er ... I'm ever so sorry, you know...'

'Thank you.' As Helena crossed the room, the poignancy of Rosalind's empty cot was unavoidable, but she looked away and tapped at the adjacent door. 'It's Mrs Faraday, Nanny.'

There came shuffling footsteps and when the door partly opened, she gazed into the tortured eyes of a woman who seemed to have aged ten years. Quietly she said, 'How are you?'

'I should be asking you that question, Madam. Not that I have any right after the way I've let you down.'

'May I come in?'

Helena went into the small neat room, trying to subdue the feelings of bitterness, even hatred she had been feeling towards the woman to whom she had entrusted her child. But even she had to admit that this was not a case of deliberate negligence.

'My first duty was to Miss Rosalind. I should never have left her side. There is still no news?'

Helena shook her head. 'I'm afraid not.' She hesitated. 'But there is something I must say, Nanny, and it is only out of concern for you. From now on, I wish you to resume taking your morning

369

coffee and afternoon tea in the Servants' Hall with the rest of the staff. It will not do at all for you to hide away from everyone.'

The broken woman sat in an armchair, her hands lying limply in her lap. 'I'll never get over it, never. I'll have to resign of course, and I doubt if anyone will trust me with their children after this.'

'You may rest assured that I shall still give you a reference.'

'Thank you, Mrs Faraday. The secret is not in what is written but in what is omitted. We both know that a discerning employer learns to read between the lines.'

Helena remained silent.

'Mrs Faraday?' Nanny Evans rose and going to a drawer at the side of her bed withdrew something and held it out. 'This was left in the perambulator.'

Helena turned to see sunshine glinting on Rosalind's silver rattle.

'Why on earth didn't the woman tell the Chief Inspector?' Jacob was furious.

'Isn't that the rattle Dorothy bought?' Beatrice said.

'Yes.' Helena was fingering its engraved image of a rabbit, tears stinging her eyes as she remembered Rosalind's delight in it.

'Surely no normal criminal would leave behind such a valuable object? I shall take it to Scotland Yard in case it might be viewed as evidence.'

The two women watched Jacob leave, then turned as a parlourmaid brought in tea. Helena shook her head as Beatrice offered her a scone.

'Please try and eat, you hardly touched your breakfast, and at luncheon only pushed your food around. You will be ill, and that will do no-one any good.'

'I'm sorry, Aunt Beatrice. I just cannot stand all this inactivity. I want to go out there, search the streets, anything! She's *my child*, I should be doing something.' Her nerves were at screaming pitch when there came a peal of the doorbell. Helena said wearily, 'I don't wish to see anyone, whoever it is.'

A moment later, the butler came into the room. 'Dr Carstairs has called, Madam. He says he has no wish to disturb you, Mrs Faraday, other than to bring a letter of condolence from Dr Haverstock. Miss Standish, if convenient he requested that he might see you for a moment? I have shown him into the morning room.'

Beatrice rose immediately. 'But of course.'

Helena could only put a hand to her throat, feeling profound relief. Nicholas was here... Surely he would to be able to help her. The letter from Dr Haverstock would be the excuse he had needed to bring him to Faraday House after reading the news of Oliver's death. But although Helena did grieve for her husband, hating the way he had suffered such a violent death, what was causing every hour to be a living nightmare was her fear and terror for her baby's safety. She would never be able to help Oliver again, but Rosalind needed her as never before.

'Helena, my dear,' Beatrice soon returned. 'I have been prescribed a sleeping draught and if you feel well enough, Dr Carstairs has suggested that you might like to see him for a few moments. It would seem sensible as he could then let Dr Haverstock know how you are.'

Helena kept her eyes lowered. 'If you think that might help.'

Beatrice smiled at her with relief. 'Yes I do.'

Helena watched her leave and then at last, the butler ushered in the tall man she had thought never to see again. As the door closed and he began to walk towards her, his step slowed and she saw his expression alter with deep concern.

Nicholas could only gaze at the young woman who rose to face him in profound shock. He had expected to find Helena pale and saddened, but never to find her so ravaged. The dark circles around her eyes, her excessive pallor, the trembling of her hands revealed the extent of her distress, and apart from his concern, he felt bewildered. Had he been wrong all these months, had he misjudged the happiness within her marriage? Had she after all been deeply in love with her husband? When they had talked together in this room all those months ago, she had evaded his question in such a way that... Nicholas felt as if his world had shifted.

She rushed to towards him. 'Oh Nicholas, I can't believe I am seeing you again.'

He pulled himself together, hating to see her suffer so. 'Helena. I am so sorry about Oliver.'

'It's dreadful. Oh, I'm so glad you've come.' Her voice caught in a sob. 'You cannot know...'

'Helena, I...'

'You don't understand – it's Rosalind...'

He stared at her in bewilderment. 'Your baby?

Is she ill?'

She shook her head. 'No, it's not that.' Her eyes full of panic, she clutched at his sleeve. 'Nicholas, she's been kidnapped.'

He stared at her in disbelief.

Her eyes brimming now with tears, she said, 'You know that Oliver was murdered just after midnight? Well, earlier that day in the park, Nanny went to help some woman who had fainted and...' her voice broke, 'someone stole Rosalind out of her pram!' Now Helena's voice became a wail. 'I don't know where she is, Nicholas; I don't even know whether she's been hurt.'

For the first time Nicholas drew her into his arms, holding her close, feeling at last her slender yet soft body against his own, and as Helena wept on his shoulder, he tried to grasp the enormity of what she had told him. Then once her sobs became quieter, he led her to the sofa and gently folding her hands inside his, said, 'I want you to tell me exactly what happened, everything.'

He listened carefully, his mind dissecting every detail. 'And you say there has been no word, no ransom demand, nothing?'

She shook her head.

'But you *have* told the police?'

She nodded, 'Papa is even now at Scotland Yard.'

Nicholas gazed at her wan face, and opened his bag. 'Helena, I want you to promise me to take this sedative that Andrew has prescribed.'

'I promise. And Nicholas, you mustn't say a word to anyone about Rosalind. I really shouldn't

373

have told you.'

'I understand. Do you still have the card I gave you, with my telephone number?'

She nodded.

'Please use it, Helena, day or night, whenever you need me.' He shook his head. 'I can't believe such a thing can happen. I mean here, in England.' He said with reluctance, 'I suppose I ought to leave.' As he watched her walk over to the bell pull, the slump of her shoulders tore at his heartstrings, but he could only promise to come again as soon as he possibly could.

When a few minutes later he left Faraday House, Nicholas was consumed with unease; because no matter how he tried to dismiss it, a creeping suspicion was growing with every second that passed, and it was so horrendous that he hardly dared to face it.

The memory of Oliver Faraday's cold blue eyes that first and only time they had met, Andrew relating Oliver's horror on first seeing Rosalind's imperfect hands, that he had even threatened to hide his own daughter away from public gaze. And even as a child he had apparently refused to play with a toy that was imperfect. To Nicholas all this tended to lead to one conclusion. Besides, he could only think of two possible reasons why a man should leave his home and his distraught wife in the middle of the night and go to the Embankment. Either he had been contacted by the kidnappers or – and may God forgive him for thinking ill of the deceased – he was himself involved in the crime. The family may not think him capable of such evil; however, were the officers at Scotland Yard aware of Oliver's true feelings towards his child?

Cora had never risen so early in her life. Nor had she ever felt so afraid. Not even on the day of the kidnapping had her nerves bothered her so much. It was just after 5 am when she let herself out of the apartment building. Her face was devoid of makeup, her hair concealed beneath a hat with a short veil and she wore a plain brown skirt and jacket, an image she often adopted when visiting the public library. Quietly she began to walk along the pavement.

Cora had thought long and hard about what she was going to do. She doubted that this Oliver Faraday's plan included someone in London playing happy families with his kid. During the last couple of days, Cora hadn't been able to get the image of that baby's sweet smile out of her head, nor how it had felt to carry her small warm body. She may have a stash of golden guineas at the bottom of the wardrobe, but she still wanted to sleep easy in her bed for the rest of her life. But twenty minutes later without a single hansom cab in sight, her stomach began to churn with anxiety. She already knew that she might be too late, but this morning could be her last chance...

And then at last with relief she heard the clop of hooves.

She told the driver to stop when they were a short distance away from Carlton House Terrace, and she walked demurely along the streets until she reached the one adjacent to it. Cora, curious to see Faraday House, forced herself to resist the temptation to look around the corner. Just because there had been nothing in the papers about the kidnapping, that didn't mean it hadn't been reported to the police. No, what she needed to do was to try not to be noticed and to watch out for her prey. Fortunately, as she felt conspicuous in the deserted street, she did not have to wait too long. The boy was about twelve, thin faced, his wrists protuding from his jacket, his cap at a jaunty angle, his lips pursed in a soundless whistle. As he ran up and down the steps of each house to deliver his newspapers, she waited until just before he turned into Carlton House Terrace, then grasped at his shoulder.

He swung round. ''Ere, what's your game?'

'Ssh. Want to earn a tanner?'

'What for?'

'Just to push this envelope through one of the doors.'

'Which door?'

'Faraday House, round this corner.'

He stared at her. 'Where that geezer lived? The one what was murdered?'

'That's right.'

He frowned. 'I'd need a shillin'.'

Cora took out the coin and held it up. 'It's a deal then?' She handed him the envelope. 'And if anyone asks you…'

Grabbing the coin, he grinned. 'I never admit ter nuthin'!'

Cora turned away, not daring to risk staying in the area a minute longer. She forced herself to walk at the same demure pace; there were a few other young women about now, mainly shop girls on their way to work, and she mingled amongst them before taking a tram and returning to her apartment building. Once safely home, she cut herself a slice of thick bread and butter spread with marmalade, and washed it down with a cup of strong sweet tea. Replenished, she sat back in her armchair satisfied that at least she had tried to make amends; the rest was in the lap of the Gods.

Cora settled further into the chair and yawned. Just forty winks, and then she would set off for the public library and have a look at an atlas.

Chapter Fifty-one

Nicholas breakfasted early the following morning. The previous evening with the terrible suspicion concerning Oliver at the forefront of his mind, he had pored over his medical books, only to be defeated in forming any conclusion because he had insufficient facts. While it would be unthinkable to raise the subject with Helena, Jacob Standish had the reputation of being a man of both intelligence and perception and Nicholas intended to go directly to Faraday House. Even if his questions – and he would need to use the utmost diplomacy – were rebuffed, there was the chance that they might lead to a fresh light being shone on the investigations.

When he arrived, he gave only a brief glance at the car outside with its waiting driver, but almost immediately the front door opened and he stood aside as Jacob Standish, followed closely by two other men, came hurrying out down the steps. Helena, behind them, gave an exclamation on seeing him and called out. 'Nicholas! There is news about Rosalind!'

Her father swung round to stare up at her in astonishment.

Helena flushed. 'I'm sorry, Papa. I told Dr Carstairs yesterday.'

The taller of the men frowned. '*Dr* Carstairs? Are you a physician?

Nicholas nodded. 'I am, and known to the family.'

'In that case, would you be willing to come with us? I will explain on the way.'

'Yes of course. I take it you have no objection, Mr Standish?'

'If you so wish. Can we please not waste any more time?' Jacob was already on his way to his own car, now drawn up behind the other.

Nicholas was ushered on to the back seat of the police car and sitting beside him, the Detective Chief Inspector introduced both himself and his sergeant who was in the passenger seat. 'Mr Standish telephoned Scotland Yard early this morning before I came on duty, and again later. Once informed, I acted immediately. An envelope was delivered by hand to Faraday House containing one sheet of paper with the words – "*the baby was taken here*" – followed by an address. That is where we are going, Dr Carstairs. I have already arranged for another car to meet us there. I just hope that your services will not be required.'

It seemed an age until Nicholas glimpsed the name of the street, a seemingly respectable tree-lined one, the houses three-storey, and as their car drew up at the number given, he could see the police car with its blue lamp drawn up further along. Seeing his glance, the Chief Inspector said, 'We shall first of all go in quietly. I shall endeavour yet again to deter Mr Standish from accompanying us, but as a member of His Majesty's Government, he does hold a certain authority.'

Out on the pavement, Jacob was adamant. 'If my granddaughter is in that house, Chief Inspector, neither you nor the King himself could prevent me from going in.'

The detective gave a sigh of resignation. 'Sergeant?'

The stockily built officer held his finger on the doorbell.

The front door with its gleaming black paint was opened by a sallow-faced maid, her hair concealed beneath a white cap.

The Chief Inspector said, 'Is your master or mistress at home?'

'Yes, Sir. I mean…'

'Who is it, Emmie?' The woman who came forward was dressed entirely in black, her pale hands devoid of rings, a bunch of keys dangling from her waist. Her eyes narrowed. 'It's all right, I'll deal with this.'

The Chief Inspector introduced himself and his sergeant.

She smiled pleasantly. 'Has there been an accident?'

'No, it is nothing like that. Are you the house-keeper?'

'Yes, I am.'

'May I see the owner, please? I suggest that it would be rather less public if you were to invite us inside.'

She hesitated then stood aside for the small group of men to enter the hall. 'I hope, Chief Inspector, that you have good reason for this. Mrs Masterson does not like to be disturbed in the mornings.'

As they waited in the hall and watched the housekeeper ascend the staircase, Nicholas glanced around at the hall, and at a corridor leading off with several doors. Then at the faint sound overhead of a baby crying, Jacob's head jerked up, his face suffused with eagerness. But already coming down the stairs with the house-keeper was a small woman fussily dressed in purple, her ample bosom adorned with pearls.

'Good morning, Chief Inspector. How can I help you?'

'I must apologise for the inconvenience, Mrs Masterson. I am afraid we have received inform-ation that a child abducted from her rightful parents was recently brought to this address.'

'That is an outrageous accusation. I cannot imagine how my late husband, Colonel Master-son, would have reacted to it. Can you vouch for the accuracy of your source?'

'In a case such as this we have to investigate every report.'

'That is as may be. But I can assure you...'

The Chief Inspector said, 'We did a few

moments ago hear a baby crying?'

'You did indeed. This house is used as a nursery for children placed here by quite high-born families who, you understand, rely on my discretion.'

'I see, that would certainly explain it. But you would have no objection to my officers searching the premises?'

'Of course not, I can only imagine how the child's poor parents must be feeling.'

While the Sergeant went out to the other car, the Chief Inspector turned to Jacob and Nicholas. 'I would be greatly obliged if you would remain here in the hall, and allow my officers to search the entire house unimpeded. Believe me if we find anything at all...'

As the other three uniformed constables came in to secure the downstairs quarters and followed Mrs Masterson to search the ground floor, the senior officers accompanied the housekeeper to the upstairs rooms. Jacob tapped his cane on the tiled floor. 'Dr Carstairs, I hope this is not a fool's errand. I mean – a Colonel's widow...?'

Nicholas was thoughtful. 'Mr Standish, we have only her word as to her status.'

They waited for what seemed an eternity, catching glimpses of the constables leaving first one room then another and another, before disappearing along a corridor. Eventually they came back to wait at the foot of the staircase for their superior officer. Mrs Masterson stood with them, a satisfied expression on her face. Once the Chief Inspector returned, he questioned his subordinates who shook their heads. Nicholas heard the words 'kitchen quarters', then the constables left.

With an exclamation of frustration, Jacob, with Nicholas following, hurried over to them. 'Well?'

'I'm sorry, Sir. We have found nothing.'

Nicholas frowned. 'There are babies of a similar age here?'

The Chief Inspector nodded. 'Four.'

Nicholas persisted. 'You checked all of their hands?'

'Yes!' His tone was sharp. 'All three of them!'

Jacob said, 'I thought you said there were four babies?'

'The fourth is of no interest to you,' Mrs Masterson said. 'She is the misfortune of a Negro servant, who is returning in disgrace to her family. She is even now waiting for a carriage to take her to the docks.'

Nicholas turned to the Chief Inspector. 'You saw this baby?'

'One of my constables did.'

Nicholas could almost feel Jacob's despondency. He thought of Helena, of her bitter disappointment, her anguish when they returned empty-handed.

'Please, Chief Inspector, would you allow me to accompany you and see the child for myself.'

He sighed. 'I don't know what you hope to achieve, but if you insist.'

Jacob stepped forward. 'In that case, I shall not remain in the background.'

The three men went down the back stairs to the small Servants' Hall, and to a neat kitchen where a harrassed looking cook, on seeing the three men, disappeared into the scullery. Seated at a

382

table was a young Negro girl dressed in travel clothes, a large and a small carpet bag by her feet. In her arms and wrapped in a shawl was a baby, who Nicholas would judge to be around three months old. She was wearing a sunbonnet, but her black skin gleamed and it only took one look for Jacob's shoulders to slump in despair. The Chief Inspector gave an expressive shrug in the direction of Nicholas.

Nicholas studied the young woman, seeing her nervousness, although that could be because of their presence, but he was sure that he could detect fear in her eyes and she held the child awkwardly, not as a mother would. He sensed the others behind him begin to move away but he hesitated, some instinct making him pause. The baby slowly began to stir and as he watched, the tiny mouth opened in a yawn, there was a flutter of eyelashes and blue eyes gazed up at him. His own narrowed and he turned swiftly to call, 'Wait!'

As the other two men returned, Nicholas took a handkerchief from his pocket. 'I need someone to prise the baby's head away from her.'

Jacob stared at him. 'What?'

The Chief Inspector looked at Nicholas. 'Doctor, are you sure about this?'

'Please, trust me.'

The Chief Inspector turned as Mrs Masterson, who had followed them, came rushing over. 'What are you doing, how dare you touch that girl!'

It was then as the Chief Inspector bent to loosen her grip that the young girl suddenly gave in, and Nicholas moistened one corner of the handkerchief with his tongue and gently rubbed it across the baby's forehead. Then he held out the white fabric with its black smudge. 'I knew as soon as she woke up. Have you ever seen a Negro with blue eyes?'

Stunned, Jacob stared first at the handkerchief then at the white patch on the baby's skin, and as the Chief Inspector with compassion stood aside, Jacob dropped his cane, removed the shawl from the baby's hands and with trembling fingers, untied the ribbons on the mittens to reveal her tiny white and unmistakeable hands. When Rosalind reached up to grasp at his beard, it took every ounce of Jacob's self-control not to give way to tears of profound joy.

Instead, as he took her away from the servant and held her protectively against him, he glared at Mrs Masterson who was now staring at him with frightened eyes. 'You, Madam, will feel the full weight of the law. You have my word on it.' He began to walk towards the door. 'And now, Chief Inspector,' he cleared his throat, 'I shall take my granddaughter home where she belongs.'

On their way back to Faraday House, with Jacob holding his tearful baby granddaughter like precious china, he and Nicholas discussed the dramatic happenings of the morning. 'It was a shame we had to distress her by rubbing the black shoe polish off her face,' Nicholas said...'

Jacob nodded. 'Yes, but necessary, I'm afraid. Otherwise there was a risk of attracting unwanted attention.' Gently he rocked Rosalind in his arms and gradually she began to calm down.

'You have been fortunate so far, Sir, with the loyalty of your staff.'

'Not my staff, Dr Carstairs, those of my late son-in-law. However, we cannot be certain they will always remain so.'

'Perhaps now that Mrs Masterson and her servants have been arrested and taken to Scotland Yard they will make a full confession,' Nicholas said. 'After all, they were caught red-handed, so there would be little point in trying to deny their crime.' He was hoping that their evidence would prove his suspicions regarding Oliver to be unfounded; after all his beloved Helena had suffered enough anguish.

Helena and Beatrice had spent the last two hours in an agony of suspense. For once Beatrice had been unable to remonstrate with her niece for pacing the drawing room, for she too had been equally distraught. And they had both been mystified as to not only who had written and delivered the note, but as to her motive. Beatrice was convinced that the cheap lined stationery and the handwriting proved the culprit was a woman.

'I've told Dorothy about it,' Helena said. Her friend had telephoned every day since returning home. 'She thinks it may be because of Oliver's death being in the newspapers.'

'Why should that make such a difference?'

'Perhaps someone thought that for me to lose both a husband and a child almost on the same day, was too much for anyone to bear.'

'That,' Beatrice said, 'is to credit whoever took Rosalind with decent Christian feelings! What I fail to understand is why she was stolen at all, if not to extract money from us. This whole business puzzles me. No, this is a falling out among thieves, I am sure of it.'

But Helena was again at the window, her hair dishevelled from her constant fingering of it, the skin on her lower lip becoming sore as she had gnawed on it so often. 'How much longer... Oh they're here, the car is coming now...' With her aunt close behind her, Helena rushed from the room, and before anyone else could reach the front door, she had opened it herself to hurry down the steps.

When she glimpsed the white shawl in her father's arms, she ran along the pavement to touch the window, uncaring of Beatrice's call to wait for the car to stop. The chauffeur drew to a halt and hurriedly opened the rear door for Jacob to hand over his precious bundle. On seeing her mother, Rosalind eagerly held up her arms and with tears of joy, Helena lifted her tiny daughter to hold her close. She breathed in the scent of her, kissing her forehead, her cheek, whispering, 'Mummy's here, my darling, you're home, you're safe.' She held her away to search her face and reassured said, 'Look, Aunt Beatrice is here too, let's take you in – all your teddies are waiting for you...'

When they all went into the hall, even the butler and footmen were smiling. Helena said over her shoulder, 'Thank you, Papa, thank you! I'm going to take her straight up to the nursery for a bath and some clean clothes.'

'I do think an examination might be advisable first,' Nicholas said.

Jacob gave a nod of approval. 'Thank you, Dr Carstairs. I would appreciate that.'

Nicholas followed Helena up the curving staircase to be met on the first landing by two beaming maids, one of whom lifted her apron to dab at her eyes, and then on to the third floor and the nursery. As a young fresh-faced girl who was bending over a cot turned and cried out 'Rosalind', a door opened in the corner of the room and a haggard woman in the uniform of a nanny came hurrying out.

'Thank God! Is she unharmed?'

'We are hoping so,' Helena said. 'At least she is safely home.'

Nicholas felt a stab of compassion as the woman sank into a nursing chair and buried her face in her hands. Helena said, 'Betsy, I shall need a bath to be prepared for her.'

'Yes, Madam. Oh, I'm so pleased she's back.'

'Thank you. Nanny, I can understand your being upset, but perhaps you and Betsy could leave while Dr Carstairs carries out his examination?'

Once alone, Helena placed Rosalind in the cot and taking off her clothes threw them on the floor with distaste. 'I shall have those burned.' Then she watched Nicholas move gentle and experienced hands over her daughter.

'She seems to be fine. It might be as well to resume her normal formula in small amounts at first at frequent intervals, at least for the first forty-eight hours.' Helena saw him frown. 'What her destiny would have been had we not arrived at the house when we did...'

'You were only just in time?'

387

As she covered Rosalind with a pink cotton sheet, he began to describe the scene in the kitchen. With Helena now staring at him in horror, he ended, 'I really am beginning to believe in fate Helena. If I hadn't come here this morning, and just at that particular time...'

Her voice was shaky. 'Nicholas, there are not the words.' She turned to him and somehow they were in each other's arms, her relief, her gratitude, her love for him, all drowning the caution she had tried so carefully to perserve. As she clung to his lean yet strong body, she could feel the warmth of his breath and at last raised her lips for his first sweet and tender kiss, swiftly followed by another so deep and full of promise, that Helena knew a line had been crossed beyond which it would be impossible ever to return.

Chapter Fifty-two

Nicholas, although aware of the immediate need to disillusion Andrew concerning his obvious hope of a future marriage between his partner and his niece, was finding it a sensitive subject to broach. Then the opportunity arose one lunch-time, as when seated in the oak-panelled room of their favourite restaurant and waiting for their oxtail soup, Andrew leaned back and said, 'Mrs Haverstock told me this morning that her sister and the girls are thinking of extending their stay in London. And I,' his eyes creased at the corners, 'have a slight suspicion that one of the reasons might be seated opposite.'

Nicholas gazed steadily at him. 'Andrew, I do hope not.'

'I don't understand, we both thought that...'

'Miss Elspeth is delightful, but I'm afraid that something has happened that changes everything. I had every intention of mentioning it to you.'

Andrew frowned. 'When you say that something has happened, am I to take it that you mean...'

Nicholas nodded. 'I offer you my apologies, Andrew. Yes, there is someone else. The situation that I find myself in arose unexpectedly, and I am not at liberty to say more. But I can assure you that nothing of a personal nature passed between myself and Miss Elspeth.'

Andrew waited until the waiter had brought their soup, and then slowly broke off a morsel of his bread roll. 'I cannot deny that I am disappointed and I know my wife will be too.' He looked across at Nicholas. 'But I know you well enough to respect your decision. I just hope you don't regret it.'

A few days after Rosalind's safe return, in response to a telephone call, Jacob instructed his chauffeur to drive him to New Scotland Yard on the Victoria Embankment and he was immediately ushered to the office of Chief Inspector Morris.

The tall figure of the detective came forward, hand outstretched. 'Good morning, Mr Standish. I'm sorry to cause you the inconvenience of coming all this way.'

'Not at all, Chief Inspector, I am sure you are a very busy man.'

'I think you will understand my reasons for not coming to Faraday House, when you hear what I have to tell you. A rather unpleasant business, I'm afraid.'

Jacob took the seat indicated before the desk, and found apprehension rising as the Chief Inspector returned to his own on the other side. He lowered himself into the chair somewhat heavily. 'I'm afraid what I have to say will come as a profound shock to you. The fact is that as a result of Mrs Masterson's statement, our investigations have uncovered irrefutable evidence linking your son-in-law to the kidnap of your granddaughter.'

Jacob felt the blood begin to pound in his temples, and gripped the silver knob of his cane so tightly that his knuckles whitened.

The Chief Inspector waited a moment then continued. 'Apparently, there was a profitable trade being carried out in that house. Babies born on the wrong side of the blanket, who would cause scandal in high places, were brought there to be smuggled out of the country, first over the Channel to France, and then elsewhere.'

Jacob's voice was hoarse. 'I find this difficult to believe. About Oliver, I mean.'

'I am afraid there is no mistake. I can only assume that your son-in-law availed himself of this service for the disposal of his own daughter. What I do not understand, Mr Standish, is why he should do such a thing.'

Jacob lowered his eyes in an attempt to conceal

how shaken he was, how horrified. 'I can only thank you for your consideration, Chief Inspector. If my daughter were to have the slightest inkling…'

'Indeed, but I would ask you again, could you give me any explanation?'

After a pause, Jacob, who could only attribute it to what he assumed to be Oliver's phobic mental illness, briefly explained. 'And his death – was that connected?'

'We have discovered nothing to indicate it. But it is still early days.'

Oliver Faraday's funeral was a sober and well-attended occasion, with a sonorous sermon as befitted such a prominent member of the local community, despairing of the decline in moral standards that had led to the manner of his death. The burial ceremony took place in the churchyard near Graylings where the Faraday family had its own small mausoleum.

In the black-draped drawing room afterwards, many of the mourners cast admiring glances towards what some described as a tragic and beautiful widow, although Dorothy whispered to Peregrine that she had already detected speculative glances. 'I suppose we can expect a few fortune hunters,' she said with scorn. 'Scavengers, that's all they are.'

Jacob was finding the day almost impossible to bear, as at his side his beloved daughter, pale in her widow's weeds, listened to well-meaning people extol the virtues of his son-in-law. As he murmured the expected platitudes, he felt not only a hypocrite, but also guilt knowing that he had allowed his political ambition to cloud his judgment. Otherwise, how could he have encouraged his daughter to marry such a man?

'You look tired, Jacob.' Angela Shirley's quiet smile later eased his nerves. 'It has been a difficult day for all of you.'

'It has indeed.' He glanced across to where Beatrice was valiantly conversing with the last remaining couple and saw her relief as the butler ushered them out. 'I imagine that my sister will be in need of a rest before dinner, whereas ... would you care to join me in taking some air?'

'I think a walk would be delightful.'

It was a week later when Jane Forrester approached Helena. 'Madam, might I have a word on a personal matter?'

'But of course, Jane. How can I help?' Helena turned from the extra cot that was now a fixture in her bedroom. She was still too fearful of Rosalind's absence from her to allow her to sleep overnight in the nursery upstairs.

Jane, after bending to give the smiling baby her silver rattle, said, 'It's about Jack, I mean Hines, Madam. He was wondering if he has your permission to return to Graylings to see Mr Crossley.'

'Yes of course, but why does he...'

Jane said quietly, 'He needs to know what his position is. He has finished sorting out Mr Faraday's clothes and belongings.'

Helena gazed at her. 'Yes, I see, but he may as well wait until we all return which will be very soon now. Jane, how is this change in his circumstances going to affect you?'

She pushed back a strand of her dark hair. 'I don't know what the future holds for us. We would like to get married, but neither of us has ever worked anywhere but in service, and very few households employ husbands and wives.'

Helena was thoughtful and later, having given Betsy instructions to watch Rosalind with extreme care, she went downstairs to the morning room to join Dorothy and Peregrine who had remained after the funeral. Dorothy was scornful. 'I can understand staff being discouraged from forming relationships within a household, but why preclude a couple already married?' She turned to her fiancé. 'Didn't you say that you intend to keep on your house in the country, besides one in town?'

He gazed at her with amusement. 'Do I detect your sharp brain at work?'

'It's just that only recently old Farthingale told me of his wish to live nearer to his daughter.' She turned to Helena. 'What if Perry were to have a word with Hines. If he likes the look of him, and they both feel he could take on the role of a butler, then maybe they could join our staff. I like your Jane, and I shall need a personal maid once I'm married.'

Helena smiled at her with relief. 'Dorothy, you're a genius.'

'That is the only reason I proposed.' Peregrine stretched out his long legs and grinned. 'I shall expect her to write all of my speeches.'

'I might even do that, if only to infiltrate them with my own political views.'

Helena said, 'Actually, Dorothy, thinking of your support for women's suffrage, you would be welcome to hold any committee meetings here. It would be a pity if your activities were to affect Perry's prospects in the House.'

'Thank you. I am even more relieved that you are to keep Faraday House. I'm sure that loathsome Selwyn expected to inherit it along with Graylings.'

'Mr McPherson told me that Papa was implacable that it should be included in my Marriage Settlement.'

'He is a formidable man, your father,' Peregrine said. 'I'm sorry we have to leave tomorrow.'

'I'm just grateful you've been able to stay,' Helena said. 'Anyway, although we can't properly entertain yet, as it's your last night we have a few guests for dinner. Mrs Shirley and Johnnie Horton you already know, but not Miss Selina Lee, who he met in Italy, nor Dr Nicholas Carstairs.' As she mentioned his name Helena glanced away, horrified to feel the colour rise in her cheeks.

'How could you not tell me?' Dorothy's voice was low so as not to disturb the sleeping baby, although she and Helena were sitting in the small parlour adjacent to the bedroom. Always perceptive, she had questioned her friend at the earliest opportunity.

'I nearly did once, at Broadway Manor, when we were in the garden and the others were playing tennis, but you were always so scathing about anything romantic, even novels. Can you imagine how foolish you would have made me feel at dreaming about a man I had seen twice, and then only briefly? I knew nothing about him, not even where he lived, or whether I would ever see him again. And,' Helena looked down at her hands, her voice becoming even lower, 'I can't explain it; the feelings I had for him were too fragile.'

Dorothy gazed at her with contrition. 'It was, I'm afraid, a case of "He jests at scars who never felt a wound", you know, from *Romeo and Juliet*. I had never been in love then.'

'It's such a relief,' Helena said, 'to feel able to confide in you at last.'

Dorothy said quietly, 'I've often wondered – were you truly happy with Oliver?'

'Do I have to answer that question?'

'Helena, you already have.'

The gathering in the dining room was subdued at first, but Johnnie's irrepressible good humour and his obvious devotion to the gentle dark-haired Selina soon lightened the atmosphere. Helena, seated at the head of the table with Nicholas on her left, hated the enforced pretence between them, conscious even as he conversed with Beatrice beside him, of his every word and smile, of his long slender fingers each time he reached for his glass.

Jacob, facing Helena at the other end of the table, was again appreciative of Angela Shirley's rare quality; that of sensing when a man had no desire for female chatter. He was quietly observant. Helena, with her black gown relieved by a double row of glowing pearls, looked breathtakingly lovely and it was such a relief to see the mantle of despair lifted from her shoulders. May God forgive him, never from *his* lips would she hear the terrible truth about the man who had fathered her child.

As Jacob gazed along the white damask table-cloth with its centrepiece of pink and cream summer roses towards his daughter and then around the table, despite his initial surprise, he felt pleased that Dr Carstairs was included in their small gathering. Neither he nor his family would ever be able to repay the debt they owed that young man. Then he saw Helena's expression soften as the doctor turned towards her with a brief smile, and to Jacob it seemed as if a silent message passed between them.

Suddenly into his mind came an image of the scene outside Faraday House the morning they left to rescue Rosalind. On seeing Dr Carstairs arrive, Helena had called out his Christian name. He had been somewhat startled at the time, and only now did he realise that since then she had reverted to using his formal address. The man was a devilish handsome chap and Jacob was beginning to frown in puzzlement when he felt Angela Shirley's soft hand on his sleeve deflecting him from his thoughts. Later when retiring for the night, he decided that the wine, having been an especially fine vintage, had merely made him imagine things. After all, his daughter had buried her husband scarcely a week before; he was doing her a disservice to think she would be so disloyal.

When Jacob returned to Broadway Manor, it was alone, Beatrice having decided to remain behind

396

at Faraday House. 'I feel that Helena will need me,' she explained. 'As you and I both know, the period after a funeral can often be the hardest time. You will make sure that little Skye is not fretting for me?'

Jacob smiled. 'You miss that little dog, don't you?'

She nodded. 'Ridiculous, isn't it?'

'Would you like me to arrange to have her brought down?'

'Jacob, would you? We are so close to the park, I am sure she would settle. And if Hewson gave you a list, perhaps one of the parlourmaids could pack up some extra clothes?'

Helena, quietly grateful, found comfort in her aunt's strength, while little Rosalind smiled at little dog's antics, and gradually the days turned into weeks, until at last, Nicholas came.

Helena was reading *The Times*, while Beatrice was embroidering a cassock for Lichfield Cathedral when the butler came into the morning room to announce him. 'Dr Carstairs has called, Madam.'

Helena laid the newspaper on her lap, her pulse racing. 'Please show him in.'

When his tall figure appeared on the threshold, Helena wondered whether he had had decided that the time had come for no more pretence, but surely, it was too soon.

Beatrice looked up. 'Good morning, Dr Carstairs.'

'Good morning, Miss Standish, Mrs Faraday. I trust I find you both well?'

397

Helena said, 'Please do join us. May I offer you some refreshment?'

'Thank you. My apologies for disturbing you, but I wanted to advise you that it might be wise to keep Rosalind at home at the moment. There is a bad outbreak of measles.' His gaze rested on Helena. 'After being involved in bringing her back to you, let us say that I feel a personal concern for her welfare.'

'Why, Dr Carstairs, how very thoughtful,' Beatrice said.

'I'm very grateful to you,' Helena said. 'Measles is a terrible disease, there was a baby who died of it in the village.'

Beatrice turned back from the bell pull. 'Yes indeed, it can affect the eyes too.' As the clock in the hall began to chime, she said, 'I hadn't realised that was the time, I must take Skye for her walk. She does so like her routine. I hope you will forgive me, Dr Carstairs.'

Once she had left the room, Helena said, 'I can only bless little Skye, she is my aunt's dog by the way.' Her voice caught in her throat. 'Nicholas, it's so wonderful to see you.'

'I just couldn't wait any longer,' his voice was intense.

'You look glowing with health.'

He smiled at her. 'I took a brisk walk in the park. I'm a great believer in the benefits of fresh air. Helena, how are you? These past weeks must have been so difficult.'

'Honestly?'

'Honestly.'

'I feel – I suppose the best way of describing it

would be to say that I feel subdued. You of all people know the truth of my marriage, yet Faraday House seems so full of Oliver's presence, and knowing the terrible way he lost his life...' she looked down at her blouse and skirt. 'Wearing black all the time is a constant reminder.'

'I've always thought it an unnecessary penance for those left behind,' he said. 'Respect for the deceased, yes, but terribly depressing for the living.'

There was a knock at the door and a few seconds later, a young parlourmaid brought in a tray. Nicholas smiled as she lifted the domed lid on a silver dish. 'Ah, warm muffins.'

'Will there be anything else, Madam?'

'No thank you, Mary.'

'If only,' Nicholas said, when she had left the room, 'we could find some way of spending time together without being interrupted by servants.'

'I know.' Helena passed him a plate, napkin and knife, her gaze lingering on the dusting of dark hairs on his hands. 'Nicholas what are we going to do? This is going to go on for months and months.'

'I can't ask you to come and see me. We must protect your reputation at all costs.'

'And if we walk together, we are bound to be seen – even I can see that would cause a scandal. It is so soon after...' she broke off and felt colour rise in her cheeks.

Nicholas said, 'Sweetheart, we are only trying to get to know each other better, you have no need to feel guilty.' He took a bite out of a muffin. 'I have an idea. Once your aunt has returned home, why not decide to take Rosalind for some sea air. You could wheel her along the promenade at around the same time each morning, and perhaps take a walk alone each afternoon, and if we consult on the dates...'

'The perfect solution,' Helena breathed. 'Nicholas, you are so clever.' Then she laughed. 'You've got butter dripping down your chin.'

'Have I?' He dabbed at it with his napkin, his eyes alight with amusement.

'I wanted to do that,' she said softly, 'but I couldn't in case the butler came in.' There was a scuffle at the door as Beatrice swept in. 'Oh, good, I hope there are some muffins left. Skye refused to go any further than just inside the park gates. Come along and meet Dr Carstairs, you naughty girl.'

Helena suppressed a sigh. It would, she knew, always be like this.

They chose Bognor Regis and it was there, despite knowing that it would be months before they could truly be together, that Helena and Nicholas made plans for their future.

'I think Easter,' she said, 'will be the best time for me to tell Papa. Perhaps at Broadway Manor. I am so looking forward to you seeing it.'

'Do I have to ask his permission to marry you?' He smiled down at her as they walked along in the sunshine and not unaware of a few envious female glances as they passed. She thought how much a slight tan suited him.

She laughed. 'No, of course not. When will you tell your mother?'

'When I see her at Christmas, but I shall swear her to secrecy. I know she will love you, just as I do, and she'll be captivated by Rosalind.'

Helena leaned forward to adjust the sunshade on the perambulator. 'The sea air seems to suit her.'

'I think it does everyone. Certainly she is a picture of health.'

'I wish I could find a useful role in life,' Helena mused as they paused to look out at a ship on the horizon, 'in the way that you have.'

'There's no reason why you shouldn't find some cause that appeals to you.' Nicholas considered. 'I know you're in favour of women's suffrage, your friend Dorothy left me in no doubt of that. I have attended quite a few meetings of the WSPU myself with a friend of mine, Nurse Barton.'

'Need I be jealous?'

He laughed. 'Not for a moment.'

'I haven't been to any public meetings, but I am now writing letters on their behalf, that sort of thing, although I'm not militant. I couldn't risk arrest because of Rosalind, not to mention embarrassing Papa.'

'Will he lend his support in the House do you think? I did gain an impression that he wasn't against women having the vote.'

'He's a fair-minded man – of course he's in favour, but he's only recently been elected, so he will have to feel his way at first.'

'How about Dorothy, won't her activities be awkward for Peregrine?'

'Not really, she's mainly involved behind the scenes, organising things, at least at the moment. I shall carry on helping in my own way, but I'm looking for something else too.'

His hand rested briefly on hers. 'I shall see you this afternoon?'

'Yes, as usual I shall leave Rosalind with Nanny.' She looked up at him. 'You know you only have to say the word, and I would come to your hotel...'

Nicholas gazed down at her, his eyes dark with desire. Then he shook his head. 'You will never know how I have to force myself to say this, but no, my darling. I want to be able to meet your father's eyes.'

'Then we shall talk and hold hands just as other lovers do – carefree and unafraid of prying eyes. Bliss.'

The flower shop was in a small side street just off the Esplanade. Cora had chosen Bognor Regis because, as she had told Sybil, if they settled in Brighton, they stood the risk of being recognised.

'I don't mean,' she explained, as they ate their paste sandwiches in the otherwise empty carriage on their journey down, 'because of the kidnapping, I'm pretty sure we got away with that, but because of Belle's.'

'You mean...'

Cora nodded, and began to pour tea from a thermos. 'Just suppose you did meet a bloke you wanted to settle down with, you know, get married and have kids with. And one day you both bumped into some punter?'

'And in Bognor that wouldn't 'appen?'

'Can't promise that, but it'll be a lot less likely.'

They had both emerged from the railway station clutching their belongings, and full of excited apprehension. But it had been a simple matter to find cheap lodgings and after spending a week inspecting empty premises, had discovered this little gem. Bow fronted, it had previously been a sweetshop, with a two-bedroomed apartment upstairs containing a sitting room and kitchen. Cora had instantly felt at home, recognising the security she had longed for all her life. She had no doubt that a good-looking girl like Sybil would eventually find a husband, but Cora was determined to remain single, to keep her independence. Sex she enjoyed too much to abandon, but any man she welcomed into her bed would now be by choice, rather than necessity. And the small business flourished, both girls working hard, and their cheerful banter bringing repeat customers.

It was one morning in late summer, when Sybil came back from her usual morning walk. They took it in turns to take exercise and to take the sea air, both still relishing the novelty. 'I saw this young couple with a perambulator,' she said as she began to tie the stems of a bunch of carnations, 'ever so good looking they were. She was in mourning though, probably lost one of her parents or something.'

'So?' Cora was carefully making a row of buttonholes.

'I took a peep at the baby as I passed. A little girl it was, sitting up and pointing at a seagull. I couldn't believe it when I saw her hands – she'd got six fingers. I've never 'eard of that before.'

'Better too many than too few.' Cora's tone was distracted.

Chapter Fifty-three

With Easter approaching, everyone at Broadway Manor was looking forward to a busy few weeks, especially in the Servants' Hall. Miss Helena coming to stay would mean more people to look after, what with a nanny, nursemaid and chauffeur, not to mention Molly. And there were bound to be other guests to entertain.

'Molly will be coming down soon,' Cook said. 'Don't forget now, you've got to call her Miss Fox, you kept forgetting last time.'

'That's right.' Enid Hewson drew her thin frame up to its full height. 'As Miss Helena's maid, Molly has her position to uphold.'

'At least she's got on – I'll never be anything but a kitchen maid.' Annie's expression was mutinous as she hung up a tea towel.

'Why don't I ask Miss Beatrice if I can train you up to be a cook?' Mrs Kemp said.

'Thanks, but even if became good enough and tried to get a job somewhere, they'd only say me face would turn the milk sour.'

Molly, who had paused halfway down the stairs, had heard most of the conversation and her heart filled with compassion. She had been so lucky; since her promotion she'd not only seen London but at some time in the future might even be able to travel abroad. Yet poor Annie's life held no promise at all.

'Here I am,' she said gaily, coming down into the kitchen, 'the prodigal daughter returns again.'

'Molly, love. It's good to see you.' Cook went forward and enfolded her in a floury embrace.

'I thought you said we couldn't call her...' Annie protested.

'Don't be daft!' Molly bent and kissed her cheek. 'At least not when I've only just arrived and Mr Bostock isn't around. How are you, Annie?'

'Better now you're here.'

'I bet you're all dying to see Miss Rosalind again.'

'We are that,' Cook said. 'Can you believe it, over a year old already, bless her! It's always a relief when they reach that age, safe and sound.'

Molly, who had been deeply shocked at the kidnap, glanced at Enid Hewson, both conscious of their strict instructions to say nothing. Jacob Standish had impressed upon them that the fewer people who knew of the crime, the less likelihood there was of it becoming public knowledge.

Helena had been back at Broadway Manor for just over a week when, as she had anticipated, Beatrice suggested inviting a few guests. 'Just for a weekend, my dear. After all, it is almost the end of your first year of mourning.'

'As you can see I have anticipated it slightly,' Helena confessed, looking down at her dove grey crêpe-de-Chine dress, 'I did weary of always wearing black. Who did you have in mind?'

'Mrs Shirley – your father does seem to find her company congenial, as I do – and...' Beatrice went on to mention a few members of familiar county families. 'And I thought perhaps the vicar and his wife might join us on Saturday evening. They have their niece staying with them, a sweet girl if a little shy. You know, Helena, she might rather suit Dorothy's brother, Hugh.'

'Then we must invite him, and he can tell us her news. The last I heard she and Peregrine were touring France.' Then Helena said casually, 'I wondered about Dr Carstairs. I don't think he's ever been to Staffordshire. He does work so hard, a weekend in the country might be refreshing for him.'

Beatrice's voice was calm. 'Certainly, Helena. I shall write to him this very afternoon.'

On the day that Nicholas was due to arrive, Helena walked along the hall of Broadway Manor and after tapping on the door of Jacob's study, went in and said, 'Am I disturbing you, Papa?'

He looked up from his chair behind his desk. 'Not at all, my dear, in fact I have some news.'

She walked across and sat in the leather chair opposite.

'Chief Inspector Morris has only a few moments ago telephoned. Oliver's gold pocket watch has been found. The police arrested two known ruffians and it was among their possessions; I would imagine that as it bore his initials and crest, their fear of discovery proved greater than their greed. The police are now convinced his attack was purely random.'

'So, it was not connected with the kidnapping after all.'

'That seems to be their conclusion. Also as far

as the two young women were concerned, the Chief Inspector's view is they must have either left the area or gone abroad, either way there is little trace of them.'

'So, it is all over?'

'It would appear so.' He closed the cap on his black fountain pen and laid it on his blotter. 'Now, what was it you wished to see me about?'

Helena somewhat nervously smoothed down her skirt. 'Next week will be the anniversary of Oliver's death.'

'Yes my dear, I hadn't forgotten.'

Helena twisted the rings on her fingers. Now that the moment had arrived, she was finding it more difficult than she had anticipated. 'Papa, I understand that in another three months, it will be considered acceptable for me to marry again.'

There was a short pause before Jacob said, 'If that is your intention, it is my duty to remind you that at the age of twenty-five Rosalind would then inherit Faraday House.'

'Yes, I know.' Helena's eyes met those of her father's. 'You have not asked who it is I am intending to marry.'

Jacob stroked his beard before replying and then he said, 'My dear, I may not be in the first flush of youth, but I have not been blind these past months in London. I would only ask that you tell me the truth, because I had my suspicions long ago and then dismissed them. Did this ... liaison between you and Dr Carstairs begin while your husband was alive?'

'No!' her tone was sharp, defensive, and then she said, 'At least... I cannot deny that I have had feelings for Nicholas for some time, but there has never been anything improper between us.'

He gave a grave nod. 'I would have expected nothing less from you. However, I feel that I should point out that the doctor is not the wealthiest of men.'

'Papa, he is not a fortune hunter, rather the reverse. Nicholas works hard and after our marriage will continue to do so.'

Jacob frowned. 'You have a considerable fortune, Helena. Selwyn may have inherited Graylings, but you have inherited your husband's personal investments. Then there was the money your mother left you. While I consider Dr Carstairs to be a man of integrity, I would be a poor father if I did not have a few misgivings.'

'We love each other, Papa.' Helena's voice was clear, her eyes steady. 'I am confident that we will be happy together.'

'And you are prepared for the fact that as the wife of a mere doctor, however well respected, you will find yourself *persona non grata* in some social circles?'

'Then I can only say that those within them reflect the hypocrisy of the whole system.'

Jacob gave a reluctant laugh. 'Answered like a true daughter of mine. Tell me, have you talked to your aunt about all this?'

Helena shook her head. 'I wasn't sure whether she would understand. However, if you had guessed, I'm wondering now whether she did also.'

Jacob gazed into the blue eyes that so reminded him of her mother, and inwardly sighed. 'It is possible, but if so she made no mention of it. I assume that Nicholas will be coming to see me?'

Helena nodded. 'I told him I wanted to talk to you first.'

'Well, I can only give you both my blessing, and I suggest that you now go ask for your aunt's.'

She got up, and coming round the desk, leaned to kiss his cheek. 'Thank you, Papa.'

He watched her leave. It had been his life-long ambition to raise the social status of the Standish family, and with Helena's first marriage, it had seemed he had achieved his goal, but he did wonder at what cost. He doubted whether he would ever know if his daughter had known any real happiness in her marriage to Oliver. As for this second marriage, perhaps the time-honoured tradition of allowing love to make its own selection might prove to be the best one after all. All he could do now was to protect Rosalind; she must never know the truth about her father. The thought of what her fate might have been if Oliver's plan had succeeded, even now had the power to give Jacob nightmares. That burden of knowledge was his and only his, for the rest of his life.

Beatrice was in the morning room, writing her list of 'matters to attend to'. She put down her pen and turned in her chair. 'Yes, my dear?'

Helena glanced towards the sofa and chairs. 'Could we perhaps sit down? There is something I need to tell you.'

Beatrice gazed at her. 'I see.'

Once they were both comfortable, Helena

hesitated, 'I don't quite know how to begin. I've been wanting to…'

Her aunt said gently, 'I take it that this is about Dr Carstairs?'

'You knew as well? I have just spoken to Papa, and…'

'My dear, we are not quite in our dotage. You had a right to your privacy, both of you. I just want you to be happy, my dear. And if a spinster like me can express an opinion on such things, I think you have found a man who will be not only a good husband, but a good father. I have a high regard for Dr Carstairs.'

'Thank you, Aunt Beatrice, so have I.'

After the morning service on Sunday morning, the others travelled back to Broadway Manor by carriage and motor, but Helena and Nicholas decided to walk, although Helena still lingered outside the church porch. 'There's someone I want you to meet,' she said. Briefly, she told him about Annie's accident.

'But Helena, what makes you think that I can do something that her own doctor cannot?'

'I don't, Nicholas, it's just that you may have some more up-to-date knowledge … ah, here she is.'

They both turned as the sturdy kitchen maid carrying a brown paper parcel came out of the church. She bobbed a curtsey on seeing Helena. 'Good morning, Miss.'

'Hello, Annie. Are you off to see your mother? Do give her my best wishes.'

'Thank you, Miss Helena.' She blushed on seeing Nicholas.

'This is Dr Carstairs.' Helena turned to him. 'Annie has worked at Broadway Manor since she was fourteen.'

Nicholas raised his hat and smiled at her. 'I hope they treat you well.'

'Oh yes, Sir. I'm very happy there.'

'Does your mother live far?'

'Not really, it's only a couple of miles along this road.'

'Good exercise, then. We are going to walk too.'

They watched her booted small figure leave, and as they turned to make their way towards the broad avenue to the estate, Nicholas said, 'That's a courageous young woman.' He was thoughtful for a few moments as they walked along. 'Tell me, could she come down to London, work at Faraday House for a while?'

'But of course.'

'Because I think I could arrange for her to be instructed how to use special cosmetics to disguise the worst of the redness.' Nicholas frowned. 'Only I'm afraid the consultation would be expensive and the cost of the products would continue to be so.'

'Nicholas, would you rather I frittered my money on new gowns and hats? No, I shall arrange for her to return to Faraday House when I do.' She smiled up at him. 'When we are married, you must tell me of people who need help, of deserving cases ... that will be the cause I have been looking for.'

'I shall never take advantage of your money, Helena.'

411

'I hope you do, Nicholas. I want to put it to good use.'

He glanced at her, proud of her honest belief that any difference between them regarding class and status should be of no consequence.

They walked along in companionable silence and then he said, 'Darling, do you realise just how rare it for us to be alone together, really alone?'

'I know. Even now I feel... Do you think anyone can see us?' She glanced around the wide avenue lined with trees, the sunlight dappling their leaves.

'Not unless you count the squirrels.' Drawing her into his arms, Nicholas gazed down into the face of the young woman he had loved from afar for so long. His lips moved over her forehead, lingering on her soft closed eyelids and then found her mouth in a kiss that was tender at first but soon became more searching and urgent. He drew away and murmured, 'Have you any idea how much I want and need you?' His lips travelled down to seek the hollow in her throat, 'Having to wait so long has been a torment.'

'I know.' Helena gazed up at him, lifting back a strand of his dark hair. 'Do you ever think that if I hadn't stood at that casement window...?'

'We would have met some other way, I'm sure of it. How else can you explain how fate kept bringing us together?'

She nestled into his shoulder. 'I can't. These last months have been so difficult since that time in Bognor – only being able to see you occasionally, and hardly ever alone. But it won't be long now, and then we'll be able to spend the rest of our lives together.'

Epilogue

It had been, Helena thought, an inspired decision to travel to London alone after their quiet wedding in Lichfield, leaving Rosalind in the care of Aunt Beatrice at Broadway Manor.

And now, as she stood in an ivory silk nightdress before the window awaiting her bridegroom, Faraday House was so silent she could almost imagine it completely empty. Their bedrooms had been redecorated and Nicholas would use the adjoining room only when he had a late call and to dress in – he had dismissed any notion of them sleeping separately. She gazed at the interconnecting door, hearing sounds of movement, watching as the handle turned, and then he was coming through, smiling at her, one hand fingering the lapel of his pale blue pyjamas.

'I feel quite decadent – silk, indeed!'

'But you like them?'

'How could I not.' Nicholas looked at Helena, her honey-coloured hair loose around her shoulders, the elegant nightdress almost a replica of the gown she had been wearing when he had first seen her. 'Darling, you look absolutely beautiful.'

Slowly she walked towards him. 'It is all as I promised,' she murmured. 'We shall have complete privacy for hours and hours.'

'Can we request that always happens?' He was slipping the strap from her shoulder, his lips moving down to the swell of her breast. 'No maid, no valet coming in each morning, not until we ring for them?'

Helena looked over at the white linen sheets and inviting bed and trailed her fingers in the dark hair of the man she loved so much. Her voice soft, she murmured, 'What a wonderful idea.'

The publishers hope that this book has given you enjoyable reading. Large Print Books are especially designed to be as easy to see and hold as possible. If you wish a complete list of our books please ask at your local library or write directly to:

Magna Large Print Books
Magna House, Long Preston,
Skipton, North Yorkshire.
BD23 4ND

This Large Print Book for the partially sighted, who cannot read normal print, is published under the auspices of

THE ULVERSCROFT FOUNDATION

KT-433-109

PRESCRIPTION MEDICINES

CHRISTINA BUNCE
& ANNE FENNELL

Capella

This edition printed 2005

For: Bookmart Limited
Registered Number 2372865
Trading as Bookmart Limited
Blaby Road, Wigston, Leicester LE18 4SE

Revised edition of title orginally published 2002.

Cover design by Alex Ingr
Text design by Chris Smith

© Arcturus Publishing Limited, 2002
Unit 26/27 Bickels Yard, 151-153 Bermondsey Street
London SE1 3HA

ISBN 1-84193-256-6

Printed and bound in China

INTRODUCTION

Medicines have been a major force in the fight against disease for many centuries. Most of us have taken some kind of medicine to treat or ward off illness.

The range of medicines at our disposal has never been greater than it is today. This book is designed as a guide to the most common conventional medicines prescribed for people both at home and in hospital. It may be that you have been given information about a medicine prescribed and have forgotten it, or it may be that you want to find out more about a drug which has been prescribed for yourself or a member of the family. Whatever your motive for searching, this book offers basic information about each medicine in layman's language.

The book lists over 400 of the most commonly prescribed medicines together with information about their actions, side effects and special precautions.

IMPORTANT
This book is not intended as a substitute for professional medical advice

HOW TO USE THIS BOOK

This book is designed to be a quick-reference guide to the medicines which are most commonly prescribed for people both at home and in hospital. The medicines are listed in alphabetical order, according to their most commonly used generic name, which is the official chemical name for a medicine and describes its main active ingredient. You can find the generic name on any medicine. If you cannot, your pharmacist will tell you.

Brand name: These are the names given to the product by a manufacturer. For instance, Aspirin is the generic name for the painkilling drug, while Anadin is one of the many brand names under which it is marketed.

Type of drug: This loosely classifies the drug, either by the type of action it has (eg, beta blocker) or the effect it has (eg, anticancer).

Uses: Describes what conditions the drug will be used for.

How it works: Where known, an explanation of how the drug works and what effect it has will be given.

Possible adverse effects: These are undesirable side effects that, as far as most drugs are concerned, will affect only a small number of people but which should always be reported. Some drugs, such as those which fight cancer, will nearly always have adverse effects that will be monitored closely by medical staff.

Availability: Unless otherwise indicated, all drugs are available only with a prescription from a doctor. The exceptions indicate whether some strengths or form of the drug are available over-the-counter as well as on prescription.

Other information: Information about the drug which will be of interest to the people taking it.

CAUTIONS : These indicate whether a drug should not be prescribed, or only prescribed with extreme caution, for children or pregnant and/or breastfeeding women. It also indicates whether the drug may affect the ability to drive or operate machinery, and whether it is advisable to consume alcohol during treatment.

If there are no indications in any of the above areas, it can be assumed that:

• **Children:** there are no commonly reported problems associated with prescribing this medication for children.

• **Pregnancy and breastfeeding:** No specific problems documented, but any medication should be taken with utmost caution by women who are either pregnant or breastfeeding, and only after professional medical or pharmaceutical advice has been sought.

• **Alcohol:** No known problems if taken with alcohol.

• **Driving and operating machinery:** There are no commonly reported problems which may impact on the ability to drive or operate machinery. However, many drugs can cause dizziness or drowsiness in a few people, so it is wise to see how the drug affects you before driving or working with dangerous machinery.

ACAMPROSATE CALCIUM
Brand name: Campral EC
Type of drug: Alcohol abuse deterrent
Uses: The treatment of people who have been diagnosed as having an addiction to alcohol. Usually used in conjunction with counselling, particularly for people who are at risk of starting to drink again.
How it works: It interferes with the chemicals in the brain which are thought to be involved in causing people to become dependent on alcohol.
Possible adverse effects: Diarrhoea, nausea, vomiting, stomach pain and loss of sex drive.
Other information: Do not take if you have liver problems. Treatment will usually be started as soon as the patient has stopped drinking and be continued for around a year.
CAUTIONS
Children: This drug is either not recommended for children, or is recommended only for children above a certain age.
Pregnancy and breastfeeding: This drug is either not recommended for use by women who are pregnant or breastfeeding, or the precise effects are not known and it should therefore only be used with caution and under medical advice.
Alcohol: Alcohol should not be consumed, or only with caution – after medical advice has been sought – while you are taking this drug.

ACARBOSE
Brand name: Glucobay
Type of drug: Anti-diabetic
Uses: The treatment of diabetes in people whose condition cannot be adequately controlled by diet or other medication.
How it works: Slows down the rate at which carbohydrates are digested, with the result that high blood sugar levels, particularly following meals, are reduced.
Possible adverse effects: Wind and occasionally diarrhoea and cramps. These will be minimised if sucrose is avoided.
Other information: Patients prescribed acarbose in addition to insulin or a sulphonylurea need to carry glucose rather than ordinary sucrose. Acarbose should always be taken in conjunction with the recommended diabetic diet.
CAUTIONS
Children: This drug is either not recommended for children, or is recommended only for children above a certain age.
Pregnancy and breastfeeding: This drug is either not recommended for use by women who are pregnant or breastfeeding, or the precise effects are not known and it should therefore only be used with caution and when advised by a doctor.

ACEBUTOLOL
Brand name: Sectral
Type of drug: Beta-blocker
Uses: A treatment for angina, abnormal heart rhythms and high blood pressure. Can also sometimes be used as a treatment for anxiety.
How it works: Works to slow and steady the heart rate. It does not cure the underlying problem, but works to control the symptoms.
Possible adverse effects: Lethargy and fatigue, cold hands and feet,

nausea and vomiting, nightmares. Sometimes a slow pulse may be noticed. A rash and/or breathlessness should always be reported to a doctor.

Other information: Acebutolol will not normally be prescribed for people with asthma or other lung disorders such as obstructive airways disease because it can make the conditions worse. It is likely that Acebutolol will need to be taken for long periods.

CAUTIONS

Children: This drug is either not recommended for children, or is recommended only for children above a certain age.

Driving and operating machinery: This drug may have some effect on your driving ability, so it is advisable not to drive or operate machinery while taking it.

ACEMETACIN
Brand name: Emflex
Type of drug: Anti-inflammatory
Uses: To treat the pain and inflammation of rheumatism and other musculoskeletal disorders.
How it works: Reduces pain and inflammation by blocking the production of prostaglandins, chemicals produced by the body which contribute to the inflammation associated with rheumatoid arthritis.
Possible adverse effects: Stomach and bowel upsets, headaches, blurred vision and dizziness, tinnitus.
Other information: Must not be taken if allergic to aspirin. Patients on long-term treatment should have an annual eye examination.

CAUTIONS

Pregnancy and breastfeeding: This drug is either not recommended for use by women who are pregnant or breastfeeding, or the precise effects are not known and it should therefore only be used with caution and under medical advice.

Driving and operating machinery: This drug may have some effect on your driving ability, so it is advisable not to drive or operate machinery while taking it.

ACETAZOLAMIDE
Brand name: Diamox, Diamox SR
Type of drug: Glaucoma treatment
Uses: Affects the chemical processes which take place in the kidneys, to produce a diuretic effect. This results in fluid being drawn out of the body.
How it works: Results in the reduction of the volume of fluid in the eye which is the main symptom of glaucoma.
Possible adverse effects: Tiredness, headache, appetite loss and tingling in the hands and feet. Stop taking the drug and call a doctor if a rash, or bruising effect, appears on the skin.
Other information: People on long-term treatment may also be prescribed a potassium supplement. Blood tests will be carried out regularly.

CAUTIONS

Pregnancy and breastfeeding: This drug is either not recommended for use by women who are pregnant or breastfeeding, or the precise effects are not known and it should therefore only be used with caution and under medical advice.

Alcohol: Alcohol should not be consumed, or only with caution – after medical advice has been sought – while you are taking this drug.

Driving and operating machinery: This drug may have some effect on your driving ability, so it is advisable not to drive or operate machinery while taking it.

ACICLOVIR
Brand name: Zovirax
Type of drug: Anti-viral
Uses: Antiviral drug available in cream, ointment and tablet form, used to treat herpes infections.
How it works: Attacks the herpes virus. Cream reduces the severity of cold sores and herpes. Tablets used to treat shingles. Ointment used for herpes infections affecting the eye. Can be given as an injection for severe infections.
Possible adverse effects: Cream can cause burning and stinging, or more rarely, a rash. Any rash should be discussed with a doctor.
Availability: Some preparations available over the counter.
Other information: Available as tablets, liquid, injection, cream and eye ointment. Injection not recommended for pregnant women. Always complete the full course.

ACITRETIN
Brand name: Neotigason
Type of drug: Oral retinoid
Uses: The treatment of extensive and severe psoriasis where other treatments have failed.
How it works: Slows down the rapid reproduction of skin cells which causes the scaling of the skin which characterises psoriasis.
Possible adverse effects: Dryness in the mouth, skin and eyes. Inflamed skin. May cause hair to thin and fall out.
Other information: Usually prescribed as capsules. Avoid getting pregnant before treatment and for at least two years after taking this drug. Avoid exposure to sunlight and sunray lamps. Liver and blood tests will be conducted during treatment to monitor effects and levels of the medication.
CAUTIONS
Children: This drug is either not recommended for children, or is recommended only for children above a certain age.
Pregnancy and breastfeeding: This drug is either not recommended for use by women who are pregnant or breastfeeding, or the precise effects are not known and it should therefore only be used with caution and under medical advice.

ACRIVASTINE
Brand name: Benadryl Allergy Relief
Type of drug: Antihistamine
Uses: A short acting antihistamine which is used for the treatment of hay fever and allergic skin conditions such as urticaria (hives).
How it works: It acts to control a runny nose, sneezing and other symptoms of nasal allergies, without causing the drowsiness which is a side effect of many other types of antihistamine treatment.
Possible adverse effects: Some people may experience drowsiness. On rare occasions can cause disturbances to the digestive system, headaches

and dry mouth. Children and elderly people are more susceptible to the adverse effects.

Other information: Has less of a sedative effect than other similar drugs, so is often prescribed for people who need to avoid becoming drowsy.

CAUTIONS

Children: This drug is either not recommended for children, or is recommended only for children above a certain age.

Alcohol: Alcohol should not be consumed, or only with caution – after medical advice has been sought – while you are taking this drug.

ADENOSINE

Brand name: Adenocor

Type of drug: Anti-arrhythmic

Uses: Treatment of some kinds of rapid heart beat (paroxysmal supraventricular tachycardia).

How it works: Acts on the heart muscle and arteries, causing the heart rate to slow down to normal.

Possible adverse effects: Facial flushing, difficulty in breathing and sneezing, chest pain, nausea, dizziness, headache.

Other information: Usually administered as an intravenous (straight into the vein) injection in hospital. Unlikely to be given to pregnant women unless in an emergency.

ADRENALINE (Epinephrine)

Brand name: Ana-Guard, EpiPen, Minijet Adrenaline,

Type of drug: Emergency treatment

Uses: For emergency treatment of anaphylactic shock and severe asthma attacks.

How it works: Reverses the dangerous effects of anaphylactic shock which include difficulty in breathing, a drop in blood pressure and swelling of the throat. It increases the blood supply to muscles, including those of the heart and lungs.

Possible adverse effects: Anxiety, breathlessness, restlessness, palpitations, rapid heartbeat, dizziness and cold hands and feet.

Other information: Patients who have a high risk of developing anaphylaxis as a result of an allergy to food or insect stings, for instance, may be advised to carry adrenaline with them at all times and understand how to inject it in case of an emergency. Special dose syringes are available for children.

ALBENDAZOLE

Brand name: Zentel

Type of drug: Anti-tapeworm

Uses: In conjunction with surgery can reduce the risk of recurrence of cysts caused by Echinococcus granulosus.

How it works: Keeps the cysts which characterise the disease at bay and prevents symptoms resulting from their effect on the surrounding tissues such as the brain, liver or lungs.

Possible adverse effects: Digestive disturbances, headache, dizziness, rash and fever.

Other information: Usually prescribed as tablets.

CAUTIONS

Pregnancy and breastfeeding: This drug is either not recommended

for use by women who are pregnant or breastfeeding, or the precise effects are not known and it should therefore only be used with caution and under medical advice.

ALENDRONIC ACID
Brand name: Fosamax
Type of drug: Biphosphonate
Uses: Treatment of osteoporosis, which affects women who have passed the menopause.
How it works: Acts on the rate of bone growth which has a role in the development of osteoporosis.
Possible adverse effects: Rarely, alendronic acid can lead to severe oesophageal reactions which may cause pain on swallowing, heartburn and chest pain, which should be reported to a doctor immediately. More common adverse effects include abdominal pain and swelling, wind and headache.
Other information: Usually prescribed as tablets.
The tablets should be taken at least 30 minutes before breakfast (and any other medication) with a full glass of water on an empty stomach. Patients should then stand or sit upright for 30 minutes and not lie down until after breakfast.
Because of the risk of gastric disturbance, alendronic acid is rarely given to people who have existing gastric problems such as ulcers or oesophageal disease.
CAUTIONS
Children: Not usually prescribed.
Pregnancy and breastfeeding: This drug is either not recommended for use by women who are pregnant or breastfeeding, or the precise effects are not known and it should therefore only be used with caution and under medical advice.

ALFACALCIDOL
Brand name: AlphaD, One-Alpha
Type of drug: Vitamin
Uses: The prevention or treatment of some kinds of bone disease which are caused by either kidney malfunction or vitamin D-resistant rickets.
How it works: Replaces vitamin D, which is essential to healthy bone growth.
Possible adverse effects: Adverse effects usually only occur as a result of overdose and include a loss of appetite, nausea and vomiting, diarrhoea, weight loss, headache, thirst and vertigo. The drug may also cause the levels of calcium in the blood to rise, but this will be monitored by regular blood tests.
Other information: Usually prescribed as tablets. Blood should be tested regularly to check calcium levels in people who are taking high doses.

ALLOPURINOL
Brand name: Caplenal, Cosuric, Rimapurinol, Xanthomaz, Zyloric
Type of drug: Gout treatment
Uses: Used as a preventative measure for people who suffer from gout. It is not usually prescribed to treat sudden flare-ups of the condition.
How it works: It inhibits the production of an enzyme which is crucial

to the formation of crystals – made from uric acid – in the joints of the body which characterises the disease. It can also be used to reduce high uric acid levels which occur as side effects of some anti-cancer treatments.

Possible adverse effects: Adverse effects are uncommon, but there may be nausea and itching. Rarely causes drowsiness, headache, fever, a metallic taste in the mouth and fever and chills.

Other information: Will often be given in conjunction with an anti-inflammatory drug, as in some cases it may increase the severity of acute attacks of the disease. Regular blood checks will be made to assess the levels of uric acid. It is advisable to drink plenty of fluids while taking this medication.

CAUTIONS

Children: This drug is either not recommended for children, or is recommended only for children above a certain age.

Pregnancy and breastfeeding: This drug is either not recommended for use by women who are pregnant or breastfeeding, or the precise effects are not known and it should therefore only be used with caution and under medical advice.

Alcohol: Alcohol should not be consumed, or only with caution – after medical advice has been sought – while you are taking this drug.

ALPROSTADIL

Brand name: Caverject, Viridal Duo

Type of drug: Prostaglandin

Uses: Treatment of impotence.

How it works: When injected into the penis it results in an erection in men who are otherwise unable to obtain or maintain an erection. The erection should last no more than an hour.

Possible adverse effects: Persistent erections or scarring of the penis, pain in testicles and bottom. Female partners of men taking this drug may occasionally experience vaginal itching and burning.

Other information: Given as an injection into the penis. The first dose should always be given by qualified medical personnel. Thereafter, self-administration is possible after tuition. The drug should not be used more often than once in 24 hours or more than three times a week. A qualified medical practitioner should be consulted if any erection lasts more than four hours.

CAUTIONS

Children: This drug is either not recommended for children, or is recommended only for children above a certain age.

Pregnancy and breastfeeding: This drug is either not recommended for use by women who are pregnant or breastfeeding, or the precise effects are not known and it should therefore only be used with caution and under medical advice.

ALTEPLASE

Brand name: Actilyse

Type of drug: Clot-buster

Uses: Treatment of heart attacks.

How it works: If administered early enough, it works to dissolve the clots which cause heart attacks and enables oxygen to reach the affected part of the heart muscle and thus prevents it from being permanently damaged.

Possible adverse effects: Can occasionally lead to bleeding from the site of the injection, nausea, vomiting, allergic skin rash and fever.
Other information: Usually administered as an intravenous infusion (also known as a drip), in hospital. It will be used with extreme caution in women who are pregnant, for people with kidney disorders or those with diabetes.
CAUTIONS
Pregnancy and breastfeeding: This drug is either not recommended for use by women who are pregnant or breastfeeding, or the precise effects are not known and it should therefore only be used with caution and under medical advice.

ALUMINIUM HYDROXIDE
Brand name: Alu-Cap, Aludrox
Type of drug: Antacid
Uses: Treatment of indigestion, heartburn, and sometimes diarrhoea. Also used to prevent these conditions.
How it works: Acts to neutralise the acid in the stomach which in turn reduces the irritant effect which causes the symptoms of the gastric problems.
Possible adverse effects: Side effects are rare and not usually serious, but include constipation, nausea and vomiting. Constipation is more likely in elderly people.
Other information: Usually taken as a liquid, which should be slightly diluted with water or fruit juice.
CAUTIONS
Pregnancy and breastfeeding: This drug is either not recommended for use by women who are pregnant or breastfeeding, or the precise effects are not known and it should therefore only be used with caution and under medical advice.

AMANTADINE
Brand name: Symmetrel
Type of drug: Parkinsonism and anti-viral treatment
Uses: It can be used as an anti-viral drug – to treat infections of influenza type A virus, and infections of the respiratory tract. It is also used to control, although not cure, the symptoms of Parkinson's disease.
How it works: Protects against influenza A and reduces the symptoms once an infection has occurred. It affects the release of the brain chemical, dopamine, which plays a crucial part in Parkinsonism. The Parkinsonism symptoms usually diminish during the first few weeks of treatment, but the effect of the drug often wears off within six to eight weeks, after which another drug will be needed to deal with the symptoms. Occasionally the effectiveness of the drug will be restored after a break from it.
Possible adverse effects: Nervousness, agitation and confusion. Dizziness, blurred vision, loss of appetite, ankle swelling and a rash are rare side effects. The drug may cause insomnia in some people, in which case it should be taken several hours before bedtime.
Other information: Usually supplied as capsules or tablets. Should be taken after meals to ensure maximum absorption. When taken as an anti-Parkinsonism treatment, it is important not to suddenly stop taking it, as this may make the symptoms of the original problem worse.
CAUTIONS
Pregnancy and breastfeeding: This drug is either not recommended

for use by women who are pregnant or breastfeeding, or the precise effects are not known and it should therefore only be used with caution and under medical advice.
Alcohol: Alcohol should not be consumed, or only with caution – after medical advice has been sought – while you are taking this drug.
Driving and operating machinery: This drug may have some effect on your driving ability, so it is advisable not to drive or operate machinery while taking it.

AMILORIDE
Brand name: Amiloride, Amilamont
Type of drug: Diuretic
Uses: Helps the body to get rid of the excess fluid that is often retained as a result of heart or liver disease and which results in high blood pressure.
How it works: Encourages more fluid to be expelled from the body as urine. The effect is not noticeable until a few hours after the pill has been taken.
Possible adverse effects: Side effects are rare, but include possible digestive disturbance, confusion, muscle weakness, rash and a dry mouth.
Other information: Can be taken as a pill or a liquid. It is best to take this medication in the afternoon, rather than evening, to prevent frequent trips to the toilet during the night. Foods high in potassium should be avoided. Unlikely to be used in patients who suffer from diabetes mellitus.
CAUTIONS
Children: This drug is either not recommended for children, or is recommended only for children above a certain age.
Pregnancy and breastfeeding: This drug is either not recommended for use by women who are pregnant or breastfeeding, or the precise effects are not known and it should therefore only be used with caution and under medical advice.
Driving and operating machinery: This drug may have some effect on your driving ability so it is advisable not to drive or operate machinery while taking it.

AMINOGLUTETHIMIDE
Brand name: Orimeten
Type of drug: Hormone antagonist
Uses: Treatment of advanced stages of breast cancer in women who have passed the menopause.
How it works: Interferes with the hormone actions, thereby starving certain types of cancerous tumours of the hormone they need to survive.
Possible adverse effects: Side effects usually occur within two weeks of treatment and include drowsiness and fever, which usually settle spontaneously.
If a rash occurs which persists for more than five days, you should consult your doctor.
Other information: Should not be used at the same time as hormonal contraception.
CAUTIONS
Children: Not usually prescribed.

Alcohol: Alcohol should not be consumed, or only with caution – after medical advice has been sought – while you are taking this drug.
Driving and operating machinery: This drug may have some effect on your driving ability, so it is advisable not to drive or operate machinery while taking it.

AMINOPHYLLINE
Brand name: Phyllocontin Continus
Type of drug: Bronchodilator
Uses: Treatment of reversible airways obstruction and asthma attacks.
How it works: Reverses the effects of airways obstruction and asthma to enable the sufferer to breathe more easily.
Possible adverse effects: Rapid heart beat, palpitations, nausea, gastric discomfort, headaches. Dizziness is quite common when people start taking this drug.
Other information: Will usually be given as a tablet. Seek medical advice before taking any other kind of medication while taking this drug.
CAUTIONS
Pregnancy and breastfeeding: This drug is either not recommended for use by women who are pregnant or breastfeeding, or the precise effects are not known and it should therefore only be used with caution.
Alcohol: Alcohol should not be consumed, or only with caution – after medical advice has been sought – while you are taking this drug.

AMIODARONE
Brand name: Cordarone X
Type of drug: Anti-arrhythmic
Uses: Used to prevent and treat a range of abnormal heart rhythms such as those which occur in Wolff-Parkinson-White syndrome, atrial fibrillation and ventricular fibrillation.
How it works: It slows the messages sent to the heart muscle, with the result that the heartbeat is slowed and steadied.
Possible adverse effects: Liver damage, thyroid problems and damage to the eyes and lungs. Also nausea, shortness of breath, a metallic taste in the mouth and a rash which is sensitive to light. The skin can also become more sensitive and burn easily in sunlight if not adequately protected. Eye drops may be prescribed for the few patients who may get visual disturbances while taking this drug.
Other information: This drug can cause the eyes to be dazzled by bright lights. It is worth wearing a sunscreen to prevent sensitised skin reacting to sunlight.
CAUTIONS
Children: This drug is either not recommended for children, or is recommended only for children above a certain age.
Pregnancy and breastfeeding: This drug is either not recommended for use by women who are pregnant or breastfeeding, or the precise effects are not known and it should therefore only be used with caution.
Driving and operating machinery: This drug may have some effect on your driving ability, so it is advisable not to drive or operate machinery while taking it.

AMITRIPTYLINE
Brand name: Elavil
Type of drug: Tricyclic antidepressant

Uses: Used in the treatment of depression which has persisted for long periods. Has also been used for the treatment of anorexia or bulimia associated with depression. Occasionally used in the treatment of bedwetting.

How it works: It inhibits the re-uptake of brain chemicals, which results in a heightening of mood. It also encourages appetite and enables users to lead a more normal daily life. Its sedative effect is also useful for people who find difficulty in sleeping at nights.

Possible adverse effects: A more sedative effect than similar drugs. Drowsiness, sweating, dry mouth, dizziness and blurred vision can be experienced. The risk of nausea can be reduced if taken with food or milk. Any troublesome side effects should be reported instantly.

Other information: Usually administered as a pill. The beneficial effects are reduced if taken by someone who is a heavy cigarette smoker. An overdose is dangerous and may lead to fits and abnormal heart rhythms. An overdose should be treated as an emergency situation. It is advisable to take this drug at bedtime in order to avoid daytime sedation. Alternatively, if taken early in the morning, a 'hangover' effect may be avoided. It may take four weeks before the beneficial effects of the medication are noticed.

CAUTIONS

Children: This drug is either not recommended for children, or is recommended only for children above a certain age.

Alcohol: Alcohol should not be consumed, or only with caution – after medical advice has been sought – while you are taking this drug.

Driving and operating machinery: This drug may have some effect on your driving ability, so it is advisable not to drive or operate machinery while taking it.

AMLODIPINE BESILATE

Brand name: Istin

Type of drug: Anti-angina and anti-hypertensive

Uses: The treatment of the chest pain associated with both chronic (ongoing) and acute (sudden worsening) angina.

How it works: Affects the electrical impulses which pass through the heart muscle and blood vessels, with the result that the heart can operate more effectively. It also dilates the blood vessels around the heart.

Possible adverse effects: May cause blood pressure to drop too low. May lead to leg and ankle swelling, which should be reported to a doctor immediately. You should also report any worsening of angina symptoms to a doctor. Can also cause dizziness and flushing.

Other information: Usually given in tablet form. You should not stop taking this drug without first discussing it with your doctor.

CAUTIONS

Children: This drug is either not recommended for children, or is recommended only for children above a certain age.

Pregnancy and breastfeeding: This drug is either not recommended for use by women who are pregnant or breastfeeding, or the precise effects are not known and it should therefore only be used with caution and under medical advice.

Alcohol: Alcohol should not be consumed, or only with caution – after medical advice has been sought – while you are taking this drug.

Driving and operating machinery: This drug may have some effect on your driving ability, so it is advisable not to drive or operate machinery while taking it.

AMOXICILLIN
Brand name: Amix, Amoram, Amoxil, Galenamox, Rimoxallin
Type of drug: Antibiotic
Uses: Penicillin antibiotic used for a wide range of infections, including respiratory and ear infections, sinusitis, skin infections and infections of the urinary tract.
How it works: Acts fast – sometimes within one or two hours – to kill the bacteria which cause infections.
Possible adverse effects: Rash and diarrhoea are relatively common. Can also cause nausea and diarrhoea. Occasionally a severe allergic reaction can occur, which results in a high fever, swelling of the mouth and tongue, itching and breathing problems. If this happens a doctor should be consulted immediately.
Other information: Usually prescribed as a pill. Can be administered intravenously (through a vein) but this will normally only happen in hospital. Maximum absorption of Amoxicillin takes place if the stomach is empty. Tablets should be chewed thoroughly or crushed and washed down with liquid to ensure the maximum beneficial effect takes place. As with any course of antibiotics the prescribed course should always be completed. You should tell your doctor any known allergy to antibiotics or anything else and whether you are on the contraceptive pill. May reduce effectiveness of contraceptive pill.

AMPHOTERICIN
Brand name: Abelcet, AmBisome, Amphocil, Fungilin, Fungizone
Type of drug: Anti-fungal
Uses: Drug used to fight fungal infections such as fungal meningitis, cystitis caused by candida, and fungal infections of the eye.
How it works: Treats infections caused by a fungus by damaging the outer, protective layer of the fungus.
Possible adverse effects: Rash and diarrhoea are relatively common. Occasionally a severe allergic reaction can occur, with high fever, swelling of the mouth and tongue, itching and breathing problems. Any signs of this should be reported to a doctor immediately.
Other information: Administered either in tablet form or as an intravenous infusion. Treatment may last for some time. You should tell your doctor about any known allergy to antibiotics or anything else and whether you are on the contraceptive pill. May reduce effectiveness of contraceptive pill.

ANASTROZOLE
Brand name: Arimidex
Type of drug: Anti-cancer
Uses: Treatment of breast cancer in women who have passed the menopause and for whom other treatments have not been successful.
How it works: Starves the cancer of certain hormones which are known to stimulate its growth.
Possible adverse effects: Hot flushes, sweating, vaginal irritation, thinning of the hair and gastric disturbances.
Other information: Will usually only be administered in hospital by staff experienced in this kind of treatment.
CAUTIONS
Pregnancy and breastfeeding: This drug is either not recommended for use by women who are pregnant or breastfeeding, or the precise

effects are not known and it should therefore only be used with caution and under medical advice.

Driving and operating machinery: This drug may have some effect on your driving ability, so it is advisable not to drive or operate machinery while taking it.

ANISTREPLASE
Brand name: Eminase
Type of drug: Clot busting
Uses: The treatment of heart attacks.
How it works: Dissolves the thrombus or lump which is blocking coronary arteries and causing a heart attack to occur.
Possible adverse effects: Flushing, internal bleeding, nausea and vomiting, a sudden drop in blood pressure and heart rate.
Other information: Should be used with caution by people with a history of heart rhythm problems. Use with caution if there is an increased risk of bleeding, for example following surgery or an injury. Will usually only be administered in hospital as an emergency treatment.
CAUTIONS
Children: This drug is either not recommended for children, or is recommended only for children above a certain age.
Pregnancy and breastfeeding: This drug is either not recommended for use by women who are pregnant or breastfeeding, or the precise effects are not known and it should therefore only be used with caution and under medical advice.

APOMORPHINE HYDROCHLORIDE
Brand name: Uprima
Type of drug: Anti-Parkinsonism
Uses: Control of some of the symptoms of Parkinsonism in patients in whom the effects of other drugs are no longer sufficient.
How it works: Helps to control some of the symptoms which have not been helped by other treatments.
Possible adverse effects: Symptoms may not improve, and can worsen. Nausea and vomiting may occur and patients may show signs of confusion.
Other information: Administered as an injection. Hospital admission is necessary for at least three days prior to treatment.
CAUTIONS
Pregnancy and breastfeeding: This drug is either not recommended for use by women who are pregnant or breastfeeding, or the precise effects are not known and it should therefore only be used with caution and under medical advice.

APRACLONIDINE
Brand name: Iopidine
Type of drug: Eye surgery preparation
Uses: Given as preparation for surgery before an eye operation.
How it works: Controls the pressure within the eyeball to increase the safety and effectiveness of surgery.
Possible adverse effects: Dry mouth and an unpleasant taste in the mouth, eye discomfort and headache.
Other information: Administered as eye drops which will usually be administered three times a day for a month.

CAUTIONS

Children: This drug is either not recommended for children, or is recommended only for children above a certain age.

Pregnancy and breastfeeding: This drug is either not recommended for use by women who are pregnant or breastfeeding, or the precise effects are not known and it should therefore only be used with caution and under medical advice.

Driving and operating machinery: This drug may have some effect on your driving ability, so it is advisable not to drive or operate machinery while taking it.

ASPIRIN

Brand name: Angettes, Caprin, Disprin, Nu-Seals Aspirin

Type of drug: Non-opioid analgesic, anti-platelet, anti-pyretic

Uses: Treatment of a wide variety of mild to moderate pain, including menstrual pain, headache, toothache. Aspirin is an effective way of treating a fever. It is also useful to control the symptoms of colds and flu. It relieves the inflammation present in conditions such as arthritis. Aspirin is thought to be helpful in the treatment of some types of heart disease.

How it works: Acts on the hypothalamus in the brain to block the generation of pain impulses. As this part of the brain also helps to control the body temperature, it causes sweating, which helps to lower the body temperature. It interferes with the clotting mechanism in the blood, which helps with the treatment of heart and circulatory conditions.

Possible adverse effects: Can cause irritation and, with long term use, bleeding in the stomach. Can also provoke asthma attacks. Rarely it can cause Reye's syndrome in children under 12 years.

Availability: Available without a prescription (over-the-counter).

Other information: Usually taken as a tablet, but also available as suppositories. Should be taken with food or milk, to protect the stomach.

CAUTIONS

Children: This drug is either not recommended for children, or is recommended only for children above a certain age.

Pregnancy and breastfeeding: This drug is either not recommended for use by women who are pregnant or breastfeeding, or the precise effects are not known and it should therefore only be used with caution and under medical advice.

Alcohol: Alcohol should not be consumed, or only with caution – after medical advice has been sought – while you are taking this drug.

ATENOLOL

Brand name: Co-tenidone, Kalten, Tenoret 50, Tenormin, Tenoretic

Type of drug: Beta-blocker

Uses: Prescribed to control hypertension (high blood pressure). Is also used to control the symptoms of angina. If administered soon after a heart attack it can be effective at minimising the damage.

How it works: Affects angina by slowing the heart rate and reducing the amount of oxygen needed by the heart. Treats angina by reducing the amount of work the heart has to do in order to effectively pump blood around the body.

Possible adverse effects: Muscle aches and tiredness are common.

Headache, nausea and a rash are also possible. Any sign of palpitations should be reported immediately. Can cause breathing difficulties, so extra caution is needed for people with asthma or bronchitis.

Other information: Will usually be prescribed as a tablet, although sometimes a liquid is the chosen option. Can react with a number of other medicines, so make sure your doctor is aware of all other medication.

CAUTIONS

Children: This drug is either not recommended for children, or is recommended only for children above a certain age.

Driving and operating machinery: This drug may have some effect on your driving ability, so it is advisable not to drive or operate machinery while taking it.

ATROPINE SULPHATE

Brand name: Lomotil, Minims Atropine

Type of drug: Anti-cholinergic and mydriatic

Uses: Atropine tablets are used to treat irritable bowel syndrome.

Atropine eye drops are used to treat uveitis, an inflammation of part of the eye.

How it works: A muscle relaxant which acts on the wall of the intestine. When used as eye drops, it enlarges the pupil in the eye.

Possible adverse effects: Blurred vision, dry mouth and thirst. Flushing and dry skin. Constipation and rash. If eye pain or palpitations occur, medical attention should be sought as a matter of urgency.

Other information: An overdose should be treated as an emergency.

CAUTIONS

Pregnancy and breastfeeding: This drug is either not recommended for use by women who are pregnant or breastfeeding, or the precise effects are not known and it should therefore only be used with caution and under medical advice.

Alcohol: Alcohol should not be consumed, or only with caution – after medical advice has been sought – while you are taking this drug.

Driving and operating machinery: This drug may have some effect on your driving ability, so it is advisable not to drive or operate machinery while taking it.

AURANOFIN

Brand name: Ridaura

Type of drug: Gold compound

Uses: The treatment of severe rheumatoid arthritis, psoriatic arthritis and systemic lupus erythematosus.

How it works: It has an anti-inflammatory effect which suppresses, and in some cases prevents, but does not cure, adult or juvenile arthritis. The precise way it works is unknown.

Possible adverse effects: Diarrhoea, which can be treated with bran. Can cause some blood problems, so a doctor should be informed immediately if there are any signs of sore throat, fever, infection, mouth ulcers or bleeding and bruising.

Other information: Pre-menopausal women should use contraception during treatment and for six months following it.

CAUTIONS

Children: This drug is either not recommended for children, or is recommended only for children above a certain age.

Pregnancy and breastfeeding: This drug is either not recommended for use by women who are pregnant or breastfeeding, or the precise effects are not known and it should therefore only be used with caution and under medical advice.

AZAPROPAZONE
Brand name: Rheumox
Type of drug: Non-steroidal and anti-inflammatory
Uses: For providing pain relief.
How it works: Is absorbed rapidly to provide pain relief. Because of its anti-inflammatory qualities, azapropazone is also particularly useful in the treatment of conditions such as osteoarthritis, rheumatoid arthritis and injuries where inflammation has resulted.
Possible adverse effects: Rash, gastrointestinal disturbances. This drug can irritate the lining of the stomach, but discomfort can be avoided if it is taken with milk or at mealtimes. Can lead to worsening of asthma in some people.
Other information: Do not take aspirin or other similar pain-relieving drugs whilst on this medication.
CAUTIONS
Pregnancy and breastfeeding: This drug is either not recommended for use by women who are pregnant or breastfeeding, or the precise effects are not known and it should therefore only be used with caution and under medical advice.
Alcohol: Alcohol should not be consumed, or only with caution – after medical advice has been sought – while you are taking this drug.

AZATHIOPRINE
Brand name: Azamune, Immunoprin, Imuran
Type of drug: Anti-rheumatic
Uses: Treatment of rheumatoid arthritis that has not responded to other types of medication.
How it works: Acts on the immune system and boosts the effect of other rheumatic drugs to relieve the symptoms of rheumatoid arthritis.
Possible adverse effects: Can affect the production of white blood cells, leaving patients at an increased risk of infection. Can also irritate the stomach. Any signs of side effects should be reported immediately.
Other information: Can be given as tablets or as an injection. Regular blood checks will be made to assess the effect of this drug.
CAUTIONS
Pregnancy and breastfeeding: This drug is either not recommended for use by women who are pregnant or breastfeeding, or the precise effects are not known and it should therefore only be used with caution and under medical advice.
Driving and operating machinery: This drug may have some effect on your driving ability, so it is advisable not to drive or operate machinery while taking it.

AZITHROMYCIN
Brand name: Zithromax
Type of drug: Antibiotic
Uses: The treatment of a wide range of infections, such as those which occur with chronic obstructive pulmonary disease, pneumonia, tonsillitis and otitis media.

How it works: Binds to part of the bacteria, preventing it from multiplying.
Possible adverse effects: Dizziness, vertigo, headache. Nausea, vomiting, diarrhoea and gastrointestinal disturbances.
Other information: Should be taken on an empty stomach – one or two hours after meals.
CAUTIONS
Children: This drug is either not recommended for children, or is recommended only for children above a certain age.

AZTREONAM
Brand name: Azactam
Type of drug: Antibiotic
Uses: Treatment of a wide range of severe infections including those affecting the lungs, urinary tract and skin.
How it works: Binds to the infectious organisms and kills them, thereby relieving the symptoms of the infection.
Possible adverse effects: Disturbances to the stomach, leading to diarrhoea and nausea. Any signs of a rash, reddening of the skin, or itching should be reported to a doctor as these could signify an allergic reaction.
Other information: Usually given as an injection in hospital.
CAUTIONS
Pregnancy and breastfeeding: This drug is either not recommended for use by women who are pregnant or breastfeeding, or the precise effects are not known and it should therefore only be used with caution and under medical advice.

BACLOFEN
Brand name: Baclospas, Lioresal
Type of drug: Muscle relaxant
Uses: A drug which relaxes muscles, thereby relieving painful spasms which occur in conditions such as multiple sclerosis or which are caused by trauma such as spinal injuries. Baclofen is also a useful treatment option for seized-up or spastic muscles that can occur following brain injury, cerebral palsy or stroke.
How it works: The exact way it works is unknown, but it is thought to act on the spinal cord and inhibit the transmission of chemicals which contribute to the spasms. It relieves symptoms but does not cure the underlying condition.
Possible adverse effects: Dizziness, drowsiness, nausea, weakness. These effects are more likely to occur in patients over 40 years of age and should be reported to a doctor immediately.
Other information: Administered either as tablets or as an injection – although the latter will only be given in hospital. May interfere with a diabetic's blood sugar levels. Do not take any other medication without checking with your doctor first.
CAUTIONS
Children: This drug is either not recommended for children, or is recommended only for children above a certain age.
Pregnancy and breastfeeding: This drug is either not recommended for use by women who are pregnant or breastfeeding, or the precise effects are not known and it should therefore only be used with caution and under medical advice.
Alcohol: Alcohol should not be consumed, or only with caution – after medical advice has been sought – while you are taking this drug.

BECLOMETASONE DIPROPIONATE
Brand name: AeroBec, Asmabec Clickhaler, Beclazone, Becloforte, Becodisks, Beconase, Becotide, EasiBreathe, Qvar
Type of drug: Corticosteroid
Uses: Prescribed as an inhalant to relieve the symptoms of severe asthma which has not responded to other treatments. It is also prescribed as a nasal spray to treat hay fever and as an ointment for some skin conditions.
How it works: Reduces inflammation and the production of mucus in the nose. Used as a preventative treatment for asthmatics.
Possible adverse effects: Occasionally fungal infections can occur in the mouth, but gargling with water after each inhalation will prevent this is most cases. Nasal discomfort and a sore throat are also possible.
Availability: Some preparations available over the counter.
Other information: Beclomethasone is unlikely to be prescribed for long periods for children.

BENDROFLUMETHIAZIDE
Brand name: Aprinox, Neo-NaClex
Type of drug: Diuretic
Uses: A diuretic (water pill) used to prevent the water retention, or oedema, caused by heart conditions or pre-menstrual bloating. It can also be used as a treatment for high blood pressure.
How it works: Works to encourage excess water to be eliminated from the body.
Possible adverse effects: The most serious side effect is that too much potassium can be expelled from the body. Rarely, cramps, lethargy and nausea may also occur. Any incidence should be discussed with your doctor.
Other information: Administered as tablets. Blood tests will be conducted regularly to check potassium levels. Potassium pills may be prescribed if the levels are too low.
CAUTIONS
Children: This drug is either not recommended for children, or is recommended only for children above a certain age.
Pregnancy and breastfeeding: This drug is either not recommended for use by women who are pregnant or breastfeeding, or the precise effects are not known and it should therefore only be used with caution and under medical advice.

BENZHEXOL
Brand name: Artane, Broflex
Type of drug: Anti-Parkinsonism
Uses: Anti-Parkinsonism drug, used to control the symptoms of Parkinson's disease and other conditions that cause tremor. Also used to treat the tremor which can be experienced as a side effect of some medicines used for psychiatric disorders.
How it works: Goes some way towards correcting the imbalance between two chemicals in the brain – dopamine and acetylcholine – which lead to Parkinsonian symptoms. It boosts the response to treatment of people already using another similar medicine, Levodopa.
Possible adverse effects: Dry mouth, nausea, dizziness and blurred vision.

Occasionally it can affect the bladder, making it difficult to pass water, in which case medical advice should be sought immediately.

Other information: Regular checks will be made on blood pressure, eyes and heart whilst taking this drug.

CAUTIONS

Children: This drug is either not recommended for children, or is recommended only for children above a certain age.

Pregnancy and breastfeeding: This drug is either not recommended for use by women who are pregnant or breastfeeding, or the precise effects are not known and it should therefore only be used with caution and under medical advice.

Alcohol: Alcohol should not be consumed, or only consumed with caution – after medical advice has been sought – while you are taking this drug.

Driving and operating machinery: This drug may have some effect on your driving ability, so it is advisable not to drive or operate machinery while taking it.

BENZOIC ACID
Brand name: Benzoic Acid Ointment, Compound, BP
Type of drug: Anti-fungal
Uses: The treatment of ringworm – athlete's foot.
How it works: When applied to the affected area it destroys the fungus which causes the problem.
Possible adverse effects: Rarely occur.
Availability: Available with or without a prescription.
Other information: Available as a cream.

BETAHISTINE
Brand name: Serc
Type of drug: Meniere's disease treatment
Uses: Most frequently used to control the nausea and vertigo attacks which are symptomatic of Meniere's disease. It can also be used to control the sound of ringing in the ears experienced by people with tinnitus.
How it works: Thought to improve the blood flow through the small blood vessels in the ear, with the result that the pressure in the inner ear is reduced.
Possible adverse effects: Nausea and indigestion. Rarely, a rash can occur, which should be reported to a doctor.
Other information: Not successful in all cases. An overdose should be treated as an emergency.

CAUTIONS

Children: This drug is either not recommended for children, or is recommended only for children above a certain age.

Pregnancy and breastfeeding: This drug is either not recommended for use by women who are pregnant or breastfeeding, or the precise effects are not known and it should therefore only be used with caution and under medical advice.

BETAMETHASONE
Brand name: Betnelan, Betnesol, Betnovate, Diprosone, Vista-Methasone
Type of drug: Corticosteroid

Uses: Main use is as an anti-inflammatory when it is given as an injection straight into the affected joints in order to alleviate the symptoms of arthritis. Is also given by mouth as part of the treatment of conditions affecting the pituitary and adrenal glands and some blood disorders. Can be applied to the skin to treat eczema and psoriasis.

How it works: Stimulates the production of enzymes in the body, which reduces the inflammation associated with arthritis and other inflammatory conditions.

Possible adverse effects: Most reactions to this drug are related to the dose and can be alleviated with adjustment. Indigestion is common and should always be reported to a doctor. Long term, large doses can lead to symptoms such as peptic ulcers, muscle weakness, delicate skin.

Other information: There is a significant difference in strength between the topical preparations (creams and ointments) and those which are given in tablet or injection form. It is not recommended that oral courses of medication are stopped suddenly.

CAUTIONS

Children: This drug is either not recommended for children, or is recommended only for children above a certain age.

Pregnancy and breastfeeding: This drug is either not recommended for use by women who are pregnant or breastfeeding, or the precise effects are not known and it should therefore only be used with caution and under medical advice.

Alcohol: Alcohol should not be consumed, or only with caution – after medical advice has been sought – while you are taking this drug.

BETHANECHOL CHLORIDE

Brand name: Myotonine

Type of drug: Cholinergic

Uses: The treatment of people who are unable to pass urine and for whom catheterisation (the passing of a tube into the bladder) is not an option.

How it works: Stimulates the nerves in the urinary tract, forcing the bladder to contract and enabling urination to take place.

Possible adverse effects: Sweating, slow pulse and intestinal discomfort.

Other information: Can be given in either injection or tablet form. Will usually be given when the patient has an empty stomach.

CAUTIONS

Pregnancy and breastfeeding: This drug is either not recommended for use by women who are pregnant or breastfeeding, or the precise effects are not known and it should therefore only be used with caution and under medical advice.

BEZAFIBRATE

Brand name: Bezalip, Bezalip-Mono

Type of drug: Lipid lowering

Uses: To lower the level of fats (lipids) in the blood which are thought to contribute to coronary heart disease, which can lead to angina, heart attacks and stroke.

How it works: Bezafibrate is prescribed with the aim of reducing the level of cholesterol in the blood as a way of preventing the onset of coronary heart disease in people who are known to have high cholesterol levels in the blood.

Possible adverse effects: Nausea, appetite loss, gastric pain. Usually short-term. Any episodes of gastric pain should be reported to a doctor.
Other information: Should to be taken in conjunction with a low fat diet. Blood tests will be performed regularly to assess the effect on the level of fat in the blood.
CAUTIONS
Children: This drug is either not recommended for children, or is recommended only for children above a certain age.
Pregnancy and breastfeeding: This drug is either not recommended for use by women who are pregnant or breastfeeding, or the precise effects are not known and it should therefore only be used with caution and under medical advice.

BICALUTAMIDE
Brand name: Casodex
Type of drug: Anti-cancer
Uses: The treatment of cancer of the prostate in patients who have advanced stages of the disease.
How it works: Changes the chemical composition of the tissue where the cancer is growing.
Possible adverse effects: Hot flushes, constipation, nausea, diarrhoea are relatively common, as is a pain in the back or pelvic area.
Other information: This drug should be taken at approximately the same time each day.
CAUTIONS
Children: This drug is either not recommended for children, or is recommended only for children above a certain age.
Pregnancy and breastfeeding: This drug is either not recommended for use by women who are pregnant or breastfeeding, or the precise effects are not known and it should therefore only be used with caution and under medical advice.

BROMOCRIPTINE
Brand name: Parlodel
Type of drug: Fertility
Uses: The treatment of both male and female infertility and a variety of menstrual problems. It is also effective for some people who are in the later stages of Parkinsonism, particularly those for whom other courses of treatment have not worked.
How it works: Prevents the pituitary gland from producing a hormone which causes some types of female infertility, breast problems and menstrual disorders. It is also used to prevent women who do not wish to breast-feed from producing milk. Stimulates the production of chemicals in the central nervous system which counteract the symptoms of Parkinsonism.
Possible adverse effects: Nausea and vomiting are the most common, but these can be minimised by taking the medication at mealtimes.
Other information: Regular blood and gynaecological tests will be conducted to assess the effectiveness of the drug.
CAUTIONS
Children: This drug is either not recommended for children, or is recommended only for children above a certain age.
Pregnancy and breastfeeding: This drug is either not recommended for use by women who are pregnant or breastfeeding, or the precise

effects are not known and it should therefore only be used with caution.
Alcohol: Alcohol should not be consumed, or only with caution – after medical advice has been sought – while you are taking this drug.
Driving and operating machinery: This drug may have some effect on your driving ability, so it is advisable not to drive or operate machinery while taking it.

BUDESONIDE
Brand name: Pulmicort
Type of drug: Anti-inflammatory
Uses: Prescribed to control the symptoms of hay fever and asthma.
How it works: Precise action is not known but it controls some of the chemicals which are involved in the development of the conditions.
Possible adverse effects: Nasal irritation, cough, nose bleeds and headache.
Other information: Will be prescribed as an inhaler. The prescribed dose should not be exceeded. It is important that patients use the correct technique when taking this medication – if in doubt check with a medical professional. This drug will not achieve its maximum level of effectiveness until it has been used for a few weeks.
CAUTIONS
Children: This drug is either not recommended for children, or is recommended only for children above a certain age.
Pregnancy and breastfeeding: This drug is either not recommended for use by women who are pregnant or breastfeeding, or the precise effects are not known and it should therefore only be used with caution and under medical advice.

BUMETANIDE
Brand name: Burinex
Type of drug: Diuretic
Uses: Used to reduce fluid retention in people who have problems such as heart failure and cirrhosis of the liver. It can also be used for people with kidney problems, unlike most diuretics.
How it works: Encourages elimination of excess fluid.
Possible adverse effects: Most side effects are due to the loss of potassium and the rapid loss of fluid and include dizziness, lethargy and muscle cramps. For this reason, bumetanide is usually given in conjunction with potassium supplements. Any sign of a rash should be reported immediately.
Other information: A diet high in fresh fruit and vegetables should be taken. Regular blood tests will be taken to monitor effectiveness.
CAUTIONS
Alcohol: Alcohol should not be consumed, or only with caution – after medical advice has been sought – while you are taking this drug.
Driving and operating machinery: This drug may have some effect on your driving ability, so it is advisable not to drive or operate machinery while taking it.

BUPRENORPHINE
Brand name: Temgesic
Type of drug: Painkiller
Uses: The alleviation of moderate to severe pain.
How it works: The precise way it works is unknown, but it is thought

to neutralise the effect of the chemicals which transmit the pain messages.

Possible adverse effects: Dizziness, drowsiness, headache, vertigo, nausea.

Other information: Will usually be prescribed as a pill which needs to be taken sublingually – allowed to dissolve under the tongue.

CAUTIONS

Pregnancy and breastfeeding: This drug is either not recommended for use by women who are pregnant or breastfeeding, or the precise effects are not known and it should therefore only be used with caution and under medical advice.

Alcohol: Alcohol should not be consumed, or only with caution – after medical advice has been sought – while you are taking this drug.

Driving and operating machinery: This drug may have some effect on your driving ability, so it is advisable not to drive or operate machinery while taking it.

BUSERELIN
Brand name: Suprefact
Type of drug: Hormone
Uses: The treatment of types of prostate cancer which depend on hormones to grow. Also used to treat endometriosis.
How it works: Deprives prostate cancer of the hormones it needs for growth. For endometriosis, it blocks the production of hormones by the ovaries and stops periods.
Possible adverse effects: In men – hot flushes, nasal irritation due to nasal spray, loss of sex drive, depression, vomiting, diarrhoea. In women – hot flushes, dry vagina, emotional swings, sore breasts and changes in breast size.
Other information: Barrier methods of contraception should be used during treatment to prevent unwanted pregnancy.
CAUTIONS
Children: Not usually prescribed.
Pregnancy and breastfeeding: This drug is either not recommended for use by women who are pregnant or breastfeeding, or the precise effects are not known and it should therefore only be used with caution and under medical advice.

CABERGOLINE
Brand name: Dostinex
Type of drug: Dopamine receptor stimulant
Uses: To halt or prevent the production of a mother's milk soon after childbirth – this is usually necessary in people who have pituitary gland disorders, a symptom of which may be a vast over-production of milk.
How it works: Inhibits the release of prolactin by the pituitary gland, which alleviates the symptoms.
Possible adverse effects: Headache, vertigo, dizziness, breast pain, weakness.
Other information: Prescribed as tablets. Use a barrier method of contraception whilst being treated with this drug.
CAUTIONS
Children: This drug is either not recommended for children, or is recommended only for children above a certain age.
Pregnancy and breastfeeding: This drug is either not recommended

for use by women who are pregnant or breastfeeding, or the precise effects are not known and it should therefore only be used with caution and under medical advice.

Driving and operating machinery: This drug may have some effect on your driving ability, so it is advisable not to drive or operate machinery while taking it.

CALCIPOTRIOL

Brand name: Dovonex
Type of drug: Synthetic vitamin
Uses: A cream, ointment or lotion for external use only, to treat moderate and severe psoriasis.
How it works: Reduces the production of skin cells that cause the symptoms of skin thickening and scaling associated with psoriasis.
Possible adverse effects: The skin may be irritated initially but this usually wears off. Long term, heavy use may affect calcium levels in the blood.
Other information: The drug is not normally used for longer than six weeks. Regular blood tests may be required to check calcium levels for people on long term treatment.
CAUTIONS
Children: This drug is either not recommended for children, or is recommended only for children above a certain age.

CALCITONIN

Brand name: Calsynar, Forcaltonin, Miacalcic
Type of drug: Thyroid hormone
Uses: An injection to relieve pain of Paget's disease and other bony disorders. Is useful for the treatment of osteoporosis. Relieves bony problems in the ear which are causing deafness. It can also be administered in the form of a nasal spray.
How it works: It regulates the blood calcium level in bones.
Possible adverse effects: Nausea, vomiting, tingling of hands, flushing, unpleasant taste and allergies.
Other information: A skin test should be carried out before use to test for allergic reactions.
CAUTIONS
Children: This drug is either not recommended for children, or is recommended only for children above a certain age.
Pregnancy and breastfeeding: This drug is either not recommended for use by women who are pregnant or breastfeeding, or the precise effects are not known and it should therefore only be used with caution and under medical advice.

CALCIUM POLYSTYRENE SULPONATE

Brand name: Calcium Resonium
Type of drug: Potassium removing
Uses: To treat people who have excess potassium in the blood due to a urinary disorder or as a result of kidney dialysis.
How it works: Once in the intestine, it exchanges calcium ions for potassium ions, thus reducing the amount of potassium in the body.
Possible adverse effects: Too much calcium in the blood or too little potassium. Because the drug is given as a resin it can cause a blockage in the intestine.

Other information: Regular blood tests will be taken to monitor the effect of the drug.
CAUTIONS
Children: This drug is either not recommended for children, or is recommended only for children above a certain age.
Pregnancy and breastfeeding: This drug is either not recommended for use by women who are pregnant or breastfeeding, or the precise effects are not known and it should therefore only be used with caution and under medical advice.

CAPREOMYCIN
Brand name: Capastat
Type of drug: Antibiotic
Uses: An injection to treat tuberculosis when other forms of drug treatment have failed.
How it works: It reduces the development of resistant bacteria.
Possible adverse effects: Vertigo, tinnitus and rashes are possible side effects.
Other information: This drug will be used with caution in people who have impaired hearing or impaired kidney function.
CAUTIONS
Pregnancy and breastfeeding: This drug is either not recommended for use by women who are pregnant or breastfeeding, or the precise effects are not known and it should therefore only be used with caution and under medical advice.

CAPTOPRIL
Brand name: Acepril, Capoten
Type of drug: ACE inhibitor
Uses: To treat and lower, high blood pressure and heart failure.
How it works: It relaxes the muscles around the blood vessels, which allows the blood vessels to dilate, thereby easing blood flow, and reducing blood pressure.
Possible adverse effects: A fall in blood pressure, dizziness, palpitations, stomach upsets, dry cough, unpleasant taste and rashes, though they usually disappear fairly quickly.
Other information: The first dose should be taken while lying down as there is a risk of falling due to the sudden drop in blood pressure.
CAUTIONS
Children: This drug is either not recommended for children, or is recommended only for children above a certain age.
Pregnancy and breastfeeding: This drug is either not recommended for use by women who are pregnant or breastfeeding, or the precise effects are not known and it should therefore only be used with caution and under medical advice.
Alcohol: Alcohol should not be consumed, or only with caution – after medical advice has been sought – while you are taking this drug.
Driving and operating machinery: This drug may have some effect on your driving ability, so it is advisable not to drive or operate machinery while taking it.

CARBACHOL
Brand name: Isopto Carbachol
Type of drug: Cholinergic

Uses: To reduce the pressure inside the eye in patients with glaucoma. It is also given after abdominal surgery to people having difficulty in emptying their bladders.

How it works: Causes contraction of the sphincter muscle in the iris and in the bladder.

Possible adverse effects: Headaches, brow pain and eye pain. Blurred vision initially.

Other information: Do not wear soft contact lenses during treatment.

CAUTIONS

Pregnancy and breastfeeding: This drug is either not recommended for use by women who are pregnant or breastfeeding, or the precise effects are not known and it should therefore only be used with caution and under medical advice.

Driving and operating machinery: This drug may have some effect on your driving ability, so it is advisable not to drive or operate machinery while taking it.

CARBAMAZEPINE

Brand name: Tegretol

Type of drug: Anti-convulsant and anti-psychotic

Uses: For the treatment of epilepsy. It is also used for severe nerve pain and for certain behaviour or psychological disorders.

How it works: Reduces the possible occurrences of fits caused by abnormal signals to the brain.

Possible adverse effects: Headache, dizziness, blurred vision, nausea, tiredness.

Other information: Considered a particularly suitable drug for treating children, because the side effects occur less frequently than with similar drugs.

CAUTIONS

Pregnancy and breastfeeding: This drug is either not recommended for use by women who are pregnant or breastfeeding, or the precise effects are not known and it should therefore only be used with caution and under medical advice.

Alcohol: Alcohol should not be consumed, or only with caution – after medical advice has been sought – while you are taking this drug.

Driving and operating machinery: This drug may have some effect on your driving ability, so it is advisable not to drive or operate machinery while taking it.

CARBARYL

Brand name: Carylderm, Derbac M, Suleo-M

Type of drug: Insecticide treatment

Uses: A solution in the form of a lotion or shampoo that is used to treat head lice.

How it works: As an insecticide it functions by interfering with the nervous system of the lice, causing their death through paralysis.

Possible adverse effects: Skin irritations are the mostly likely side effect from using this product, so it should not be used more than once a week, for three weeks only.

Other information: Should not be used for long periods. Several different preparations should be used to treat head lice, as the lice become easily resistant to insecticides.

CARBENOXOLONE
Brand name: Bioplex, Bioral Gel
Type of drug: Anti-ulcer
Uses: Originally used for the treatment of gastric and duodenal ulcers, now mainly used for treating mouth ulcers.
How it works: It stimulates the production of mucus and also protects the mucosal barrier from gastric juices and so aids the healing of ulcers.
Possible adverse effects: May cause salt and water retention which can lead to swelling and blood pressure problems.
Availability: Prescription needed for mouthwash but not for gel.
Other information: For patients with heart disease, kidney disease or low blood potassium, use with caution.
CAUTIONS
Children: This drug is either not recommended for children, or is recommended only for children above a certain age.
Pregnancy and breastfeeding: This drug is either not recommended for use by women who are pregnant or breastfeeding, or the precise effects are not known and it should therefore only be used with caution and under medical advice.
Alcohol: Alcohol should not be consumed, or only with caution – after medical advice has been sought – while you are taking this drug.

CARBIMAZOLE
Brand name: Neo-Mercazole
Type of drug: Anti-thyroid
Uses: Used for people with an overactive thyroid or after thyroid surgery.
How it works: It reduces the production of thyroid hormones.
Possible adverse effects: Nausea, headaches, joint pain, and skin rashes.
Other information: Sore throat, mouth ulcers or fevers should be reported to a doctor immediately.
CAUTIONS
Pregnancy and breastfeeding: This drug is either not recommended for use by women who are pregnant or breastfeeding, or the precise effects are not known and it should therefore only be used with caution and under medical advice.
Driving and operating machinery: This drug may have some effect on your driving ability, so it is advisable not to drive or operate machinery while taking it.

CARBOCISTEINE
Brand name: Mucodyne
Type of drug: Mucolytic
Uses: To facilitate expectoration in patients with excess sticky sputum. Also used to treat glue ear in children.
How it works: It facilitates expectoration by reducing sputum viscosity.
Possible adverse effects: Nausea, stomach upsets and rashes.
Other information: Do not use if the patient is suffering from an active peptic ulcer.
CAUTIONS
Pregnancy and breastfeeding: This drug is either not recommended for use by women who are pregnant or breastfeeding, or the precise effects are not known and it should therefore only be used with caution and under medical advice.

CARBOPROST
Brand name: Hemabate
Type of drug: Prostaglandin
Uses: To treat haemorrhage after childbirth due to the failure of the womb to contract.
How it works: Stimulates the uterus to contract, as it does during labour.
Possible adverse effects: Nausea, vomiting, and diarrhoea. Pain and redness at the site of the injection.
Other information: Will only be administered in hospital, as an injection.
CAUTIONS
Children: Unlikely to be prescribed.
Pregnancy and breastfeeding: This drug is either not recommended for use by women who are pregnant or breastfeeding, or the precise effects are not known and it should therefore only be used with caution and under medical advice.

CARISOPRODOL
Brand name: Carisoma
Type of drug: Muscle relaxant
Uses: To relieve chronic muscular spasms.
How it works: Prescribed as pills which have a sedative effect on muscles, thus causing them to relax.
Possible adverse effects: Drowsiness is the most commonly experienced side effect. It can also cause nausea, headache, flushes and rashes, insomnia and depressive reactions.
Other information: Not suitable for long term use. Also use with caution in conjunction with sleeping drugs, sedatives, anti-depressants and oral contraceptives. Should be stored away from direct heat and light. Do not take more than the prescribed dose.
CAUTIONS
Children: This drug is either not recommended for children, or is recommended only for children above a certain age.
Pregnancy and breastfeeding: This drug is either not recommended for use by women who are pregnant or breastfeeding, or the precise effects are not known and it should therefore only be used with caution and under medical advice.
Alcohol: Alcohol should not be consumed, or only with caution — after medical advice has been sought – while you are taking this drug.
Driving and operating machinery: This drug may have some effect on your driving ability, so it is advisable not to drive or operate machinery while taking it.

CARNITINE
Brand name: Carnitor
Type of drug: Thyroid hormone
Uses: To treat a deficiency of carnitine, a chemical which is vital in the process of changing fat to energy, due to genetic defects or dialysis.
How it works: It helps to transport long-chain fatty acids into cells to be burned to produce energy.
Possible adverse effects: Nausea, vomiting, stomach pain and diarrhoea.
Other information: Use with caution if there is impaired kidney function.

CAUTIONS
Pregnancy and breastfeeding: This drug is either not recommended for use by women who are pregnant or breastfeeding, or the precise effects are not known and it should therefore only be used with caution and under medical advice.

CARVEDILOL
Brand name: Eucardic
Type of drug: Alpha- and beta-blocker
Uses: A drug to treat high blood pressure and heart failure.
How it works: It acts to dilate the blood vessels throughout the body, with the result that blood pressure is lowered.
Possible adverse effects: Dizziness – particularly on standing up – possibility of disturbed vision, headache, fatigue and stomach upsets.
Other information: Prescribed as tablets. Dosage must not be stopped or interrupted without medical approval. Contact lens wearers may experience problems from dry eyes.
CAUTIONS
Children: This drug is either not recommended for children, or is recommended only for children above a certain age.
Pregnancy and breastfeeding: This drug is either not recommended for use by women who are pregnant or breastfeeding, or the precise effects are not known and it should therefore only be used with caution and under medical advice.
Driving and operating machinery: This drug may have some effect on your driving ability, so it is advisable not to drive or operate machinery while taking it.

CEFACLOR
Brand name: Distaclor
Type of drug: Antibiotic
Uses: Antibiotic used to treat a variety of bacterial infections of the respiratory tract, sinuses, skin, soft tissue, ear and urinary tract.
How it works: Attacks a wide range of infective organisms.
Possible adverse effects: Diarrhoea is the most common side effect, but should not be severe. Other serious side effects may indicate an allergic reaction and should be reported.
Other information: Take the full course of the drug even if the infection appears to have cleared up.
CAUTIONS
Pregnancy and breastfeeding: This drug is either not recommended for use by women who are pregnant or breastfeeding, or the precise effects are not known and it should therefore only be used with caution and under medical advice.

CEFALEXIN
Brand name: Ceporex, Keflex
Type of drug: Antibiotic
Uses: Antibiotic most commonly used for treatment of bronchitis, cystitis and some skin infections.
How it works: Targeted at specific, rather than a wide range of infections.
Possible adverse effects: Diarrhoea. May trigger an allergic reaction in people who are sensitive to penicillin.

Other information: May reduce the effect of oral contraceptives.
CAUTIONS
Pregnancy and breastfeeding: This drug is either not recommended for use by women who are pregnant or breastfeeding, or the precise effects are not known and it should therefore only be used with caution and under medical advice.

CETIRIZINE
Brand name: Zirtek
Type of drug: Antihistamine
Uses: The treatment of hayfever and other similar allergies.
How it works: Inhibits the production of histamine which leads to the symptoms of an allergic reaction.
Possible adverse effects: Drowsiness, dizziness, headaches and stomach upsets.
Availability: Prescription needed for liquid but not for tablets.
Other information: Can be prescribed as tablets or as a syrup.
CAUTIONS
Children: This drug is either not recommended for children, or is recommended only for children above a certain age.
Pregnancy and breastfeeding: This drug is either not recommended for use by women who are pregnant or breastfeeding, or the precise effects are not known and it should therefore only be used with caution and under medical advice.
Alcohol: Alcohol should not be consumed, or only with caution – after medical advice has been sought – while you are taking this drug.
Driving and operating machinery: This drug may have some effect on your driving ability, so it is advisable not to drive or operate machinery while taking it.

CHLOMETHIAZOLE
Brand name: Heminevrin
Type of drug: Hypnotic
Uses: As a treatment for epilepsy, insomnia and the symptoms of alcohol withdrawal.
How it works: Has a hypnotic, sedative-like, effect.
Possible adverse effects: Nasal congestion accompanied by sneezing, headache, nausea, vomiting, stomach upsets.
Other information: Not suitable for patients with chest problems or for alcoholics who continue to drink.
CAUTIONS
Pregnancy and breastfeeding: This drug is either not recommended for use by women who are pregnant or breastfeeding, or the precise effects are not known and it should therefore only be used with caution and under medical advice.
Alcohol: Alcohol should not be consumed, or only with caution – after medical advice has been sought – while you are taking this drug.
Driving and operating machinery: This drug may have some effect on your driving ability, so it is advisable not to drive or operate machinery while taking it.

CHLORAL HYDRATE
Brand name: Chloral Mixture, BP Chloral Elixir, Peadiatric, BP, Welldorm

Type of drug: Sleep inducing
Uses: For short term treatment of sleeplessness.
How it works: Acts on the central nervous system to induce drowsiness.
Possible adverse effects: Headache, nausea, dizziness, drowsiness, nightmares. Can irritate and upset the stomach.
Other information: If taking the drug for longer than four weeks, do not suddenly stop taking it. Withdrawal symptoms may well occur, so a gradual reduction in dosage is recommended.
CAUTIONS
Pregnancy and breastfeeding: This drug is either not recommended for use by women who are pregnant or breastfeeding, or the precise effects are not known and it should therefore only be used with caution and under medical advice.
Alcohol: Alcohol should not be consumed, or only with caution – after medical advice has been sought – while you are taking this drug.
Driving and operating machinery: This drug may have some effect on your driving ability, so it is advisable not to drive or operate machinery while taking it.

CHLORAMBUCIL
Brand name: Leukeran
Type of drug: Anti-cancer
Uses: For treating various cancers, in particular leukaemia, ovarian cancer and Hodgkin's disease.
How it works: Acts on the DNA within the cell to prevent the cancerous cells from multiplying.
Possible adverse effects: Nausea, vomiting, diarrhoea and rashes.
Other information: Blood will be taken regularly to monitor the effect of this medication. Also best to avoid aspirin derivatives. A barrier contraceptive is also advised.
CAUTIONS
Pregnancy and breastfeeding: This drug is either not recommended for use by women who are pregnant or breastfeeding, or the precise effects are not known and it should therefore only be used with caution and under medical advice.

CHLORAMPHENICOL
Brand name: Kemicetine, Minims Chloramphenicol
Type of drug: Antibiotic
Uses: Used topically to treat acne, ear and eye infections. Occasionally administered by mouth or injection to treat more serious conditions such as meningitis, typhoid or pneumonia
How it works: Treats infection by bacterial organisms.
Possible adverse effects: Can very occasionally cause blood disorders and is usually only used after other treatments have failed.
Other information: Take the full course of the drug even if the infection has cleared up.
CAUTIONS
Pregnancy and breastfeeding: This drug is either not recommended for use by women who are pregnant or breastfeeding, or the precise effects are not known and it should therefore only be used with caution and under medical advice.

CHLORDIAZEPOXIDE
Brand name: Librium, Tropium
Type of drug: Anti-anxiety
Uses: To treat anxiety and tension and to encourage sleep. It can also be used to treat the symptoms of alcohol withdrawal. Also helps to ease muscular spasms.
How it works: Depresses activity in the part of the brain which is thought to control anxiety and tension by changing the chemical activity there.
Possible adverse effects: Drowsiness, confusion, nausea, constipation, menstrual irregularities and decreased libido.
Other information: Not suitable for a long-term solution as the drug can be habit-forming, but it also loses its effectiveness after a time. Treatment is usually limited to two weeks.
CAUTIONS
Children: This drug is either not recommended for children, or is recommended only for children above a certain age.
Pregnancy and breastfeeding: This drug is either not recommended for use by women who are pregnant or breastfeeding, or the precise effects are not known and it should therefore only be used with caution and under medical advice.
Alcohol: Alcohol should not be consumed, or only consumed with caution – after medical advice has been sought – while you are taking this drug.
Driving and operating machinery: This drug may have some effect on your driving ability, so it is advisable not to drive or operate machinery while taking it.

CHLOROQUINE
Brand name: Avloclor, Nivaquine
Type of drug: Anti-malarial and anti-rheumatic
Uses: For prevention and treatment of malaria. It is also used to treat rheumatoid arthritis.
How it works: An oral dose usually clears up the infection within a few days. Injections may be needed for a severe attack.
Possible adverse effects: Nausea, headache, diarrhoea and abdominal pain.
Other information: Prolonged use of the drug could lead to serious damage of the retina which could progress to blindness. Regular eye checks should be carried out.
CAUTIONS
Driving and operating machinery: This drug may have some effect on your driving ability, so it is advisable not to drive or operate machinery while taking it.

CHLORPROMAZINE
Brand name: Chloractil, Largactil
Type of drug: Anti-psychotic
Uses: Used to treat schizophrenia, mania and other conditions which result in confused or abnormal behaviour.
How it works: Has an anti-psychotic effect which reduces aggression and promotes more tranquil behaviour.
Possible adverse effects: Drowsiness, increase in weight, blurred vision, dizziness and tremors.

Other information: Avoid exposure to sunlight. Take drug exactly as prescribed.
CAUTIONS
Children: This drug is either not recommended for children, or is recommended only for children above a certain age.
Pregnancy and breastfeeding: This drug is either not recommended for use by women who are pregnant or breastfeeding, or the precise effects are not known and it should therefore only be used with caution and under medical advice.
Alcohol: Alcohol should not be consumed, or only with caution – after medical advice has been sought – while you are taking this drug.
Driving and operating machinery: This drug may have some effect on your driving ability, so it is advisable not to drive or operate machinery while taking it.

CHLORPROPAMIDE
Brand name: Diabinese, Glymese
Type of drug: Anti-diabetic
Uses: Taken by mouth to treat maturity onset diabetes.
How it works: Lowers blood sugar levels by increasing the production of insulin and encouraging the uptake of sugar into the body.
Possible adverse effects: Rare, but include feeling faint, weakness, sweating and confusion.
Other information: Regular monitoring of urine and blood sugar is required.
CAUTIONS
Children: This drug is either not recommended for children, or is recommended only for children above a certain age.
Pregnancy and breastfeeding: This drug is either not recommended for use by women who are pregnant or breastfeeding, or the precise effects are not known and it should therefore only be used with caution and under medical advice.
Alcohol: Alcohol should not be consumed, or only with caution – after medical advice has been sought – while you are taking this drug.

CHORIONIC GONADOTROPHIN
Brand name: Choragon, Pregnyl, Profasi
Type of drug: Infertility treatment
Uses: The treatment of female infertility where the problem is due to an inability to ovulate.
How it works: It encourages the ovaries to produce hormones which are essential to conception and stimulates ovulation, which usually occurs within 18 hours of administration by injection.
Possible adverse effects: Abdominal pain or swelling may occur but this should pass off soon after treatment.
Other information: Patients offered this treatment should be aware of the increased likelihood of multiple births as several eggs may be released at once.
CAUTIONS
Children: Unlikely to be prescribed.
Pregnancy and breastfeeding: This drug is either not recommended for use by women who are pregnant or breastfeeding, or the precise effects are not known and it should therefore only be used with caution and under medical advice.

Alcohol: Alcohol should not be consumed, or only with caution – after medical advice has been sought – while you are taking this drug.
Driving and operating machinery: This drug may have some effect on your driving ability, so it is advisable not to drive or operate machinery while taking it.

CILAZAPRIL
Brand name: Vascace
Type of drug: ACE inhibitor
Uses: Used in conjunction with other drugs, to treat high blood pressure and chronic heart failure.
How it works: It is rapidly metabolised in the stomach and enables the blood vessels to dilate, with the result that blood pressure is lowered.
Possible adverse effects: Headache, dizziness, fatigue, rash, dry cough.
Other information: Use with caution if patients have impaired kidney or liver function.
CAUTIONS
Pregnancy and breastfeeding: This drug is either not recommended for use by women who are pregnant or breastfeeding, or the precise effects are not known and it should therefore only be used with caution and under medical advice.

CIMETIDINE
Brand name: Acitak, Dyspamet, Peptimax, Phimetin, Tagamet, Ultec, Zita
Type of drug: Anti-ulcer
Uses: To treat ulcers of the stomach and duodenum.
How it works: This drug reduces the secretion of gastric acid, and pepsin – an enzyme which helps in the digestion of protein. It thereby promotes healing of the stomach lining where the ulcers occur.
Possible adverse effects: Headaches, dizziness, confusion, hallucinations and sometimes diarrhoea.
Availability: Available with a prescription or without (over the counter).
Other information: Patients receiving anti-coagulants and anti-convulsant drugs need to take extra caution with this drug.
CAUTIONS
Pregnancy and breastfeeding: This drug is either not recommended for use by women who are pregnant or breastfeeding, or the precise effects are not known and it should therefore only be used with caution and under medical advice.

CIPROFIBRATE
Brand name: Modalim
Type of drug: Lipid lowering
Uses: Used to lower blood cholesterol and fat levels.
How it works: Lowers the levels of fat in the blood, with the result that the risk of developing coronary artery disease is low.
Possible adverse effects: Stomach upsets, dizziness, headache and fatigue. Possible hair loss and impotence. Any unexplained muscle weakness or pain should be reported immediately.
Other information: A barrier method of contraception should be used whilst on this medication. Use with great caution in patients with any impairment of liver or kidney function.
CAUTIONS
Pregnancy and breastfeeding: This drug is either not recommended

for use by women who are pregnant or breastfeeding, or the precise effects are not known and it should therefore only be used with caution and under medical advice.

CIPROFLOXACIN
Brand name: Ciproxin, Ciloxan
Type of drug: Anti-bacterial
Uses: To treat infections of the chest, intestine and urinary tract. Also a single dose treatment for gonorrhoea.
How it works: Acts on the DNA of the bacteria to stop them replicating.
Possible adverse effects: Nausea, vomiting, diarrhoea and abdominal pain occasionally.
Other information: Patients are advised to drink plenty of fluids while taking this drug.
CAUTIONS
Children: This drug is either not recommended for children, or is recommended only for children above a certain age.
Pregnancy and breastfeeding: This drug is either not recommended for use by women who are pregnant or breastfeeding, or the precise effects are not known and it should therefore only be used with caution and under medical advice.
Alcohol: Alcohol should not be consumed, or only with caution – after medical advice has been sought – while you are taking this drug.
Driving and operating machinery: This drug may have some effect on your driving ability, so it is advisable not to drive or operate machinery while taking it.

CISPLATIN
Brand name: Cisplatin
Type of drug: Anti-cancer
Uses: An effective treatment for cancer of the ovaries and testicular cancer in particular. Also for cancers of the bladder, head, neck and lung, and for bone cancer in children.
How it works: Acts on the DNA of the cancer cells to prevent them replicating.
Possible adverse effects: Severe nausea and vomiting, impairment of kidney function. Also tinnitus and damage to hearing.
Other information: This drug is usually administered as an injection. Anti-emetics are often given at the same time if nausea and vomiting are very severe.
CAUTIONS
Pregnancy and breastfeeding: This drug is either not recommended for use by women who are pregnant or breastfeeding, or the precise effects are not known and it should therefore only be used with caution and under medical advice.

CITALOPRAM
Brand name: Cipramil
Type of drug: Antidepressant
Uses: To treat depression and anxiety.
How it works: Lifts the mood, enabling people to take part in normal activities of daily living.
Possible adverse effects: Nausea, vomiting, stomach upsets and

diarrhoea. Appetite and weight changes, insomnia, dizziness and drowsiness.

Other information: Use with caution if patient has kidney, heart or epileptic problems. Also do not take if in a manic phase of manic depression.

CAUTIONS

Children: This drug is either not recommended for children, or is recommended only for children above a certain age.

Pregnancy and breastfeeding: This drug is either not recommended for use by women who are pregnant or breastfeeding, or the precise effects are not known and it should therefore only be used with caution and under medical advice.

CLARITHROMYCIN

Brand name: Klaricid

Type of drug: Antibiotic

Uses: To treat respiratory tract infections such as tonsillitis and bronchitis.

How it works: Attaches itself to the bacteria, preventing them from replicating.

Possible adverse effects: Headaches, nausea, diarrhoea, abdominal discomfort.

Other information: Do not stop before the end of the prescribed course. Use with caution in patients with impaired kidney function.

CAUTIONS

Children: This drug is either not recommended for children, or is recommended only for children above a certain age.

Pregnancy and breastfeeding: This drug is either not recommended for use by women who are pregnant or breastfeeding, or the precise effects are not known and it should therefore only be used with caution and under medical advice.

CLINDAMYCIN

Brand name: Dalacin C

Type of drug: Antibiotic

Uses: Used to treat joint and bone infections such as osteomyelitis and other severe infections like peritonitis.

How it works: Inhibits the replication of the bacteria and kills them.

Possible adverse effects: Abdominal discomfort, nausea, and vomiting. Rashes and occasionally a thrush infection may develop. If severe diarrhoea or colitis results, stop use immediately.

Other information: Capsules should be taken with a full glass of water.

CAUTIONS

Pregnancy and breastfeeding: This drug is either not recommended for use by women who are pregnant or breastfeeding, or the precise effects are not known and it should therefore only be used with caution and under medical advice.

CLOBETASONE

Brand name: Eumovate, Trimovate

Type of drug: Corticosteroid

Uses: Used to treat eczema, psoriasis and dermatitis.

How it works: Has an anti-inflammatory, anti-pus forming and vasoconstrictive action which removes the discomfort of the condition.

Possible adverse effects: Worsening of skin condition, thinning of the skin if used for excessively long periods.

Other information: A water-based cream is usually prescribed for moist or weeping eczema; an ointment is more likely for dry and scaly patches.

CLOMIFENE

Brand name: Clomid

Type of drug: Infertility treatment

Uses: Treatment of infertility in women where ovulation is not taking place because of inadequate levels of the necessary hormones.

How it works: Following a five-day course of tablets, the release of eggs (ovulation) is stimulated by the increased levels of the necessary hormones.

Possible adverse effects: Hot flushes and abdominal discomfort, headaches, insomnia and depression. Visual impairment is possible but rare.

Other information: Multiple pregnancies are a possible result of this treatment. Must not be used for longer than six monthly cycles, otherwise the risk of ovarian cancer may be increased.

CAUTIONS

Children: This drug is either not recommended for children, or is recommended only for children above a certain age.

CLOMIPRAMINE

Brand name: Anafranil, Anafranil SR

Type of drug: Tricyclic antidepressant

Uses: Long term treatment of depression, irrational fears and obsessive behaviour.

How it works: Changes the chemical balance in the brain to lift the mood, increases the appetite and stimulates an improved interest in day-to-day living.

Possible adverse effects: Dry mouth, constipation, drowsiness, hot flushes and dizziness.

Other information: Avoid using over-the-counter medications that contain antihistamines and decongestants.

CAUTIONS

Children: This drug is either not recommended for children, or is recommended only for children above a certain age.

Pregnancy and breastfeeding: This drug is either not recommended for use by women who are pregnant or breastfeeding, or the precise effects are not known and it should therefore only be used with caution and under medical advice.

Alcohol: Alcohol should not be consumed, or only with caution – after medical advice has been sought – while you are taking this drug.

Driving and operating machinery: This drug may have some effect on your driving ability, so it is advisable not to drive or operate machinery while taking it.

CLONAZEPAM

Brand name: Rivotril

Type of drug: Anti-epilepsy

Uses: Prevention and treatment of epileptic fits, particularly in children.

How it works: Has an anti-convulsant action that helps to prevent muscle spasms and seizures.

Possible adverse effects: Drowsiness and dizziness.

Other information: The anticonvulsant effect tends to lessen after several months of use.

CAUTIONS

Pregnancy and breastfeeding: This drug is either not recommended for use by women who are pregnant or breastfeeding, or the precise effects are not known and it should therefore only be used with caution and under medical advice.

Alcohol: Alcohol should not be consumed, or only with caution – after medical advice has been sought – while you are taking this drug.

Driving and operating machinery: This drug may have some effect on your driving ability, so it is advisable not to drive or operate machinery while taking it.

CLONIDINE

Brand name: Catapres, Catapres Perlongets, Dixarit

Type of drug: Anti-hypertensive, anti-migraine

Uses: To help prevent migraine attacks; also used for controlling menopausal flushing and helping with drug withdrawal symptoms.

How it works: Reduces the impulses from the brain that are thought to raise the blood pressure and increases activity in the area which is thought to decrease blood pressure.

Possible adverse effects: Drowsiness, dizziness, fatigue, nausea and dry mouth. Most side effects decrease during long term therapy.

Other information: Patient should be informed to report any excessive weight gain. Do not stop taking this drug suddenly except on medical advice.

CAUTIONS

Children: This drug is either not recommended for children, or is recommended only for children above a certain age.

Pregnancy and breastfeeding: This drug is either not recommended for use by women who are pregnant or breastfeeding, or the precise effects are not known and it should therefore only be used with caution and under medical advice.

Alcohol: Alcohol should not be consumed, or only with caution – after medical advice has been sought – while you are taking this drug.

Driving and operating machinery: This drug may have some effect on your driving ability, so it is advisable not to drive or operate machinery while taking it.

CLOZAPINE

Brand name: Clozaril

Type of drug: Anti-psychotic

Uses: To treat people with schizophrenia who have not responded to other treatments.

How it works: Helps to control the symptoms of the disorder, with the result that the sufferer can hopefully live a more conventionally normal life.

Possible adverse effects: Drowsiness, confusion, fatigue, dry mouth, constipation, blurred vision and nausea.

Other information: It can take up to three weeks for the benefits of this drug to be felt. Regular blood tests are required as this drug can produce a life-threatening fall in the white blood count.

CAUTIONS
Children: This drug is either not recommended for children, or is recommended only for children above a certain age.
Pregnancy and breastfeeding: This drug is either not recommended for use by women who are pregnant or breastfeeding, or the precise effects are not known and it should therefore only be used with caution and under medical advice.
Alcohol: Alcohol should not be consumed, or only with caution – after medical advice has been sought – while you are taking this drug.
Driving and operating machinery: This drug may have some effect on your driving ability, so it is advisable not to drive or operate machinery while taking it.

CO-AMILOFRUSE
Brand name: Burinex A, Fru-Co, Frumil, Lasoride
Type of drug: Diuretic
Uses: Used to treat oedema associated with heart failure; also high blood pressure and liver and kidney disease. It is also used when it is particularly important to avoid a fall in blood potassium levels.
How it works: Inhibits salt reabsorption in the kidneys, with the result that fluid is expelled from the body more effectively.
Possible adverse effects: Stomach and bowel upsets. Rashes.
Other information: Should be used with caution by patients with kidney and liver impairments and those with diabetes.
CAUTIONS
Pregnancy and breastfeeding: This drug is either not recommended for use by women who are pregnant or breastfeeding, or the precise effects are not known and it should therefore only be used with caution and under medical advice.

CO-AMILOZIDE
Brand name: Amil-Co, Moduret 25, Moduretic, Navispare
Type of drug: Diuretic
Uses: Used to treat high blood pressure, congestive heart failure and liver complaints.
How it works: Encourages the expulsion of excess fluid from the body, thereby reducing the blood pressure.
Possible adverse effects: Rashes and over-sensitivity to sunlight, blood disorders and gout.
Other information: Caution must be used if treating patients with liver and kidney impairments and diabetics.
CAUTIONS
Pregnancy and breastfeeding: This drug is either not recommended for use by women who are pregnant or breastfeeding, or the precise effects are not known and it should therefore only be used with caution and under medical advice.

CO-AMOXICLAV
Brand name: Augmentin
Type of drug: Antibiotic
Uses: Used to treat infections of the respiratory tract, genito-urinary, abdominal infections and severe dental infection.
How it works: Kills the bacteria which are causing the infection.
Possible adverse effects: Liver damage, skin disorders and dizziness

and headaches are all possible side effects. Patients must be warned about becoming jaundiced, which can occur up to six weeks after stopping the drug.

Other information: Should not be used for more than two weeks at a time.

CO-PROXAMOL

Brand name: Cosalgesic, Distalgesic
Type of drug: Painkiller
Uses: Painkiller used to relieve mild to moderate pain.
How it works: Controls pain that has not responded to paracetamol or other mild painkillers.
Possible adverse effects: Side effects are rare, but can include dizziness and nausea. Can be habit forming if taken for long periods.
Other information: Overdose is dangerous because breathing can be affected.

CAUTIONS

Children: This drug is either not recommended for children, or is recommended only for children above a certain age.
Pregnancy and breastfeeding: This drug is either not recommended for use by women who are pregnant or breastfeeding, or the precise effects are not known and it should therefore only be used with caution and under medical advice.
Alcohol: Alcohol should not be consumed, or only with caution – after medical advice has been sought – while you are taking this drug.
Driving and operating machinery: This drug may have some effect on your driving ability, so it is advisable not to drive or operate machinery while taking it.

CO-TRIMOXAZOLE

Brand name: Fectrim, Septrin
Type of drug: Anti-bacterial
Uses: The treatment of stubborn infections, particularly of the lung and bladder. Can also be used as treatment for some types of pneumonia.
How it works: Uses the combined force of two antibacterial drugs to combat the infection.
Possible adverse effects: Nausea, vomiting and rash.
Other information: Long term use of this drug could lead to folic acid deficiency, so supplements should be taken. It is also important to drink plenty of fluids. Blood tests will be taken to monitor blood composition.
CAUTIONS

Pregnancy and breastfeeding: This drug is either not recommended for use by women who are pregnant or breastfeeding, or the precise effects are not known and it should therefore only be used with caution and under medical advice.

CODEINE

Brand name: Codeine
Type of drug: Opioid analgesic, anti-diarrhoeal, cough suppressant
Uses: Painkiller for treatment of mild to moderate pain and occasionally to prevent coughing.
How it works: Acts as a mild opium-type painkiller, similar to morphine, to treat mild to moderate pain.
Possible adverse effects: Constipation is common. Other side effects

such as nausea and drowsiness are rare and will usually stop if the dose is reduced.

Other information: Can be habit forming if taken for long periods; usually only prescribed for short term relief. Can be supplied in either tablet, liquid or injection form.

CAUTIONS

Pregnancy and breastfeeding: This drug is either not recommended for use by women who are pregnant or breastfeeding, or the precise effects are not known and it should therefore only be used with caution and under medical advice.

Alcohol: Alcohol should not be consumed, or only with caution – after medical advice has been sought – while you are taking this drug.

Driving and operating machinery: This drug may have some effect on your driving ability, so it is advisable not to drive or operate machinery while taking it.

COLCHICINE

Brand name: Colchicine

Type of drug: Gout treatment

Uses: Used to relieve joint pain and inflammation in attacks of gout.

How it works: Decreases the deposits of uric acid in the joints which lead to the symptoms of the condition.

Possible adverse effects: Nausea, vomiting and abdominal pain. Possible diarrhoea. Any side effects should be reported.

Other information: This drug is most effective when taken at the first sign of an attack.

CAUTIONS

Children: This drug is either not recommended for children, or is recommended only for children above a certain age.

Pregnancy and breastfeeding: This drug is either not recommended for use by women who are pregnant or breastfeeding, or the precise effects are not known and it should therefore only be used with caution and under medical advice.

Alcohol: Alcohol should not be consumed, or only with caution – after medical advice has been sought – while you are taking this drug.

COLESTYRAMINE

Brand name: Questran, Questran Light

Type of drug: Lipid lowering

Uses: To treat people who have high levels of cholesterol or fat in their blood, and who are at risk from heart disease.

How it works: It is a resin that binds acids in the intestine to prevent their reabsorption. This action results in a reduction of cholesterol levels in the blood.

Possible adverse effects: Can cause nausea, constipation and general abdominal discomfort.

Other information: Vitamin absorption is reduced while taking this drug, so vitamin supplements of A, D and K are advised. Regular blood checks will help monitor the cholesterol level.

CAUTIONS

Children: This drug is either not recommended for children, or is recommended only for children above a certain age.

Alcohol: Alcohol should not be consumed, or only with caution – after medical advice has been sought – while you are taking this drug.

CONJUGATED OESTROGENS
Brand name: Premarin
Type of drug: Hormone
Uses: These naturally occurring female sex hormones are used to relieve the symptoms of the menopause and to treat and prevent osteoporosis and breast cancer.
How it works: When given by mouth, they relieve the hot flushes and sweating.
Possible adverse effects: Nausea, sore breasts and weight changes.
Other information: The drug is taken in a cyclic dosing schedule.
CAUTIONS
Children: This drug is either not recommended for children, or is recommended only for children above a certain age.
Pregnancy and breastfeeding: This drug is either not recommended for use by women who are pregnant or breastfeeding, or the precise effects are not known and it should therefore only be used with caution and under medical advice.

CYCLOPENTHIAZIDE
Brand name: Navidrex
Type of drug: Diuretic
Uses: The treatment of water retention which occurs with some liver and kidney disorders, pre-menstrual problems and long-term heart failure.
How it works: Has a diuretic effect which results in excess water being removed from the body and prevents it from being absorbed into the tissues, causing oedema.
Possible adverse effects: The drug causes the body to lose potassium, in which case supplements will be prescribed. It can also cause loss of appetite and nausea.
Other information: A diet rich in potassium or potassium supplements is recommended while taking this drug. Blood tests will be taken regularly to monitor potassium levels.
CAUTIONS
Alcohol: Alcohol should not be consumed, or only with caution – after medical advice has been sought – while you are taking this drug.

CYCLOPENTOLATE
Brand name: Minims Cyclopentolate, Mydrilate
Type of drug: Anticholinergic
Uses: Used for dilating the pupil of the eye for examination purposes.
How it works: The drug prevents the sphincter muscle of the eye from responding.
Possible adverse effects: Stinging and irritation of the eye and possible conjunctivitis. Headaches and confusion.
Other information: A darker pigmented eye is more resistant; care should be taken not to overdose.
CAUTIONS
Driving and operating machinery: This drug may have some effect on your driving ability, so it is advisable not to drive or operate machinery while taking it.

CYCLOPHOSPHAMIDE
Brand name: Endoxana

Type of drug: Anti-cancer
Uses: Used for treating cancers, in particular leukaemia, lymphomas and tumours. Can also be used to treat rheumatoid arthritis.
How it works: Prevents the cancer cells from dividing and therefore reproducing. Also kills the cells.
Possible adverse effects: Nausea, vomiting and diarrhoea. Abdominal pain and possible anorexia. Reversible hair loss. Because this drug reduces the production of blood cells, abnormal bleeding may occur and resistance to infection is reduced.
Other information: Patients to inform the doctor if any fever or infection occurs. A barrier contraceptive is recommended during treatment.
CAUTIONS
Pregnancy and breastfeeding: This drug is either not recommended for use by women who are pregnant or breastfeeding, or the precise effects are not known and it should therefore only be used with caution and under medical advice.

CYCLOSERINE
Brand name: Cycloserine
Type of drug: Antibiotic
Uses: Used to treat pulmonary tuberculosis; it is usually given in combination with other drugs.
How it works: Has one of two actions on the bacteria, depending on the susceptibility of the organism; it can either retard the multiplication of the bacteria or kill them.
Possible adverse effects: Headache, dizziness, drowsiness, confusion and depression. A rash or any other unusual effects should be reported to a doctor.
Other information: Treatment is likely to be continued for up to two years. This medication should be taken after meals to minimise irritation of the stomach.
CAUTIONS
Pregnancy and breastfeeding: This drug is either not recommended for use by women who are pregnant or breastfeeding, or the precise effects are not known and it should therefore only be used with caution and under medical advice.
Alcohol: Alcohol should not be consumed, or only with caution – after medical advice has been sought – while you are taking this drug.
Driving and operating machinery: This drug may have some effect on your driving ability, so it is advisable not to drive or operate machinery while taking it.

CYCLOSPORIN
Brand name: Neoral, Sandimmun
Type of drug: Immunosuppressant
Uses: Given to prevent organ rejection following transplants. It is also prescribed in severe cases of eczema and psoriasis and rheumatoid arthritis where other drugs have failed to help.
How it works: Suppresses the body's ability to defend itself against infection and what it perceives as foreign matter. It is therefore used after transplant surgery of organs such as the heart, kidney, and liver to reduce the occurrence of organ rejection.
Possible adverse effects: Nausea, headaches, confusion, overgrowth of

gums, fatigue, anaemia and diarrhoea. Increased susceptibility to infection.

Other information: It is important that kidney, liver and blood levels are regularly monitored. Patients should report any unusual symptoms immediately.

CAUTIONS

Children: This drug is either not recommended for children, or is recommended only for children above a certain age.

Pregnancy and breastfeeding: This drug is either not recommended for use by women who are pregnant or breastfeeding, or the precise effects are not known and it should therefore only be used with caution and under medical advice.

CYPROTERONE ACETATE
Brand name: Androcur, Cyprostat
Type of drug: Hormone
Uses: Used for treating prostate cancer in men and severe acne in women. Used in individuals who have misdirected male libido. Also used with oestrogen as a contraceptive, though not normally prescribed.
How it works: Cyproterone Acetate is a synthetic sex hormone that has effects similar to those of the female hormone progesterone. It is used to correct an imbalance of hormones which are thought to contribute to the above conditions.
Possible adverse effects: Reduces sex drive and stops sperm production. May cause testicles to shrink and be painful, and produce swelling of the breasts. Weight changes will probably occur. These effects usually diminish during treatment.
Other information: Should not be used by patients who have a history of thrombosis, diabetes or anaemia.

CAUTIONS

Children: This drug is either not recommended for children, or is recommended only for children above a certain age.

Pregnancy and breastfeeding: This drug is either not recommended for use by women who are pregnant or breastfeeding, or the precise effects are not known and it should therefore only be used with caution and under medical advice.

Alcohol: Alcohol should not be consumed, or only with caution – after medical advice has been sought – while you are taking this drug.

Driving and operating machinery: This drug may have some effect on your driving ability, so it is advisable not to drive or operate machinery while taking it.

CYTARABINE
Brand name: Cytarabine
Type of drug: Anti-cancer
Uses: Used to treat several types of acute leukaemia.
How it works: Prevents the cancer cells from replicating.
Possible adverse effects: Nausea, vomiting, diarrhoea, mouth ulcers and skin rashes can occur. Increased susceptibility to infection.
Other information: Blood tests should be regularly carried out to monitor the impact of treatment. Large amounts of fluid should be drunk during treatment.

CAUTIONS

Pregnancy and breastfeeding: This drug is either not recommended

for use by women who are pregnant or breastfeeding, or the precise effects are not known and it should therefore only be used with caution and under medical advice.

DACARBAZINE
Brand name: DTIC-Dome
Type of drug: Anti-cancer
Uses: Used to treat malignant melanomas and Hodgkin's disease.
How it works: Administered as an injection to prevent the cancer cells from replicating.
Possible adverse effects: Severe nausea and vomiting, together with a loss of appetite, are relatively common. A flu-like illness may occur a week after treatment. Reduced ability to fight off infection. Loss of hair, which will grow back after treatment. Any sign of bleeding should be reported immediately.
Other information: Patient should avoid people with infections and all products containing aspirin.
CAUTIONS
Pregnancy and breastfeeding: This drug is either not recommended for use by women who are pregnant or breastfeeding, or the precise effects are not known and it should therefore only be used with caution and under medical advice.

DALTEPARIN SODIUM
Brand name: Fragmin
Type of drug: Anticoagulant
Uses: Used to prevent the formation of blood clots in the veins of patients undergoing surgery and who have been identified as being at high risk.
How it works: Alters the clotting mechanism of the blood to make the formation of clots less likely.
Possible adverse effects: Rashes. Unusual bruising may occur which can indicate bleeding and should be reported immediately.
Other information: Avoid any products containing aspirin.
CAUTIONS
Children: This drug is either not recommended for children, or is recommended only for children above a certain age.
Pregnancy and breastfeeding: This drug is either not recommended for use by women who are pregnant or breastfeeding, or the precise effects are not known and it should therefore only be used with caution and under medical advice.

DANAZOL
Brand name: Danol
Type of drug: Synthetic hormone
Uses: Treatment of endometriosis, breast pain, male breast swelling and lumpy breasts in women.
How it works: It reduces the growth rate of abnormal breast tissue which causes discomfort in both men and women. It causes the abnormal endometrial tissue which occurs in endometriosis to be destroyed.
Possible adverse effects: Mainly occur when high doses are prescribed; they include swelling of the feet and ankles, weight gain, acne, and in women, unusual hair growth and voice changes. Nausea, rash, dizziness

and flushing may also occur. Menstrual periods will usually be disrupted or halted.

Other information: A barrier contraceptive should be used during treatment.

CAUTIONS

Children: This drug is either not recommended for children, or is recommended only for children above a certain age.

Pregnancy and breastfeeding: This drug is either not recommended for use by women who are pregnant or breastfeeding, or the precise effects are not known and it should therefore only be used with caution and under medical advice.

DANTRON

Brand name: Capsuvac, Codalax, Normax

Type of drug: Laxative

Uses: To treat constipation particularly in the elderly, the terminally ill and patients with serious heart conditions, where straining would be dangerous.

How it works: Increases intestinal motility, which enables the stool to be passed more easily.

Possible adverse effects: Abdominal cramps, nausea and vomiting. Avoid prolonged contact with skin, as irritation can occur. Urine may be coloured red.

Other information: Must not be used if bowel is obstructed.

CAUTIONS

Children: This drug is either not recommended for children, or is recommended only for children above a certain age.

Pregnancy and breastfeeding: This drug is either not recommended for use by women who are pregnant or breastfeeding, or the precise effects are not known and it should therefore only be used with caution and under medical advice.

DANTROLENE

Brand name: Dantrium

Type of drug: Muscle relaxant

Uses: It is used to help relieve muscular spasms produced by conditions such as stroke, multiple sclerosis and injuries of the spinal cord.

How it works: Acts on the skeletal muscles to produce a relaxant effect.

Possible adverse effects: Drowsiness, dizziness, weakness and fatigue. Headaches and insomnia.

Other information: It is advised to avoid excessive exposure to sunlight.

CAUTIONS

Children: This drug is either not recommended for children, or is recommended only for children above a certain age.

Pregnancy and breastfeeding: This drug is either not recommended for use by women who are pregnant or breastfeeding, or the precise effects are not known and it should therefore only be used with caution and under medical advice.

Alcohol: Alcohol should not be consumed, or only with caution – after medical advice has been sought – while you are taking this drug.

Driving and operating machinery: This drug may have some effect on your driving ability, so it is advisable not to drive or operate machinery while taking it.

DESFERRIOXAMINE
Brand name: Desferal
Type of drug: Antidote for iron poisoning
Uses: Used in treating iron poisoning, usually due to multiple blood transfusions. Also when there is too much aluminium in the body due to kidney dialysis.
How it works: The drug joins with the iron and the combination is then excreted in the urine.
Possible adverse effects: Abdominal pain, diarrhoea, shock and a drop in blood pressure, dizziness, allergic skin reactions.
Other information: Treatment should be stopped if the patient develops an infection.
CAUTIONS
Pregnancy and breastfeeding: This drug is either not recommended for use by women who are pregnant or breastfeeding, or the precise effects are not known and it should therefore only be used with caution.

DESMOPRESSIN
Brand name: DDAVP, Desmospray, Desmotabs
Type of drug: Antidiuretic hormone
Uses: Treatment of diabetes insipidus and nocturnal bedwetting (enuresis) in children.
How it works: A synthetic hormone that replaces a hormone which is lacking in people with diabetes insipidus. It also controls the production of urine by correcting the patient's hormonal deficiency.
Possible adverse effects: Fluid retention, headache, nausea, vomiting.
Other information: Fluid intake must be strictly observed.
CAUTIONS
Pregnancy and breastfeeding: This drug is either not recommended for use by women who are pregnant or breastfeeding, or the precise effects are not known and it should therefore only be used with caution and under medical advice.
Alcohol: Alcohol should not be consumed, or only with caution – after medical advice has been sought – while you are taking this drug.

DEXAMETHASONE
Brand name: Decadron
Type of drug: Corticosteroid
Uses: To treat rheumatic, allergic and inflammatory disorders such as rheumatoid arthritis, asthma and emphysema. Drops are used to treat eye inflammation.
How it works: Reduces the inflammation which occurs with the above condition.
Possible adverse effects: In the short term not too many side effects, but long-term use of corticosteroids can have many side effects.
Other information: People taking this drug are advised not to wear soft contact lenses.
CAUTIONS
Pregnancy and breastfeeding: This drug is either not recommended for use by women who are pregnant or breastfeeding, or the precise effects are not known and it should therefore only be used with caution and under medical advice.
Alcohol: Alcohol should not be consumed, or only with caution – after medical advice has been sought – while you are taking this drug.

DEXAMFETAMINE
Brand name: Dexadrine
Type of drug: Amphetamine
Uses: Used to treat narcolepsy, an uncontrollable tendency to fall asleep.
How it works: Acts on the nervous system to have a stimulant effect in adults, increasing alertness. However, this drug can have a sedative effect on children, so it is sometimes used to calm hyperactive children.
Possible adverse effects: Insomnia, dizziness, headache.
Other information: Not to be given if there is a history of drug or alcohol abuse. Not for people with glaucoma.
CAUTIONS
Pregnancy and breastfeeding: This drug is either not recommended for use by women who are pregnant or breastfeeding, or the precise effects are not known and it should therefore only be used with caution and under medical advice.
Alcohol: Alcohol should not be consumed, or only with caution – after medical advice has been sought – while you are taking this drug.
Driving and operating machinery: This drug may have some effect on your driving ability, so it is advisable not to drive or operate machinery while taking it.

DEXFENFLURAMINE
Brand name: Adifax
Type of drug: Appetite suppressant
Uses: The treatment of severe obesity.
How it works: Suppresses the appetite.
Possible adverse effects: Nausea, constipation or diarrhoea, drowsiness, dizziness, headache. Heart problems.
Other information: This drug is no longer available on the NHS.
CAUTIONS
Children: This drug is either not recommended for children, or is recommended only for children above a certain age.
Pregnancy and breastfeeding: This drug is either not recommended for use by women who are pregnant or breastfeeding, or the precise effects are not known and it should therefore only be used with caution and under medical advice.
Alcohol: Alcohol should not be consumed, or only with caution – after medical advice has been sought – while you are taking this drug.

DIAZEPAM
Brand name: Dialar, Diazemuls, Rimapam, Stesolid, Tensium, Valclair, Valium
Type of drug: Benzodiazepine anti-anxiety drug, anticonvulsant
Uses: To treat tension, nervousness and insomnia. It can also be used to treat epileptic fits.
How it works: Stimulates a chemical in the brain that helps control emotion and has a muscle-relaxant effect.
Possible adverse effects: Drowsiness and unsteadiness. Confusion.
Other information: It can be habit forming and if taken over a longer time its effect diminishes.
CAUTIONS
Pregnancy and breastfeeding: This drug is either not recommended for use by women who are pregnant or breastfeeding, or the precise

effects are not known and it should therefore only be used with caution and under medical advice.

Alcohol: Alcohol should not be consumed, or only with caution – after medical advice has been sought – while you are taking this drug.

Driving and operating machinery: This drug may have some effect on your driving ability, so it is advisable not to drive or operate machinery while taking it.

DIAZOXIDE
Brand name: Eudemine
Type of drug: Anti-hypertensive
Uses: To treat a severe rise in blood pressure associated with kidney disease. It is also used to treat low blood sugar.
How it works: Relaxes the smooth muscles, enabling the blood vessels to expand, thereby lowering the blood pressure. Inhibits the production of insulin, which keeps blood sugar levels low.
Possible adverse effects: Rapid beating of the heart (palpitations), raised blood sugar, fall in blood pressure, fluid and salt retention.
Other information: Blood sugar levels should be checked regularly.
CAUTIONS
Pregnancy and breastfeeding: This drug is either not recommended for use by women who are pregnant or breastfeeding, or the precise effects are not known and it should therefore only be used with caution and under medical advice.

DICLOFENAC
Brand name: Diclomax SR, Motifene, Rhumalgan, Volraman, Voltarol
Type of drug: Anti-inflammatory
Uses: Used to treat the mild to moderate pain of rheumatoid arthritis and osteoarthritis, gout, menstrual pain and post-operative pain.
How it works: Has an anti-inflammatory effect and similar pain killing actions to paracetamol.
Possible adverse effects: Irritation of the stomach, dizziness, drowsiness, irritability and insomnia.
Other information: Salt intake should be restricted during treatment with this drug.
CAUTIONS
Children: This drug is either not recommended for children, or is recommended only for children above a certain age.
Pregnancy and breastfeeding: This drug is either not recommended for use by women who are pregnant or breastfeeding, or the precise effects are not known and it should therefore only be used with caution and under medical advice.
Alcohol: Alcohol should not be consumed, or only with caution – after medical advice has been sought – while you are taking this drug.

DICYCLOMINE
Brand name: Merbentyl
Type of drug: Anti-emetic and anti-psychotic
Uses: To relieve the symptoms of irritable bowel syndrome.
How it works: Relaxes the muscles in order to relieve the painful abdominal cramps associated with the above conditions. It does not cure the underlying condition.
Possible adverse effects: Headaches, drowsiness and insomnia.

Other information: This medication is usually taken in conjunction with other drugs and treatments such as dietary changes.
CAUTIONS
Pregnancy and breastfeeding: This drug is either not recommended for use by women who are pregnant or breastfeeding, or the precise effects are not known and it should therefore only be used with caution and under medical advice.
Alcohol: Alcohol should not be consumed, or only with caution – after medical advice has been sought – while you are taking this drug.
Driving and operating machinery: This drug may have some effect on your driving ability, so it is advisable not to drive or operate machinery while taking it.

DIDANOSINE (ddI)
Brand name: Videx
Type of drug: Anti-viral drug for AIDS
Uses: To lessen the impact of AIDS-related infections.
How it works: Delays the onset of AIDS by boosting the body's ability to fight infection. The severity of infections associated with the disease is lessened. It is not a cure for the underlying disease.
Possible adverse effects: Headaches, nausea, vomiting, abdominal pain, tingling or numbness in the hands or feet. Fatigue is also common.
Other information: Long-term effects are not known, so regular blood and other tests will be conducted during treatment. The drug should be taken on an empty stomach.
CAUTIONS
Children: This drug is either not recommended for children, or is recommended only for children above a certain age.
Pregnancy and breastfeeding: This drug is either not recommended for use by women who are pregnant or breastfeeding, or the precise effects are not known and it should therefore only be used with caution and under medical advice.
Alcohol: Alcohol should not be consumed, or only with caution – after medical advice has been sought – while you are taking this drug.

DIFLUNISAL
Brand name: Dolobid
Type of drug: Nonsteroidal anti-inflammatory
Uses: To alleviate the symptoms of rheumatic diseases and menstrual pain.
How it works: Works in a similar way to aspirin to relieve pain and reduce inflammation.
Possible adverse effects: Stomach pains, nausea, vomiting, diarrhoea, indigestion, dizziness, insomnia, headache and fatigue.
Other information: Do not use if allergic to aspirin, or have active peptic ulcers. Take medication whole.
CAUTIONS
Children: This drug is either not recommended for children, or is recommended only for children above a certain age.
Pregnancy and breastfeeding: This drug is either not recommended for use by women who are pregnant or breastfeeding, or the precise effects are not known and it should therefore only be used with caution and under medical advice.

DIGOXIN
Brand name: Lanoxin
Type of drug: Heart disorder treatment
Uses: To treat congestive heart failure and heart rhythm problems.
How it works: Slows down the heart, with the effect that it pumps blood more effectively.
Possible adverse effects: Side effects are usually caused by excessive dosage and include nausea, vomiting, diarrhoea, abdominal pain, headache, visual disturbances, fatigue and drowsiness. Any sign of palpitations should be reported immediately.
Other information: Patient needs to be aware that it is not advisable to take other over-the-counter products that are high in sodium. In case of an overdose, seek medical advice immediately.

DIHYDROCODEINE
Brand name: Co-dydramol, DF 118, DHC Continus, Paramol, Remedeine
Type of drug: Opioid analgesic
Uses: To relieve mild to moderate pain; also used as a cough suppressant.
How it works: Acts to block the part of the brain that perceives pain.
Possible adverse effects: Nausea, vomiting, headache, dizziness and constipation.
Other information: Can occasionally produce dependence similar to that of morphine.
CAUTIONS
Children: This drug is either not recommended for children, or is recommended only for children above a certain age.
Pregnancy and breastfeeding: This drug is either not recommended for use by women who are pregnant or breastfeeding, or the precise effects are not known and it should therefore only be used with caution and under medical advice.
Alcohol: Alcohol should not be consumed, or only with caution – after medical advice has been sought – while you are taking this drug.

DILTIAZEM
Brand name: Adizem, Angiozem, Calcicard, Dilzem, Slozem, Tildiem
Type of drug: Calcium channel blocker, anti-hypertensive
Uses: Treatment of angina and high blood pressure.
How it works: Interferes with the electrical signals of the heart and dilates the blood vessels, thus reducing the pressure within them.
Possible adverse effects: Dizziness, headache, nausea and slowed heartbeat, usually controlled by dosage change.
Other information: Continue with drug even if feeling well. Report symptoms of dizziness.
CAUTIONS
Children: This drug is either not recommended for children, or is recommended only for children above a certain age.
Pregnancy and breastfeeding: This drug is either not recommended for use by women who are pregnant or breastfeeding, or the precise effects are not known and it should therefore only be used with caution and under medical advice.
Alcohol: Alcohol should not be consumed, or only with caution – after medical advice has been sought – while you are taking this drug.

Driving and operating machinery: This drug may have some effect on your driving ability, so it is advisable not to drive or operate machinery while taking it.

DIPHENOXYLATE
Brand name: None
Type of drug: Opioid antidiarrhoeal
Uses: Treatment for violent bouts of diarrhoea.
How it works: Reduces contractions of the bowel and therefore the frequency of bowel movements. It is not suitable for diarrhoea caused by infection or poisons.
Possible adverse effects: Bloated abdomen and nausea, rashes, drowsiness and dizziness. There is risk of addiction because it is chemically related to the opiate painkillers.
Other information: Available in tablet or liquid form. An adequate level of liquid must be taken during bouts of diarrhoea.
CAUTIONS
Children: This drug is either not recommended for children, or is recommended only for children above a certain age.
Pregnancy and breastfeeding: This drug is either not recommended for use by women who are pregnant or breastfeeding, or the precise effects are not known and it should therefore only be used with caution and under medical advice.
Alcohol: Alcohol should not be consumed, or only with caution – after medical advice has been sought – while you are taking this drug.
Driving and operating machinery: This drug may have some effect on your driving ability, so it is advisable not to drive or operate machinery while taking it.

DIPIPANONE
Brand name: Diconal
Type of drug: Opioid analgesic
Uses: For moderate pain relief.
How it works: Alleviates the pain at the same time as producing a less sedative effect than many similar drugs.
Possible adverse effects: Nausea, vomiting, dizziness, constipation. Can occasionally cause dependence.
Other information: Should not be used by patients with severe respiratory disorders.
CAUTIONS
Children: This drug is either not recommended for children, or is recommended only for children above a certain age.

DIPIVEFRINE HYDROCHLORIDE
Brand name: Propine
Type of drug: Sympathomimetic
Uses: To treat open-angle glaucoma.
How it works: Reduces the pressure inside the eye.
Possible adverse effects: Stinging of the eyes.
Other information: Do not wear soft contact lenses.
CAUTIONS
Driving and operating machinery: This drug may have some effect on your driving ability, so it is advisable not to drive or operate machinery while taking it.

DIPYRIDAMOLE
Brand name: Cerebrovase, Modaplate, Persantin
Type of drug: Anti-platelet
Uses: To prevent thrombosis (the formation of blood clots).
How it works: It 'thins' the blood in patients who have had heart valve replacement surgery, and reduces the possibility of blood clots.
Possible adverse effects: Nausea, headache, dizziness, faintness.
Other information: Patient may have to take drug for several months. Antacids should only be taken at the same time as this drug on the advice of a doctor.
CAUTIONS
Pregnancy and breastfeeding: This drug is either not recommended for use by women who are pregnant or breastfeeding, or the precise effects are not known and it should therefore only be used with caution and under medical advice.
Driving and operating machinery: This drug may have some effect on your driving ability, so it is advisable not to drive or operate machinery while taking it.

DISODIUM ETIDRONATE
Brand name: Didronel, Didronel PMO
Type of drug: Bone disorders treatment
Uses: To treat Paget's disease, and in combination with calcium tablets it is also used to treat osteoporosis.
How it works: Reduces the activity of the bone cells, thus stopping the progress of the disease.
Possible adverse effects: Diarrhoea and nausea.
Other information: Should be taken on an empty stomach.
CAUTIONS
Children: This drug is either not recommended for children, or only for children above a certain age.
Pregnancy and breastfeeding: This drug is either not recommended for use by women who are pregnant or breastfeeding, or the precise effects are not known and it should therefore only be used with caution and under medical advice.

DISODIUM PAMIDRONATE
Brand name: Aredia Dry Powder
Type of drug: Bisphosphonate
Uses: The treatment of Paget's disease and osteoporosis and bone pain associated with breast cancer.
How it works: Reduces blood calcium levels which are associated with the above conditions.
Possible adverse effects: Nausea, diarrhoea, muscle and joint pains, flu-like symptoms.
Other information: Calcium and vitamin D supplements are recommended.
CAUTIONS
Pregnancy and breastfeeding: This drug is either not recommended for use by women who are pregnant or breastfeeding, or the precise effects are not known and it should therefore only be used with caution and under medical advice.
Driving and operating machinery: This drug may have some effect on your driving ability, so it is advisable not to drive or operate machinery while taking it.

DISOPYRAMIDE
Brand name: Dirythmin SA, Rythmodan
Type of drug: Anti-arrhythmia
Uses: To treat disorders of heart rhythm such as tachycardia (rapid pulse) and atrial fibrillation.
How it works: Reduces the activity of the heart muscle and acts on the electrical impulses in the heart to encourage a normal heart rhythm.
Possible adverse effects: Stomach and bowel upsets, dry mouth, blurred vision.
Other information: Blood pressure level, blood sugar and potassium levels must be watched out for and monitored.
CAUTIONS
Pregnancy and breastfeeding: This drug is either not recommended for use by women who are pregnant or breastfeeding, or the precise effects are not known and it should therefore only be used with caution.

DISULFIRAM
Brand name: Antabuse
Type of drug: Alcohol abuse deterrent
Uses: To treat people who are chronically addicted to alcohol.
How it works: Works as a deterrent. If alcohol is taken at the same time as disulfiram, the two react to produce unpleasant effects such as palpitations, nausea and fainting. Unconsciousness may also occur.
Possible adverse effects: Drowsiness, fatigue, nausea and vomiting.
Other information: Alcohol in any form must not be consumed under any circumstances. The patient is advised to carry a card warning of the effects of this drug.
CAUTIONS
Children: This drug is either not recommended for children, or is recommended only for children above a certain age.
Pregnancy and breastfeeding: This drug is either not recommended for use by women who are pregnant or breastfeeding, or the precise effects are not known and it should therefore only be used with caution and under medical advice.
Alcohol: Alcohol should not be consumed while you are taking this drug.
Driving and operating machinery: This drug may have some effect on your driving ability, so it is advisable not to drive or operate machinery while taking it.

DITHRANOL
Brand name: Dithrocream, Micanol, Psorin
Type of drug: Psoriasis treatment
Uses: To treat moderate to severe psoriasis.
How it works: Restores excessive skin growth to normal; sometimes accompanied by ultraviolet treatments to boost its effect.
Possible adverse effects: Skin irritation.
Availability: Available with or without a prescription (over-the-counter).
Other information: The cream/ointment can be applied for short periods each day and then washed off. May stain clothes and linen. Keep away from the eyes and nose. Beneficial effect may not be felt for a few weeks.

CAUTIONS
Children: This drug is either not recommended for children, or is recommended only for children above a certain age.

DOBUTAMINE
Brand name: Dobutrex, Posiject
Type of drug: Sympathomimetic
Uses: The treatment of heart failure following a heart attack, heart surgery and shock.
How it works: Stimulates heart muscle without increasing the heart rate.
Possible adverse effects: Rapid beating of heart. An unexpected rise in blood pressure may indicate an overdose.
Other information: Usually only administered in intensive care units in hospital. Use with caution for patients with very low blood pressure.

DOMPERIDONE
Brand name: Motilium
Type of drug: Anti-emetic
Uses: Treatment of nausea and vomiting caused by gastrointestinal problems or as side effects from other medication.
How it works: Stops nausea without causing sedation.
Possible adverse effects: This drug is used because side effects from it are rare.
Other information: Not prescribed for long-term treatment.
CAUTIONS
Pregnancy and breastfeeding: This drug is either not recommended for use by women who are pregnant or breastfeeding, or the precise effects are not known and it should therefore only be used with caution and under medical advice.

DOPEXAMINE
Brand name: Dopacard
Type of drug: Sympathomimetic
Uses: Used to treat heart failure, particularly that associated with heart surgery.
How it works: Acts on the cardiac muscle and dilates the cardiac blood vessels to improve the flow of blood to the heart.
Possible adverse effects: Rapid beating of the heart; high doses may cause nausea, vomiting, headache, anginal pain.
Other information: Usually administered in an intensive care unit in hospital.
CAUTIONS
Pregnancy and breastfeeding: This drug is either not recommended for use by women who are pregnant or breastfeeding, or the precise effects are not known and it should therefore only be used with caution and under medical advice.
Alcohol: Alcohol should not be consumed, or only with caution – after medical advice has been sought – while you are taking this drug.

DORNASE ALFA
Brand name: Pulmozyme
Type of drug: Mucolytic enzyme
Uses: To treat cystic fibrosis.

How it works: Improves pulmonary function and helps to reduce the frequency of moderate to severe respiratory infections in patients with cystic fibrosis. The enzyme helps to breakdown and remove the sticky secretions of the lungs.

Possible adverse effects: Sore throat, hoarseness, voice changes, skin rash.

Other information: The drug is administered through inhalation using a jet-nebuliser.

CAUTIONS

Pregnancy and breastfeeding: This drug is either not recommended for use by women who are pregnant or breastfeeding, or the precise effects are not known and it should therefore only be used with caution and under medical advice.

DORZOLAMIDE

Brand name: Trusopt

Type of drug: Anti-glaucoma

Uses: To treat raised pressure in the eyes in open-angled glaucoma.

How it works: Inhibits the production of aqueous humour (the jelly-like fluid within the eye), thus reducing the pressure within the eye.

Possible adverse effects: Stinging and sore eyes, blurred vision, headache.

Other information: Do not wear soft contact lenses.

CAUTIONS

Pregnancy and breastfeeding: This drug is either not recommended for use by women who are pregnant or breastfeeding, or the precise effects are not known and it should therefore only be used with caution and under medical advice.

DOSULEPIN

Brand name: Dothapax, Prepadine, Prothiaden

Type of drug: Tricyclic antidepressant

Uses: A long-term treatment for depression.

How it works: Improves mood and interest in day-to-day living and encourages sleep if taken at night.

Possible adverse effects: Drowsiness, sweating and dry mouth sometimes occur during early days of treatment.

Other information: Can take several weeks for full beneficial effects to be realised.

CAUTIONS

Children: This drug is either not recommended for children, or is recommended only for children above a certain age.

Pregnancy and breastfeeding: This drug is either not recommended for use by women who are pregnant or breastfeeding, or the precise effects are not known and it should therefore only be used with caution and under medical advice.

Alcohol: Alcohol should not be consumed, or only with caution – after medical advice has been sought – while you are taking this drug.

Driving and operating machinery: This drug may have some effect on your driving ability, so it is advisable not to drive or operate machinery while taking it.

DOXAZOSIN

Brand name: Cardura

Type of drug: Vasodilator and anti-hypertensive
Uses: To treat high blood pressure (hypertension) and sometimes used for the treatment of enlarged prostate gland.
How it works: Dilates blood vessels, allowing more blood to pass.
Possible adverse effects: Dizziness on standing up. Headache, nausea and general fatigue.
Other information: The first treatment will cause a marked drop in blood pressure which will cause the patient to feel faint and dizzy.
CAUTIONS
Children: This drug is either not recommended for children, or is recommended only for children above a certain age.
Pregnancy and breastfeeding: This drug is either not recommended for use by women who are pregnant or breastfeeding, or the precise effects are not known and it should therefore only be used with caution and under medical advice.
Alcohol: Alcohol should not be consumed, or only with caution – after medical advice has been sought – while you are taking this drug.
Driving and operating machinery: This drug may have some effect on your driving ability, so it is advisable not to drive or operate machinery while taking it.

DOXORUBICIN
Brand name: Doxorubicin
Type of drug: Anti cancer
Uses: Used to treat many types of leukaemia, Hodgkin's disease, and many other cancers.
How it works: Acts on the DNA within the cancer cells to prevent them from replicating.
Possible adverse effects: Nausea and vomiting are the most common side effects of this drug after initial injection. Urine may be stained red. Lowered resistance to infection.
Other information: Blood will be carefully monitored to assess the impact of the drug. Patients should stay away from people with infections during a course of this treatment.
CAUTIONS
Pregnancy and breastfeeding: This drug is either not recommended for use by women who are pregnant or breastfeeding, or the precise effects are not known and it should therefore only be used with caution and under medical advice.

DOXYCYCLINE
Brand name: Cyclodox, Demix, Doxylar, Vibramycin
Type of drug: Antibiotic
Uses: Treatment of urinary, respiratory, eye, prostate and gut infections. Occasionally used for malaria and acne.
How it works: Antibiotic.
Possible adverse effects: Rarely causes nausea, vomiting and increased sensitivity to sun which may result in a rash.
Other information: Avoid excessive exposure to sunlight.
CAUTIONS
Pregnancy and breastfeeding: This drug is either not recommended for use by women who are pregnant or breastfeeding, or the precise effects are not known and it should therefore only be used with caution and under medical advice.

DYDROGESTERONE
Brand name: Duphaston, Duphaston HRT
Type of drug: Female sex hormone
Uses: Treatment of menstrual disorders and as part of hormone replacement therapy (HRT).
How it works: Synthetic hormone similar to progesterone.
Possible adverse effects: Irregular periods and bleeding between periods.
Other information: Dosage is taken on selective days during the menstrual cycle.
CAUTIONS
Children: This drug is either not recommended for children, or is recommended only for children above a certain age.
Driving and operating machinery: This drug may have some effect on your driving ability, so it is advisable not to drive or operate machinery while taking it.

ENALAPRIL
Brand name: Innovace
Type of drug: Vasodilator and anti-hypertensive
Uses: Treatment of hypertension and heart failure.
How it works: Dilates the blood vessels, with the result that the pressure within them is lowered.
Possible adverse effects: Dizziness and headache which usually subside after initial treatment. Possible rashes.
Other information: After first treatment patient will have to lie down for a few hours. Blood and urine tests will be periodically taken.
CAUTIONS
Children: This drug is either not recommended for children, or is recommended only for children above a certain age.
Pregnancy and breastfeeding: This drug is either not recommended for use by women who are pregnant or breastfeeding, or the precise effects are not known and it should therefore only be used with caution and under medical advice.
Alcohol: Alcohol should not be consumed, or only consumed with caution – after medical advice has been sought— while you are taking this drug.
Driving and operating machinery: This drug may have some effect on your driving ability, so it is advisable not to drive or operate machinery while taking it.

ENOXAPARIN
Brand name: Clexane
Type of drug: Anti-coagulant
Uses: The prevention of deep-vein thrombosis.
How it works: Acts on the clotting mechanism of the blood to stop clots forming.
Possible adverse effects: Nausea, confusion. Any sign of unusual bruising or bleeding should be reported.
Other information: Administered as an injection, usually in hospital.
CAUTIONS
Children: This drug is either not recommended for children, or is recommended only for children above a certain age.
Pregnancy and breastfeeding: This drug is either not recommended

for use by women who are pregnant or breastfeeding, or the precise effects are not known and it should therefore only be used with caution and under medical advice.

ENOXIMONE
Brand name: Perfan
Type of drug: Anti-emetic and anti-psychotic
Uses: Used to treat congestive heart failure.
How it works: Acts on the heart muscle to increase the heart's ability to pump blood around the body. Alleviates the symptoms, but is not a cure for the condition.
Possible adverse effects: Fall in blood pressure, irregular heart rhythm, nausea and vomiting, diarrhoea, headache.
Other information: Administered as an injection, usually in hospital.
CAUTIONS
Pregnancy and breastfeeding: This drug is either not recommended for use by women who are pregnant or breastfeeding, or the precise effects are not known and it should therefore only be used with caution and under medical advice.

EPHEDRINE
Brand name: CAM
Type of drug: Bronchodilator and decongestant
Uses: To treat the symptoms of respiratory problems.
How it works: It relaxes the muscles surrounding the airways to ease breathing difficulties.
Possible adverse effects: Anxiety and insomnia and restlessness, occasionally palpitations if taken by mouth.
Other information: Prolonged use is not recommended.
CAUTIONS
Pregnancy and breastfeeding: This drug is either not recommended for use by women who are pregnant or breastfeeding, or the precise effects are not known and it should therefore only be used with caution and under medical advice.
Driving and operating machinery: This drug may have some effect on your driving ability, so it is advisable not to drive or operate machinery while taking it.

EPINEPHRINE (Adrenaline)
Brand name: Ana-Guard, EpiPen, Mini-I-Jet Epinephrine
Type of drug: Stimulant
Uses: Used as an emergency treatment for acute heart failure and anaphylactic shock. Also given as eye drops to treat glaucoma.
How it works: Stimulates part of the nervous system, with the result that it relaxes smooth muscle within the lungs, stimulates the heart to beat more effectively and lowers pressure within the eyeball that is symptomatic of glaucoma.
Possible adverse effects: Dry mouth, nervousness, palpitations, headache and blurred vision.
Other information: Can be administered as an injection, inhaler and eye drops. If used for glaucoma, soft contact lenses should not be worn.
CAUTIONS
Pregnancy and breastfeeding: This drug is either not recommended for use by women who are pregnant or breastfeeding, or the precise

effects are not known and it should therefore only be used with caution and under medical advice.

EPOPROSTENOL
Brand name: Flolan
Type of drug: Anti-coagulant
Uses: During kidney dialysis.
How it works: Used to prevent the blood clotting during kidney dialysis, by stopping platelets from sticking together.
Possible adverse effects: Flushing, headache and a drop in blood pressure.
Other information: Given as an intravenous drip during dialysis.
CAUTIONS
Pregnancy and breastfeeding: This drug is either not recommended for use by women who are pregnant or breastfeeding, or the precise effects are not known and it should therefore only be used with caution and under medical advice.

ERGOCALCIFEROL
Brand name: Calciferol, Vitamin D2
Type of drug: Vitamin
Uses: Prevention and treatment of certain types of vitamin D deficiency.
How it works: Delivers vitamin D to people who are deficient for a number of reasons, including inadequate diet, malabsorption problems or long-term liver disease.
Possible adverse effects: Loss of appetite, nausea and vomiting, diarrhoea, weight loss, sweating, headache and thirst.
Availability: Some preparations are available over the counter.
Other information: Blood tests will be taken regularly to monitor the impact of the drug.
CAUTIONS
Pregnancy and breastfeeding: This drug is either not recommended for use by women who are pregnant or breastfeeding, or the precise effects are not known and it should therefore only be used with caution and under medical advice.

ERGOMETRINE
Brand name: Syntometrine
Type of drug: Prostaglandin
Uses: Used to prevent bleeding from the uterus after childbirth.
How it works: Causes contractions of the uterus, thus helping the blood vessels to heal and therefore stop bleeding.
Possible adverse effects: Nausea, vomiting, headache, dizziness, palpitations.
Other information: Given as an injection after childbirth.

ERGOTAMINE
Brand name: Medihaler-Ergotamine, Cafergot, Migril
Type of drug: Migraine treatment
Uses: To treat migraine in people for whom traditional pain relief is not effective.
How it works: Narrows the blood vessels around the skull and prevents pulsing effect which often accompanies migraine.

Possible adverse effects: Nausea and stomach upset. Can reduce circulation to the hands and feet and should not be taken by people known to have poor circulation.

Other information: Most effective when taken at the first indication of a migraine attack, when the 'aura' is perceived.

CAUTIONS

Children: This drug is either not recommended for children, or is recommended only for children above a certain age.

Pregnancy and breastfeeding: This drug is either not recommended for use by women who are pregnant or breastfeeding, or the precise effects are not known and it should therefore only be used with caution and under medical advice.

Driving and operating machinery: This drug may have some effect on your driving ability, so it is advisable not to drive or operate machinery while taking it.

ERYTHROMYCIN

Brand name: Erymax, Erythrocin, Erythroped, Rommix, Stiemycin

Type of drug: Antibiotic

Uses: Treatment of a range of bacterial infections, including those of the throat, ear and lungs. Can also be helpful in treating acne.

How it works: Kills the organisms which are causing the infection.

Possible adverse effects: Nausea and vomiting; also abdominal discomfort.

Other information: Can be administered as tablets, capsules, liquid, injection or as a solution to be applied to the skin.

CAUTIONS

Pregnancy and breastfeeding: This drug is either not recommended for use by women who are pregnant or breastfeeding, or the precise effects are not known and it should therefore only be used with caution and under medical advice.

ERYTHROPOIETIN

Brand name: Eprex

Type of drug: Kidney hormone

Uses: To treat anaemia due to kidney failure.

How it works: The drug stimulates the body to produce red blood cells, which people with kidney failure cannot do in the right quantity.

Possible adverse effects: Increased blood pressure, headache, dizziness.

Other information: Regular blood tests will be required to measure blood composition.

CAUTIONS

Pregnancy and breastfeeding: This drug is either not recommended for use by women who are pregnant or breastfeeding, or the precise effects are not known and it should therefore only be used with caution and under medical advice.

Alcohol: Alcohol should not be consumed, or only consumed with caution – after medical advice has been sought – while you are taking this drug.

ESTRAMUSTINE

Brand name: Estracyt

Type of drug: Anti-cancer

Uses: To treat cancer of the prostate gland.
How it works: The hormone affects the cancerous cells.
Possible adverse effects: Nausea, vomiting, diarrhoea. Breast tenderness and hair thinning may also occur.
Other information: Treatment with this drug may continue for up to three months. Milk, milk products and calcium-rich foods can impair the absorption of the drug.
CAUTIONS
Pregnancy and breastfeeding: This drug is either not recommended for use by women who are pregnant or breastfeeding, or the precise effects are not known and it should therefore only be used with caution and under medical advice

ETAMSYLATE
Brand name: Dicynene
Type of drug: Haemostatic
Uses: To stop heavy menstrual bleeding and to prevent bleeding in premature low birth-weight babies.
How it works: Corrects blood clotting malfunction.
Possible adverse effects: Nausea, headache and rashes.
Other information: In patients with heavy periods the drug will usually be given as tablets, to be taken during menstruation; for low birth-weight babies, it will be given as an injection.
CAUTIONS
Pregnancy and breastfeeding: This drug is either not recommended for use by women who are pregnant or breastfeeding, or the precise effects are not known and it should therefore only be used with caution and under medical advice.

ETHAMBUTOL
Brand name: Myambutol
Type of drug: Anti-tuberculous
Uses: Treatment of tuberculosis.
How it works: Works in conjunction with other drugs to attack the organisms that cause the infection.
Possible adverse effects: Side effects are uncommon, but this drug can occasionally cause eye problems such as temporary colour blindness.
Other information: Regular eye tests will be conducted.
CAUTIONS
Children: This drug is either not recommended for children, or is recommended only for children above a certain age.
Pregnancy and breastfeeding: This drug is either not recommended for use by women who are pregnant or breastfeeding, or the precise effects are not known and it should therefore only be used with caution and under medical advice.
Driving and operating machinery: This drug may have some effect on your driving ability, so it is advisable not to drive or operate machinery while taking it.

ETHOSUXIMIDE
Brand name: Emeside, Zarontin
Type of drug: Anti-convulsant
Uses: Treatment of certain types of epilepsy, particularly petit mal (daydreaming type episodes).

How it works: Has an anti-convulsant effect.
Possible adverse effects: Rare except when levels of the drug in the blood become too high.
Other information: Can reduce the production of blood cells.
CAUTIONS
Pregnancy and breastfeeding: This drug is either not recommended for use by women who are pregnant or breastfeeding, or the precise effects are not known and it should therefore only be used with caution and under medical advice.
Alcohol: Alcohol should not be consumed, or only with caution – after medical advice has been sought – while you are taking this drug.
Driving and operating machinery: This drug may have some effect on your driving ability, so it is advisable not to drive or operate machinery while taking it.

FACTOR VIII FRACTION, FREEZE DRIED
Brand name: Alphanate, Monoclate-P, Replenate, 8Y, High Potency Factor VIII Concentrate
Type of drug: Haemophilia treatment
Uses: To control bleeding in people with haemophilia.
How it works: Replaces a chemical vital for blood clotting, which is deficient in people with haemophilia.
Possible adverse effects: Fever, chills, flushing, tingling which may indicate an allergic reaction.
Other information: Administered via an intravenous infusion (drip) in hospital.

FAMCICLOVIR
Brand name: Famvir
Type of drug: Anti-viral
Uses: Used to treat herpes zoster, shingles, herpes simplex, genital herpes.
How it works: Enters the cells of the virus and acts to prevent them from replicating.
Possible adverse effects: Headache and nausea.
Other information: Treatment is most effective when started within 48 hours of onset.
CAUTIONS
Children: This drug is either not recommended for children, or is recommended only for children above a certain age.
Pregnancy and breastfeeding: This drug is either not recommended for use by women who are pregnant or breastfeeding, or the precise effects are not known and it should therefore only be used with caution and under medical advice.

FAMOTIDINE
Brand name: Pepcid, Pepcid AC
Type of drug: Anti-ulcer
Uses: Used to treat duodenal and gastric ulcers.
How it works: Inhibits the production of the stomach acids which are causing the lining of the gut to ulcerate.
Possible adverse effects: Headache, dizziness and stomach and bowel upsets.
Availability: Available with or without a prescription.

Other information: Treatment will be more beneficial if the dose is taken at bedtime.
CAUTIONS
Children: This drug is either not recommended for children, or is recommended only for children above a certain age.
Pregnancy and breastfeeding: This drug is either not recommended for use by women who are pregnant or breastfeeding, or the precise effects are not known and it should therefore only be used with caution and under medical advice.

FELODIPINE
Brand name: Plendil
Type of drug: Anti-hypertensive
Uses: Used to treat high blood pressure and angina.
How it works: Causes the blood vessels to relax and dilate – or widen – which means that the pressure inside them is lowered.
Possible adverse effects: Headache, dizziness, palpitations and fatigue. Has also been connected with mild gum problems.
Other information: Not to be used by patients who have low blood pressure or a fast heart rate. The medication is given in tablet form. The tablets should be swallowed whole and not crushed or chewed. Do not take any other over-the-counter products while taking this medication without first consulting a doctor.
CAUTIONS
Pregnancy and breastfeeding: This drug is either not recommended for use by women who are pregnant or breastfeeding, or the precise effects are not known and it should therefore only be used with caution and under medical advice.

FENBUFEN
Brand name: Lederfen,
Type of drug: Non-steroidal anti-inflammatory
Uses: The relief of inflammation, pain and stiffness which occurs with rheumatoid arthritis, osteoarthritis and gout.
How it works: Acts to relieve the inflammation which causes the symptoms of inflammatory diseases at the same time as treating the pain which often accompanies them.
Possible adverse effects: Like other non-steroidal anti-inflammatories, Fenbufen can irritate the lining of the stomach and other parts of the intestine. Any sign of blood in the vomit or faeces should be reported immediately, as should episodes of wheezing or breathlessness whilst taking this medication.
Other information: Prescribed as tablets or capsules. It is important not to take more than the prescribed dose. Do not take aspirin or other anti-inflammatory drugs except under the advice of a doctor.
CAUTIONS
Children: This drug is either not recommended for children, or is recommended only for children above a certain age.
Pregnancy and breastfeeding: This drug is either not recommended for use by women who are pregnant or breastfeeding, or the precise effects are not known and it should therefore only be used with caution and under medical advice.
Alcohol: Alcohol should not be consumed, or only consumed with caution – after medical advice has been sought – while you are taking this drug.

FENFLURAMINE/DEXFENFLURAMINE
Brand name: [Fenfluramine] Ponderax, [Dexfenfluramine] Adifax
Type of drug: Appetite suppressant
Uses: Used in the treatment of severe obesity.
How it works: The drugs increase the activity of serotonin (a chemical in the brain) with the result that the psychological desire to eat is reduced.
Possible adverse effects: Drowsiness, dizziness, headache, stomach disorders.
Other information: This drug has to be taken in conjunction with a strict diet, under medical supervision, and should be prescribed for no more than three months.
CAUTIONS
Children: This drug is either not recommended for children, or is recommended only for children above a certain age.
Pregnancy and breastfeeding: This drug is either not recommended for use by women who are pregnant or breastfeeding, or the precise effects are not known and it should therefore only be used with caution and under medical advice.
Alcohol: Alcohol should not be consumed, or only with caution – after medical advice has been sought – while you are taking this drug.
Driving and operating machinery: This drug may have some effect on your driving ability, so it is advisable not to drive or operate machinery while taking it.

FENOFIBRATE
Brand name: Lipantil
Type of drug: Lipid lowering
Uses: To lower the cholesterol and fat levels.
How it works: Action is thought to stimulate the breakdown of part of the proteins contained within the fats which are in the blood.
Possible adverse effects: Nausea and stomach upsets, headache, dizziness. Sometimes it can cause episodes of muscle pain and weakness, which should be reported.
Other information: Usually prescribed as capsules which should be taken with meals to maximise benefits. Not recommended for patients with kidney or gall bladder problems. Patient must also diet and exercise whilst taking this medication.
CAUTIONS
Children: This drug is either not recommended for children, or is recommended only for children above a certain age.
Pregnancy and breastfeeding: This drug is either not recommended for use by women who are pregnant or breastfeeding, or the precise effects are not known and it should therefore only be used with caution and under medical advice.

FENTANYL
Brand name: Durogesic, Sublimaze
Type of drug: Opioid analgesic
Uses: Its main use is to relieve pain during surgical operations. However, it can also be used to manage long-term pain in people for whom other painkillers are not sufficient.
How it works: Has a similar action to morphine in that it alters the patient's perception of what pain is, so that it is no longer felt.

Possible adverse effects: Depression of respiration, slowing of pulse rate, and nausea and vomiting. Side effects can occur 12 hours after administration of this medication.

Other information: Given by injection in hospital or for people with long-term pain problems, by a patch, which is attached to the skin and which delivers the dosage over 72 hours. Patients are taught how to use the patch. Soaps, oils and lotions should be avoided on the patch area.

CAUTIONS

Pregnancy and breastfeeding: This drug is either not recommended for use by women who are pregnant or breastfeeding, or the precise effects are not known and it should therefore only be used with caution and under medical advice.

Alcohol: Alcohol should not be consumed, or only consumed with caution, after medical advice has been sought, while taking this drug.

Driving and operating machinery: This drug may have some effect on your driving ability, so it is advisable not to drive or operate machinery while taking it.

FENTICONAZOLE

Brand name: Lomexin
Type of drug: Anti-fungal
Uses: Used in pessaries for vaginal infections which are caused by the fungus, vaginal candidiasis.
How it works: An anti-infective treatment which attacks the fungus which is the cause of the infection.
Possible adverse effects: Mild skin irritation.
Other information: Prescribed as pessaries. Care should be taken with contraception as this medication damages latex condoms and diaphragms.
Always complete the prescribed course of treatment.

CAUTIONS

Children: This drug is either not recommended for children, or is recommended only for children above a certain age.

Pregnancy and breastfeeding: This drug is either not recommended for use by women who are pregnant or breastfeeding, or the precise effects are not known and it should therefore only be used with caution and under medical advice.

FILGRASTIM

Brand name: Neupogen
Type of drug: Immunity booster
Uses: To reduce the risk of infection in people who have had chemotherapy for certain types of cancer and as part of the treatment for some other blood disorders.
How it works: It stimulates the bone marrow to produce white blood cells, which boosts the body's ability to fight off infection.
Possible adverse effects: Rarely, can affect the heart rhythm. More commonly, can cause skeletal pain, fever, tiredness, nausea and diarrhoea.
Other information: This medication is usually prescribed as an injection or in vials. Patients taking it are instructed in the techniques of self-administration.

CAUTIONS

Pregnancy and breastfeeding: This drug is either not recommended

for use by women who are pregnant or breastfeeding, or the precise effects are not known and it should therefore only be used with caution and under medical advice.

FINASTERIDE
Brand name: Proscar
Type of drug: Anti-androgens
Uses: Used mainly to treat men with enlarged prostate glands, although is also a treatment for first-stage cancer of the prostate.
How it works: Affects the balance of hormones present in the prostate, with the effect that the prostate does not enlarge.
Possible adverse effects: Impotence, decreased libido, breast tenderness and rash.
Other information: Women of childbearing age must avoid handling the tablets. The use of condoms is recommended if the sexual partner is pregnant or is likely to become pregnant, as the drug is excreted in semen. The effect of treatment with this drug may not become apparent for several months.
CAUTIONS
Children: This drug is either not recommended for children, or is recommended only for children above a certain age.

FLAVOXATE
Brand name: Urispas 200
Type of drug: Anti-cholinergic
Uses: The drug is used as an anti-spasmodic to help incontinence and other urinary tract problems.
How it works: Acts on the smooth muscle in the urinary tract, with the result that the bladder is able to hold more urine and the pain associated with urinary problems is controlled.
Possible adverse effects: Drowsiness and headache, diarrhoea and fatigue.
Other information: Must not be used if there is a prostate problem.
CAUTIONS
Children: This drug is either not recommended for children, or is recommended only for children above a certain age.
Driving and operating machinery: This drug may have some effect on your driving ability, so it is advisable not to drive or operate machinery while taking it.

FLECAINIDE
Brand name: Tambocor
Type of drug: Anti-arrhythmic
Uses: Used to treat heart rhythm disorders (arrhythmia) such as paroxysmal supraventricular tachycardia and atrial fibrillation.
How it works: Affects the electrical impulses in the heart, with the result that a more regular and normal rhythm is re-established.
Possible adverse effects: Dizziness and visual disturbances, nausea and vomiting. Occasionally difficulty in breathing can occur.
Other information: Treatment will usually be started in hospital.
CAUTIONS
Children: This drug is either not recommended for children, or is recommended only for children above a certain age.
Pregnancy and breastfeeding: This drug is either not recommended

for use by women who are pregnant or breastfeeding, or the precise effects are not known and it should therefore only be used with caution and under medical advice.

FLUCONAZOLE
Brand name: Diflucan
Type of drug: Anti-fungal
Uses: To treat thrush (candidiasis) and other infections such as those which occur in the urinary tract or gut and are caused by a fungus. Is also used to treat some types of meningitis and as a preventative treatment for patients undergoing bone marrow transplants.
How it works: Interferes with the individual cells which make up the fungus, with the result that it can no longer grow.
Possible adverse effects: Irritation of the gastrointestinal tract, resulting in nausea, abdominal pain or diarrhoea.
Availability: Some preparations are available over the counter.
Other information: Usually administered as capsules or liquid, but can also be given as an injection. For patients who may suffer a relapse of meningitis this drug may be administered indefinitely.
CAUTIONS
Children: This drug is either not recommended for children, or is recommended only for children above a certain age.
Pregnancy and breastfeeding: This drug is either not recommended for use by women who are pregnant or breastfeeding, or the precise effects are not known and it should therefore only be used with caution and under medical advice.

FLUCYTOSINE
Brand name: Ancotil
Type of drug: Anti-fungal
Uses: To treat yeast and fungal infections.
How it works: Penetrates the cells which make up the fungus and interferes with their ability to multiply.
Possible adverse effects: Nausea, vomiting, diarrhoea and rashes. Can occasionally cause bleeding in the gut. Any signs of blood in vomit or faeces, or bruising, should be reported straight away.
Other information: Treatment may need to be maintained over a long period.
CAUTIONS
Pregnancy and breastfeeding: This drug is either not recommended for use by women who are pregnant or breastfeeding, or the precise effects are not known and it should therefore only be used with caution and under medical advice.

FLUDARABINE
Brand name: Fludara
Type of drug: Anti-cancer
Uses: Used in the treatment of chronic leukaemia, and some types of lymphoma in patients who have not responded to other treatments.
How it works: Affects the DNA of the cancer cells, with the result that they are unable to multiply, thus preventing the tumour from growing.
Possible adverse effects: Blood disorders and lowering of immunity are the most common side effects. Fatigue, visual disturbances, nausea, vomiting and fever are also possible.

Other information: It is advisable to stay away from people with infections whilst on this medication, as your immunity will be reduced.
CAUTIONS
Children: This drug is either not recommended for children, or is recommended only for children above a certain age.

FLUDROCORTISONE
Brand name: Florinef
Type of drug: Mineralocorticoid
Uses: Treatment of disorders of the adrenal glands, which are situated just above the kidneys and which are crucial in the production of hormones which affect the breakdown of carbohydrates and electrolytes as well as the sex glands.
How it works: The replacement of substances usually produced by the adrenal glands.
Possible adverse effects: Hypertension, sodium and water retention and potassium loss. Muscle weakness, numbness, appetite loss and nausea may be signs of electrolyte imbalance and should be reported. A doctor should also be informed of significant weight gain or headaches.
Other information: It is important not to miss doses or to double dose if one is forgotten.
CAUTIONS
Children: This drug is either not recommended for children, or is recommended only for children above a certain age.

FLUMAZENIL
Brand name: Anexate
Type of drug: Benzodiazepine antagonist
Uses: Given following a general anaesthetic.
How it works: Used to reverse the sedative effects of benzodiazepines, used for anaesthesia.
Possible adverse effects: Nausea, vomiting, flushing, rise in blood pressure and heart rate.
Other information: Usually given as an injection to hospital in-patients.
CAUTIONS
Children: This drug is either not recommended for children, or is recommended only for children above a certain age.
Pregnancy and breastfeeding: This drug is either not recommended for use by women who are pregnant or breastfeeding, or the precise effects are not known and it should therefore only be used with caution and under medical advice.
Driving and operating machinery: This drug may have some effect on your driving ability, so it is advisable not to drive or operate machinery while taking it.

FLUOROURACIL
Brand name: Efudix
Type of drug: Anti-cancer
Uses: To treat various cancers, including those which affect the stomach, breast, bladder and pancreas.
How it works: Prevents the DNA in the cancer cells replicating.
Possible adverse effects: Nausea, vomiting, diarrhoea, rashes and dermatitis. Bleeding from the digestive system can occur, so any signs of blood in vomit or faeces should be reported straight away.

Other information: Usually given as an injection, in hospital, as it is not absorbed sufficiently if taken by mouth. Patients are advised to wear sunscreens, as the drug increases sensitivity to sunlight. People with infections should also be avoided.

CAUTIONS

Pregnancy and breastfeeding: This drug is either not recommended for use by women who are pregnant or breastfeeding, or the precise effects are not known and it should therefore only be used with caution and under medical advice.

Alcohol: Alcohol should not be consumed, or only with caution – after medical advice has been sought – while you are taking this drug.

Driving and operating machinery: This drug may have some effect on your driving ability, so it is advisable not to drive or operate machinery while taking it.

FLUOXETINE
Brand name: Prozac
Type of drug: Antidepressant
Uses: To treat depression, binge eating (bulimia nervosa), panic disorder, alcohol dependence (rarely) and other psychiatric problems.
How it works: Changes the chemicals in the brain, with the result that patients have an elevated mood and feel more able to take an interest in day-to-day living.
Possible adverse effects: Headache, nausea, restlessness, inability to sleep and stomach upsets. Any sign of a rash or hives should be reported instantly, as should a loss of appetite.
Other information: Side effects decrease in time.

CAUTIONS

Children: This drug is either not recommended for children, or is recommended only for children above a certain age.

Pregnancy and breastfeeding: This drug is either not recommended for use by women who are pregnant or breastfeeding, or the precise effects are not known and it should therefore only be used with caution and under medical advice.

Driving and operating machinery: This drug may have some effect on your driving ability, so it is advisable not to drive or operate machinery while taking it.

FLUPENTIXOL
Brand name: Depixol, Fluanxol
Type of drug: Anti-psychotic
Uses: To treat schizophrenia and other similar disorders, and mild to moderate depression.
How it works: Tranquillises the patient and reduces hallucinations and other psychotic symptoms without having a sedative effect.
Possible adverse effects: Blurred vision, dizziness, nausea, drowsiness, weight gain, palpitations, tremors, Parkinsonism.
Other information: This medication should be used with caution by patients with heart disease. The control of severe symptoms may take up to six months.

CAUTIONS

Children: This drug is either not recommended for children, or is recommended only for children above a certain age.

Pregnancy and breastfeeding: This drug is either not recommended

for use by women who are pregnant or breastfeeding, or the precise effects are not known and it should therefore only be used with caution and under medical advice.

Alcohol: Alcohol should not be consumed, or only with caution – after medical advice has been sought – while you are taking this drug.

Driving and operating machinery: This drug may have some effect on your driving ability, so it is advisable not to drive or operate machinery while taking it.

FLUPHENAZINE
Brand name: Modecate, Moditen, Motival
Type of drug: Anti-psychotic
Uses: To treat psychotic disorders – those in which the sufferer loses contact with reality.
How it works: Blocks the production of brain chemicals which contribute to the symptoms of psychosis – hallucinations and delusions.
Possible adverse effects: Dizziness, drowsiness and possible weight gain.
Other information: Patient must report any rashes that appear while on the medication.
CAUTIONS
Children: This drug is either not recommended for children, or is recommended only for children above a certain age.
Alcohol: Alcohol should not be consumed, or only with caution – after medical advice has been sought – while you are taking this drug.
Driving and operating machinery: This drug may have some effect on your driving ability, so it is advisable not to drive or operate machinery while taking it.

FLURBIPROFEN
Brand name: Froben, Froben SR
Type of drug: Nonsteroidal anti-inflammatory
Uses: Mainly used to treat and relieve pain in rheumatoid arthritis and osteoarthritis. Also used for severe menstrual pain and used in an eye solution to relieve inflammation after eye surgery.
How it works: Has an anti-inflammatory and pain-relieving effect which is useful for the treatment of continuous pain and discomfort.
Possible adverse effects: Headache, dizziness, nausea, oedema. **Other information:** Patient to take drug with food or milk to minimise stomach upset, and to report any unusual side effects.
CAUTIONS
Children: This drug is either not recommended for children, or is recommended only for children above a certain age.
Pregnancy and breastfeeding: This drug is either not recommended for use by women who are pregnant or breastfeeding, or the precise effects are not known and it should therefore only be used with caution and under medical advice.
Driving and operating machinery: This drug may have some effect on your driving ability, so it is advisable not to drive or operate machinery while taking it.

FLUTAMIDE
Brand name: Drogenil
Type of drug: Anti-cancer

Uses: The treatment of cancer of the prostate.
How it works: Bombards the tumour with hormones that inhibit its growth.
Possible adverse effects: Tenderness and enlargement of the breasts. Diarrhoea and impotence. Nausea, vomiting, headache, insomnia. Can cause fluid retention, which can aggravate heart disease.
Other information: Some symptoms of the disease may worsen before the treatment starts to be effective.
CAUTIONS
Children: This drug is either not recommended for children, or is recommended only for children above a certain age.

FLUTICASONE PROPIONATE
Brand name: Cutivate, Flixonase, Flixotide
Type of drug: Corticosteroid
Uses: Treatment of asthma and allergic rhinitis.
How it works: As a corticosteroid drug.
Possible adverse effects: Rare, but can irritate the nasal passages if taken as a spray, or encourage fungal infection of the throat if taken by inhaler. Any burning or irritation should be reported.
Other information: May be prescribed as an ointment, cream, nasal spray or inhaler. Creams and ointments should be applied sparingly. Keep away from eyes, around genital and rectal area and any skin creases. Rinse mouth after inhaling the steroids. Avoid contact with those infected with chickenpox or measles and consult a doctor if you come into contact with either of these diseases.
CAUTIONS
Children: This drug is either not recommended for children, or is recommended only for children above a certain age.
Pregnancy and breastfeeding: This drug is either not recommended for use by women who are pregnant or breastfeeding, or the precise effects are not known and it should therefore only be used with caution and under medical advice.

FLUVOXAMINE
Brand name: Faverin
Type of drug: Antidepressant
Uses: To treat depression and obsessive-compulsive disorders.
How it works: Affects the balance of chemicals in the brain thought to be connected to the development of obsessive-compulsive problems.
Possible adverse effects: Nausea, vomiting, abdominal pain. Headache, dizziness and insomnia.
Other information: Smoking may decrease the effectiveness of this drug.
CAUTIONS
Children: This drug is either not recommended for children, or is recommended only for children above a certain age.
Pregnancy and breastfeeding: This drug is either not recommended for use by women who are pregnant or breastfeeding, or the precise effects are not known and it should therefore only be used with caution and under medical advice.
Alcohol: Alcohol should not be consumed, or only consumed with caution – after medical advice has been sought – while you are taking this drug.

Driving and operating machinery: This drug may have some effect on your driving ability, so it is advisable not to drive or operate machinery while taking it.

FOLIC ACID
Brand name: Folic acid (non-proprietary)
Type of drug: Vitamin
Uses: For the treatment of some types of anaemia and the prevention of congenital disorders.
How it works: Stimulates the production of blood cells, which are deficient in anaemia. When taken during the early days of pregnancy it prevents neural tube defects, such as spina bifida, developing in the womb. Also given to people with some types of chronic blood disorders.
Possible adverse effects: Possible allergic rash.
Other information: Should not be used to treat pernicious anaemia or vitamin B12 deficiencies. Not to be used in cancer patients. Dietary sources of folic acid are available.

FOLLITROPIN ALFA and BETA
Brand name: [Alfa] Gonal-F, [Beta] Puregon
Type of drug: Hormone
Uses: In assisted fertility treatments, for women who do not ovulate and who have not responded to other treatments.
How it works: This synthetic hormone stimulates the ovaries to produce eggs.
Possible adverse effects: Rarely, it can lead to an over-stimulation of the ovaries which may result in abdominal swelling and pain, nausea, vomiting and diarrhoea. Multiple pregnancies, pain at the injection site and allergic reactions are also possible.
Other information: Given by an injection under the surface of the skin. Should be used with caution by women with ovarian cysts or thyroid disorders.

FORMOTEROL
Brand name: Foradil, Oxis
Type of drug: Bronchodilator
Uses: The treatment of moderate to severe asthma.
How it works: It has a bronchodilating action – by relaxing the muscles surrounding the airways in the lungs it can relieve the symptoms of asthma.
Possible adverse effects: A fine tremor, palpitations and headaches.
Other information: Levels of potassium in the blood will be regularly monitored.
CAUTIONS
Pregnancy and breastfeeding: This drug is either not recommended for use by women who are pregnant or breastfeeding, or the precise effects are not known and it should therefore only be used with caution and under medical advice.

FOSCARNET
Brand name: Foscavir
Type of drug: Anti-viral
Uses: Used to treat serious viral infections such as cytomegalovirus, a

herpes virus, and retinitis in AIDS patients.

How it works: Affects the DNA to stop the virus from replicating.

Possible adverse effects: Anaemia, nausea, vomiting, diarrhoea, abdominal pain, headache and fatigue.

Other information: Blood calcium level and kidney function tests need to be carried out every other day. Patient must report any tingling and numbness.

CAUTIONS

Children: This drug is either not recommended for children, or is recommended only for children above a certain age.

Pregnancy and breastfeeding: This drug is either not recommended for use by women who are pregnant or breastfeeding, or the precise effects are not known and it should therefore only be used with caution and under medical advice.

FOSINOPRIL

Brand name: Staril

Type of drug: ACE inhibitor

Uses: Used to treat high blood pressure (hypertension) and heart failure.

How it works: Reduces constriction in the arteries and reduces the amount of blood being pumped around the body.

Possible adverse effects: Dizziness, stomach and bowel upsets, palpitations and fatigue. Fever or a sore throat should be reported to a doctor.

Other information: This medication should be taken one hour before, or two hours after, any food or antacids.

CAUTIONS

Children: This drug is either not recommended for children, or is recommended only for children above a certain age.

Pregnancy and breastfeeding: This drug is either not recommended for use by women who are pregnant or breastfeeding, or the precise effects are not known and it should therefore only be used with caution and under medical advice.

FRUSEMIDE FUROSEMIDE

Brand name: Froop, Lasix, Rusyde

Type of drug: Loop diuretic and anti-hypertensive

Uses: Treatment of fluid retention (oedema) which is usually caused by heart failure or lung and kidney disorders.

How it works: Acts on a part of the kidney to promote the excretion of excess fluid and body salts.

Possible adverse effects: Serious problems unlikely, but loss of potassium can lead to muscle cramps and dizziness.

Other information: You may be advised to wear sunscreens, as some people can develop an increased sensitivity to sunlight which does not occur until 10 days after exposure to the sun.

CAUTIONS

Pregnancy and breastfeeding: This drug is either not recommended for use by women who are pregnant or breastfeeding, or the precise effects are not known and it should therefore only be used with caution.

Alcohol: Alcohol should not be consumed, or only with caution – after medical advice has been sought – while you are taking this drug.

Driving and operating machinery: This drug may have some effect

on your driving ability, so it is advisable not to drive or operate machinery while taking it.

GABAPENTIN
Brand name: Neurotin
Type of drug: Anti-epilepsy
Uses: The treatment of epilepsy.
How it works: Acts as an anti-convulsant by damping down the electrical activity which takes place within the brain cells and works to prevent any build-up of electrical activity which could lead to a seizure.
Possible adverse effects: Drowsiness, dizziness, ataxia, fatigue. Headache, nausea, and vomiting.
Other information: First dose to be taken at bedtime to minimise drowsiness and dizziness. It is not advisable to stop taking this drug suddenly – the dosage should be reduced over at least a week.
CAUTIONS
Children: This drug is either not recommended for children, or is recommended only for children above a certain age.
Pregnancy and breastfeeding: This drug is either not recommended for use by women who are pregnant or breastfeeding, or the precise effects are not known and it should therefore only be used with caution and under medical advice.
Driving and operating machinery: This drug may have some effect on your driving ability, so it is advisable not to drive or operate machinery while taking it.

GANCICLOVIR
Brand name: Cymevene
Type of drug: Anti-viral
Uses: To treat serious infections such as cytomegalovirus, herpes and retinitis.
How it works: Prevents the replication of infected cells.
Possible adverse effects: Blood disorders, rashes, fever, nausea, vomiting, headache, confusion, drowsiness. Any signs of fever, easy bruising or bleeding should be reported immediately.
Other information: More than one course of this drug may be necessary to keep the infection at bay.
CAUTIONS
Children: This drug is either not recommended for children, or is recommended only for children above a certain age.
Pregnancy and breastfeeding: This drug is either not recommended for use by women who are pregnant or breastfeeding, or the precise effects are not known and it should therefore only be used with caution and under medical advice.

GEMFIBROZIL
Brand name: Lopid
Type of drug: Lipid lowering
Uses: To lower cholesterol and fat levels in the blood in patients for whom a change of diet and other drugs have not worked.
How it works: Reduces the amount of cholesterol in the blood and prevents it from building up again.
Possible adverse effects: Stomach upsets, rash, headache, dizziness.
Other information: Must not be taken by people with alcohol

problems, gallstones or kidney impairment. A fat-lowering diet and exercise regime should be maintained whilst on medication. Take with food to minimise the risk of gastric problems.

CAUTIONS

Children: This drug is either not recommended for children, or is recommended only for children above a certain age.

Pregnancy and breastfeeding: This drug is either not recommended for use by women who are pregnant or breastfeeding, or the precise effects are not known and it should therefore only be used with caution and under medical advice.

Alcohol: Alcohol should not be consumed, or only consumed with caution – after medical advice has been sought – while you are taking this drug.

GENTAMICIN

Brand name: Cidomycin, Garamycin, Genticin, Minims Gentamicin

Type of drug: Antibiotic

Uses: Available as an injection for the treatment of serious infections such as those which affect the lungs, urinary tract, brain (meningitis) and female reproductive system. It is also available as drops and ointment for the treatment of ear and eye infections.

How it works: Binds on to the bacteria and prevents them from replicating.

Possible adverse effects: Seizures, nausea and vomiting, sweatiness and dizziness. The most common side effect of using the creams is a skin irritation, which should be reported.

Other information: Injections are not recommended if pregnant or breastfeeding. Tests will be taken regularly to monitor the effect of the drug.

CAUTIONS

Pregnancy and breastfeeding: This drug is either not recommended for use by women who are pregnant or breastfeeding, or the precise effects are not known and it should therefore only be used with caution and under medical advice.

GESTRINONE

Brand name: Dimetriose

Type of drug: Endometriosis treatment

Uses: To treat endometriosis.

How it works: Affects the production of hormones in a way that causes the unwanted deposits of endometrial tissue responsible for the symptoms of the condition to shrink.

Possible adverse effects: Fluid retention, weight gain, acne. Stomach and bowel upsets, voice change, change in breast size.

Other information: Menstruation will stop while you are taking this medication. A barrier method of contraception should be used.

CAUTIONS

Children: This drug is either not recommended for children, or is recommended only for children above a certain age.

Pregnancy and breastfeeding: This drug is either not recommended for use by women who are pregnant or breastfeeding, or the precise effects are not known and it should therefore only be used with caution and under medical advice.

GESTONORONE
Brand name: Depostat, Gestronol Caproate
Type of drug: Progestogens
Uses: To treat cancer of the womb. Also used in males to shrink cancer of the prostate gland.
How it works: As a hormone, affects the ability of the cancer to grow.
Possible adverse effects: Fluid retention, acne, rash, weight gain, breast discomfort, stomach upsets, insomnia depression.
Other information: Given as an injection.

GLIBENCLAMIDE
Brand name: Daonil, Euglucon, Semi-Daonil
Type of drug: Oral anti-diabetic
Uses: Used as treatment and maintenance therapy for people with late (maturity) onset diabetes.
How it works: Stimulates the production of insulin by cells in the pancreas and encourages the body to take up sugar, thereby reducing the amount of sugar in the blood.
Possible adverse effects: These are rare and are usually linked to the level of sugar present in the blood. Feeling faint, weak, confused and sweaty. May have stomach upset and headaches.
Other information: A low fat, low carbohydrate diet should be adhered to whilst taking this drug. Blood and urine tests will be taken regularly to monitor the effectiveness of the medication regime. The effectiveness of this medication may be reduced at times of severe stress or other injury and so may need to be supplemented with insulin.
CAUTIONS
Children: This drug is either not recommended for children, or is recommended only for children above a certain age.
Pregnancy and breastfeeding: This drug is either not recommended for use by women who are pregnant or breastfeeding, or the precise effects are not known and it should therefore only be used with caution.
Alcohol: Alcohol should not be consumed, or only consumed with caution – after medical advice has been sought – while you are taking this drug.
Driving and operating machinery: This drug may have some effect on your driving ability, so it is advisable not to drive or operate machinery while taking it.

GLICLAZIDE
Brand name: Diamicron
Type of drug: Oral anti-diabetic
Uses: Used as treatment and maintenance therapy for people with late (maturity) onset diabetes.
How it works: Stimulates the production of insulin by cells in the pancreas and encourages the body to take up sugar, thereby reducing the amount of sugar in the blood.
Possible adverse effects: Rare, but include weakness, confusion, sweating and headache.
Other information: As well as adhering to a low carbohydrate and low fat diet, it is important to exercise regularly while being treated for diabetes. The effectiveness of this medication may be reduced at times of severe stress or injury and so may need to be supplemented with insulin.

CAUTIONS
Children: This drug is either not recommended for children, or is recommended only for children above a certain age.
Pregnancy and breastfeeding: This drug is either not recommended for use by women who are pregnant or breastfeeding, or the precise effects are not known and it should therefore only be used with caution and under medical advice.
Alcohol: Alcohol should not be consumed, or only with caution – after medical advice has been sought – while you are taking this drug.
Driving and operating machinery: This drug may have some effect on your driving ability, so it is advisable not to drive or operate machinery while taking it.

GLYCERYL TRINITRATE (GTN)
Brand name: Coro-Nitro Pump Spray, Glytrin Spray, GTN 300 mcg, Nitrolingual Pumpspray, Nitrocine, Nitromin, Nitronal, Nitro-Dur, Percutol, Trintek
Type of drug: Anti-angina
Uses: To relieve the symptoms of angina. It is not a cure.
How it works: Dilates the blood vessels and enables more blood to reach the heart. It relieves the pain which occurs as the heart muscle is starved of oxygen which is carried by the blood.
Possible adverse effects: Flushing, headache, fainting after first dose.
Other information: Regular checks on the blood pressure are required with this medication. The drug can be taken in tablet form (slow release), which is placed under the tongue, or as a skin patch, capsule, spray or ointment.
CAUTIONS
Children: This drug is either not recommended for children, or is recommended only for children above a certain age.
Pregnancy and breastfeeding: This drug is either not recommended for use by women who are pregnant or breastfeeding, or the precise effects are not known and it should therefore only be used with caution and under medical advice.
Alcohol: Alcohol should not be consumed, or only with caution – after medical advice has been sought – while you are taking this drug.
Driving and operating machinery: This drug may have some effect on your driving ability, so it is advisable not to drive or operate machinery while taking it.

GONADORELIN
Brand name: GnRH, LH-RH, HRF
Type of drug: Hormone
Uses: Used for treating the absence of periods and infertility problems.
How it works: It increases the levels of certain types of hormones in the blood, with the result that ovulation is stimulated.
Possible adverse effects: Possible nausea, headache, abdominal pain, increased menstrual bleeding.
Other information: Women taking this drug should be warned that multiple pregnancies are a possibility.
CAUTIONS
Children: This drug is either not recommended for children, or is recommended only for children above a certain age.
Pregnancy and breastfeeding: This drug is either not recommended

for use by women who are pregnant or breastfeeding, or the precise effects are not known and it should therefore only be used with caution and under medical advice.

GONADOTROPHIN – See Human Menopausal Gonadotrophins and Chorionic Gonadotrophin

GOSERELIN
Brand name: Zoladex
Type of drug: Gonadorelin analogues
Uses: To treat hormone-related cancers such as those which occur in the prostate and breast. Is also used to treat endometriosis.
How it works: Stimulates changes to hormone levels, thus starving cancerous tumours and preventing the growths which are symptomatic of endometriosis from growing.
Possible adverse effects: Menopause-like symptoms, headache. On rare occasions a rash may appear, which should be reported to a doctor. In both men and women it can lead to a loss of libido.
Other information: Use a non-hormonal contraceptive whilst on a course of this medication.
CAUTIONS
Pregnancy and breastfeeding: This drug is either not recommended for use by women who are pregnant or breastfeeding, or the precise effects are not known and it should therefore only be used with caution and under medical advice.

GRANISETRON
Brand name: Kytril
Type of drug: Anti-emetic
Uses: To treat nausea and vomiting induced by anti-cancers (chemotherapy) and radiotherapy.
How it works: Blocks the messages to the brain which stimulate the feelings of nausea and instinct to vomit.
Possible adverse effects: Constipation, diarrhoea, headache and rash.
Other information: Report to a doctor any sign of an anaphylactic reaction such as swelling around the lips and face, difficulty in breathing and a rash.
CAUTIONS
Pregnancy and breastfeeding: This drug is either not recommended for use by women who are pregnant or breastfeeding, or the precise effects are not known and it should therefore only be used with caution and under medical advice.

GRISEOFULVIN
Brand name: Grisovin
Type of drug: Anti-fungal
Uses: To treat fungal infections of the nails, hair and skin.
How it works: Disrupts the ability of the fungal cell to divide and therefore grow. Also helps the skin to resist the fungus.
Possible adverse effects: Headache, nausea, vomiting, rashes and dizziness. Can alter the taste sensation.
Other information: Supplied as tablets or capsules. Pregnancy must be avoided until after one month of stopping treatment. Men must not father a child within six months of stopping the treatment. Should be

taken around meal times to minimise stomach upset.
CAUTIONS
Pregnancy and breastfeeding: This drug is either not recommended for use by women who are pregnant or breastfeeding, or the precise effects are not known and it should therefore only be used with caution and under medical advice.
Alcohol: Alcohol should not be consumed, or only with caution – after medical advice has been sought – while you are taking this drug.
Driving and operating machinery: This drug may have some effect on your driving ability, so it is advisable not to drive or operate machinery while taking it.

GUANETHIDINE MONOSULPHATE
Brand name: Ismelin
Type of drug: Anti-hypertensive
Uses: To treat moderate to severe high blood pressure and the signs and symptoms of an overactive thyroid gland (thyrotoxicosis).
How it works: Acts on the peripheral parts of the body to prevent the walls of blood vessels constricting, thereby easing the flow of blood through them.
Possible adverse effects: Most common is diarrhoea and a drop in blood pressure which leads to dizziness and faintness. Hot showers and sudden changes of position should be avoided to minimise the possibility of side effects occurring.
Other information: Take medical advice before taking other over-the-counter preparations. Do not double up on doses if you forget to take one.
CAUTIONS
Children: This drug is either not recommended for children, or is recommended only for children above a certain age.
Pregnancy and breastfeeding: This drug is either not recommended for use by women who are pregnant or breastfeeding, or the precise effects are not known and it should therefore only be used with caution and under medical advice.
Driving and operating machinery: This drug may have some effect on your driving ability, so it is advisable not to drive or operate machinery while taking it.

HALOPERIDOL
Brand name: Dozic, Haldol, Serenace
Type of drug: Anti-psychotic
Uses: To treat schizophrenia, manias and dementia. Also a short-term treatment for severe anxiety.
How it works: Reduces the violent and aggressive symptoms of schizophrenia and other illnesses where delusions and hallucinations occur. It controls the symptoms rather than curing the disease.
Possible adverse effects: Side effects experienced are abnormal involuntary movements and stiffness of face and limbs, headaches, confusion, dizziness and drowsiness.
Other information: This drug should not be used at the same time as other anti-depressants.
CAUTIONS
Children: This drug is either not recommended for children, or is recommended only for children above a certain age.

Pregnancy and breastfeeding: This drug is either not recommended for use by women who are pregnant or breastfeeding, or the precise effects are not known and it should therefore only be used with caution and under medical advice.

Alcohol: Alcohol should not be consumed, or only with caution – after medical advice has been sought – while you are taking this drug.

Driving and operating machinery: This drug may have some effect on your driving ability, so it is advisable not to drive or operate machinery while taking it.

HEPARIN

Brand name: Calciparine, Minihep, Monoparin, Multiparin, Fragmin, Innohep

Type of drug: Anti-coagulant

Uses: Prevents formation of blood clots and assists in their breakdown.

How it works: Dissolves existing blood clots before they can reach vital organs such as the brain. It can also be used to prevent blood clots forming during procedures such as surgery and dialysis.

Possible adverse effects: Excessive bleeding is a risk, so the dosage will be monitored carefully. Bruising may appear around the site of the injection.

Other information: Heparin will usually only be given in hospital, by injection. Patient must avoid aspirin and aspirin derivatives.

CAUTIONS

Pregnancy and breastfeeding: This drug is either not recommended for use by women who are pregnant or breastfeeding, or the precise effects are not known and it should therefore only be used with caution and under medical advice.

Driving and operating machinery: This drug may have some effect on your driving ability, so it is advisable not to drive or operate machinery while taking it.

HOMATROPINE HYDROBROMIDE

Brand name: Homatropine

Type of drug: Anti-cholinergic

Uses: Preparation for eye surgery.

How it works: Affects the muscles within the eye, with the result that the pupil is dilated and remains so for around 12 hours.

Possible adverse effects: Local irritation and stinging.

Other information: Not to be used for patients with closed-angle glaucoma.

CAUTIONS

Children: This drug is either not recommended for children, or is recommended only for children above a certain age.

Pregnancy and breastfeeding: This drug is either not recommended for use by women who are pregnant or breastfeeding, or the precise effects are not known and it should therefore only be used with caution and under medical advice.

Driving and operating machinery: This drug may have some effect on your driving ability, so it is advisable not to drive or operate machinery while taking it.

HUMAN MENOPAUSAL GONADOTROPHINS

Brand name: Menopur, Menonal, Menogon

Type of drug: Gonadotrophin
Uses: To treat infertility due to an insufficiency of the pituitary gland; also given to women who have not responded to other infertility treatments.
How it works: Stimulates the ovaries. The preparation is produced from purified extracts of urine from women who have passed the menopause.
Possible adverse effects: Headache, fatigue, irritability, depression.
Other information: Patient must be told about possibility of multiple pregnancy.

HYDRALAZINE
Brand name: Apresoline
Type of drug: Anti-hypertensive
Uses: To treat moderate to severe high blood pressure.
How it works: Acts on the smooth muscle of the veins and has a relaxant effect which causes the blood pressure to fall.
Possible adverse effects: Increase in heart rate, fluid retention, nausea, vomiting, headache.
Other information: Take medication with meals to enhance drug absorption and minimise gastric irritation.
CAUTIONS
Children: This drug is either not recommended for children, or is recommended only for children above a certain age.
Pregnancy and breastfeeding: This drug is either not recommended for use by women who are pregnant or breastfeeding, or the precise effects are not known and it should therefore only be used with caution and under medical advice.
Driving and operating machinery: This drug may have some effect on your driving ability, so it is advisable not to drive or operate machinery while taking it.

HYDROCHLOROTHIAZIDE
Brand name: HydroSaluric
Type of drug: Diuretic
Uses: Used to treat fluid retention (oedema) in people who have heart failure, kidney, liver or pre-menstrual problems. Is also used as a treatment for high blood pressure.
How it works: Affects the kidneys, with the result that the excretion of sodium and water is increased and the excess passed out.
Possible adverse effects: Rare, except if associated with an excess loss of potassium. Possible stomach and bowel upsets.
Other information: Take medication with food to avoid gastric upset. To avoid having to pass water during the night, do not take at bedtime. Do not take any over-the-counter medication without first discussing it with your doctor.
CAUTIONS
Pregnancy and breastfeeding: This drug is either not recommended for use by women who are pregnant or breastfeeding, or the precise effects are not known and it should therefore only be used with caution and under medical advice.
Alcohol: Alcohol should not be consumed, or only with caution – after medical advice has been sought – while you are taking this drug.
Driving and operating machinery: This drug may have some effect

on your driving ability, so it is advisable not to drive or operate machinery while taking it.

HYDROCORTISONE
Brand name: Colifoam, Corlan, Dioderm, Efcortelan, Efcortesol, Hydrocortistab, Hydrocortone, Solu-Cortef
Type of drug: Corticosteroid
Uses: Used to suppress allergies and severe inflammations.
How it works: Replaces natural hormones where the adrenal glands are not producing sufficient quantities. Suppresses inflammatory reaction in other conditions.
Possible adverse effects: Indigestion, abdominal discomfort, weight gain, acne. Prolonged high dosage of this medication can produce serious side effects such as diabetes and glaucoma, so is avoided where possible.
Availability: Prescription needed except for preparations.
Other information: People on long-term treatment are advised to carry a treatment card in case of emergency. Regular checks will be made on blood pressure if hydrocortisone is being given by mouth.
CAUTIONS
Alcohol: Alcohol should not be consumed, or only with caution – after medical advice has been sought – while you are taking this drug.

HYDROXOCOBALAMIN
Brand name: Cobalin-H, Neo-Cytamen
Type of drug: Vitamin
Uses: Used to treat pernicious anaemia and other vitamin B12 deficient anaemias.
How it works: Replaces the vitamin B12, which is deficient in people suffering with anaemia.
Possible adverse effects: Itching, hot flushes, nausea and dizziness. Rarely, allergic reactions may occur.
Other information: Administered as an injection. Treatment will usually be for life.

HYDROXYAPATITE
Brand name: Ossopan
Type of drug: Calcium and phosphorous supplement
Uses: To treat calcium deficiency.
How it works: Replaces calcium which is lost through disorders such as osteoporosis, rickets and osteomalacia and through inadequate intake in the diet. It may also be used during breastfeeding.
Possible adverse effects: Mild gastro-intestinal disturbances, changes to the heart rhythm.
Availability: Available with or without a prescription (over the counter).
Other information: Can be given in tablet or injection form. This drug will not be used for people who have a history of kidney problems.

IBUPROFEN
Brand name: Arthrofen, Brufen, Ebufac, Fenbid, Ibufac, Ibugel, Ibuleve, Inoven, Motrin, Nurofen
Type of drug: Non-steroidal anti-inflammatory
Uses: Treatment of the symptoms of conditions such as osteo- and rheumatoid arthritis, back pain and gout. Also effective for headaches,

menstrual pain, soft tissue injuries and backache.

How it works: Relieves pain, inflammation and stiffness.

Possible adverse effects: Heartburn and indigestion, which can be minimised by taking it with food or milk. Rarely, Ibuprofen can cause nausea and vomiting.

Availability: Available with or without a prescription (over the counter).

Other information: Available as tablets, slow release tablets, capsules, liquid, granules or cream.

CAUTIONS

Pregnancy and breastfeeding: This drug is either not recommended for use by women who are pregnant or breastfeeding, or the precise effects are not known and it should therefore only be used with caution and under medical advice.

Alcohol: Alcohol should not be consumed, or only with caution – after medical advice has been sought – while you are taking this drug.

IDARUBICIN

Brand name: Zavedos

Type of drug: Anti-cancer

Uses: To part-treat some types of leukaemia; used with other medications.

How it works: Inhibits part of the chemical process which takes place as the disease progresses.

Possible adverse effects: Headache, nausea, vomiting, cramps, diarrhoea, hair loss, fever, rash on palms and soles. Patients are at an increased risk of infection whilst on this treatment, so symptoms such as a sore throat or fever should be reported immediately. Increased risk of bleeding.

Other information: Administered as an intravenous infusion (drip).

CAUTIONS

Children: This drug is either not recommended for children, or is recommended only for children above a certain age.

Pregnancy and breastfeeding: This drug is either not recommended for use by women who are pregnant or breastfeeding, or the precise effects are not known and it should therefore only be used with caution and under medical advice.

Alcohol: Alcohol should not be consumed, or only with caution – after medical advice has been sought – while you are taking this drug.

IDOXURIDINE

Brand name: Herpid

Type of drug: Anti-viral

Uses: Treatment of herpes infections of the eye.

How it works: Blocks the ability of the virus to reproduce.

Possible adverse effects: These occur rarely, but adverse effects include irritation, burning and pain in the eye. A mild swelling of the eyelid may also be experienced. Any signs of an adverse reaction should be reported immediately.

Other information: Administered as eye drops. Not recommended for long-term use because of the risk of eye damage. Do not mix with any other solutions or medication. Avoid sharing towels and flannels with others to prevent the infection from spreading. Always wash hands before and after application.

CAUTIONS

Children: This drug is either not recommended for children, or is recommended only for children above a certain age.

Pregnancy and breastfeeding: This drug is either not recommended for use by women who are pregnant or breastfeeding, or the precise effects are not known and it should therefore only be used with caution and under medical advice.

IMIPRAMINE
Brand name: Tofranil
Type of drug: Tricyclic anti-depressant
Uses: Prescribed for the long-term treatment of depression. It is also sometimes prescribed to treat children who have a night-time bedwetting problem.
How it works: A tricyclic anti-depressant which helps to improve mood and appetite at the same time as stimulating an interest in everyday activities which usually diminishes with depression.
Possible adverse effects: Sweating, dry mouth, blurred vision and constipation. Should be taken with milk or food if it appears to upset the stomach.
Other information: The full effects of the drug may not be experienced for up to four weeks after starting treatment. Less sedating than many anti-depressants. An overdose should be treated as a medical emergency.
CAUTIONS
Pregnancy and breastfeeding: This drug is either not recommended for use by women who are pregnant or breastfeeding, or the precise effects are not known and it should therefore only be used with caution and under medical advice.
Alcohol: Alcohol should not be consumed, or only with caution – after medical advice has been sought – while you are taking this drug.

INDAPAMIDE
Brand name: Natrilix
Type of drug: Diuretic
Uses: For the treatment of high blood pressure and oedema due to heart failure.
How it works: Affects the kidneys and encourages excess water to be expelled from the body.
Possible adverse effects: Headache, dizziness and vertigo, particularly on standing up. Occasionally a rash may appear.
Other information: Will be dispensed as tablets.
CAUTIONS
Children: This drug is either not recommended for children, or is recommended only for children above a certain age.
Pregnancy and breastfeeding: This drug is either not recommended for use by women who are pregnant or breastfeeding, or the precise effects are not known and it should therefore only be used with caution and under medical advice.

INDOMETACIN
Brand name: Flexin Continus, Indocid, Indolar, Rheumacin LA, Slo-Indo
Type of drug: Non-steroidal anti-inflammatory, gout treatment
Uses: Treatment of conditions such as rheumatoid arthritis, osteoarthritis, ankylosing spondylitis, gout and bursitis.
How it works: Has an anti-inflammatory effect.

Possible adverse effects: As with all non-steroidal anti-inflammatories, there is a risk of irritation of the gut. Also, headaches, dizziness and nausea.

Other information: Do not take aspirin or similar medication without consulting a doctor first.

CAUTIONS

Children: This drug is either not recommended for children, or is recommended only for children above a certain age.

Pregnancy and breastfeeding: This drug is either not recommended for use by women who are pregnant or breastfeeding, or the precise effects are not known and it should therefore only be used with caution and under medical advice.

Alcohol: Alcohol should not be consumed, or only with caution – after medical advice has been sought – while you are taking this drug.

Driving and operating machinery: This drug may have some effect on your driving ability, so it is advisable not to drive or operate machinery while taking it.

INOSINE PRANOBEX

Brand name: Imunovir

Type of drug: Anti-viral

Uses: Given by mouth to treat infections caused by the herpes virus, including herpes simplex and genital herpes. Can also be used to treat some brain infections caused by the virus.

How it works: Attacks the virus, but does not eradicate it.

Possible adverse effects: Nausea, vomiting, headache, dizziness.

Other information: The course of treatment is likely to last for up to a month for genital herpes infections and for 14 days for other infections.

CAUTIONS

Children: This drug is either not recommended for children, or is recommended only for children above a certain age.

Pregnancy and breastfeeding: This drug is either not recommended for use by women who are pregnant or breastfeeding, or the precise effects are not known and it should therefore only be used with caution.

INSULIN

Brand name: Humalog, Actrapid, Insulatard, Mixtard, Monotard, Ultratard, Velosulin, Humulin, Hypurin, Pork Insulatard, Pork Mixtard, Rapitard MC, Semitard MC

Type of drug: Anti-diabetic

Uses: Treatment of diabetes mellitus. It is the only effective treatment for juvenile onset diabetes.

How it works: Provides the body with the hormone insulin, which is made in the pancreas and which is lacking in diabetics. Insulin is crucial if the body is to be able to metabolise and use sugar.

Possible adverse effects: Most of the adverse effects are associated with a low blood sugar level (hypoglycaemia), and include light-headedness, confusion, sweating and dizziness. These can usually be prevented by a correction to the dose. Serious allergic reactions are rare.

Other information: An overdose should be reported to a doctor immediately. People prescribed insulin should carry some kind of warning card. Do not take any other medication without consulting a doctor, as it may contain sugar.

CAUTIONS
Alcohol: Alcohol should not be consumed, or only with caution – after medical advice has been sought – while you are taking this drug.

INTERFERON
Brand name: Betaferon, Immukin, Intron A, Roferon-A, Viraferon
Type of drug: Anti-viral and anticancer
Uses: There are three types of Interferon. Interferon Alpha is used to treat leukaemias, some cancers and active hepatitis. Interferon Beta is used for multiple sclerosis. Interferon gamma is used with antibiotics for people with granulomatous disease.
How it works: Interferon are substances which have been infected by viruses and are effective at resisting other types of infections.
Possible adverse effects: Headache, listlessness, dizziness and sleepiness, digestive upsets and fever are relatively common.
Other information: Administered as an injection in hospital. Frequent blood tests will be taken to monitor the impact of this medication.
CAUTIONS
Children: This drug is either not recommended for children, or is recommended only for children above a certain age.
Pregnancy and breastfeeding: This drug is either not recommended for use by women who are pregnant or breastfeeding, or the precise effects are not known and it should therefore only be used with caution and under medical advice.

IPECACUANHA
Brand name: Ipecacuanha Emetic Mixture, Paediatric
Type of drug: Emetic
Uses: Used to induce vomiting in people who have either deliberately or accidentally swallowed poisonous substances.
How it works: Irritates the lining of the gut to the point where vomiting occurs. It usually results in the stomach being completely empty within 30 minutes of ingesting dose.
Availability: Available with or without a prescription (over-the-counter).
Other information: This drug will only be used with caution and should never be used in people who are not conscious. Should be taken with water, with a dose repeated after 20 minutes if necessary.

IPRATROPIUM BROMIDE
Brand name: Atrovent, Rinatec
Type of drug: Bronchodilator
Uses: Treatment of lung problems such as chronic bronchitis.
How it works: Usually given by nebuliser or inhaler to relax the muscles of the airways to aid easier breathing. Also prescribed as a nasal spray for the treatment of a persistent runny nose due to an allergic reaction.
Possible adverse effects: Rare, except for dry mouth and throat.
Other information: Should be used with caution by people with glaucoma.

ISOCARBOXAZID
Brand name: Isocarboxazid
Type of drug: Anti-depressant

Uses: To treat depressive illness.

How it works: Enables people with depressive illnesses to lead more normal lives.

Possible adverse effects: Can interact with certain types of food such as cheese, pickled herring, broad beans, Bovril, Oxo and Marmite to cause a headache and high blood pressure. These foods should therefore be avoided. Hypotension (low blood pressure) leading to feelings of dizziness. Also drowsiness, dryness of the mouth.

Other information: Do not eat any food which you do not believe to be fresh whilst on this medication.

CAUTIONS

Children: This drug is either not recommended for children, or is recommended only for children above a certain age.

Alcohol: Alcohol should not be consumed, or only with caution – after medical advice has been sought – while you are taking this drug.

Driving and operating machinery: This drug may have some effect on your driving ability, so it is advisable not to drive or operate machinery while taking it.

ISONIAZID

Brand name: Isonaizid

Type of drug: Anti-tuberculous drug

Uses: Used on its own to prevent tuberculosis and in conjunction with other drugs as a treatment for the disease.

How it works: Interferes with the cell wall of the bacteria to stop them reproducing.

Possible adverse effects: Problems are rare but should be reported because of the risk of liver damage.

Other information: Therapy is likely to continue for at least 18 months. Should be taken on an empty stomach. Medical advice should always be sought if an overdose is taken.

CAUTIONS

Pregnancy and breastfeeding: This drug is either not recommended for use by women who are pregnant or breastfeeding, or the precise effects are not known and it should therefore only be used with caution.

Alcohol: Alcohol should not be consumed, or only with caution – after medical advice has been sought – while you are taking this drug.

ISOPRENALINE

Brand name: Medihaler-iso, Saventrine

Type of drug: Bronchodilator

Uses: To treat the symptoms of lung conditions such as asthma, bronchitis and emphysema. It also improves the transmission of electrical signals that take place in the heart.

How it works: Expands the small air passages in the lungs and relieves bronchospasm. If given as an injection, can treat some heart conditions.

Possible adverse effects: Side effects such as dry mouth, tremor and agitation usually disappear once the body has become used to the drug. Palpitations should be reported to a doctor.

Other information: Seek medical attention in all cases of overdose.

CAUTIONS

Pregnancy and breastfeeding: This drug is either not recommended for use by women who are pregnant or breastfeeding, or the precise

effects are not known and it should therefore only be used with caution and under medical advice.

Driving and operating machinery: This drug may have some effect on your driving ability, so it is advisable not to drive or operate machinery while taking it.

ISOSORBIDE DINITRATE/MONONITRATE

Brand name: Angitak, Cedocard Retard, Isoket Retard, Isoket, Elantan, Ismo, Isotrate, Monit, Istard, MCR50, Modisal XL, Monomax, Monsorb XL 60

Type of drug: Nitrate vasodilator and anti-angina

Uses: Treatment of angina and occasionally heart failure.

How it works: Acts to dilate the blood vessels around the heart, enabling the blood to flow more freely and oxygen to reach the heart.

Possible adverse effects: Headache, dizziness and flushing are relatively common, but usually pass off. Occasionally a sudden drop in blood pressure occurs.

Other information: Blood pressure will be regularly monitored.

CAUTIONS

Children: This drug is either not recommended for children, or is recommended only for children above a certain age.

Pregnancy and breastfeeding: This drug is either not recommended for use by women who are pregnant or breastfeeding, or the precise effects are not known and it should therefore only be used with caution and under medical advice.

Alcohol: Alcohol should not be consumed, or only with caution – after medical advice has been sought – while you are taking this drug.

ISOTRETINOIN

Brand name: Isotrex, Roaccutane

Type of drug: Acne treatment

Uses: Treatment of severe acne which has not responded to other types of treatment.

How it works: Reduces the production of skin oils by the sebaceous glands. Also has an anti-inflammatory action.

Possible adverse effects: Most people experience dryness of the eye, nose and mouth, together with flaking skin. Any episodes of abdominal pain and diarrhoea or bloody faeces should be reported immediately.

Other information: A course of treatment usually lasts for 16-20 weeks. Should be taken with, or shortly after, meals, to minimise gastric discomfort. Women should take extra care to avoid pregnancy whilst on this medication.

CAUTIONS

Children: This drug is either not recommended for children, or is recommended only for children above a certain age.

Pregnancy and breastfeeding: This drug is either not recommended for use by women who are pregnant or breastfeeding, or the precise effects are not known and it should therefore only be used with caution and under medical advice.

Alcohol: Alcohol should not be consumed, or only with caution – after medical advice has been sought – while you are taking this drug.

ISRADIPINE

Brand name: Prescal

Type of drug: Anti-emetic and anti-psychotic
Uses: The long-term treatment of high blood pressure.
How it works: Changes the chemicals in the heart muscle with the result that the blood vessels around the heart increase in size and the blood can flow more easily.
Possible adverse effects: Dizziness, headache.
Other information: Any episodes of palpitations or irregular heart beat should be reported.
CAUTIONS
Children: This drug is either not recommended for children, or is recommended only for children above a certain age.
Pregnancy and breastfeeding: This drug is either not recommended for use by women who are pregnant or breastfeeding, or the precise effects are not known and it should therefore only be used with caution and under medical advice.

ITRACONAZOLE
Brand name: Sporanox
Type of drug: Anti-fungal
Uses: The treatment of severe fungal infections.
How it works: Attaches itself to the fungal cells and prevents them replicating.
Possible adverse effects: Nausea is the most common. Liver problems can sometimes occur, so any sign of jaundice, unusually dark urine or nausea should be reported.
Other information: The capsules should be taken with food to maximise absorption and therefore effectiveness.
CAUTIONS
Children: This drug is either not recommended for children, or is recommended only for children above a certain age.
Pregnancy and breastfeeding: This drug is either not recommended for use by women who are pregnant or breastfeeding, or the precise effects are not known and it should therefore only be used with caution and under medical advice.

KETOCONAZOLE
Brand name: Nizoral
Type of drug: Anti-fungal
Uses: Treatment of severe fungal infections which have spread through the body. It is also given to treat skin infections caused by the candida yeast.
How it works: Kills the organisms that are causing the symptoms.
Possible adverse effects: Nausea is common but can be controlled if the drug is taken with meals.
Other information: Do not take over-the-counter preparations to try and dispel nausea.
CAUTIONS
Pregnancy and breastfeeding: This drug is either not recommended for use by women who are pregnant or breastfeeding, or the precise effects are not known and it should therefore only be used with caution and under medical advice.
Alcohol: Alcohol should not be consumed, or only consumed with caution – after medical advice has been sought – while you are taking this drug.

KETOPROFEN
Brand name: Ketocid, Ketovail, Ketozip, Larafen, Orudis, Oruvail
Type of drug: Non-steroidal anti-inflammatory
Uses: To relieve the symptoms of rheumatoid arthritis, osteoarthritis and ankylosing spondylitis. This medication is also used to relieve pain associated with menstruation or injury.
How it works: The anti-inflammatory action of this drug relieves the pain and stiffness which are characteristic features of the above-mentioned conditions.
Possible adverse effects: Gastro-intestinal irritation leading to nausea, heartburn or abdominal pain. Black or bloodstained faeces should be reported immediately.
Availability: Available with or without a prescription (over-the-counter).
Other information: Do not take over-the-counter medication whilst on this drug without discussing it with your doctor first. It is advisable to wear a sunscreen whilst on this drug, as it can increase sensitivity to sunlight.
CAUTIONS
Children: This drug is either not recommended for children, or is recommended only for children above a certain age.
Alcohol: Alcohol should not be consumed, or only with caution – after medical advice has been sought – while you are taking this drug.
Driving and operating machinery: This drug may have some effect on your driving ability, so it is advisable not to drive or operate machinery while taking it.

KETOROLAC TROMETAMOL
Brand name: Toradol
Type of drug: Painkiller
Uses: The short-term treatment of moderately severe, acute pain.
How it works: Acts as a non-steroidal anti-inflammatory to alleviate pain.
Possible adverse effects: Drowsiness, sedative effect, pain at injection site. Can irritate the stomach and gut leading to indigestion and abdominal discomfort which should be reported.
Other information: Supplied as either tablets or injection. Aspirin and products containing aspirin should be avoided.
CAUTIONS
Children: This drug is either not recommended for children, or is recommended only for children above a certain age.
Pregnancy and breastfeeding: This drug is either not recommended for use by women who are pregnant or breastfeeding, or the precise effects are not known and it should therefore only be used with caution and under medical advice.
Alcohol: Alcohol should not be consumed, or only consumed with caution – after medical advice has been sought – while you are taking this drug.

KETOTIFEN
Brand name: Zaditen
Type of drug: Anti-allergy
Uses: The prevention of asthma and hay fever.
How it works: Inhibits the production of histamine, a naturally

occurring substance which gives rise to the symptoms of allergic conditions.

Possible adverse effects: Drowsiness, dry mouth, weight gain and dizziness.

Other information: Tablets should be taken with food.

CAUTIONS

Pregnancy and breastfeeding: This drug is either not recommended for use by women who are pregnant or breastfeeding, or the precise effects are not known and it should therefore only be used with caution and under medical advice.

Driving and operating machinery: This drug may have some effect on your driving ability, so it is advisable not to drive or operate machinery while taking it.

LABETALOL
Brand name: Trandate
Type of drug: Beta-blocker
Uses: The treatment of high blood pressure.
How it works: Has a relaxant effect by slowing and steadying the heart rate. It also allows the blood vessels to dilate, easing the flow of blood.
Possible adverse effects: Dizziness – particularly on standing up. Scalp tingling may be experienced during the early days of therapy.
Other information: Supplied as tablets or injection.
CAUTIONS
Children: This drug is either not recommended for children, or is recommended only for children above a certain age.

LACTULOSE
Brand name: Duphalac, Lactugal, Regulose
Type of drug: Laxative
Uses: The treatment of constipation.
How it works: Softens the faeces by increasing the amount of water in the bowel.
Possible adverse effects: Stomach cramps and wind may occur during the early days of treatment but they usually pass off. Discuss with your doctor if diarrhoea occurs.
Availability: Available without a prescription (over-the-counter).
Other information: Available in liquid or powder form.

LAMIVUDINE
Brand name: Epivir
Type of drug: Anti-viral
Uses: Used at the same time as other drugs to treat infection with the HIV virus.
How it works: Acts on the DNA to prevent the virus from replicating. When used in conjunction with other drugs it can suppress or delay the emergence of resistant strains of the virus.
Possible adverse effects: Headache, tiredness, dizziness, sleeplessness, fever, chills, bone and muscle pain, nausea, diarrhoea and vomiting. Can cause pancreatitis in children.
Other information: The long-term effects of this drug are unknown but the benefits of it are thought to outweigh the risks that come with this uncertainty. It is crucial to take this drug exactly as prescribed.
CAUTIONS

Pregnancy and breastfeeding: This drug is either not recommended for use by women who are pregnant or breastfeeding, or the precise effects are not known and it should therefore only be used with caution and under medical advice.

LAMOTRIGINE
Brand name: Lamictal
Type of drug: Anti-convulsant
Uses: The treatment of epilepsy.
How it works: Restores the balance of chemicals in the brain, with the result that epileptic seizures are reduced.
Possible adverse effects: Rare, but include rash, visual disturbances, headache and a lack of co-ordination. A rash may occur during the early days of treatment which will usually resolve itself but should be reported.
Other information: Supplied as tablets. Blood tests will be taken regularly to assess the effect of the drug.
CAUTIONS
Children: This drug is either not recommended for children, or is recommended only for children above a certain age.
Pregnancy and breastfeeding: This drug is either not recommended for use by women who are pregnant or breastfeeding, or the precise effects are not known and it should therefore only be used with caution.
Alcohol: Alcohol should not be consumed, or only with caution – after medical advice has been sought – while you are taking this drug.
Driving and operating machinery: This drug may have some effect on your driving ability, so it is advisable not to drive or operate machinery while taking it.

LANSOPRAZOLE
Brand name: Zoton
Type of drug: Proton pump inhibitor
Uses: The treatment of duodenal ulcers, stomach ulcers and reflux oesophagitis.
How it works: Reduces the production of gastric acid which causes the symptoms of the problems.
Possible adverse effects: Gastric disturbances, headache and skin irritation.
Other information: Supplied as capsules which should be taken before meals. Capsules should not be chewed, but swallowed whole.
CAUTIONS
Children: This drug is either not recommended for children, or is recommended only for children above a certain age.
Pregnancy and breastfeeding: This drug is either not recommended for use by women who are pregnant or breastfeeding, or the precise effects are not known and it should therefore only be used with caution and under medical advice.

LEUPRORELIN
Brand name: Prostap SR, Prostap 3
Type of drug: Anti-cancer
Uses: The treatment of serious cancer of the prostate. Sometimes also used to treat endometriosis.
How it works: Prevents the production of male hormones to produce

an effect similar to castration, with the result that the cancer cells can no longer reproduce.

Possible adverse effects: Similar for both men and women. Decreased libido, hot flushes, sweating, tiredness and nausea.

Other information: Do not use an oral contraceptive whilst on this medication.

CAUTIONS

Children: This drug is either not recommended for children, or is recommended only for children above a certain age.

Pregnancy and breastfeeding: This drug is either not recommended for use by women who are pregnant or breastfeeding, or the precise effects are not known and it should therefore only be used with caution and under medical advice.

LEVOCABASTINE

Brand name: Livostin

Type of drug: Anti-allergy

Uses: To reduce the symptoms which occur with hay fever.

How it works: Acts rapidly to alleviate the runny nose and eyes which are symptomatic of hay fever.

Possible adverse effects: Headache, tiredness, sleeplessness.

Other information: Available as nasal spray and eye drops. Do not use the eye drops at the same time as wearing soft contact lenses.

CAUTIONS

Children: This drug is either not recommended for children, or is recommended only for children above a certain age.

LEVODOPA

Brand name: Brocadopa, Larodopa

Type of drug: Parkinsonism treatment

Uses: To treat the symptoms of Parkinson's disease.

How it works: Becomes transformed into dopamine, a chemical which is deficient in people with Parkinson's disease. Although it can effectively relieve many of the symptoms of Parkinson's disease, it is not a cure for the condition.

Possible adverse effects: These can be severe and include nausea, dizziness, palpitations, digestive disturbance, nervousness, dark-coloured urine.

Other information: Levodopa is usually prescribed with other drugs which help minimise its side effects. Its benefits usually diminish with time.

CAUTIONS

Children: This drug is either not recommended for children, or is recommended only for children above a certain age.

Pregnancy and breastfeeding: This drug is either not recommended for use by women who are pregnant or breastfeeding, or the precise effects are not known and it should therefore only be used with caution and under medical advice.

Driving and operating machinery: This drug may have some effect on your driving ability, so it is advisable not to drive or operate machinery while taking it.

LIOTHYRONINE

Brand name: Tetroxin

Type of drug: Thyroid hormone

Uses: The treatment of thyroid deficiency conditions.
How it works: Replaces the hormone produced by the thyroid gland which is deficient in conditions such as cretinism and myxoedema.
Possible adverse effects: Insomnia, tremor, heart rhythm disturbances. Any sign of a headache or diarrhoea should be reported.
Other information: The drug should be stored in a warm place to prevent it from deteriorating. The drug should be taken at the same time each day.

LISINOPRIL
Brand name: Carace, Zestril, Zestoretic
Type of drug: ACE inhibitor
Uses: Most commonly used as a treatment for mild to severe high blood pressure. Can also be used for people with heart failure and those who have had a heart attack.
How it works: Reduces the body's ability to retain sodium and water, which is one of the main causes of high blood pressure.
Possible adverse effects: Dizziness, headache, fatigue, nasal congestion and a dry cough. Any signs of light-headedness or infection should be reported.
Other information: Do not take any over-the-counter products – especially to treat a cold – without checking with your doctor first. Do not use salt substitutes which contain potassium.
CAUTIONS
Children: This drug is either not recommended for children, or is recommended only for children above a certain age.

LITHIUM
Brand name: Camcolit, Li-liquid, Liskonum, Litarex, Priadel
Type of drug: Anti-manic
Uses: Treatment of mania associated with manic depression. It is also occasionally used for the treatment of severe depression.
How it works: Prevents the intensity of mood swings between the manic and depressive stages of the disorder.
Possible adverse effects: Nausea, vomiting and tremor. These side-effects are usually caused by high levels of the drug circulating in the body and should be reported to your doctor, because it may be necessary to reduce the dosage.
Other information: It may take two to three weeks for this drug to take effect. An overdose should be treated as an emergency. Long-term treatment (more than five years) can lead to kidney problems.
CAUTIONS
Children: This drug is either not recommended for children, or is recommended only for children above a certain age.
Pregnancy and breastfeeding: This drug is either not recommended for use by women who are pregnant or breastfeeding, or the precise effects are not known and it should therefore only be used with caution and under medical advice.
Alcohol: Alcohol should not be consumed, or only with caution – after medical advice has been sought – while you are taking this drug.
Driving and operating machinery: This drug may have some effect on your driving ability, so it is advisable not to drive or operate machinery while taking it.

LOFEPRAMINE
Brand name: Gamanil
Type of drug: Tricyclic anti-depressant
Uses: The long-term treatment of depression.
How it works: It improves the mood, energy levels and interest in day-to-day living without the sedative effects of many similar drugs.
Possible adverse effects: These are relatively uncommon but include sweating and flushing.
Other information: Smoking while taking this drug may reduce its beneficial effects. Do not stop taking this drug suddenly.
CAUTIONS
Children: This drug is either not recommended for children, or is recommended only for children above a certain age.
Pregnancy and breastfeeding: This drug is either not recommended for use by women who are pregnant or breastfeeding, or the precise effects are not known and it should therefore only be used with caution and under medical advice.
Alcohol: Alcohol should not be consumed, or only with caution – after medical advice has been sought – while you are taking this drug.
Driving and operating machinery: This drug may have some effect on your driving ability, so it is advisable not to drive or operate machinery while taking it.

LOFEXIDINE
Brand name: BritLofex
Type of drug: Anti-emetic and anti-psychotic
Uses: The management of symptoms which addicts experience during withdrawal from heroin or other opium-based drugs.
How it works: Acts on the central nervous system to produce a relaxant effect without the corresponding fall in blood pressure which can occur with similar drugs.
Possible adverse effects: Drowsiness, dry mouth, throat and nose, slow pulse.
Other information: Will be supplied as tablets.
CAUTIONS
Children: This drug is either not recommended for children, or is recommended only for children above a certain age.
Pregnancy and breastfeeding: This drug is either not recommended for use by women who are pregnant or breastfeeding, or the precise effects are not known and it should therefore only be used with caution and under medical advice.
Alcohol: Alcohol should not be consumed, or only with caution – after medical advice has been sought – while you are taking this drug.
Driving and operating machinery: This drug may have some effect on your driving ability, so it is advisable not to drive or operate machinery while taking it.

LOSARTAN POTASSIUM
Brand name: Cozaar
Type of drug: Anti-hypertensive
Uses: The treatment of high blood pressure.
How it works: Blocks the production of chemicals which cause the blood vessels to constrict.
Possible adverse effects: Dizziness, fall in blood pressure on standing

after sitting or lying down. Diarrhoea and insomnia.
Other information: Patient should avoid sodium substitutes.
CAUTIONS
Children: This drug is either not recommended for children, or is recommended only for children above a certain age.
Pregnancy and breastfeeding: This drug is either not recommended for use by women who are pregnant or breastfeeding, or the precise effects are not known and it should therefore only be used with caution and under medical advice.

MAPROTILINE
Brand name: Ludiomil
Type of drug: Anti-depressant
Uses: The treatment of depression when there is also a need for a sedative effect.
How it works: Has a sedative effect at the same time as raising the patient's mood, stimulates appetite and generally enables the patient to lead a more normal daily life.
Possible adverse effects: Dry mouth, blurred vision, drowsiness, rapid beating of the heart, constipation.
Other information: Not for patients who have heart problems or for those with suicidal tendencies.
CAUTIONS
Children: This drug is either not recommended for children, or is recommended only for children above a certain age.
Pregnancy and breastfeeding: This drug is either not recommended for use by women who are pregnant or breastfeeding, or the precise effects are not known and it should therefore only be used with caution and under medical advice.
Alcohol: Alcohol should not be consumed, or only with caution – after medical advice has been sought – while you are taking this drug.
Driving and operating machinery: This drug may have some effect on your driving ability, so it is advisable not to drive or operate machinery while taking it.

MEBEVERINE
Brand name: Colofac
Type of drug: Anti-spasmodic
Uses: The alleviation of episodes of painful spasms in the bowel which often occur with conditions such as irritable bowel syndrome.
How it works: Acts on the muscles in the bowel wall and on the nerves which send messages to it, with the result that the bowel wall muscles relax and the spasms are halted.
Possible adverse effects: Side effects are rare, but constipation can occur.
Other information: Take medication with plenty of water. Should not be taken just before bedtime.
CAUTIONS
Pregnancy and breastfeeding: This drug is either not recommended for use by women who are pregnant or breastfeeding, or the precise effects are not known and it should therefore only be used with caution and under medical advice.

MEDROXYPROGESTERONE
Brand name: Depo-Provera, Farlutal, Provera

Type of drug: Female sex hormone
Uses: Used to treat a range of disorders related to the menstrual cycle, including endometriosis. It is also used in conjunction with other drugs to treat cancer of the breast, uterus and prostate.
How it works: Mimics the action of the female sex hormone, progesterone, the lack of which is thought to be a key factor in disorders of this type.
Possible adverse effects: Rare, but include weight gain, swollen ankles and sore breasts.
Other information: Long-term use of this drug may increase the risk of blood clots in the leg veins.
CAUTIONS
Children: This drug is either not recommended for children, or is recommended only for children above a certain age.
Pregnancy and breastfeeding: This drug is either not recommended for use by women who are pregnant or breastfeeding, or the precise effects are not known and it should therefore only be used with caution and under medical advice.

MEFENAMIC ACID
Brand name: Dysman, Ponstan
Type of drug: Non-steroidal anti-inflammatory
Uses: To treat headache, toothache, menstruation pains, rheumatoid arthritis and osteoarthritis.
How it works: Relieves the pain and inflammation associated with the above conditions.
Possible adverse effects: Drowsiness, indigestion, nausea and diarrhoea. The most common side effect is an irritation of the stomach and gut. A rash, or black or bloodstained faeces should be reported to a doctor.
Other information: Blood tests will be taken at regular intervals to monitor the effect of this medication.
CAUTIONS
Pregnancy and breastfeeding: This drug is either not recommended for use by women who are pregnant or breastfeeding, or the precise effects are not known and it should therefore only be used with caution and under medical advice.
Alcohol: Alcohol should not be consumed, or only with caution – after medical advice has been sought – while you are taking this drug.
Driving and operating machinery: This drug may have some effect on your driving ability, so it is advisable not to drive or operate machinery while taking it.

MEFLOQUINE
Brand name: Lariam
Type of drug: Anti-malarial
Uses: To prevent and treat malaria.
How it works: It is effective against all human types of malaria, including choloroquine-resistant and other persistent strains.
Possible adverse effects: Side effects can be serious in some patients. Dizziness, headache, confusion, hallucinations, nausea, vomiting and diarrhoea. Also sleep disorders. Any signs of depression or confusion may indicate a toxic effect and the drug should be discontinued.
Other information: This drug should not be taken on an empty

stomach and always taken with a large glass of water.
CAUTIONS
Children: This drug is either not recommended for children, or is recommended only for children above a certain age.
Pregnancy and breastfeeding: This drug is either not recommended for use by women who are pregnant or breastfeeding, or the precise effects are not known and it should therefore only be used with caution and under medical advice.
Alcohol: Alcohol should not be consumed, or only with caution – after medical advice has been sought – while you are taking this drug.
Driving and operating machinery: This drug may have some effect on your driving ability, so it is advisable not to drive or operate machinery while taking it.

MEGESTROL
Brand name: Megace
Type of drug: Female sex hormone and anti-cancer
Uses: The treatment of cancer of the breast and uterus.
How it works: Helps to inhibit growth and therefore reduces the size of the tumour.
Possible adverse effects: Weight gain. Also nausea, vomiting and diarrhoea.
Other information: Could increase risk of blood clots in leg veins.
CAUTIONS
Children: This drug is either not recommended for children, or is recommended only for children above a certain age.
Pregnancy and breastfeeding: This drug is either not recommended for use by women who are pregnant or breastfeeding, or the precise effects are not known and it should therefore only be used with caution and under medical advice.

MELATONIN
Brand name: Melatonin
Type of drug: Hormone
Uses: To induce sleep and help the body re-adjust to its normal circadian (day-night) rhythm. Useful to treat jet lag and for blind people and for shift workers to alter the body clock.
How it works: It is a natural hormone which affects the pineal gland which controls the natural sleep/wake rhythms of the body.
Possible adverse effects: Drowsiness.
Other information: Not commercially available in the United Kingdom.
CAUTIONS
Children: This drug is either not recommended for children, or is recommended only for children above a certain age.
Pregnancy and breastfeeding: This drug is either not recommended for use by women who are pregnant or breastfeeding, or the precise effects are not known and it should therefore only be used with caution and under medical advice.
Alcohol: Alcohol should not be consumed, or only with caution – after medical advice has been sought – while you are taking this drug.
Driving and operating machinery: This drug may have some effect on your driving ability, so it is advisable not to drive or operate machinery while taking it.

MERCAPTOPURINE
Brand name: Puri-Nethol
Type of drug: Anti-cancer
Uses: The treatment of lymphoblastic and myeloblastic leukaemias.
How it works: Affects the DNA and RNA of cancer cells and kills them.
Possible adverse effects: Nausea, vomiting, mouth ulcers and diarrhoea.
Other information: Regular blood counts are required, as drug can interfere with blood cell production. Anaemia and other blood disorders could result.
CAUTIONS
Pregnancy and breastfeeding: This drug is either not recommended for use by women who are pregnant or breastfeeding, or the precise effects are not known and it should therefore only be used with caution and under medical advice.
Alcohol: Alcohol should not be consumed, or only with caution – after medical advice has been sought – while you are taking this drug.

MESALAZINE
Brand name: Asacol, Pentasa, Salofalk
Type of drug: Chronic diarrhoea treatment
Uses: Treatment of mild to moderate cases of inflammatory bowel diseases such as ulcerative colitis and Crohn's disease.
How it works: Inhibits the production of chemicals which are key factors in the development of the disease, with the result that the inflammation of the bowel which is associated with an attack is relieved. It also has a role in preventing acute attacks.
Possible adverse effects: Nausea, abdominal pain and diarrhoea.
Other information: If medication is in the form of tablets patients are advised to swallow them whole, not chew or crush them. If given as a suppository, it should be retained for as long as possible.
CAUTIONS
Children: This drug is either not recommended for children, or is recommended only for children above a certain age.
Pregnancy and breastfeeding: This drug is either not recommended for use by women who are pregnant or breastfeeding, or the precise effects are not known and it should therefore only be used with caution and under medical advice.

METARAMINOL
Brand name: Aramine
Type of drug: Anti-hypotensive
Uses: Used to treat a fall in blood pressure.
How it works: Increases the resistance of blood vessels and constricts them, with the result that the pressure within them is increased.
Possible adverse effects: Dizziness, headache, rapid beating of the heart or a prolonged rise in blood pressure.
Other information: Patient should report any adverse reaction quickly.
CAUTIONS
Children: This drug is either not recommended for children, or is recommended only for children above a certain age.
Pregnancy and breastfeeding: This drug is either not recommended for use by women who are pregnant or breastfeeding, or the precise

effects are not known and it should therefore only be used with caution and under medical advice.

METFORMIN
Brand name: Glucophage, Glucamet, Orabet
Type of drug: Anti-diabetic
Uses: Used in the management of late onset diabetes in cases where the pancreas is still producing some insulin.
How it works: Reduces the production of sugar and lowers the amount of glucose which is absorbed from the gut into the bloodstream.
Possible adverse effects: Appetite loss, nausea, abdominal discomfort. Dizziness, sweatiness and confusion could indicate that the blood sugar level has dropped too far.
Other information: Should be taken in conjunction with a low sugar, low fat, diabetic diet. Do not take any over-the-counter products without prior consultation with your doctor.
CAUTIONS
Children: This drug is either not recommended for children, or is recommended only for children above a certain age.
Pregnancy and breastfeeding: This drug is either not recommended for use by women who are pregnant or breastfeeding, or the precise effects are not known and it should therefore only be used with caution and under medical advice.
Alcohol: Alcohol should not be consumed, or only with caution – after medical advice has been sought – while you are taking this drug.

METHADONE
Brand name: Methadosc, Physeptone
Type of drug: Opioid analgesic
Uses: For the treatment of severe pain and for heroin addiction.
How it works: Its chemical similarity to morphine makes methadone an effective painkiller. It is also used as a substitute for morphine during the detoxification process of people who are addicted to heroin.
Possible adverse effects: Constipation, drowsiness, nausea and vomiting.
Other information: Not suitable for patients with respiratory problems.
CAUTIONS
Children: This drug is either not recommended for children, or is recommended only for children above a certain age.
Pregnancy and breastfeeding: This drug is either not recommended for use by women who are pregnant or breastfeeding, or the precise effects are not known and it should therefore only be used with caution and under medical advice.
Driving and operating machinery: This drug may have some effect on your driving ability, so it is advisable not to drive or operate machinery while taking it.

METHANAMINE HIPPURATE
Brand name: Hiprex
Type of drug: Anti-fungal
Uses: To treat recurrent infections of the urinary system.
How it works: Forms formaldehyde in the urine, in which the infected organisms cannot survive.
Possible adverse effects: Stomach and bowel upsets, bladder irritation and rash.

Other information: Administered in tablet form. This drug is now only used rarely.
CAUTIONS
Pregnancy and breastfeeding: This drug is either not recommended for use by women who are pregnant or breastfeeding, or the precise effects are not known and it should therefore only be used with caution and under medical advice.

METHOCARBAMOL
Brand name: Robaxin, Robaxisal Forte
Type of drug: Muscle relaxant
Uses: To treat muscular pain and spasms.
How it works: Acts on the brain and spinal cord to relieve painful spasms in skeletal muscles.
Possible adverse effects: Drowsiness, dizziness, confusion and nausea.
Other information: Urine may change colour. Patient should change position slowly to avoid dizziness. Beware of over-the-counter preparations that contain alcohol.
CAUTIONS
Children: This drug is either not recommended for children, or is recommended only for children above a certain age.
Pregnancy and breastfeeding: This drug is either not recommended for use by women who are pregnant or breastfeeding, or the precise effects are not known and it should therefore only be used with caution and under medical advice.
Alcohol: Alcohol should not be consumed, or only with caution – after medical advice has been sought – while you are taking this drug.
Driving and operating machinery: This drug may have some effect on your driving ability, so it is advisable not to drive or operate machinery while taking it.

METHYLCELLULOSE
Brand name: Celevac
Type of drug: Laxative and antidiarrhoeal
Uses: To treat chronic constipation, particularly that associated with diverticular disease and irritable bowel syndrome.
How it works: It works by absorbing up to 25 times its volume of water, with the result that faeces are softened and easier to pass through the gut. It also bulks out diarrhoea. It is not absorbed into the intestine.
Possible adverse effects: Flatulence, abdominal discomfort.
Availability: Available with or without a prescription (over the counter).
Other information: Take medication with plenty of water. Should not take dosage just before bedtime.

METHYLDOPA
Brand name: Aldomet, Dopamet
Type of drug: Anti-hypertensive
Uses: To treat high blood pressure.
How it works: Decreases peripheral resistance of the circulatory system, thus reducing the pressure of blood within the blood vessels.
Possible adverse effects: Drowsiness, dry mouth, depression, headaches, diarrhoea and fluid retention.
Other information: Will usually be prescribed together with a diuretic.

Taking drug at bedtime minimises its effects. Do not take other over-the- counter preparations unless checked with a doctor first.
CAUTIONS
Alcohol: Alcohol should not be consumed or only with caution (after medical advice has been sought) while you are taking this drug.
Driving and operating machinery: This drug may have some effect on your driving ability, so it is advisable not to drive or operate machinery while taking it.

METHYLPHENIDATE
Brand name: Ritalin
Type of drug: Stimulant
Uses: Controversial medication used to treat children who have been diagnosed as having attention deficit hyperactivity disorder.
How it works: Although a stimulant, the drug has the effect of calming hyperactive children.
Possible adverse effects: Stomach and bowel upsets, nervousness and insomnia. Drug has been associated with growth suppression.
Other information: Tablets must not be chewed or crushed. Not recommended for children under six years of age. Caffeine should be avoided.
CAUTIONS
Pregnancy and breastfeeding: This drug is either not recommended for use by women who are pregnant or breastfeeding, or the precise effects are not known and it should therefore only be used with caution and under medical advice.
Alcohol: Alcohol should not be consumed or only with caution – after medical advice has been sought – while you are taking this drug.
Driving and operating machinery: This drug may have some effect on your driving ability, so it is advisable not to drive or operate machinery while taking it.

METHYSERGIDE
Brand name: Deseril
Type of drug: Anti-migraine
Uses: To help prevent recurrent migraine, cluster and other vascular headaches.
How it works: Constricts the blood vessels around the brain. Its pain-killing properties are thought to result from the impact the drug has on the patient's perception of pain.
Possible adverse effects: Nausea, drowsiness and dizziness, vomiting, abdominal discomfort and weight gain.
Other information: Patient to take drug with food. Report any tingling or numbness in hands or feet.
CAUTIONS
Children: This drug is either not recommended for children, or is recommended only for children above a certain age.
Pregnancy and breastfeeding: This drug is either not recommended for use by women who are pregnant or breastfeeding, or the precise effects are not known and it should therefore only be used with caution and under medical advice.
Alcohol: Alcohol should not be consumed, or only with caution – after medical advice has been sought – while you are taking this drug.
Driving and operating machinery: This drug may have some effect

on your driving ability, so it is advisable not to drive or operate machinery while taking it.

METOCLOPRAMIDE
Brand name: Gastrobid Continus, Gastroflux, Gastromax, Maxolon, Metramid, Parmid, Primperan
Type of drug: Anti-emetic
Uses: To relieve the nausea and vomiting associated with chemotherapy and to alleviate the symptoms of a hiatus hernia.
How it works: Acts directly on the gut to increase the speed at which food is propelled through the stomach and intestine.
Possible adverse effects: Drowsiness, headache, dizziness, restlessness and bowel upsets. Report any involuntary movements.
Other information: This medication should be taken 30 minutes before eating.
CAUTIONS
Pregnancy and breastfeeding: This drug is either not recommended for use by women who are pregnant or breastfeeding, or the precise effects are not known and it should therefore only be used with caution and under medical advice.
Alcohol: Alcohol should not be consumed or only with caution – after medical advice has been sought – while you are taking this drug.
Driving and operating machinery: This drug may have some effect on your driving ability, so it is advisable not to drive or operate machinery while taking it.

METRONIDAZOLE
Brand name: Anabact, Flagyl, Metrogel, Metrolyl, Metrotop, Metrozol, Rozex, Vaginyl, Zadstat
Type of drug: Anti-bacterial and anti-protozoal
Uses: Treatment of a variety of infections, particularly those affecting the abdomen, pelvis and mouth, pressure sores and leg ulcers.
How it works: Invades the infecting organisms – protozoa and bacteria – and prevents them from replicating.
Possible adverse effects: Nausea, loss of appetite and dark urine.
Other information: The importance of maintaining good hygiene is necessary to prevent re-infection.
CAUTIONS
Pregnancy and breastfeeding: This drug is either not recommended for use by women who are pregnant or breastfeeding, or the precise effects are not known and it should therefore only be used with caution and under medical advice.
Alcohol: Alcohol should not be consumed, or only with caution – after medical advice has been sought – while you are taking this drug.
Driving and operating machinery: This drug may have some effect on your driving ability, so it is advisable not to drive or operate machinery while taking it.

MIANSERIN
Brand name: Mianserin hydrochloride
Type of drug: Anti-depressant
Uses: Treatment of severe depression, particularly that associated with insomnia.

How it works: Improves mood, energy levels and appetite and generally stimulates a renewed interest in day-to-day activities. The accompanying sedative effect means it is particularly useful for depressed patients who also have trouble sleeping.

Possible adverse effects: Drowsiness, tremor, sweating and light-headedness when standing from a sitting or lying down position.

Other information: It may take up to four weeks before the full beneficial effects of the medication are felt. A full blood count is required every month. The patient should report signs of sore throat or infection immediately.

CAUTIONS

Children: This drug is either not recommended for children, or is recommended only for children above a certain age.

Pregnancy and breastfeeding: This drug is either not recommended for use by women who are pregnant or breastfeeding, or the precise effects are not known and it should therefore only be used with caution and under medical advice.

Alcohol: Alcohol should not be consumed, or only consumed with caution – after medical advice has been sought – while you are taking this drug.

Driving and operating machinery: This drug may have some effect on your driving ability, so it is advisable not to drive or operate machinery while taking it.

MIFEPRISTONE

Brand name: Mifegyne
Type of drug: Hormone
Uses: To induce an abortion up to 63 days of gestation.
How it works: This drug reversibly competes with progesterone (which protects the embryo) and so causes the death of the embryo.
Possible adverse effects: Malaise, fainting, nausea, headache. Vomiting, rashes and sometimes severe vaginal bleeding.
Other information: Aspirin or similar medication must not be taken for at least 8-12 days after taking this drug.

CAUTIONS

Children: Unlikely to be prescribed.

MILRINONE

Brand name: Primacor
Type of drug: Phosphodiesterase inhibitor
Uses: Used in treatment of severe congestive heart failure.
How it works: Acts on the chemicals which control the cardiac muscle to increase the pumping effectiveness of the heart muscle.
Possible adverse effects: Headache and hypotension, angina and disorders of the heart rhythm.
Other information: Will usually be administered in hospital as an injection.

CAUTIONS

Children: This drug is either not recommended for children, or is recommended only for children above a certain age.

Pregnancy and breastfeeding: This drug is either not recommended for use by women who are pregnant or breastfeeding, or the precise effects are not known and it should therefore only be used with caution and under medical advice.

MINOCYCLINE
Brand name: Aknemin, Blemix, Cyclomin, Minocin MR, Minogal
Type of drug: Tetracycline antibiotic
Uses: To treat infections such as pneumonia, gonorrhoea and other sexually transmitted diseases. Also given to people with chronic bronchitis to prevent infection.
How it works: The drug is widely distributed throughout the body and binds to the bacterial cell wall, preventing the organisms from multiplying.
Possible adverse effects: Nausea and dizziness.
Other information: A glass of water should be taken after each dose to wash it through the oesophagus.
CAUTIONS
Children: This drug is either not recommended for children, or is recommended only for children above a certain age.
Pregnancy and breastfeeding: This drug is either not recommended for use by women who are pregnant or breastfeeding, or the precise effects are not known and it should therefore only be used with caution.
Driving and operating machinery: This drug may have some effect on your driving ability, so it is advisable not to drive or operate machinery while taking it.

MINOXIDIL
Brand name: Loniten, Regaine
Type of drug: Anti-hypertensive
Uses: Treatment of high blood pressure and a treatment for hair loss.
How it works: Increases the size of the blood vessels to reduce blood pressure. Increases hair growth, an effect which is now being put to use as Monixidil is increasingly prescribed as a treatment for baldness.
Possible adverse effects: Fluid retention and increased heart rate, for which a diuretic and beta-blocker will usually be prescribed. Prolonged use may lead to ankle swelling.
Availability: Prescription needed except for scalp lotions.
Other information: Usually supplied as tablets, but a solution will be used for baldness treatment.
CAUTIONS
Pregnancy and breastfeeding: This drug is either not recommended for use by women who are pregnant or breastfeeding, or the precise effects are not known and it should therefore only be used with caution and under medical advice.
Alcohol: Alcohol should not be consumed, or only with caution – after medical advice has been sought – while you are taking this drug.
Driving and operating machinery: This drug may have some effect on your driving ability, so it is advisable not to drive or operate machinery while taking it.

MISOPROSTOL
Brand name: Cytotec
Type of drug: Anti-ulcer
Uses: Treatment and prevention of gastric and duodenal ulcers.
How it works: Reduces the amount of acid produced in the stomach with the result that the ulcerated areas have a chance to heal.
Possible adverse effects: Diarrhoea and indigestion. These can be minimised if preparations containing magnesium are avoided.

Other information: Side effects may be reduced if each dose is taken with food. Ulcers will usually heal after a few weeks of treatment.
CAUTIONS
Children: This drug is either not recommended for children, or is recommended only for children above a certain age.
Pregnancy and breastfeeding: This drug is either not recommended for use by women who are pregnant or breastfeeding, or the precise effects are not known and it should therefore only be used with caution and under medical advice.

MITOMYCIN
Brand name: Mitomycin C Kyowa
Type of drug: Anti-cancer
Uses: To treat upper gastro-intestinal cancers, including those of the stomach and pancreas.
How it works: Acts as a cytotoxic (poisonous to cancer) antibiotic. Acts on the DNA in the cancer cells to promote their death.
Possible adverse effects: Headache, drowsiness, fatigue, nausea. Ability to fight off infections will be impaired, so any sign of a fever should be reported.
Other information: Prolonged use causes delayed bone marrow damage. Patient should avoid exposure to people with infections.

MOCLOBEMIDE
Brand name: Manerix
Type of drug: Anti-depressant
Uses: Treatment of depression.
How it works: Acts as a Monoamine Oxidase Inhibitor Antidepressant. Heightens mood, improves energy levels, and restores interest in life.
Possible adverse effects: Side effects such as sleep disturbances, headache and dizziness are usually only temporary. Because of unpleasant interactions, certain types of food should be avoided, including those containing large amounts of caffeine, yeast extract, and pickled herring, liver, dry sausages, game, bean pods and textured vegetable proteins.
Other information: Can take up to two weeks to lift depression.
CAUTIONS
Children: This drug is either not recommended for children, or is recommended only for children above a certain age.
Pregnancy and breastfeeding: This drug is either not recommended for use by women who are pregnant or breastfeeding, or the precise effects are not known and it should therefore only be used with caution and under medical advice.
Alcohol: Alcohol should not be consumed, or only with caution – after medical advice has been sought – while you are taking this drug.
Driving and operating machinery: This drug may have some effect on your driving ability, so it is advisable not to drive or operate machinery while taking it.

MOEXIPRIL
Brand name: Perdix
Type of drug: Anti-hypertensive
Uses: To treat raised blood pressure.
How it works: Inhibits the production of a chemical which constricts

the blood vessels, with the result that the vessels dilate and the pressure within them is reduced.

Possible adverse effects: Dizziness, headache, fatigue, disorders of the heart rhythm and angina.

Other information: Patients should take dose on an empty stomach. Avoid products that contain potassium. Report any fevers or a sore throat immediately.

CAUTIONS

Pregnancy and breastfeeding: This drug is either not recommended for use by women who are pregnant or breastfeeding, or the precise effects are not known and it should therefore only be used with caution and under medical advice.

MORACIZINE

Brand name: Ethmozine
Type of drug: Anti-arrhythmic
Uses: For treatment of life-threatening ventricular arrhythmias.
How it works: Affects the electrical currents which control the heart beat, with the result that the heart rate is normalised.
Possible adverse effects: Dizziness, headache, fatigue, gastro-intestinal disturbances. Chest pain and palpitations.
Other information: Supplied as tablets.

CAUTIONS

Children: This drug is either not recommended for children, or is recommended only for children above a certain age.

Pregnancy and breastfeeding: This drug is either not recommended for use by women who are pregnant or breastfeeding, or the precise effects are not known and it should therefore only be used with caution and under medical advice.

MORPHINE

Brand name: MST Continus, MXL, Oramorph, Sevredol
Type of drug: Opioid analgesic
Uses: The relief of severe pain such as that caused by cancer, heart attack or injury.
How it works: Acts rapidly to alter the patient's perception of pain, with the result that it is no longer perceived.
Possible adverse effects: Nausea, vomiting and constipation are common.
Other information: Dependence may occur if the medication is taken for extended periods. Tablets should be swallowed whole and not broken or crushed.

CAUTIONS

Alcohol: Alcohol should not be consumed, or only with caution, and in moderation – after medical advice has been sought – while you are taking this drug.

Driving and operating machinery: This drug may have some effect on your driving ability, so it is advisable not to drive or operate machinery while taking it.

MOXONIDINE

Brand name: Physiotens
Type of drug: Anti-hypertensive
Uses: To treat mild to moderate hypertension.

How it works: Stimulates certain receptors on the blood pressure centres in the brain, causing blood vessels to dilate and blood pressure to fall.
Possible adverse effects: Headache, dry mouth, dizziness, nausea, drowsiness.
Other information: Do not stop taking this drug suddenly.
CAUTIONS
Pregnancy and breastfeeding: This drug is either not recommended for use by women who are pregnant or breastfeeding, or the precise effects are not known and it should therefore only be used with caution and under medical advice.
Alcohol: Alcohol should not be consumed, or only with caution – after medical advice has been sought – while you are taking this drug.

MYCOPHENOLATE MOFETIL
Brand name: CellCept
Type of drug: Immuno-suppressant
Uses: Given to prevent rejection of a kidney following a transplant operation.
How it works: Acts on the immune system to prevent it perceiving the kidney as a foreign body and attacking it.
Possible adverse effects: Vomiting, diarrhoea, headache, dizziness.
Other information: Capsules are to be swallowed whole, not chewed or crushed.
CAUTIONS
Pregnancy and breastfeeding: This drug is either not recommended for use by women who are pregnant or breastfeeding, or the precise effects are not known and it should therefore only be used with caution and under medical advice.

NABILONE
Brand name: Cesamet
Type of drug: Anti-emetic
Uses: To treat nausea and vomiting in patients undergoing cancer treatment.
How it works: Closely related – chemically – to cannabis, its precise actions are unknown but it is thought to act on the part of the brain which controls nausea and vomiting to alter the patient's perception of pain.
Possible adverse effects: Drowsiness, vertigo, dry mouth, depression and euphoria.
Other information: Patients should be made aware that this drug can cause mood and behavioural changes.
CAUTIONS
Pregnancy and breastfeeding: This drug is either not recommended for use by women who are pregnant or breastfeeding, or the precise effects are not known and it should therefore only be used with caution and under medical advice.
Alcohol: Alcohol should not be consumed, or only with caution – after medical advice has been sought – while you are taking this drug.
Driving and operating machinery: This drug may have some effect on your driving ability, so it is advisable not to drive or operate machinery while taking it.

NAFARELIN
Brand name: Synarel
Type of drug: Gonadorelin analogues
Uses: To treat endometriosis.
How it works: It stimulates the release of pituitary hormones which reduce the levels of female hormones and relieve the symptoms of endometriosis.
Possible adverse effects: Irregular bleeding, nausea, vomiting and constipation.
Other information: Sexual intercourse is best avoided or a form of barrier contraception should be used. Avoid use of nasal decongestants for at least 30 minutes after treatment.
CAUTIONS
Pregnancy and breastfeeding: This drug is either not recommended for use by women who are pregnant or breastfeeding, or the precise effects are not known and it should therefore only be used with caution and under medical advice.

NAPROXEN
Brand name: Arthrosin, Arthroxen, Laraflex, Naprosyn, Nycopren, Prosaid, Synflex, Timpron, Valrox
Type of drug: Non-steroidal anti-inflammatory.
Uses: To treat the symptoms of conditions such as rheumatoid arthritis, ankylosing spondylitis and osteoarthritis. Also useful in the treatment of gout, migraine and pain following surgery.
How it works: Non-steroidal, anti-inflammatory action which reduces pain, stiffness and inflammation associated with the above conditions.
Possible adverse effects: Gastrointestinal problems such as indigestion and nausea should soon diminish.
Other information: Any sign of blood in the faeces should be reported immediately. Can take up to two weeks to work effectively.
CAUTIONS
Pregnancy and breastfeeding: This drug is either not recommended for use by women who are pregnant or breastfeeding, or the precise effects are not known and it should therefore only be used with caution and under medical advice.
Driving and operating machinery: This drug may have some effect on your driving ability, so it is advisable not to drive or operate machinery while taking it.

NEDOCROMIL SODIUM
Brand name: Tilade aerosol
Type of drug: Anti-inflammatory
Uses: To treat mild to moderate bronchial asthma.
How it works: Has an anti-inflammatory and anti-allergic action on the cells in the airways within the lungs.
Possible adverse effects: Unpleasant taste in the mouth, coughing, throat irritation, nausea, stomach and bowel upsets.
Other information: Should not be used instead of drugs which have a bronchodilator drug. Benefits may not be apparent until after a week of use.
CAUTIONS
Pregnancy and breastfeeding: This drug is either not recommended for use by women who are pregnant or breastfeeding, or the precise

effects are not known and it should therefore only be used with caution and under medical advice.

NEFOPAM
Brand name: Acupan
Type of drug: Non-opioid analgesic
Uses: To relieve pain associated with surgery, injury or cancer.
How it works: Acts quickly to reduce the brain's perception of pain without interfering with breathing or leading to dependence, as is the case with many drugs which have a similar effect.
Possible adverse effects: Nausea and dry mouth, which can often be alleviated by a change to the dosage regime.
Other information: Supplied in tablet or injection form. A harmless pink discoloration of the urine may occur.
CAUTIONS
Children: This drug is either not recommended for children, or is recommended only for children above a certain age.
Pregnancy and breastfeeding: This drug is either not recommended for use by women who are pregnant or breastfeeding, or the precise effects are not known and it should therefore only be used with caution and under medical advice.
Alcohol: Alcohol should not be consumed, or only with caution – after medical advice has been sought – while you are taking this drug.
Driving and operating machinery: This drug may have some effect on your driving ability, so it is advisable not to drive or operate machinery while taking it.

NEOMYCIN
Brand name: Nivemycin, Mycifradin
Type of drug: Antibiotic
Uses: Treatment of infections of the skin and mucous membranes. Also used to sterilise the bowel in preparation for surgery.
How it works: Binds to the bacteria, thus preventing them from replicating.
Possible adverse effects: Possible skin reactions to creams. Do not apply to sore or open wounds.
Other information: Supplied as tablets.
CAUTIONS
Pregnancy and breastfeeding: This drug is either not recommended for use by women who are pregnant or breastfeeding, or the precise effects are not known and it should therefore only be used with caution and under medical advice.

NEOSTIGMINE
Brand name: Prostigmin
Type of drug: Muscle stimulant
Uses: To treat myasthenia gravis, a rare autoimmune condition. Can also relieve urinary retention and temporary paralysis of the bowel.
How it works: Enhances the transmission of nerve messages to the muscles, which are weakened by the disease to the point of being unable to work.
Possible adverse effects: Abdominal cramps, excessive saliva, dizziness, drowsiness, nausea, headache, sweating, blurred vision, diarrhoea.

Other information: It is recommended taking the drug with food or milk to minimise side effects.

CAUTIONS

Pregnancy and breastfeeding: This drug is either not recommended for use by women who are pregnant or breastfeeding, or the precise effects are not known and it should therefore only be used with caution and under medical advice.

Driving and operating machinery: This drug may have some effect on your driving ability, so it is advisable not to drive or operate machinery while taking it.

NICARDIPINE

Brand name: Cardene

Type of drug: Anti-hypertensive

Uses: To treat angina and raised blood pressure.

How it works: Alters the electrical activity in the heart, with the result that the blood vessels dilate, increasing the blood flow through the heart.

Possible adverse effects: Dizziness, headache, palpitations, nausea, abdominal discomfort.

Other information: Avoid grapefruit juice. Supplied as capsules or given as an injection.

CAUTIONS

Children: This drug is either not recommended for children, or is recommended only for children above a certain age.

Pregnancy and breastfeeding: This drug is either not recommended for use by women who are pregnant or breastfeeding, or the precise effects are not known and it should therefore only be used with caution and under medical advice.

NICORANDIL

Brand name: Ikorel

Type of drug: Anti-angina

Uses: To alleviate the symptoms of angina.

How it works: Widens both veins and arteries, with the result that more oxygenated blood can reach the heart muscle and the heart's workload is lessened.

Possible adverse effects: Headache, nausea, flushing and palpitations.

Other information: Supplied as tablets.

CAUTIONS

Children: This drug is either not recommended for children, or is recommended only for children above a certain age.

Pregnancy and breastfeeding: This drug is either not recommended for use by women who are pregnant or breastfeeding, or the precise effects are not known and it should therefore only be used with caution and under medical advice.

Alcohol: Alcohol should not be consumed, or only with caution – after medical advice has been sought – while you are taking this drug.

Driving and operating machinery: This drug may have some effect on your driving ability, so it is advisable not to drive or operate machinery while taking it.

NICOTINIC ACID

Brand name: Nicotinic acid

Type of drug: Lipid lowering
Uses: Used to treat high levels of fat in the blood. Helps to improve circulatory problems such as Raynaud's disease and chilblains.
How it works: Has a vasodilator effect, meaning that the drug widens blood vessels and increases blood flow. Lowers blood cholesterol and fat levels.
Possible adverse effects: Flushing and headaches, dizziness and palpitations.
Availability: Available with or without a prescription (over-the-counter).
Other information: A low fat diet is recommended if drug is taken to help reduce fat levels.
CAUTIONS
Pregnancy and breastfeeding: This drug is either not recommended for use by women who are pregnant or breastfeeding, or the precise effects are not known and it should therefore only be used with caution and under medical advice.
Driving and operating machinery: This drug may have some effect on your driving ability, so it is advisable not to drive or operate machinery while taking it.

NIFEDIPINE
Brand name: Adalat, Adalat Retard, Adipine, Angiopine, Calcilat, Coracten, Nifensar XL, Tensipine MR
Type of drug: Anti-angina and anti-hypertensive
Uses: Treatment of angina and high blood pressure.
How it works: Affects electrical conduction of the heart with the result that the blood vessels are widened, causing the blood pressure to fall. It also makes the pumping action of the heart more effective.
Possible adverse effects: Headache, dizziness, ankle swelling. Can cause blood pressure to drop too low and to cause ankle swelling.
Other information: Patient should swallow medication whole, not chew or crush the capsules.
CAUTIONS
Children: This drug is either not recommended for children, or is recommended only for children above a certain age.
Pregnancy and breastfeeding: This drug is either not recommended for use by women who are pregnant or breastfeeding, or the precise effects are not known and it should therefore only be used with caution.
Alcohol: Alcohol should not be consumed, or only with caution – after medical advice has been sought – while you are taking this drug.
Driving and operating machinery: This drug may have some effect on your driving ability, so it is advisable not to drive or operate machinery while taking it.

NITROFURANTOIN
Brand name: Furadantin, Macrobid, Macrodantin
Type of drug: Anti-bacterial
Uses: To treat initial and recurrent urinary tract infections.
How it works: At lower doses it prevents the organisms causing the infection from replicating. At higher doses it kills them.
Possible adverse effects: Side effects are common and include stomach irritation and upset, nausea and vomiting, anorexia, diarrhoea. Urine may be discoloured.

Other information: Take with milk or food to minimise side effects.
CAUTIONS
Pregnancy and breastfeeding: This drug is either not recommended for use by women who are pregnant or breastfeeding, or the precise effects are not known and it should therefore only be used with caution.

NIZATIDINE
Brand name: Axid, Zinga
Type of drug: H2-receptor antagonist
Uses: To treat gastric and duodenal ulcers, gastro-oesophageal reflux and heartburn.
How it works: Reduces the production of gastric acid, the main factor in causing the problems.
Possible adverse effects: Diarrhoea and other gastrointestinal disturbances, headaches and dizziness.
Availability: Available with or without a prescription (over-the-counter).
Other information: Do not smoke whilst taking this medication, as it increases the production of gastric acid and therefore lessens the effectiveness of the treatment.
CAUTIONS
Children: This drug is either not recommended for children, or is recommended only for children above a certain age.
Pregnancy and breastfeeding: This drug is either not recommended for use by women who are pregnant or breastfeeding, or the precise effects are not known and it should therefore only be used with caution and under medical advice.

NORADRENALINE
Brand name: Levophed
Type of drug: Sympathomimetic
Uses: Used as an emergency treatment for a sudden fall in blood pressure and/or cardiac arrest.
How it works: Causes the blood vessels to constrict, thus raising the pressure within them.
Possible adverse effects: Hypertension, headache, palpitations, disorders of heart rhythm.
Other information: Must not be given to patients with raised blood pressure. Usually administered as an injection or intravenous infusion (drip) in hospital.
CAUTIONS
Children: This drug is either not recommended for children, or is recommended only for children above a certain age.
Pregnancy and breastfeeding: This drug is either not recommended for use by women who are pregnant or breastfeeding, or the precise effects are not known and it should therefore only be used with caution and under medical advice.
Alcohol: Alcohol should not be consumed, or only with caution – after medical advice has been sought – while you are taking this drug.
Driving and operating machinery: This drug may have some effect on your driving ability, so it is advisable not to drive or operate machinery while taking it.

NORETHISTERONE
Brand name: Menzol, Micronor, Noriday, Noristerat, Primolut N, Utovlan

Type of drug: Female sex hormone
Uses: To treat a range of menstrual disorders, including endometriosis. Is also an ingredient of the contraceptive pill. Can be used to treat certain types of breast cancer.
How it works: Acts in a similar way to the female hormone progesterone.
Possible adverse effects: Breakthrough bleeding in between normal periods.
Other information: Given as an injection or in tablet form. Blood tests to check liver function may be conducted at intervals during treatment.
CAUTIONS
Children: This drug is either not recommended for children, or is recommended only for children above a certain age.
Pregnancy and breastfeeding: This drug is either not recommended for use by women who are pregnant or breastfeeding, or the precise effects are not known and it should therefore only be used with caution and under medical advice.

NORFLOXACIN
Brand name: Utinor
Type of drug: Antibiotic
Uses: To treat infections of the urinary tract.
How it works: Acts on the DNA in the infected organism to prevent it replicating.
Possible adverse effects: Nausea, heartburn, abdominal cramps, diarrhoea, headache, dizziness, anxiety.
Other information: The patient is advised to take this medication one hour before – or two hours after – meals or antacids.
CAUTIONS
Pregnancy and breastfeeding: This drug is either not recommended for use by women who are pregnant or breastfeeding, or the precise effects are not known and it should therefore only be used with caution and under medical advice.
Driving and operating machinery: This drug may have some effect on your driving ability, so it is advisable not to drive or operate machinery while taking it.

NYSTATIN
Brand name: Nystamont, Nystan
Type of drug: Anti-fungal
Uses: To treat yeast infections such as thrush, and other infections of the skin, mouth, throat, gut and vagina.
How it works: Acts against infections caused by fungi, by either preventing them from replicating or killing them.
Possible adverse effects: These are uncommon and usually pass off quickly.
Other information: Good hygiene is essential to prevent re-infection. Vaginal tablets can be used by pregnant women up to six weeks before the due date. Always finish the course prescribed in order to minimise the risk of re-infection.

OCTREOTIDE
Brand name: Sandostatin
Type of drug: Hormone

Uses: To treat acromegaly – abnormal growth of the hands, feet and face due to excessive pituitary gland activity caused by a tumour.

How it works: Mimics the action of naturally occurring chemicals, with the result that the symptoms are decreased. It is not known if the drug affects the tumour directly.

Possible adverse effects: Gastrointestinal disturbances, abdominal pain, nausea, vomiting, diarrhoea.

Other information: This drug can cause gallstones, so patient is advised to report serious abdominal discomfort promptly.

CAUTIONS

Pregnancy and breastfeeding: This drug is either not recommended for use by women who are pregnant or breastfeeding, or the precise effects are not known and it should therefore only be used with caution and under medical advice.

OESTRADIOL

Brand name: Climaval, Estraderm, Estrapak, FemSeven, Menorest, Oestrogel, Progynova, Vagifem, Zumenon

Type of drug: Female sex hormone

Uses: Treatment of the symptoms of the menopause and post-menopausal period.

How it works: Replaces hormones lost during the menopause, with the result that symptoms such as hot flushes, night sweats and vaginal dryness are lessened.

Possible adverse effects: Symptoms similar to those experienced during the early stages of pregnancy, including nausea, sore breasts and weight gain. Skin patches sometimes can cause a local rash.

Other information: Available as tablets, pessaries, skin gel, skin patches, implants and vaginal ring. Often given with a progestogen.

CAUTIONS

Children: This drug is either not recommended for children, or is recommended only for children above a certain age.

Pregnancy and breastfeeding: This drug is either not recommended for use by women who are pregnant or breastfeeding, or the precise effects are not known and it should therefore only be used with caution and after medical advice.

OESTROGEN – See under Conjugated Oestrogen

OFLOXACIN

Brand name: Tarivid

Type of drug: Anti-bacterial

Uses: To treat infections of the urinary tract, the lower respiratory tract, the genital tract and infections of the eyes such as conjunctivitis.

How it works: Interferes with the DNA of the infected organism, preventing it from replicating.

Possible adverse effects: Dizziness, sleep disorders, headache, nervousness, visual disturbances. Stinging and irritation of the eye.

Other information: Patient should be advised to drink plenty of fluids. Also must discontinue drug if a rash or similar allergic reaction occurs. Prolonged exposure to the sun should be avoided. If being treated for eye infection, do not wear soft contact lenses.

CAUTIONS

Children: This drug is either not recommended for children, or is recommended only for children above a certain age.

Pregnancy and breastfeeding: This drug is either not recommended for use by women who are pregnant or breastfeeding, or the precise effects are not known and it should therefore only be used with caution and under medical advice.

Alcohol: Alcohol should not be consumed, or only with caution – after medical advice has been sought – while you are taking this drug.

Driving and operating machinery: This drug may have some effect on your driving ability, so it is advisable not to drive or operate machinery while taking it.

OLANZAPINE
Brand name: Zyprexa
Type of drug: Anti-psychotic
Uses: The management of manifestations of psychotic disorders such as schizophrenia.
How it works: Alters the chemicals in the brain, with the result that paranoia and hallucinations are lessened and speech, thought and mood are improved.
Possible adverse effects: Dizziness, drowsiness, increased appetite, weight gain, dry mouth and blurred vision.
Other information: Patient is not to have any over-the-counter preparations unless advised by a doctor.
CAUTIONS
Children: This drug is either not recommended for children, or is recommended only for children above a certain age.
Pregnancy and breastfeeding: This drug is either not recommended for use by women who are pregnant or breastfeeding, or the precise effects are not known and it should therefore only be used with caution and under medical advice.
Alcohol: Alcohol should not be consumed, or only with caution – after medical advice has been sought – while you are taking this drug.
Driving and operating machinery: This drug may have some effect on your driving ability, so it is advisable not to drive or operate machinery while taking it.

OMEPRAZOLE
Brand name: Losec
Type of drug: Anti-ulcer
Uses: Treatment of stomach ulcers, reflux oesophagitis and, in conjunction with other drugs, of the Helicobacter pylori bacteria.
How it works: Reduces the amount of acid that the stomach produces by about 70 per cent. When given in conjunction with antibiotics it is effective at eradicating the Helicobacter pylori bacteria that are known to cause many gastric ulcers.
Possible adverse effects: Headache, dizziness, nausea, flatulence, constipation and diarrhoea.
Other information: Patients are advised to take the drug exactly as prescribed; also to take it before meals and not to crush the capsules, but to swallow them whole.
CAUTIONS
Children: This drug is either not recommended for children, or is recommended only for children above a certain age.
Pregnancy and breastfeeding: This drug is either not recommended

for use by women who are pregnant or breastfeeding, or the precise effects are not known and it should therefore only be used with caution and under medical advice.

Alcohol: Alcohol should not be consumed, or only with caution – after medical advice has been sought – while you are taking this drug.

ONDANSETRON
Brand name: Zofran
Type of drug: Anti-emetic
Uses: To treat post-operative nausea and vomiting and nausea resulting from chemotherapy treatment.
How it works: Precise action is not known, but it is most effective if given prior to the dose of chemotherapy that causes nausea and vomiting.
Possible adverse effects: Headache, fatigue, constipation, flushing.
Other information: Administered either as tablets or as an injection.
CAUTIONS
Pregnancy and breastfeeding: This drug is either not recommended for use by women who are pregnant or breastfeeding, or the precise effects are not known and it should therefore only be used with caution and under medical advice.

ORPHENADRINE
Brand name: Biorphen, Disipal, Norflex
Type of drug: Muscle relaxant
Uses: Treatment of symptoms of Parkinson's disease.
How it works: Acts on the part of the brain which controls muscle tone, with the result that muscle stiffness and spasm, which are characteristic of Parkinsonism, are relieved.
Possible adverse effects: Dry mouth, blurred vision, insomnia, confusion, headache, difficulty in passing water.
Other information: Patient should be warned that some over-the-counter preparations contain alcohol and so should be used cautiously.
CAUTIONS
Children: This drug is either not recommended for children, or is recommended only for children above a certain age.
Pregnancy and breastfeeding: This drug is either not recommended for use by women who are pregnant or breastfeeding, or the precise effects are not known and it should therefore only be used with caution and under medical advice.
Alcohol: Alcohol should not be consumed or only with caution – after medical advice has been sought – while you are taking this drug.
Driving and operating machinery: This drug may have some effect on your driving ability, so it is advisable not to drive or operate machinery while taking it.

OXITROPIUM
Brand name: Oxivent
Type of drug: Bronchodilator
Uses: The alleviation of the symptoms of respiratory disease such as chronic bronchitis and asthma.
How it works: Relieves the constriction of the airways which is characteristic of chronic obstructive pulmonary disease.
Possible adverse effects: Rarely, dry mouth and irritation of the throat.

Other information: The medication is delivered through an inhaler. Patient is advised not to exceed prescribed dose. Should not be used by people with glaucoma.
CAUTIONS
Children: This drug is either not recommended for children, or is recommended only for children above a certain age.
Pregnancy and breastfeeding: This drug is either not recommended for use by women who are pregnant or breastfeeding, or the precise effects are not known and it should therefore only be used with caution and under medical advice.

OXYBUTYNIN
Brand name: Cystrin, Ditropan
Type of drug: Anti-spasmodic
Uses: To treat the frequency and urgency to pass urine which is associated with incontinence.
How it works: Increases bladder capacity by diminishing the unwanted muscle contractions which cause the problem.
Possible adverse effects: Dizziness, blurred vision, dry mouth, abdominal discomfort.
Other information: Drug will be discontinued periodically to see if the patient still requires it.
CAUTIONS
Pregnancy and breastfeeding: This drug is either not recommended for use by women who are pregnant or breastfeeding, or the precise effects are not known and it should therefore only be used with caution and under medical advice.
Driving and operating machinery: This drug may have some effect on your driving ability, so it is advisable not to drive or operate machinery while taking it.

PANTOPRAZOLE
Brand name: Protium
Type of drug: Protein pump inhibitor
Uses: For treating stomach ulcers.
How it works: Blocks the production of stomach acid, excessive amounts of which cause gastric ulcers.
Possible adverse effects: Headache, abdominal pain, diarrhoea, dizziness, itching and rash.
Other information: Administered either as an injection or as tablets.
CAUTIONS
Children: This drug is either not recommended for children, or is recommended only for children above a certain age.
Pregnancy and breastfeeding: This drug is either not recommended for use by women who are pregnant or breastfeeding, or the precise effects are not known and it should therefore only be used with caution and under medical advice.

PAROXETINE
Brand name: Seroxat
Type of drug: Anti-depressant
Uses: Treatment of mild to moderate depression, panic disorders and obsessive-compulsive disorders.
How it works: Has an anti-depressant action which results in a

heightening of mood and an improved ability to lead a normal daily life.
Possible adverse effects: Nausea and sweating, weakness, inability to
sleep and shaking.
Other information: Some symptoms of withdrawal may be experienced
if the drug is stopped suddenly.
CAUTIONS
Children: This drug is either not recommended for children, or is
recommended only for children above a certain age.
Pregnancy and breastfeeding: This drug is either not recommended
for use by women who are pregnant or breastfeeding, or the precise
effects are not known and it should therefore only be used with caution
and under medical advice.
Alcohol: Alcohol should not be consumed, or only with caution – after
medical advice has been sought – while you are taking this drug.
Driving and operating machinery: This drug may have some effect
on your driving ability, so it is advisable not to drive or operate
machinery while taking it.

PENICILLAMINE
Brand name: Distamine, Pendramine
Type of drug: Anti-rheumatic drug
Uses: To treat rheumatic disease; also used as an antidote to treat
copper and lead poisoning.
How it works: Slows or halts the progression of rheumatoid arthritis.
Possible adverse effects: Nausea, anorexia, vomiting, mouth ulcers.
Kidney problems.
Other information: The patient taking this drug should drink large
quantities of water. It may be a few weeks before the benefits are felt.
Sore throat or unexplained rashes or fevers   must be reported
immediately.
CAUTIONS
Pregnancy and breastfeeding: This drug is either not recommended
for use by women who are pregnant or breastfeeding, or the precise
effects are not known and it should therefore only be used with caution
and under medical advice.

PENTAMIDINE
Brand name: Pentacarinat
Type of drug: Anti-protazoal
Uses: To treat pneumonia caused by pneumocystis carinii, in HIV,
AIDS, chemotherapy and other immunosuppressed patients.
How it works: Precise action unknown, but is thought to affect the
DNA of the infective organism and parts of the organism's metabolic
process.
Possible adverse effects: Can cause severe side effects, hypotension,
hypoglycaemia, rapid heart beat. Other effects are dizziness, headache,
confusion.
Other information: This treatment will be delivered in hospital under
close supervision.
CAUTIONS
Children: This drug is either not recommended for children, or is
recommended only for children above a certain age.
Pregnancy and breastfeeding: This drug is either not recommended
for use by women who are pregnant or breastfeeding, or the precise

effects are not known and it should therefore only be used with caution and under medical advice.

Alcohol: Alcohol should not be consumed, or only with caution – after medical advice has been sought – while you are taking this drug.

Driving and operating machinery: This drug may have some effect on your driving ability, so it is advisable not to drive or operate machinery while taking it.

PENTAZOCINE
Brand name: Fortagesic, Fortral
Type of drug: Opioid analgesic
Uses: To treat moderate to severe pain.
How it works: Exact mechanism of action is unknown.
Possible adverse effects: Dizziness, nausea, vomiting. Respiratory depression is possible. Patient should report rash, confusion or any other serious side effect immediately.
Other information: Physical dependence is possible.
CAUTIONS
Pregnancy and breastfeeding: This drug is either not recommended for use by women who are pregnant or breastfeeding, or the precise effects are not known and it should therefore only be used with caution and under medical advice.
Alcohol: Alcohol should not be consumed, or only consumed with caution – after medical advice has been sought – while you are taking this drug.
Driving and operating machinery: This drug may have some effect on your driving ability, so it is advisable not to drive or operate machinery while taking it.

PERGOLIDE
Brand name: Celance
Type of drug: Dopaminergic drug
Uses: To treat the symptoms of Parkinson's disease.
How it works: Reduces tremor and rigidity and improves movement in sufferers.
Possible adverse effects: Headache, sleepiness, hallucinations and confusion, fall in blood pressure.
Other information: Patient should be warned of the adverse effects, mainly hallucination and confusion.
CAUTIONS
Children: This drug is either not recommended for children, or is recommended only for children above a certain age.
Pregnancy and breastfeeding: This drug is either not recommended for use by women who are pregnant or breastfeeding, or the precise effects are not known and it should therefore only be used with caution and under medical advice.
Driving and operating machinery: This drug may have some effect on your driving ability, so it is advisable not to drive or operate machinery while taking it.

PERINDOPRIL
Brand name: Coversyl
Type of drug: ACE inhibitor
Uses: Used to treat raised blood pressure and congestive heart failure.

How it works: Reduces constriction of the arteries and lowers blood volume, with the result that the blood pressure falls.

Possible adverse effects: Too much of a fall in blood pressure, leading to light-headedness and dizziness. Nausea, flushing.

Other information: Supplied as tablets.

CAUTIONS

Pregnancy and breastfeeding: This drug is either not recommended for use by women who are pregnant or breastfeeding, or the precise effects are not known and it should therefore only be used with caution and under medical advice.

PETHIDINE

Brand name: Pethidine

Type of drug: Opioid analgesic

Uses: For moderate to severe pain, such as during labour and after an operation.

How it works: Takes effect quickly, but lasts for a shorter time than alternative pain relief.

Possible adverse effects: Dizziness, sweating, dry mouth, nausea, confusion, vomiting.

Other information: Potentially habit-forming, although this is unlikely to be a problem if the drug is used appropriately.

CAUTIONS

Pregnancy and breastfeeding: This drug is either not recommended for use by women who are pregnant or breastfeeding, or the precise effects are not known and it should therefore only be used with caution and under medical advice.

Alcohol: Alcohol should not be consumed, or only with caution – after medical advice has been sought – while you are taking this drug.

Driving and operating machinery: This drug may have some effect on your driving ability, so it is advisable not to drive or operate machinery while taking it.

PHENINDIONE

Brand name: Dindevan

Type of drug: Anti-coagulant

Uses: To prevent and treat deep-vein thrombosis, atrial fibrillation and pulmonary embolism.

How it works: Alters the composition of the blood, making it 'thinner'.

Possible adverse effects: Haemorrhage, rash, diarrhoea, nausea.

Other information: Supplied as tablets. Urine may be discoloured.

CAUTIONS

Children: This drug is either not recommended for children, or is recommended only for children above a certain age.

Pregnancy and breastfeeding: This drug is either not recommended for use by women who are pregnant or breastfeeding, or the precise effects are not known and it should therefore only be used with caution and under medical advice.

Alcohol: Alcohol should not be consumed, or only with caution – after medical advice has been sought – while you are taking this drug.

Driving and operating machinery: This drug may have some effect on your driving ability, so it is advisable not to drive or operate machinery while taking it.

PHENOBARBITAL
Brand name: Phenobarbitol Sodium, Gardenal Sodium
Type of drug: Anti-convulsant
Uses: To treat all forms of epilepsy other than sufferers who have a sense of absence (absence seizures).
How it works: Suppresses the spread of seizure activity in the brain and acts as a depressant.
Possible adverse effects: Drowsiness, lethargy, weakness, depression.
Other information: Patient must not stop taking the drug suddenly, as some symptoms of withdrawal may be experienced.
CAUTIONS
Children: This drug is either not recommended for children, or is recommended only for children above a certain age.
Pregnancy and breastfeeding: This drug is either not recommended for use by women who are pregnant or breastfeeding, or the precise effects are not known and it should therefore only be used with caution and under medical advice.
Alcohol: Alcohol should not be consumed, or only with caution – after medical advice has been sought – while you are taking this drug.
Driving and operating machinery: This drug may have some effect on your driving ability, so it is advisable not to drive or operate machinery while taking it.

PHENOXYMETHYLPENICILLIN
Brand name: Stabillin V-K, Tenkicin
Type of drug: Penicillin antibiotic
Uses: Used to treat a wide variety of infections. Respiratory tract, tonsillitis, pharyngitis, ear and gum infections. Also scarlet fever, rheumatic fever and sickle cell disease.
How it works: A synthetic drug which destroys the organisms that are causing the infection.
Possible adverse effects: Nausea, diarrhoea, itching, rashes, joint pain. Long-term use may increase the risk of infections with thrush.
Other information: Not for patients who are allergic to penicillin.

PHENTERMINE
Brand name: Duromine, Ionamin
Type of drug: Appetite suppressant
Uses: For use only in severe cases of obesity.
How it works: Suppresses the appetite and boosts energy levels.
Possible adverse effects: Dizziness, drowsiness, confusion, dry mouth headache. Risk of dependence.
Other information: Patients are advised to swallow the medication whole, not to chew or crush the tablet. Should also avoid caffeine-containing drinks. Patients should report if they suffer palpitations or dyspnoea.
CAUTIONS
Children: This drug is either not recommended for children, or is recommended only for children above a certain age.
Pregnancy and breastfeeding: This drug is either not recommended for use by women who are pregnant or breastfeeding, or the precise effects are not known and it should therefore only be used with caution and under medical advice.
Alcohol: Alcohol should not be consumed, or only with caution – after

medical advice has been sought – while you are taking this drug.
Driving and operating machinery: This drug may have some effect on your driving ability, so it is advisable not to drive or operate machinery while taking it.

PHENYLBUTAZONE
Brand name: Butacote
Type of drug: Non-steroidal anti-inflammatory
Uses: To treat rheumatic diseases such as ankylosing spondylitis. Also can be used as a pain relief treatment and reduces high temperature.
How it works: Has a pain-killing and anti-inflammatory effect and is effective at treating continuous or regular pain.
Possible adverse effects: Salt retention, interferes with several enzyme processes. If sore throat, mouth ulcers, fevers or bruising occur, notify a doctor immediately.
Other information: Do not take if allergic to aspirin.
CAUTIONS
Children: This drug is either not recommended for children, or is recommended only for children above a certain age.
Pregnancy and breastfeeding: This drug is either not recommended for use by women who are pregnant or breastfeeding, or the precise effects are not known and it should therefore only be used with caution and under medical advice.

PHENYLEPHRINE
Brand name: Minims Phenylephrine
Type of drug: Decongestant
Uses: Used to treat hay fever and colds, to dilate the pupils and as a treatment for a fall in blood pressure.
How it works: Has a decongestant action. Constricts the blood vessels in the eye and dilates the pupils.
Possible adverse effects: Raised blood pressure, headache. Stinging of the eye in eye-treatment.
Availability: Available with or without a prescription (over the counter).
Other information: Prolonged use of the nasal spray may result in rebound congestion.
CAUTIONS
Children: This drug is either not recommended for children, or is recommended only for children above a certain age.
Pregnancy and breastfeeding: This drug is either not recommended for use by women who are pregnant or breastfeeding, or the precise effects are not known and it should therefore only be used with caution and under medical advice.
Driving and operating machinery: This drug may have some effect on your driving ability, so it is advisable not to drive or operate machinery while taking it.

PHENYTOIN
Brand name: Epanutin, Pentran
Type of drug: Anti-convulsant
Uses: Treatment of epilepsy, migraine and some abnormal heart rhythms.
How it works: Reduces the abnormal electrical discharges within the brain that lead to seizures.

Possible adverse effects: Dizziness, confusion, nausea and vomiting, difficulty in sleeping. Most adverse effects only occur with long-term use.

Other information: Patient should take drug with food or milk to minimise side effects. A higher dose of contraceptive will be required.

CAUTIONS

Pregnancy and breastfeeding: This drug is either not recommended for use by women who are pregnant or breastfeeding, or the precise effects are not known and it should therefore only be used with caution and under medical advice.

Alcohol: Alcohol should not be consumed, or only with caution – after medical advice has been sought – while you are taking this drug.

Driving and operating machinery: This drug may have some effect on your driving ability, so it is advisable not to drive or operate machinery while taking it.

PILOCARPINE

Brand name: Minims Pilocarpine, Ocusert Pilo, Salagen, Sno Pilo

Type of drug: Glaucoma treatment

Uses: Treatment of acute and chronic glaucoma.

How it works: Narrows the pupil within the eye. Can be given as slow release Ocuserts, which are put under the eyelid once a week.

Possible adverse effects: Changes to vision, including blurring and poor sight at night. Headaches and irritation of the eye are also possible.

Other information: Prescribed as eye drops and Ocuserts (slow-release inserts which are placed under the eyelid once a week).

CAUTIONS

Driving and operating machinery: This drug may have some effect on your driving ability, so it is advisable not to drive or operate machinery while taking it.

PIPERAZINE

Brand name: Expelix, Pripsen

Type of drug: Anthelmintic

Uses: To treat infestations of threadworm and roundworm.

How it works: Paralyses the worms and enables the body to eliminate them.

Possible adverse effects: Very rare. Consult a doctor if there are any signs of a rash, or itching.

Availability: Available with or without a prescription (over the counter).

Other information: Roundworm treatment is usually completed in one dose, but it may need to be repeated in severe cases. Threadworm treatment may take up to seven days. Follow the instructions carefully.

CAUTIONS

Pregnancy and breastfeeding: This drug is either not recommended for use by women who are pregnant or breastfeeding, or the precise effects are not known and it should therefore only be used with caution and under medical advice.

Driving and operating machinery: This drug may have some effect on your driving ability, so it is advisable not to drive or operate machinery while taking it.

PIROXICAM

Brand name: Feldene, Flamatrol, Kentene, Larapram, Piroflam, Pirozip.

Type of drug: Non-steroidal anti-inflammatory, gout treatment
Uses: Relieves the symptoms of osteoarthritis, rheumatoid arthritis, and ankylosing spondylitis.
How it works: Reduces pain, stiffness and inflammation which occur with the above conditions. Does not cure the underlying condition.
Possible adverse effects: Stomach pain and nausea.
Other information: Patient should avoid aspirin and seek medical approval with other over-the-counter preparations.
CAUTIONS
Pregnancy and breastfeeding: This drug is either not recommended for use by women who are pregnant or breastfeeding, or the precise effects are not known and it should therefore only be used with caution and under medical advice.
Alcohol: Alcohol should not be consumed, or only with caution – after medical advice has been sought – while you are taking this drug.
Driving and operating machinery: This drug may have some effect on your driving ability, so it is advisable not to drive or operate machinery while taking it.

PIZOTIFEN
Brand name: Sanomigran
Type of drug: Anti-migraine
Uses: Used to treat migraine, vascular and cluster headaches.
How it works: Works in a similar way to some anti-depressants. It is thought to block the effect of some of the chemicals that act on the blood vessels in the brain.
Possible adverse effects: Drowsiness, increased appetite, weight gain.
Other information: Can cause weight gain during long periods of use.
CAUTIONS
Pregnancy and breastfeeding: This drug is either not recommended for use by women who are pregnant or breastfeeding, or the precise effects are not known and it should therefore only be used with caution and under medical advice.
Alcohol: Alcohol should not be consumed, or only with caution – after medical advice has been sought – while you are taking this drug.
Driving and operating machinery: This drug may have some effect on your driving ability, so it is advisable not to drive or operate machinery while taking it.

PODOPHYLLOTOXIN
Brand name: Condyline, Warticon
Type of drug: Wart and callus preparation
Uses: Used to treat external genital warts.
How it works: Kills the causative organism and destroys the wart.
Possible adverse effects: Can cause considerable skin irritation. Severe toxicity can occur if there is excessive use of the medication.
Other information: Should be washed off the treated area after six hours. Protect skin around the affected area with a soft paraffin preparation.
CAUTIONS
Children: This drug is either not recommended for children, or is recommended only for children above a certain age.
Pregnancy and breastfeeding: This drug is either not recommended for use by women who are pregnant or breastfeeding, or the precise

effects are not known and it should therefore only be used with caution and under medical advice.

PRAVASTATIN
Brand name: Lipostat
Type of drug: Lipid lowering
Uses: Used to treat people with raised blood cholesterol levels.
How it works: Prevents the formation of cholesterol which is associated with coronary artery disease.
Possible adverse effects: Nausea, constipation, flatulence, insomnia, dizziness, chest pain, fatigue.
Other information: Patient should be instructed to eat a low fat, low cholesterol diet and take exercise. A doctor should be notified of any adverse aches and pains. Drug is best taken at bedtime.
CAUTIONS
Children: This drug is either not recommended for children, or is recommended only for children above a certain age.
Pregnancy and breastfeeding: This drug is either not recommended for use by women who are pregnant or breastfeeding, or the precise effects are not known and it should therefore only be used with caution and under medical advice.
Alcohol: Alcohol should not be consumed, or only with caution – after medical advice has been sought – while you are taking this drug.

PRAZOSIN
Brand name: Alphavase, Hypovase
Type of drug: Anti-hypertensive
Uses: Used as a treatment for high blood pressure and conditions caused by poor circulation, such as Raynaud's disease. Also given to relieve symptoms associated with an enlarged prostate gland.
How it works: Relaxes the blood vessel walls, enabling more blood to flow through.
Possible adverse effects: Dizziness and fainting on first rising. Nausea, headache, faintness and drowsiness. First dose may cause a dramatic drop in blood pressure and will be given when the patient is lying down.
Other information: Patient should seek medical approval before taking any over-the-counter preparations. Must not stop taking drug suddenly.
CAUTIONS
Children: This drug is either not recommended for children, or is recommended only for children above a certain age.
Pregnancy and breastfeeding: This drug is either not recommended for use by women who are pregnant or breastfeeding, or the precise effects are not known and it should therefore only be used with caution and under medical advice.
Alcohol: Alcohol should not be consumed, or only with caution – after medical advice has been sought – while you are taking this drug.
Driving and operating machinery: This drug may have some effect on your driving ability, so it is advisable not to drive or operate machinery while taking it.

PREDNISOLONE
Brand name: Deltacortril, Deltastab, Minims prednisolone, Precortisyl, Predenema, Predfoam, Pred Forte, Predsol
Type of drug: Corticosteroid

Uses: Corticosteroid used to treat a range of skin diseases, allergies, some blood disorders, inflammatory bowel disease and arthritis.

How it works: Stimulates the production of enzymes needed to reduce the inflammatory response. Suppresses the immune system by reducing activity and volume of the lymphatic system, thus reducing the inflammatory response.

Possible adverse effects: Indigestion and acne. More serious side effects are possible when taken for long periods. These include diabetes and glaucoma. Discuss with your doctor.

Other information: Alcohol can increase the risk of peptic ulcers.

CAUTIONS

Children: This drug is either not recommended for children, or is recommended only for children above a certain age.

Alcohol: Alcohol should not be consumed, or only with caution – after medical advice has been sought – while you are taking this drug.

PROBENECID
Brand name: Benemid
Type of drug: Gout treatment
Uses: Used to treat gout.

How it works: It increases the excretion of uric acid by the kidneys, which results in the reduction of the raised blood uric acid levels which are symptomatic of the condition.

Possible adverse effects: Nausea, vomiting, sore gums and increased passing of urine.

Other information: Do not use with aspirin. Patient should drink 8-10 glasses of fluid daily.

PROCHLORPERAZINE
Brand name: Buccastem, Proziere, Stemetil
Type of drug: Anti-emetic and anti-psychotic
Uses: Control of nausea and vomiting which occurs with some ear disorders. Can also be used as a tranquilliser for psychiatric disorders.

How it works: Acts on the central nervous system to relieve symptoms, but is not a cure.

Possible adverse effects: Drowsiness, dry mouth, dizziness and involuntary movements similar to those seen in people with Parkinson's disease.

Other information: Patient should avoid excessive exposure to sun and to extreme temperatures.

CAUTIONS

Pregnancy and breastfeeding: This drug is either not recommended for use by women who are pregnant or breastfeeding, or the precise effects are not known and it should therefore only be used with caution and under medical advice.

Alcohol: Alcohol should not be consumed, or only with caution – after medical advice has been sought – while you are taking this drug.

Driving and operating machinery: This drug may have some effect on your driving ability, so it is advisable not to drive or operate machinery while taking it.

PROCYCLIDINE
Brand name: Arpicolin, Kemadrin
Type of drug: Anti-Parkinsonism

Uses: To treat some of the symptoms of Parkinson's disease.
How it works: Relieves muscle rigidity and excess salivation. It is particularly effective in the early stages of the disease.
Possible adverse effects: Dizziness, dry mouth, constipation, blurred vision.
Other information: Prolonged use of this drug can cause glaucoma.
CAUTIONS
Children: This drug is either not recommended for children, or is recommended only for children above a certain age.
Pregnancy and breastfeeding: This drug is either not recommended for use by women who are pregnant or breastfeeding, or the precise effects are not known and it should therefore only be used with caution and under medical advice.
Alcohol: Alcohol should not be consumed, or only with caution – after medical advice has been sought – while you are taking this drug.
Driving and operating machinery: This drug may have some effect on your driving ability, so it is advisable not to drive or operate machinery while taking it.

PROGESTERONE
Brand name: Cyclogest, Gestone
Type of drug: Female sex hormone
Uses: Used for the treatment of amenorrhoea and as an contraceptive.
How it works: As a contraceptive it suppresses ovulation.
Possible adverse effects: Acne, rashes, fluid retention, weight changes, gastrointestinal disturbances.
Other information: A doctor should be consulted if there is any excessive bleeding.
CAUTIONS
Children: Unlikely to be prescribed.
Pregnancy and breastfeeding: This drug is either not recommended for use by women who are pregnant or breastfeeding, or the precise effects are not known and it should therefore only be used with caution and under medical advice.

PROGUANIL
Brand name: Paludrine
Type of drug: Anti-malarial
Uses: As protection against malaria in infected areas.
How it works: Prevents development of the disease, but may need to be taken in conjunction with other drugs in order to be effective.
Possible adverse effects: These are rare, but may include stomach irritation, which usually settles with continued treatment.
Availability: Available with or without a prescription (over-the-counter).
Other information: The drug should be taken one week before travelling and for four weeks after returning. Care should be taken to avoid getting bitten.
CAUTIONS
Pregnancy and breastfeeding: This drug is either not recommended for use by women who are pregnant or breastfeeding, or the precise effects are not known and it should therefore only be used with caution and under medical advice.

PROMETHAZINE
Brand name: Avomine, Phenergan, Sominex
Type of drug: Antihistamine, anti-emetic
Uses: Used to treat nausea, various skin allergies and motion sickness.
How it works: Has an effect similar to that of antihistamines. Relieves itching and can also relieve nausea and vomiting caused by inner ear problems such as Meniere's disease and travel sickness. Its sedative effect means it is also given as a premedication before surgery.
Possible adverse effects: Drowsiness, dry mouth and blurred vision.
Availability: Available with or without a prescription (over-the-counter).
Other information: For motion sickness the patient should take the drug 30-60 minutes before travelling.
CAUTIONS
Pregnancy and breastfeeding: This drug is either not recommended for use by women who are pregnant or breastfeeding, or the precise effects are not known and it should therefore only be used with caution and under medical advice.
Alcohol: Alcohol should not be consumed, or only with caution – after medical advice has been sought – while you are taking this drug.
Driving and operating machinery: This drug may have some effect on your driving ability, so it is advisable not to drive or operate machinery while taking it.

PROPAFENONE
Brand name: Arythmol
Type of drug: Anti-arrhythmic
Uses: Is used to treat disorders of heart rhythm.
How it works: Changes the chemicals which determine the heart rhythm to slow and steady the heartbeat.
Possible adverse effects: Constipation, blurred vision, dizziness, dry mouth, nausea, vomiting and fatigue.
Other information: Patient should report any signs of infection.
CAUTIONS
Pregnancy and breastfeeding: This drug is either not recommended for use by women who are pregnant or breastfeeding, or the precise effects are not known and it should therefore only be used with caution and under medical advice.

PROPRANOLOL
Brand name: Angilol, Apsolol, Berkolol, Beta-Prograne, Cardinol, Inderal, Inderal-LA, Propanix
Type of drug: Beta-blocker and anti-anxiety
Uses: Used to treat high blood pressure, and heart disorders, such as angina and arrhythmia. The drug can also be used to control the symptoms associated with an overactive thyroid and severe anxiety. Also used to prevent migraines.
How it works: Reduces the amount of action needed by the heart, reduces the heart rate, dilates the blood vessels, with the result that the heart rate is slowed and steadied.
Possible adverse effects: Tiredness and nausea usually only last for a short time.
Other information: Patient to check with doctor before taking any other over-the-counter preparations.

CAUTIONS
Children: This drug is either not recommended for children, or is recommended only for children above a certain age.
Pregnancy and breastfeeding: This drug is either not recommended for use by women who are pregnant or breastfeeding, or the precise effects are not known and it should therefore only be used with caution and under medical advice.

PROPYLTHIOURACIL
Brand name: Propylthiouracil
Type of drug: Anti-thyroid
Uses: The management of an overactive thyroid.
How it works: Helps to restore normal function to the thyroid gland.
Possible adverse effects: Skin rashes and itches. Sometimes the ability to fight infection may be reduced, so any sign of a sore throat or mouth ulceration should be reported to a doctor.
Other information: Regular blood tests will monitor effect on thyroid function.
CAUTIONS
Pregnancy and breastfeeding: This drug is either not recommended for use by women who are pregnant or breastfeeding, or the precise effects are not known and it should therefore only be used with caution and under medical advice.

PYRAZINAMIDE
Brand name: Rifater, Zinamide
Type of drug: Anti-tuberculous
Uses: Used in conjunction with other drugs to treat tuberculosis.
How it works: Acts on the bacteria which are causing the infection.
Possible adverse effects: Liver damage with fever, nausea and vomiting.
Other information: Patient should be made fully aware of all side effects and report any immediately. Treatment may be continued for up to 18 months.
CAUTIONS
Children: This drug is either not recommended for children, or is recommended only for children above a certain age.
Pregnancy and breastfeeding: This drug is either not recommended for use by women who are pregnant or breastfeeding, or the precise effects are not known and it should therefore only be used with caution and under medical advice.

PYRIDOSTIGMINE
Brand name: Mestinon
Type of drug: Anti-cholinesterases
Uses: To treat myasthenia gravis, a rare autoimmune condition.
How it works: Acts as a muscle stimulant to improve the muscle tone by strengthening the signals sent down the nerves which are faulty in this condition.
Possible adverse effects: Nausea, vomiting, diarrhoea and abdominal cramps, sweating and increased saliva.
Other information: Tablets should be swallowed whole, not chewed or crushed. Patient should be taught to how to evaluate any changes in muscle strength.

CAUTIONS
Children: This drug is either not recommended for children, or is recommended only for children above a certain age.
Pregnancy and breastfeeding: This drug is either not recommended for use by women who are pregnant or breastfeeding, or the precise effects are not known and it should therefore only be used with caution and under medical advice.
Driving and operating machinery: This drug may have some effect on your driving ability, so it is advisable not to drive or operate machinery while taking it.

PYRIMETHAMINE
Brand name: Daraprim
Type of drug: Anti-malarial
Uses: To treat infections with malaria. Not used in the prevention of malaria.
How it works: Treats infections which are resistant to other antimalarial drugs. Usually given in conjunction with other drugs to increase the power.
Possible adverse effects: Skin rashes and insomnia. Long-term use may lead to folic acid deficiency.
Other information: Blood will be tested regularly and vitamin supplements may be given during treatment.
CAUTIONS
Children: This drug is either not recommended for children, or is recommended only for children above a certain age.
Pregnancy and breastfeeding: This drug is either not recommended for use by women who are pregnant or breastfeeding, or the precise effects are not known and it should therefore only be used with caution and under medical advice.

QUINAPRIL
Brand name: Accupro, Accuretic
Type of drug: ACE inhibitor
Uses: To treat raised blood pressure and congestive heart failure.
How it works: Dilates the blood vessels, reduces sodium and water retention, with the result that the blood pressure is lowered.
Possible adverse effects: Chest pain, nausea, indigestion, abdominal pains, headache, insomnia, blurred vision.
Other information: Drug should be taken on an empty stomach. Patient should avoid salt substitutes. Patient should take care in hot weather, or if taking exercise, to avoid over-heating and dehydration.
CAUTIONS
Children: This drug is either not recommended for children, or is recommended only for children above a certain age.
Pregnancy and breastfeeding: This drug is either not recommended for use by women who are pregnant or breastfeeding, or the precise effects are not known and it should therefore only be used with caution and under medical advice.

QUINIDINE
Brand name: Kinidin Durules
Type of drug: Anti-arrhythmic
Uses: To treat disorders of heart rhythm such as atrial fibrillation,

paroxysmal supraventricular tachycardia and premature atrial contractions.

How it works: Acts on the electrical impulses in the heart to enable it to beat more steadily and effectively.

Possible adverse effects: Vertigo, headache, nausea, diarrhoea, fever.

Other information: Patient must report rash, fever, ringing in the ears or visual disturbances.

CAUTIONS

Pregnancy and breastfeeding: This drug is either not recommended for use by women who are pregnant or breastfeeding, or the precise effects are not known and it should therefore only be used with caution and under medical advice.

QUININE

Brand name: Quinine

Type of drug: Anti-malarial and muscle relaxant

Uses: For the treatment of malaria and it is also used to treat nocturnal leg cramps.

How it works: Is often an effective treatment for malaria when other treatments have failed. Also has a muscle relaxant effect.

Possible adverse effects: Tinnitus, headache, nausea, hot and flushed skin.

Other information: If the patient suffers from hearing impairment it should be reported it immediately.

CAUTIONS

Driving and operating machinery: This drug may have some effect on your driving ability, so it is advisable not to drive or operate machinery while taking it.

RALTITREXED

Brand name: Tomudex

Type of drug: Anti-cancer

Uses: To treat cancer of the colon.

How it works: Prevents the cancer cells from dividing and therefore from multiplying.

Possible adverse effects: Blood disorders and stomach and bowel upsets. Anaemia and impaired liver function can occur but they do not produce symptoms and are reversible.

Other information: Given by intravenous infusions. Regular blood counts will be carried out.

CAUTIONS

Pregnancy and breastfeeding: This drug is either not recommended for use by women who are pregnant or breastfeeding, or the precise effects are not known and it should therefore only be used with caution and under medical advice.

RAMIPRIL

Brand name: Tritace

Type of drug: ACE inhibitor and anti-hypertensive

Uses: To treat high blood pressure and heart failure after a heart attack.

How it works: Dilates the blood vessels so that blood can flow around the body more freely.

Possible adverse effects: Nausea, dizziness, cough, headache.

Other information: Blood pressure and heart function will be regularly checked.

CAUTIONS
Children: This drug is either not recommended for children, or is recommended only for children above a certain age.
Pregnancy and breastfeeding: This drug is either not recommended for use by women who are pregnant or breastfeeding, or the precise effects are not known and it should therefore only be used with caution and under medical advice.
Alcohol: Alcohol should not be consumed, or only with caution – after medical advice has been sought – while you are taking this drug.
Driving and operating machinery: This drug may have some effect on your driving ability, so it is advisable not to drive or operate machinery while taking it.

RANITIDINE
Brand name: Zantac
Type of drug: Anti-ulcer
Uses: Treatment of stomach and duodenal ulcers. Used in conjunction with other drugs to treat the Helicobacter pylori infection. Also used to treat reflux oesophagitis.
How it works: Reduces the amount of acid produced and thus enables the ulcers to heal.
Possible adverse effects: Rare, but occasional headaches.
Other information: Patient must swallow medication whole with water.
CAUTIONS
Alcohol: Alcohol should not be consumed, or only with caution – after medical advice has been sought – while you are taking this drug.

RIFABUTIN
Brand name: Mycobutin
Type of drug: Anti-tuberculous
Uses: To treat tuberculosis, often in patients who are suffering from HIV or AIDS.
How it works: The drug has an antibiotic action and will often be used in conjunction with other drugs for maximum effect.
Possible adverse effects: Nausea and vomiting, abdominal pain, diarrhoea.
Other information: Can interact with oral contraceptives.
CAUTIONS
Children: This drug is either not recommended for children, or is recommended only for children above a certain age.
Pregnancy and breastfeeding: This drug is either not recommended for use by women who are pregnant or breastfeeding, or the precise effects are not known and it should therefore only be used with caution and under medical advice.

RIFAMPICIN
Brand name: Rifadin, Rimactane
Type of drug: Anti-tuberculous
Uses: To treat tuberculosis (TB) and leprosy.
How it works: Has an antibiotic action and is used in conjunction with other anti-TB drugs to maximise effect.
Possible adverse effects: Headache, fatigue, and orange-red coloured urine.
Other information: May render oral contraceptives ineffective and disrupt menstrual cycle.

CAUTIONS

Children: This drug is either not recommended for children, or is recommended only for children above a certain age.

Pregnancy and breastfeeding: This drug is either not recommended for use by women who are pregnant or breastfeeding, or the precise effects are not known and it should therefore only be used with caution and under medical advice.

Alcohol: Alcohol should not be consumed, or only with caution – after medical advice has been sought – while you are taking this drug.

RISPERIDONE

Brand name: Risperdal
Type of drug: Anti-emetic and anti-psychotic
Uses: Treatment of long-term psychiatric disorders such as schizophrenia.
How it works: Affects the chemicals in the brain, with the result that symptoms such as hallucinations, though disturbances and aggression are reduced. Reduces the tendency to become emotionally and socially withdrawn; also helps with other symptoms such as anxiety and depression.
Possible adverse effects: Insomnia, anxiety, headache, poor concentration.
Other information: If used for a long time, some movement disorders may occur.

CAUTIONS

Pregnancy and breastfeeding: This drug is either not recommended for use by women who are pregnant or breastfeeding, or the precise effects are not known and it should therefore only be used with caution and under medical advice.

Alcohol: Alcohol should not be consumed, or only with caution – after medical advice has been sought – while you are taking this drug.

Driving and operating machinery: This drug may have some effect on your driving ability, so it is advisable not to drive or operate machinery while taking it.

RITONAVIR

Brand name: Norvir
Type of drug: Anti-viral
Uses: To treat HIV infection.
How it works: Inhibits the activity of an enzyme which is vital for the survival of the HIV virus.
Possible adverse effects: Nausea, vomiting, diarrhoea, flushing, weakness, headache.
Other information: Patient to report use of any other over-the-counter preparations in case of drug interactions.

CAUTIONS

Children: This drug is either not recommended for children, or is recommended only for children above a certain age.

Pregnancy and breastfeeding: This drug is either not recommended for use by women who are pregnant or breastfeeding, or the precise effects are not known and it should therefore only be used with caution and under medical advice.

ROPINIROLE
Brand name: Requip
Type of drug: Anti-Parkinsonism
Uses: To treat some of the signs and symptoms of Parkinson's disease.
How it works: Thought to stimulate the part of the brain that is not working effectively in patients with Parkinson's disease.
Possible adverse effects: Nausea, vomiting, abdominal pains, sleepiness and oedema. Occasionally hallucinations may occur.
Other information: The patient should be warned to rise slowly immediately after sitting or lying down to avoid becoming dizzy. Nausea will be minimised if this drug is taken with food.
CAUTIONS
Children: This drug is either not recommended for children, or is recommended only for children above a certain age.
Pregnancy and breastfeeding: This drug is either not recommended for use by women who are pregnant or breastfeeding, or the precise effects are not known and it should therefore only be used with caution and under medical advice.
Alcohol: Alcohol should not be consumed, or only consumed with caution – after medical advice has been sought – while you are taking this drug.
Driving and operating machinery: This drug may have some effect on your driving ability, so it is advisable not to drive or operate machinery while taking it.

SALBUTAMOL
Brand name: Aerolin, Airomir, Asmaven, Maxivent, Salamol Easi-Breathe, Ventodisks, Ventolin, Volmax
Type of drug: Bronchodilator
Uses: To treat lung disorders (eg, asthma, chronic bronchitis emphysema).
How it works: Improves air flow through the lungs, enabling the sufferer to breathe more easily.
Possible adverse effects: Muscle tremor, anxiety and restlessness.
Other information: If requiring more than eight puffs in 24 hours, consult your doctor.
CAUTIONS
Pregnancy and breastfeeding: This drug is either not recommended for use by women who are pregnant or breastfeeding, or the precise effects are not known and it should therefore only be used with caution and under medical advice.
Driving and operating machinery: This drug may have some effect on your driving ability, so it is advisable not to drive or operate machinery while taking it.

SALMETEROL
Brand name: Serevent
Type of drug: Bronchodilator
Uses: Long-term maintenance treatment of people with asthma.
How it works: Dilates the airways to enable the sufferer to breathe more easily.
Possible adverse effects: Tremor, headaches, palpitations.
Other information: This medication is not to appropriate for the relief of acute attacks of asthma; another type of medication should be used

in those cases. Salmeterol should not be used more than twice daily; if the drug does not meet your requirements, consult your doctor.

CAUTIONS

Pregnancy and breastfeeding: This drug is either not recommended for use by women who are pregnant or breastfeeding, or the precise effects are not known and it should therefore only be used with caution and under medical advice.

SAQUINAVIR

Brand name: Invirase
Type of drug: Anti-viral
Uses: To treat HIV infection.
How it works: Prevents the HIV virus from reaching maturity.
Possible adverse effects: Nausea, vomiting, headache, diarrhoea, abdominal discomfort.
Other information: The drug is best taken two hours after a full meal. This drug will usually be given in conjunction with other medication.

CAUTIONS

Children: This drug is either not recommended for children, or is recommended only for children above a certain age.

Pregnancy and breastfeeding: This drug is either not recommended for use by women who are pregnant or breastfeeding, or the precise effects are not known and it should therefore only be used with caution and under medical advice.

SERTINDOLE

Brand name: Serdolect
Type of drug: Anti-psychotic
Uses: Used to treat schizophrenia.
How it works: Reduces the symptoms of the disorder.
Possible adverse effects: Insomnia, anxiety, headache, drowsiness, blurred vision, nausea.
Other information: Not prescribed for new patients, although people already treated with this drug will continue with it.

CAUTIONS

Pregnancy and breastfeeding: This drug is either not recommended for use by women who are pregnant or breastfeeding, or the precise effects are not known and it should only be used with caution, after medical advice.

SERTRALINE

Brand name: Lustral
Type of drug: Anti-depressant
Uses: Treatment of depression.
How it works: Improves the mood, increases energy and stimulates an interest in day-to-day living without the sedative effects of similar drugs.
Possible adverse effects: Nausea and diarrhoea.
Other information: Patient should check with the doctor before using other over-the-counter preparations.

CAUTIONS

Children: This drug is either not recommended for children, or is recommended only for children above a certain age.

Pregnancy and breastfeeding: This drug is either not recommended for use by women who are pregnant or breastfeeding, or the precise

effects are not known and it should only be used with caution, after medical advice.

Alcohol: Alcohol should not be consumed, or only consumed with caution – after medical advice has been sought – while you are taking this drug.

Driving and operating machinery: This drug may have some effect on your driving ability, so it is advisable not to drive or operate machinery while taking it.

SILDENAFIL
Brand name: Viagra
Type of drug: Impotence treatment
Uses: Treatment of erectile dysfunction.
How it works: Enables impotent men to attain and maintain an erection.
Possible adverse effects: Indigestion, headache, flushing, dizziness, visual disturbances, nasal congestion.
Other information: Should not be used at the same time as other impotence treatments or for people with heart problems. This drug will not be prescribed on the NHS unless the problem is caused by a medical disorder.
CAUTIONS
Alcohol: Alcohol should not be consumed, or only consumed with caution – after medical advice has been sought – while you are taking this drug.
Driving and operating machinery: This drug may have some effect on your driving ability, so it is advisable not to drive or operate machinery while taking it.

SIMVASTATIN
Brand name: Zocor
Type of drug: Lipid lowering
Uses: Treatment of people who have high levels of fat in their blood and who are at risk of developing heart disease.
How it works: Lowers level of cholesterol in the blood, particularly in people who have not responded to other forms of treatment and who are at risk of developing heart disease.
Possible adverse effects: Nausea and diarrhoea are rare and will usually resolve, but prolonged treatment can damage the liver.
Other information: Regular tests to assess liver function will be carried out.
CAUTIONS
Children: This drug is either not recommended for children, or is recommended only for children above a certain age.
Pregnancy and breastfeeding: This drug is either not recommended for use by women who are pregnant or breastfeeding, or the precise effects are not known and it should therefore only be used with caution and under medical advice.
Alcohol: Alcohol should not be consumed, or only consumed with caution – after medical advice has been sought – while you are taking this drug.

SODIUM AUROTHIOMALATE
Brand name: Myocrisin
Type of drug: Anti-rheumatic

Uses: To treat progressive rheumatoid arthritis.
How it works: Slows and halts progression of the disease, but does not repair damage that has already occurred.
Possible adverse effects: Side effects can be serious, such as blood disorders, rashes and impaired kidney function and mouth ulcers.
Other information: Patient should report a sore throat, mouth ulcers, fever, infection, rashes, immediately. The drug can take several months to reach full effectiveness.

SODIUM CROMOGLYCATE
Brand name: Cromogem, Intal, Nalcrom, Opticrom, Rynacrom
Type of drug: Anti-allergy
Uses: Used to treat allergies and asthma.
How it works: Reduces the frequency and severity of asthma attacks which are brought on by cold air or exercise. Also effective as a preventive treatment for hay fever and conjunctivitis.
Possible adverse effects: Coughing, wheezing and throat irritation.
Availability: Available with or without a prescription (over-the-counter).
Other information: This medication is not effective for the relief of an asthmatic attack. May take up to six weeks for benefits to be felt.

SOMATROPIN
Brand name: Genotropin, Humatrope, Norditropin, Saizen, Zomacton
Type of drug: Pituitary hormone
Uses: To treat growth problems caused by a deficiency in growth hormone produced by the pituitary gland.
How it works: A synthetic form of growth hormone, it performs the same function – promoting normal growth and development. It stimulates skeletal, linear bone, muscle and organ growth.
Possible adverse effects: These are rare but include headache and nausea.
Other information: Treatment will continue throughout childhood until an acceptable height is reached. Treatment may be stopped for a few months and then restarted depending on rate of growth.
CAUTIONS
Pregnancy and breastfeeding: This drug is either not recommended for use by women who are pregnant or breastfeeding, or the precise effects are not known and it should therefore only be used with caution and under medical advice.

SPIRONOLACTONE
Brand name: Aldactone, Laractone, Spiroctan, Spirolone, Spirospare
Type of drug: Potassium-sparing diuretic
Uses: Treatment of fluid build-up (oedema) caused by heart failure. Also used to treat oedema caused by liver and kidney problems and some kinds of pre-menstrual syndrome.
How it works: Acts on the kidneys to encourage the expulsion of excess fluid from the body.
Possible adverse effects: Nausea.
Other information: Blood tests will be taken regularly to check kidneys are working.
CAUTIONS
Pregnancy and breastfeeding: This drug is either not recommended

for use by women who are pregnant or breastfeeding, or the precise effects are not known and it should therefore only be used with caution and under medical advice.

Driving and operating machinery: This drug may have some effect on your driving ability, so it is advisable not to drive or operate machinery while taking it.

STAVUDINE
Brand name: Zerit
Type of drug: Anti-viral
Uses: To treat HIV infections.
How it works: Acts on the DNA of the virus to inhibit its replication.
Possible adverse effects: Headache, fever, dizziness, nausea, abdominal upsets.
Other information: Patient should report any tingling or numbness in limbs.
CAUTIONS
Children: This drug is either not recommended for children, or is recommended only for children above a certain age.
Pregnancy and breastfeeding: This drug is either not recommended for use by women who are pregnant or breastfeeding, or the precise effects are not known and it should therefore only be used with caution and under medical advice.

STILBOESTROL
Brand name: Apstil
Type of drug: Female sex hormone and anti-cancer
Uses: To treat cancer of the breast in women after the menopause. Also occasionally used to treat prostate cancer in men.
How it works: A synthetic hormone, it suppresses the effects of male sex hormones.
Possible adverse effects: In women it can cause nausea, vomiting, sore breasts, swollen ankles and withdrawal bleeding. In men it can lead to impotence.
Other information: There is a risk of gallstones with long-term use of this drug.
CAUTIONS
Children: This drug is either not recommended for children, or is recommended only for children above a certain age.
Pregnancy and breastfeeding: This drug is either not recommended for use by women who are pregnant or breastfeeding, or the precise effects are not known and it should therefore only be used with caution and under medical advice.

STREPTOKINASE
Brand name: Kabikinase, Streptase
Type of drug: Thrombolytic
Uses: Used to treat life-threatening deep-vein thrombosis and pulmonary embolisms.
How it works: An enzyme which dissolves the blood clots and is particularly effective at dissolving recently formed ones. It is also used in conjunction with other drugs to treat wounds and ulcers.
Possible adverse effects: Nausea, vomiting, bleeding. It can cause allergic reactions, so any sign of this should be reported to a doctor.

Other information: Usually given as an injection but is supplied in powder form for the treatment of wounds.

CAUTIONS

Children: This drug is either not recommended for children, or is recommended only for children above a certain age.

Pregnancy and breastfeeding: This drug is either not recommended for use by women who are pregnant or breastfeeding, or the precise effects are not known and it should therefore only be used with caution and under medical advice.

Alcohol: Alcohol should not be consumed, or only with caution – after medical advice has been sought – while you are taking this drug.

Driving and operating machinery: This drug may have some effect on your driving ability, so it is advisable not to drive or operate machinery while taking it.

SUCRALFATE

Brand name: Antepsin

Type of drug: Ulcer-healing

Uses: To promote the healing of gastric and duodenal ulcers.

How it works: Forms a barrier over the ulcer which protects it from further attack by stomach acid and gives it the opportunity to heal.

Possible adverse effects: Constipation, diarrhoea, nausea, indigestion and gastric discomfort.

Other information: This medication should be taken on an empty stomach at least one hour before meals.

CAUTIONS

Children: This drug is either not recommended for children, or is recommended only for children above a certain age.

Pregnancy and breastfeeding: This drug is either not recommended for use by women who are pregnant or breastfeeding, or the precise effects are not known and it should therefore only be used with caution and under medical advice.

Alcohol: Alcohol should not be consumed, or only consumed with caution – after medical advice has been sought – while you are taking this drug.

SULCONAZOLE NITRATE

Brand name: Exelderm

Type of drug: Anti-fungal

Uses: To treat fungal skin infections such as those which cause athlete's foot.

How it works: Inhibits the growth of fungi and yeast.

Possible adverse effects: Skin irritation.

Other information: Avoid contact with the eyes. Relief should be apparent within a few days, but the full course of treatment should be completed to prevent re-occurrence.

SULFASALAZINE

Brand name: Salazopyrin

Type of drug: Inflammatory bowel disease and anti-rheumatic drug

Uses: Treatment of conditions which cause inflammation of the bowel, such as ulcerative colitis and Crohn's disease. Can also be beneficial in the treatment of rheumatoid arthritis.

How it works: Has an anti-inflammatory effect.

Possible adverse effects: Adverse effects are more likely with high doses. Nausea, appetite loss, headache and joint pain. May cause orange or yellow urine.

Other information: It is important to drink a lot of fluid when taking this medication. Treatment will often be long-term.

CAUTIONS

Pregnancy and breastfeeding: This drug is either not recommended for use by women who are pregnant or breastfeeding, or the precise effects are not known and it should therefore only be used with caution and under medical advice.

SUMATRIPTAN

Brand name: Imigran

Type of drug: Anti-migraine

Uses: Relieves acute migraine attacks without the need to identify an aura.

How it works: Stops the blood vessels in the brain from dilating – the cause of migraine attacks.

Possible adverse effects: Most disappear within an hour. Include tingling, flushing and a heavy feeling.

Other information: Should only be used to treat attacks, not as a preventive measure.

CAUTIONS

Children: This drug is either not recommended for children, or is recommended only for children above a certain age.

Pregnancy and breastfeeding: This drug is either not recommended for use by women who are pregnant or breastfeeding, or the precise effects are not known and it should only be used with caution, after medical advice.

Driving and operating machinery: This drug may have some effect on your driving ability, so it is advisable not to drive or operate machinery while taking it.

TACALCITOL

Brand name: Curatoderm

Type of drug: Anti-psoriasis

Uses: To treat psoriasis.

How it works: Slows down the division of keratin-making cells in the skin and thus prevents the formation of the plaques which are characteristic of psoriasis.

Possible adverse effects: Local skin irritation.

Other information: Wash hands immediately after use and avoid contact with the eyes. Can affect hormonal contraception.

CAUTIONS

Children: This drug is either not recommended for children, or is recommended only for children above a certain age.

Pregnancy and breastfeeding: This drug is either not recommended for use by women who are pregnant or breastfeeding, or the precise effects are not known and it should therefore only be used with caution and under medical advice.

TAMOXIFEN

Brand name: Emblon, Fentamox, Noltam, Nolvadex, Oestrifen, Tamofen

Type of drug: Anti-cancer
Uses: Used to treat breast cancer.
How it works: The exact mechanism of this medication is unknown, but it is thought to block some of the hormonal action that the cancer cells require for survival.
Possible adverse effects: Nausea, vomiting, diarrhoea.
Other information: A barrier contraceptive is recommended during treatment.
CAUTIONS
Children: This drug is either not recommended for children, or is recommended only for children above a certain age.
Pregnancy and breastfeeding: This drug is either not recommended for use by women who are pregnant or breastfeeding, or the precise effects are not known and it should therefore only be used with caution and under medical advice.
Driving and operating machinery: This drug may have some effect on your driving ability, so it is advisable not to drive or operate machinery while taking it.

TAMSULOSIN
Brand name: Flomax MR
Type of drug: Urinary retention treatment
Uses: Used to relieve the symptoms of urinary retention.
How it works: It relaxes the muscles in the bladder neck, with the result that urine flow is improved.
Possible adverse effects: Dizziness, headache, decrease in blood pressure.
Other information: Patient should not chew or crush the tablets. Patient should get up slowly from bed or chair at the beginning of therapy.
CAUTIONS
Pregnancy and breastfeeding: This drug is either not recommended for use by women who are pregnant or breastfeeding, or the precise effects are not known and it should therefore only be used with caution and under medical advice.
Driving and operating machinery: This drug may have some effect on your driving ability, so it is advisable not to drive or operate machinery while taking it.

TEMAZEPAM
Brand name: Normison
Type of drug: Sleeping aid
Uses: Treatment of insomnia.
How it works: Depresses the action of part of the brain. Acts within 30 minutes and has a short-term effect to help induce sleep.
Possible adverse effects: Occasional daytime drowsiness.
Other information: Should only be taken for short periods as can be habit-forming.
CAUTIONS
Pregnancy and breastfeeding: This drug is either not recommended for use by women who are pregnant or breastfeeding, or the precise effects are not known and it should therefore only be used with caution and under medical advice.
Alcohol: Alcohol should not be consumed, or only with caution – after

medical advice has been sought – while you are taking this drug.
Driving and operating machinery: This drug may have some effect on your driving ability, so it is advisable not to drive or operate machinery while taking it.

TENOXICAM
Brand name: Mobiflex
Type of drug: Non-steroidal anti-inflammatory
Uses: To treat pain in rheumatic disease and similar disorders.
How it works: Has an anti-inflammatory effect which alleviates the symptoms but does not treat the underlying condition.
Possible adverse effects: Irritates the stomach, so can cause nausea, diarrhoea and occasionally bleeding. Any sign of these should be reported to a doctor.
Other information: Supplied either as an injection or as tablets.
CAUTIONS
Children: This drug is either not recommended for children, or is recommended only for children above a certain age.

TERAZOSIN
Brand name: Hytrin
Type of drug: Anti-hypertensive
Uses: To treat mild to moderate raised blood pressure. Also used to treat urinary tract blockages.
How it works: Relaxes the smooth muscle of blood vessels to enable the blood to flow more freely through them.
Possible adverse effects: Dizziness, light-headedness, low blood pressure, headache, fatigue, oedema.
Other information: Dizziness may occur with the first dose.
CAUTIONS
Driving and operating machinery: This drug may have some effect on your driving ability, so it is advisable not to drive or operate machinery while taking it.

TERBINAFINE
Brand name: Lamisil
Type of drug: Anti-fungal
Uses: To treat fungal skin infections such as athlete's foot, jock itch or ringworm.
How it works: Causes the fungal cells to die.
Possible adverse effects: Abdominal discomfort.
Other information: Avoid contact with eyes, nose and mouth. Use only as directed.
CAUTIONS
Pregnancy and breastfeeding: This drug is either not recommended for use by women who are pregnant or breastfeeding, or the precise effects are not known and it should therefore only be used with caution and under medical advice.

TERBUTALINE
Brand name: Bricanyl, Monovent
Type of drug: Bronchodilator
Uses: Treatment of lung spasms associated with asthma, bronchitis and emphysema.

How it works: Acts on the muscles within the lungs, with the result that the small airways of the lungs are expanded.

Possible adverse effects: Nausea, anxiety, tremor and nervousness.

Other information: If drug produces no relief the patient should report immediately. Must also check use of over-the-counter preparations.

CAUTIONS

Children: This drug is either not recommended for children, or is recommended only for children above a certain age.

Pregnancy and breastfeeding: This drug is either not recommended for use by women who are pregnant or breastfeeding, or the precise effects are not known and it should therefore only be used with caution and under medical advice.

Driving and operating machinery: This drug may have some effect on your driving ability, so it is advisable not to drive or operate machinery while taking it.

TERFENADINE

Brand name: Aller-eze, Boots Antihistamine Tablets, Histafen, Seldane, Terfenor, Terfex, Terfinax, Triludan.

Type of drug: Antihistamine

Uses: For the relief of rhinitis and hayfever and other similar allergies. Also for skin allergies such as hives.

How it works: Acts in the same way as other antihistamines, but without the accompanying sedative effect. Reduces sneezing and irritation of the eyes and nose.

Possible adverse effects: Rare, although indigestion and abdominal pain can occur in some cases.

Availability: Most of this drug type are available with or without a prescription (over-the-counter). Triludan, however, is available only with a prescription from a doctor.

Other information: Patient should avoid grapefruit juice. Patients who have arrhythmias should avoid this medication.

CAUTIONS

Pregnancy and breastfeeding: This drug is either not recommended for use by women who are pregnant or breastfeeding, or the precise effects are not known and it should therefore only be used with caution and under medical advice.

Alcohol: Alcohol should not be consumed, or only consumed with caution – after medical advice has been sought – while you are taking this drug.

Driving and operating machinery: This drug may have some effect on your driving ability, so it is advisable not to drive or operate machinery while taking it.

TESTOSTERONE

Brand name: Primoteston Depot, Restandol, Sustanon, Virormone

Type of drug: Male sex hormone

Uses: It is used to treat under-development of the testes in males. It is also used to treat cancer of the breast in women.

How it works: Compensates for deficiency in hormone.

Possible adverse effects: Increase in weight, prostate abnormalities, headache, nausea, depression.

Other information: Regular checks will be made to monitor the effect of treatment.

CAUTIONS
Children: This drug is either not recommended for children, or is recommended only for children above a certain age.
Pregnancy and breastfeeding: This drug is either not recommended for use by women who are pregnant or breastfeeding, or the precise effects are not known and it should therefore only be used with caution and under medical advice.

TETRACYCLINE
Brand name: Achromycin, Sustamycin, Tetrabid, Tetrachel, Topicycline
Type of drug: Tetracycline antibiotic
Uses: To treat chest infections such as bronchitis, and other types of infection such as acne.
How it works: Prevents the bacteria from multiplying.
Possible adverse effects: Nausea, vomiting, diarrhoea, headache and dizziness.
Other information: Discontinue use of the drug if the condition stays the same.
CAUTIONS
Children: This drug is either not recommended for children, or is recommended only for children above a certain age.
Pregnancy and breastfeeding: This drug is either not recommended for use by women who are pregnant or breastfeeding, or the precise effects are not known and it should therefore only be used with caution and under medical advice.

THEOPHYLLINE
Brand name: Lasma Nuelin, Theo-Dur, Uniphyllin Continus; [aminophylline] Pecram, Phyllocontin Continus
Type of drug: Bronchodilator
Uses: Treatment and prevention of acute lung spasms in people with asthma, bronchitis and emphysema.
How it works: Allows the air passages to expand and stimulates the heart and the nervous system to recover.
Possible adverse effects: Headache, nausea, vomiting and anxiety – usually related to dosage.
Availability: Available without a prescription (over-the-counter).
Other information: Often given as a slow-release preparation. Overdose should be treated as a medical emergency.
CAUTIONS
Pregnancy and breastfeeding: This drug is either not recommended for use by women who are pregnant or breastfeeding, or the precise effects are not known and it should only be used with caution, after medical advice.
Alcohol: Alcohol should not be consumed, or only consumed with caution – after medical advice has been sought – while you are taking this drug.

THIABENDAZOLE
Brand name: Mintezol
Type of drug: Anthelmintic
Uses: To treat infections with, among others, roundworm, threadworm, pinworm and whipworm.
How it works: Kills the infective organisms.

Possible adverse effects: Anorexia, nausea and vomiting, diarrhoea, headache and drowsiness.
Other information: Good hygiene is vital to prevent re-infection.
CAUTIONS
Pregnancy and breastfeeding: This drug is either not recommended for use by women who are pregnant or breastfeeding, or the precise effects are not known and it should only be used with caution, after medical advice.
Driving and operating machinery: This drug may have some effect on your driving ability, so it is advisable not to drive or operate machinery while taking it.

THIORIDAZINE
Brand name: Melleril, Rideril
Type of drug: Anti-psychotic
Uses: Treatment of a range of psychiatric problems, including schizophrenia, mania, dementia.
How it works: Has a tranquillising effect which reduces aggression and abnormal behaviour.
Possible adverse effects: Drowsiness, dry mouth, blocked nose. Can cause eye problems if taken in large doses.
Other information: If sore throat, dizziness or difficulty in urinating, develops your doctor should be informed immediately.
CAUTIONS
Pregnancy and breastfeeding: This drug is either not recommended for use by women who are pregnant or breastfeeding, or the precise effects are not known and it should therefore only be used with caution and under medical advice.
Alcohol: Alcohol should not be consumed or only consumed with caution – after medical advice has been sought – while you are taking this drug.
Driving and operating machinery: This drug may have some effect on your driving ability, so it is advisable not to drive or operate machinery while taking it.

THYROXINE
Brand name: Eltroxin
Type of drug: Thyroid hormone
Uses: Treatment of an under-active thyroid gland.
How it works: Replaces vital hormones which are not being produced by the thyroid gland. Also prescribed for some people with thyroid cancer.
Possible adverse effects: Rare, and usually related to dosage.
Other information: Regular blood tests will be taken.

TIBOLONE
Brand name: Livial
Type of drug: Hormone replacement therapy
Uses: To treat the symptoms of the menopause, including sweating, depression, decreased sex drive and hot flushes.
How it works: Replaces hormones which are depleted after either a naturally occurring menopause or one brought on by surgical treatment.
Possible adverse effects: Rare. Vaginal bleeding is possible if prescribed within one year of the menopause.
Other information: Not used as a way of preventing osteoporosis. Not

usually prescribed within 10 months of the last period. Unlike other HRT it does not need to be taken in conjunction with progestogen.
CAUTIONS
Children: This drug is either not recommended for children, or is recommended only for children above a certain age.
Pregnancy and breastfeeding: This drug is either not recommended for use by women who are pregnant or breastfeeding, or the precise effects are not known and it should therefore only be used with caution and under medical advice.

TILUDRONIC ACID
Brand name: Skelid
Type of drug: Bisphosphonate
Uses: To treat Paget's disease.
How it works: Promotes normal bone formation.
Possible adverse effects: Stomach pain, nausea, diarrhoea, dizziness and headache.
Other information: The patient must avoid food for two hours before and after taking this medication. Also, calcium products and antacids should be avoided.
CAUTIONS
Children: This drug is either not recommended for children, or is recommended only for children above a certain age.
Pregnancy and breastfeeding: This drug is either not recommended for use by women who are pregnant or breastfeeding, or the precise effects are not known and it should therefore only be used with caution and under medical advice.

TIMOLOL
Brand name: Betim, Blocadren, Glaucol, Timoptol
Type of drug: Anti-hypertensive
Uses: Treatment of high blood pressure (hypertension), heart attack, glaucoma and to prevent migraine.
How it works: Slows and steadies the heartbeat, prevents heart muscle damage and reduces blood pressure.
Possible adverse effects: Tiredness, blurred vision, headache.
Other information: Administered as tablets, or eye drops if given for glaucoma.
CAUTIONS
Children: This drug is either not recommended for children, or is recommended only for children above a certain age.
Pregnancy and breastfeeding: This drug is either not recommended for use by women who are pregnant or breastfeeding, or the precise effects are not known and it should therefore only be used with caution and under medical advice.
Alcohol: Alcohol should not be consumed or only consumed with caution – after medical advice has been sought – while you are taking this drug.
Driving and operating machinery: This drug may have some effect on your driving ability, so it is advisable not to drive or operate machinery while taking it.

TIOCONAZOLE
Brand name: Trosyl

Type of drug: Anti-fungal
Uses: Used to treat fungal infections of the skin and vagina.
How it works: Alters the cell wall of the fungus and disables it.
Possible adverse effects: Skin irritations, burning discharge.
Other information: Pessaries should be inserted high into the vagina. Sexual intercourse should be avoided during treatment to minimise the risk of re-infection.
CAUTIONS
Pregnancy and breastfeeding: This drug is either not recommended for use by women who are pregnant or breastfeeding, or the precise effects are not known and it should therefore only be used with caution and under medical advice.

TOLBUTAMIDE
Brand name: Rastinon
Type of drug: Anti-diabetic
Uses: Treatment of diabetes in adults who are still producing small amounts of insulin.
How it works: Stimulates the pancreas to produce more insulin.
Possible adverse effects: Dizziness, clamminess, which may indicate that the blood sugar is too low.
Other information: Should be taken in conjunction with a diabetic diet. Urine will be tested regularly for sugar. An overdose should be treated as a medical emergency.
CAUTIONS
Children: This drug is either not recommended for children, or is recommended only for children above a certain age.
Pregnancy and breastfeeding: This drug is either not recommended for use by women who are pregnant or breastfeeding, or the precise effects are not known and it should therefore only be used with caution and under medical advice.
Alcohol: Alcohol should not be consumed, or only consumed with caution – after medical advice has been sought – while you are taking this drug.

TRANDOLAPRIL
Brand name: Gopten, Odrik
Type of drug: ACE inhibitor
Uses: To treat mild to moderate raised blood pressure.
How it works: Acts as a vasodilator which enables the blood to flow more freely and the pressure to be lowered.
Possible adverse effects: Low blood pressure, light-headedness, dizziness, headache, fatigue.
Other information: Patient should report immediately any signs of infection, sore throat, swelling, difficulty in breathing. Also best to avoid sodium substitutes. Caution must be exercised in hot weather.
CAUTIONS
Children: This drug is either not recommended for children, or is recommended only for children above a certain age.
Pregnancy and breastfeeding: This drug is either not recommended for use by women who are pregnant or breastfeeding, or the precise effects are not known and it should therefore only be used with caution and under medical advice.

TRANEXAMIC ACID
Brand name: Cykolkapron
Type of drug: Anti-fibrinolytic
Uses: To treat bleeding in various situations, menorrhagia, dental extractions, nose bleeds.
How it works: Affects the clotting mechanism of the blood to prevent unwanted bleeding.
Possible adverse effects: Nausea, vomiting, diarrhoea, and drop in blood pressure. Report any visual disturbances immediately to your medical practitioner.
Other information: Regular eye tests will be performed on people undergoing long-term treatment.

TRAZODONE
Brand name: Molipaxin
Type of drug: Anti-depressant
Uses: Treatment of depression, particularly for people who have difficulty in sleeping.
How it works: Lifts the mood and restores interest in day-to-day living.
Possible adverse effects: Less likely than with many anti-depressants, but some people experience drowsiness.
Other information: It is advisable to lie down for 30 minutes after taking medication.
CAUTIONS
Children: This drug is either not recommended for children, or is recommended only for children above a certain age.
Pregnancy and breastfeeding: This drug is either not recommended for use by women who are pregnant or breastfeeding, or the precise effects are not known and it should therefore only be used with caution and under medical advice.
Alcohol: Alcohol should not be consumed, or only consumed with caution – after medical advice has been sought – while taking this drug.
Driving and operating machinery: This drug may have some effect on your driving ability, so it is advisable not to drive or operate machinery while taking it.

TRETINOIN
Brand name: Retin-A, Retinova
Type of drug: Vitamin A derivative
Uses: Topical treatment for acne and, in some cases, wrinkles.
How it works: Promotes the growth of healthy skin cells.
Possible adverse effects: Skin irritation and sensitivity, including peeling and redness.
Other information: Avoid excessive exposure to the sun and wear a sunscreen during treatment. Follow the instructions carefully.
CAUTIONS
Pregnancy and breastfeeding: This drug is either not recommended for use by women who are pregnant or breastfeeding, or the precise effects are not known and it should therefore only be used with caution and under medical advice.

TRIAMCINOLONE ACETONIDE
Brand name: Adcortyl
Type of drug: Corticosteroid

Uses: Topical treatment of severe inflammatory skin conditions for which other treatments have failed to work.

How it works: Suppresses the body's inflammatory response which causes the condition and thus alleviates the symptoms of eczema without providing a cure.

Possible adverse effects: Worsening of any skin infection present, skin irritation.

Other information: Supplied as a cream, ointment or paste. Follow the instructions carefully.

CAUTIONS

Children: This drug is either not recommended for children, or is recommended only for children above a certain age.

Pregnancy and breastfeeding: This drug is either not recommended for use by women who are pregnant or breastfeeding, or the precise effects are not known and it should therefore only be used with caution and under medical advice.

TRIAMTERENE

Brand name: Dytac, Dytide, Frusene, Kalspare, Triamax Co, Triam-Co

Type of drug: Diuretic

Uses: Treatment of high blood pressure (hypertension) and oedema.

How it works: Acts on the kidneys to encourage the body to eliminate excess fluid.

Possible adverse effects: Rare. Can stain urine blue, but this is harmless.

Other information: Supplied as capsules.

CAUTIONS

Pregnancy and breastfeeding: This drug is either not recommended for use by women who are pregnant or breastfeeding, or the precise effects are not known and it should therefore only be used with caution and under medical advice.

TRIMEPRAZINE

Brand name: Vallergan

Type of drug: Antihistamine

Uses: To help relieve itching.

How it works: Suppresses the allergic symptoms, one of which is the itching sensation.

Possible adverse effects: Drowsiness, dizziness, headache.

Other information: A sunscreen should be worn during treatment because of the photosensitising effect of this medication.

CAUTIONS

Pregnancy and breastfeeding: This drug is either not recommended for use by women who are pregnant or breastfeeding, or the precise effects are not known and it should therefore only be used with caution and under medical advice.

Alcohol: Alcohol should not be consumed, or only with caution – after medical advice has been sought – while you are taking this drug.

Driving and operating machinery: This drug may have some effect on your driving ability, so it is advisable not to drive or operate machinery while taking it.

TRIMETHOPRIM

Brand name: Ipral, Monotrim, Trimogal, Trimopan, Triprimix,

Bactrim, Chemotrim, Comixco
Type of drug: Anti-bacterial
Uses: Treatment of infections, particularly of the urinary tract and respiratory tract.
How it works: Has an anti-bacterial effect: destroys the infective organism.
Possible adverse effects: Rare when taken on its own, but rash, nausea and a sore throat are possible.
Other information: Often taken together with another antibacterial drug, sulphamethoxazole.
CAUTIONS
Pregnancy and breastfeeding: This drug is either not recommended for use by women who are pregnant or breastfeeding, or the precise effects are not known and it should only be used with caution, after medical advice.

TRIPTORELIN
Brand name: De-capeptyl SR
Type of drug: Hormone antagonist
Uses: Used to treat advanced prostate cancer and endometriosis.
How it works: In cancer it neutralises the male sex hormones which the tumour needs to survive. In endometriosis it reduces the production of female hormones.
Possible adverse effects: Nausea, vomiting, diarrhoea, dry mouth.
Other information: Should not be used by women at high risk of developing osteoporosis.

URSODEOXYCHOLIC ACID
Brand name: Destolit, Ursofalk
Type of drug: Bile acid preparation
Uses: Treatment of gallstones.
How it works: A naturally occurring chemical, it affects cholesterol levels, with the effect that the gallstones dissolve within three to 18 months.
Possible adverse effects: Rare, but can include diarrhoea, indigestion and a rash.
Other information: Oral contraceptives may not be so effective. Ultrasound examinations may be carried out to check progress of treatment.
CAUTIONS
Children: This drug is either not recommended for children, or is recommended only for children above a certain age.
Pregnancy and breastfeeding: This drug is either not recommended for use by women who are pregnant or breastfeeding, or the precise effects are not known and it should therefore only be used with caution and under medical advice.

VALPROATE
Brand name: Convulex (valproic acid), Epilim, Orlept
Type of drug: Anti-convulsant
Uses: Treatment of several different types of epilepsy.
How it works: Reduces electrical activity in the brain to prevent epileptic seizures.
Possible adverse effects: Side effects are very uncommon.

Other information: Blood will be tested to monitor levels in the blood.
CAUTIONS
Pregnancy and breastfeeding: This drug is either not recommended for use by women who are pregnant or breastfeeding, or the precise effects are not known and it should therefore only be used with caution and under medical advice.
Alcohol: Alcohol should not be consumed, or only consumed with caution – after medical advice has been sought – while you are taking this drug.
Driving and operating machinery: This drug may have some effect on your driving ability, so it is advisable not to drive or operate machinery while taking it.

VALPROIC ACID
Brand name: Depakote
Type of drug: Anti-convulsant
Uses: For treatment of bipolar disorder.
How it works: Alters the chemicals in the brain.
Possible adverse effects: Gastric irritation, nausea, tremor, oedema, hair loss.
Other information: Patient should swallow tablets whole. May take a week for treatment to be effective.
CAUTIONS
Pregnancy and breastfeeding: This drug is either not recommended for use by women who are pregnant or breastfeeding, or the precise effects are not known and it should therefore only be used with caution and under medical advice.
Alcohol: Alcohol should not be consumed, or only consumed with caution – after medical advice has been sought – while you are taking this drug.
Driving and operating machinery: This drug may have some effect on your driving ability, so it is advisable not to drive or operate machinery while taking it.

VENLAFAXINE
Brand name: Efexor
Type of drug: Anti-depressant
Uses: To treat depression.
How it works: Improves mood, energy levels and interest in daily life.
Possible adverse effects: Nausea, dizziness, lethargy, blurred vision, weight loss. Blood pressure can increase.
Other information: Patient to check before buying any over-the-counter preparations. Patient to report any rashes or other allergic reactions.
CAUTIONS
Children: This drug is either not recommended for children, or is recommended only for children above a certain age.
Pregnancy and breastfeeding: This drug is either not recommended for use by women who are pregnant or breastfeeding, or the precise effects are not known and it should therefore only be used with caution and under medical advice.
Alcohol: Alcohol should not be consumed, or only with caution – after medical advice has been sought – while you are taking this drug.
Driving and operating machinery: This drug may have some effect

on your driving ability, so it is advisable not to drive or operate machinery while taking it.

VERAPAMIL
Brand name: Berkatens, Cordilox, Securon-SR, Univer
Type of drug: Anti-angina, anti-arrhythmic, anti-hypertensive
Uses: Treatment of heart problems such as high blood pressure, rhythm disorders and angina.
How it works: Interferes with the electrical signals in the heart and the blood vessels. Reduces the frequency of angina attacks.
Possible adverse effects: Headache, constipation, nausea, swollen ankles.
Other information: Patient must report any shortness of breath or swelling of hands and feet.
CAUTIONS
Pregnancy and breastfeeding: This drug is either not recommended for use by women who are pregnant or breastfeeding, or the precise effects are not known and it should therefore only be used with caution and under medical advice.
Alcohol: Alcohol should not be consumed, or only consumed with caution – after medical advice has been sought – while you are taking this drug.
Driving and operating machinery: This drug may have some effect on your driving ability, so it is advisable not to drive or operate machinery while taking it.

VIGABATRIN
Brand name: Sabril
Type of drug: Anti-convulsant
Uses: For the treatment of epilepsy.
How it works: Affects the chemicals in the brain so that epileptic seizures are minimised.
Possible adverse effects: Drowsiness, dizziness and fatigue.
Other information: Patients should report any visual disturbances.
CAUTIONS
Pregnancy and breastfeeding: This drug is either not recommended for use by women who are pregnant or breastfeeding, or the precise effects are not known and it should therefore only be used with caution and under medical advice.
Driving and operating machinery: This drug may have some effect on your driving ability, so it is advisable not to drive or operate machinery while taking it.

WARFARIN
Brand name: Marevan
Type of drug: Anti-coagulant
Uses: To prevent blood clots.
How it works: 'Thins' the blood to stop the formation of clots which can settle in the lung, heart, brain and legs.
Possible adverse effects: Bleeding. Any signs of blood in the vomit or faeces or unexplained bruising should be reported to your doctor as soon as possible.
Other information: Caution must be taken to avoid any injuries, as these could cause excessive bleeding.

CAUTIONS
Pregnancy and breastfeeding: This drug is either not recommended for use by women who are pregnant or breastfeeding, or the precise effects are not known and it should therefore only be used with caution and under medical advice.
Alcohol: Alcohol should not be consumed, or only with caution – after medical advice has been sought – while you are taking this drug.
Driving and operating machinery: This drug may have some effect on your driving ability, so it is advisable not to drive or operate machinery while taking it.

ZALCITABINE (ddC)
Brand name: Hivid
Type of drug: AIDS and immune deficiency drug
Uses: Treatment of AIDS and other disorders of the immune system.
How it works: Interferes with the genetic material of the virus to stop it replicating.
Possible adverse effects: Bowel problems, nausea, loss of appetite, stomach pain and fatigue. The drug can adversely affect the nerves, pancreas or liver.
Other information: Blood tests are taken regularly to assess the treatment's effect on the liver and pancreas. The drug is usually taken in conjunction with two other drugs (zidovudine and didanosine). A barrier contraceptive is recommended.
CAUTIONS
Children: This drug is either not recommended for children, or is recommended only for children above a certain age.
Pregnancy and breastfeeding: This drug is either not recommended for use by women who are pregnant or breastfeeding, or the precise effects are not known and it should therefore only be used with caution and under medical advice.
Alcohol: Alcohol should not be consumed, or only consumed with caution – after medical advice has been sought – while you are taking this drug.

ZIDOVUDINE
Brand name: Retrovir
Type of drug: AIDS and immune deficiency treatment
Uses: Treatment of AIDS.
How it works: Reduces the frequency and severity of infections associated with AIDS. Used as treatment for and prevention of infections.
Possible adverse effects: Anaemia (characterized by paleness, shortness of breath and fatigue). Also, nausea, headache, tiredness, and loss of appetite.
Other information: A blood transfusion may be necessary.
CAUTIONS
Pregnancy and breastfeeding: This drug is either not recommended for use by women who are pregnant or breastfeeding, or the precise effects are not known and it should therefore only be used with caution and under medical advice.

ZOLPIDEM
Brand name: Stilnoct
Type of drug: Sleeping aid

Uses: To treat insomnia in the short term.

How it works: Has a hypnotic effect in order to induce sleep without having the muscle relaxant properties of other sleeping aids.

Possible adverse effects: Diarrhoea, nausea and vomiting. Vertigo and dizziness.

Other information: Drug should not be taken with or after a meal. Patient should report when drug no longer effective.

CAUTIONS

Children: This drug is either not recommended for children, or is recommended only for children above a certain age.

Pregnancy and breastfeeding: This drug is either not recommended for use by women who are pregnant or breastfeeding, or the precise effects are not known and it should therefore only be used with caution and under medical advice.

Alcohol: Alcohol should not be consumed, or only consumed with caution – after medical advice has been sought – while you are taking this drug.

Driving and operating machinery: This drug may have some effect on your driving ability, so it is advisable not to drive or operate machinery while taking it.

ZOPICLONE

Brand name: Zimovane

Type of drug: Sleeping aid

Uses: Treatment of insomnia (difficulty in sleeping). It is particularly suitable for sleeplessness which is due to international travel or shift work and not accompanied by anxiety.

How it works: Has a hypnotic effect which helps to induce sleep.

Possible adverse effects: Bitter taste in the mouth, daytime sleepiness.

Other information: For infrequent use only, as can be habit-forming after even one week.

CAUTIONS

Children: This drug is either not recommended for children, or is recommended only for children above a certain age.

Pregnancy and breastfeeding: This drug is either not recommended for use by women who are pregnant or breastfeeding, or the precise effects are not known and it should therefore only be used with caution and under medical advice.

Alcohol: Alcohol should not be consumed, or only consumed with caution – after medical advice has been sought – while you are taking this drug.

Driving and operating machinery: This drug may have some effect on your driving ability, so it is advisable not to drive or operate machinery while taking it.